THE CANDLE AND THE FLAME

BY NAFIZA AZAD

SCHOLASTIC INC.

The novel uses the following Fijian Muslim nomenclature *djinni* to refer to the singular of the species and *Djinn* to the plural.

ISBN 978-1-338-60446-7

12 11 10 9 8 7 6 5 4 3 2 1   19 20 21 22 23 24

Printed in the U.S.A.   23

Originally published in hardcover by Scholastic Press, May 2019

This edition first printing, September 2019

Book design by Abby Dening

For Ammi and Abbu

TABLE OF CONTENTS

DRAMATIS PERSONAE

Fatima

Sunaina (Fatima's adoptive sister)

Achal Kaur (Fatima's employer)

Laali (Sunaina and Fatima's adopted grandmother)

Sanchit Goundar (landowner)

Ruchika Goundar (Sanchit's daughter)

Janab Jamshid (advisor to Maharajah Aarush)

Indra (one of the companions of Maharani Aruna)

The Alifs
Asma (mother), Ali (father)

Adila, Azizah, Amirah (the Alif sisters)

The Ifrit
Firdaus (the Name Giver)

Ghazala (Firdaus's daughter)

Zulfikar (the Emir of Noor City)

Anwar (the Wazir of Noor City)

Mansoor (a lieutenant in the Ifrit army)

Tali (a soldier in the Ifrit army)

The Raees (the leader of the Ifrit)

The Royal Family
Maharajah Aarush (the king of Qirat)

Maharani Aruna (the queen of Qirat)

Rajkumar Vihaan (the crown prince)

Rajmata Ekta (the dowager queen)

Jayanti (the previous maharajah's older sister)

Rajkumari Bhavya (a princess of Qirat)

Rajkumar Aaruv (a prince of Qirat)

PROLOGUE

The desert sings of loss, always loss, and if you stand quiet with your eyes closed, it will grieve you too.

Perhaps it is the comfort that the shared sense of sorrow brings that draws her to the desert. Perhaps it is the silence unbroken but for the wind sifting through the grains of sand on the dunes. Or maybe it is the wide desert sky, the blue of which peers into her soul and finds things there better left to the darkness.

Ghazala doesn't know which of these things attracts her the most, but since the day she lost everything, the desert has been a balm to all her hurts. This place with its emptiness and the promise of heat glimmering underneath the sand lies in Qirat, a country divided almost perfectly between the desert and the forest. Every chance she gets, Ghazala slips away from the fiery landscape of her home, from Al-Naar, to soothe herself with the unchanging panorama of the desert. The humans call this place the Desert of Sadness; they believe that the land grieves for the forests that once stood on it.

In the moment before she transforms from a being of smokeless fire to a being of flesh and blood, Ghazala often thinks she can hear the land's lament. If she told her father this, he would call her fanciful and ask her to pay more attention to the act of transformation instead. When a djinni becomes flesh and blood, she dons her Name and feels her fire flow into a shape that is uniquely hers. The

Ifrit clan of the Djinn have the ability to bring over material objects when transforming. Ghazala has her oud slung over her shoulder from a strap she attached to it for times when the silence is a bit too loud.

At this moment, she stands with her hands clenched into fists, breathing hard. The transformation is not difficult if done properly, but when performed in a rush, the physical toll is considerable. As soon as Ghazala has her breath back, she masks her fire, the fire that defines every djinni, no matter their clan and physical shape. She pulls the heat deep within herself so no other djinni will be able to sense it. Her father has often impressed upon her the importance of caution, especially in a world that is, for all intents and purposes, strange to her.

Judging from the position of the sun, it is late afternoon. Very soon the sky will put on a show that few will have the pleasure of experiencing. Ghazala walks down the sand dune she appeared on, her pace slow and her direction arbitrary. She doesn't ever plan her excursions to the human world; they are escapes from the demands *her* world makes on her.

Her father would be sad at the admission, but when Ghazala lost her daughter, her life lost its honey; she lost any desire she ever had to be who she is. All she has, all she clings to, are memories, and to fully indulge in those, Ghazala needs the desert's plentiful silence.

She walks aimlessly, trekking up and down sand dunes without leaving footprints, immersed in the memory of the first time she held her daughter. The sun begins its descent, and Ghazala reluctantly thinks about returning home.

A sudden scream splits the silence before it is cut off. The quiet following the scream is heavy with sinister anticipation. Ghazala rapidly moves toward the place the scream came from. It doesn't occur to her to be afraid of what she'll find on the other side; what more, apart from her life, can she lose now?

Ghazala knows she is too late long before she reaches the top of the final sand dune. The stench of freshly spilled blood permeates the air and prepares her for the sight that awaits her at the bottom of the dune. The remains of a derailed caravan train are scattered on the desert floor; the bodies of four camels lie in various positions, as though a vicious wind picked them up and threw them down again. Ghazala climbs down the dune slowly; her breath hitches when she sees the dead. Scattered among their colorful material possessions are the corpses of three men and four women, one elderly. Ghazala looks closer at the bodies, noting the slashes that ripped each one from stomach to neck. Whatever did this was extremely vicious and strong. In fact—Ghazala straightens when a frisson of danger dances down her spine—this looks very much like the work of the Shayateen. She looks around but finds the area deserted except for the corpses and herself. Shayateen have never made forays into the human world as far as she knows. Why would they start now?

Ghazala gazes upon the empty faces of the dead for a long moment. Who were they? Where were they going? Will anyone know they died? Will anyone mourn them? She turns her attention to the task of burying them; it is the least she can do. A little nudge to the sand with her fire has the desert pulling the bodies into its depths. She says a prayer for them, asking her Lord to show their souls mercy. The camels she leaves for the vultures. The senselessness of the deaths angers her, gouging into wounds she thought were healed.

She is ready to leave, when a glimmer of gold attracts her attention. A beautifully woven rug has slid off one of the camels and lies bunched up on the desert floor. The quality of its weaving is far superior to anything Ghazala has ever seen before. The scent of blood strengthens as she nears the rug, and Ghazala wonders, for the first time, where the attackers went. The idea that they could be lurking nearby doesn't scare her; in fact, she would welcome the chance to give action to her burgeoning anger.

Her senses sharpen when her masked fire flares in recognition of kin. Ghazala blinks twice before she realizes that before her, hidden underneath the rug, is a Qareen. The Qareen are a clan of diminutive Djinn. Each human has one Qareen bonded to them; this is the service their Creator demands of the Qareen.

This Qareen is grievously injured and fading quickly. Unlike the Ifrit and the Shayateen, the Qareen need no names to anchor them to earth; their bond with their humans takes care of that.

"I am Ifrit," Ghazala says to the Qareen, her words meant as a statement of friendship. "Can I ease your way, brother?" She assumes the human he is bonded to is already dead.

"Will you get this child to safety?" the Qareen responds in a reedy voice.

Ghazala peers closer into the gloom underneath the rug and sees now what she failed to see before. A girl child, around four years of age, lies curled into herself.

"I tried to take the brunt of the attack, but I couldn't stop them. They killed everyone else and wouldn't hear of mercy even for a child," the Qareen says in a voice choked with anguish. He twists his smoky body to face Ghazala and beseeches her. "Her name is Fatima. Save her, daughter of Ifrit, I beg you."

Ghazala reaches into the shelter provided by the rug and gently picks up the child who whimpers at the contact. The Qareen, almost transparent now, follows. Ghazala's heart lurches at the warm weight of a child in her arms. How many months has it been since she has felt this warmth? She thinks of her sweet Shuruq and holds the human child a bit closer. The child has dusky skin, curly black hair, and gold eyes wide with pain and fear. Ghazala lifts the child's dress and sucks in a breath at the sight of the wound on her stomach. A slash from a sword has cut her deeply.

"I think my time has come," the Qareen whispers, and fades entirely before Ghazala can respond. The child jolts as though she felt the separation. Ghazala looks down at the girl, and the girl looks back at her with eyes that seem far too old on such a young face.

"I suppose I will save you now," Ghazala tells her solemnly, and smiles when the child blinks. The best idea would be to take the child to a human city. The only one nearby is the city of Noor. Ghazala hoists the child up against her shoulders. If she travels in the Djinn way, she'll get there faster. Before she can make a move, however, she is struck hard from behind. The breath rushes out of her. The child falls from her arms and onto the ground.

Ghazala whirls around to see a trio of armed Shayateen in front of her. They are awash in blood; blood on their hands, their clothes, and around their mouths. Ghazala edges closer to the crying child. She is struck by a cruel sense of déjà vu. The heat of the sand, the glare of the sun, the blood on her hands, and Shuruq's final cry. Ghazala draws in a shuddering breath and forces herself into the present. She reminds herself that *this* child is still alive.

The Shayateen look as human as she does, and these three in particular have assumed attractive faces. The only inhuman things about them are their eyes with black irises that cover all the white. Malice emanates from them, malodorous and corrosive. Ghazala braces herself.

She knows she is outnumbered. Were she by herself, she would discard her name and flow back into her djinni form, where she is the strongest she ever is. But she cannot fail the child. Not again.

Ghazala lets go of her mental hold on her fire, hoping knowledge of her Ifrit nature will hold the Shayateen at bay.

The Shaitan on her right moves toward the child. Ghazala pulls her sword from its scabbard and lifts it in warning. The other two rush Ghazala. She dances out of the way but not before one of the Shayateen stabs her in the side. Her blood splatters, and the Shaitan reaches for it.

The Shaitan screams as her blood, the blood of an Ifrit, undoes him. That is the power the Ifrit have in the human world. Their blood is toxic to the Shayateen, a fact with which the Shaitan is becoming intimately acquainted. His name is ripped from him, and he turns to ash before their eyes.

The other two Shayateen have frozen, disbelief on their faces. Ghazala stares at them, the sword in her hand wavering. Her wound must be deep because she is losing strength quickly. The other two Shayateen look uncertain, and Ghazala waits, wondering if she is going to have to fling her blood at them. The taller of the Shayateen snarls, and Ghazala takes a deep breath.

But their resolve is lost. They flee, leaving dust in their wake, and Ghazala's sword falls. She runs to the child, whose cries have become sniffles, and gathers her up in her arms once again, kissing her cheeks and murmuring consolation.

The child has lost a lot of blood, and the fever that was a threat has now bloomed in her cheeks. Ghazala grits her teeth against her own pain and clutches the child closer before setting off for the city. She travels in the Djinn way—in desert tornados that cover long distances quickly. She reaches the city just before the gates close at nightfall. Ghazala doesn't notice the child's silence until much too late.

When she shifts the child in her arms, she realizes that the eyes she admired are closed and the child's breath is shallow. Ghazala sees Shuruq dying all over again. Her mouth opens, and her grief, usually so carefully controlled, escapes. She drops to her knees and rocks the child, wishing she could pray her well.

Her wound twinges, warning that she also is losing too much blood. Ghazala looks down at the child's face and remembers something her father told her about the forbidden rite of transferring Djinn fire. Ghazala cannot let another child die. She cannot look grief in the face again.

The decision is much easier than it should be.

Jagan is nearly at the city gates when the sound of a child crying makes him turn and peer into the darkness. A girl child, about four years old, is sitting on the ground at the side of the road, crying. In the dim light afforded by the torches at the gates, Jagan can see dark stains on her clothes. She clutches some kind of musical instrument in her arms, hugging it as if it were a favored toy.

He looks around cautiously, knowing better than to accept innocence by appearance alone. Then the child looks up and sees Jagan. Her cries peter off, and she regards him with eyes that are remarkable in both color and expression. Even in the semidarkness, Jagan can see the clarity in her eyes. He walks toward her cautiously. When she doesn't sprout horns or fangs, he crouches down to her height.

"Where are your parents?" he asks her. She doesn't respond. All right.

"What are you doing?" The silence continues.

"What is your name?"

The child moves slightly, and Jagan swallows. Then she rewards him with a smile. "My name is Fatima."

PART ONE

CHAPTER 1

Fourteen years later . . .

The muezzin's call pierces the thinning night air, extracting Fatima from dreams of fire and blood. Her eyes open to the darkness, and for a moment, she is caught in the dark space between sleep and wakefulness. This space is filled with beautiful snarling faces, fear as vast as the night sky, and grief only just realized.

The call to prayer comes once again, and this time tips Fatima fully into the land of the living. She sits up in bed with a gasp and glances across the room to where her sister is sleeping. Fatima watches her sister breathe until her own breathing calms. Satisfied that Sunaina is not going to stir anytime soon, Fatima slips out of the charpai and pulls on a shalwar under the tunic she usually sleeps in. She moves swiftly out of the bedroom and into the bathroom, where she performs wudu in front of the shaky but clean sink. Her ablutions complete, she leaves the apartment with a dupatta on her head, a lamp in her hand, and a prayer mat under her arm for the open rooftop of the building in which she lives.

The rooftop is deserted, as it usually is at this time of the morning. Other faithful Muslims in the building she lives in prefer to pray in the comfort of their homes. Fatima places the lamp on the mid-level wall that runs around the rooftop and gazes out at the expanse of the desert. Northern Taaj Gul, so called because the buildings in this area are built of rosy pink stone, is right next to the wall that surrounds the entire city of Noor. The circumference of the city wall is rumored to be undetermined, as the city is immense and, people like to claim, immeasurable. Fatima spreads her prayer mat, pointing it north toward the Kaba. The time before dawn is precious, as the air has a delicious chill to it that the sun doesn't allow during the day. Jama Masjid is lit up like a beacon; from her vantage point on the rooftop, Fatima can see groups of boys and men making their way to it for the Fajr prayer. Turning her back to the city, she, too, prays the four rakats of Fajr, bowing down with her hands on her knees for the ruqu before touching her forehead to the ground in a sajdah. After the prayer, which culminates in a dua, she gathers her belongings and returns to the apartment, where Sunaina is still sleeping. Briefly, Fatima considers returning to bed but shakes her head and stifles her yawns. She has an errand to run.

Their apartment is on the seventh floor of the building and is probably one of the shabbiest. It is, however, the only one the sisters can afford. Their apartment is one large room that has been sectioned into three different parts by thin wooden walls. The tiniest section, in the corner with a window high up on the wall, is the bathroom, which comes equipped with plumbing thanks to the Emir of Noor City who made indoor plumbing mandatory. The other section is their modest sleeping quarters, in which they have squeezed in two charpais and little else. The largest area serves as a kitchen, a dining room, and a living area.

The apartment is humble. However, compared to the street they used to live on, it is an unimaginable luxury. A chest of drawers in the living area contains their clothes. Fatima rummages in the top drawer before pulling out a clean beige tunic and matching shalwar. She binds her breasts and changes quickly, grimacing at how uncomfortable the binding is. She doesn't aim to dress like a man so much as she tries to focus attention away from her femininity. Living on the streets has left her wary of people who attempt to turn it into a weakness.

The flame in the lamp is flickering when Fatima finishes getting ready for her next excursion. With her eyes kohled and a red ambi-patterned turban wrapped around her head, she can pass for an affluent young scholar from Shams Gali. She nods at herself in the mirror and leaves the apartment with no sound apart from the click of the lock as she closes the front door behind her.

Outside, the air still has the chilly flavor of a desert night, though orange streaks in the horizon warn of the approaching heat. The sizable amount of foot traffic on the streets belies the early hour. The city of Noor never sleeps. As one of the more profitable stops on the Silk Road, a steady stream of caravans enters or leaves the city at all times of the day or night. The merchants do not just bring goods to be traded but also people who either want to visit the city of the Djinn or who want to live here. The Bayars, dressed in stately robes, jostle for space on the same sidewalk that the Han people in their white hanboks do. From the melodic Urdu to the breathy Nihon-go, the cadence of a thousand different languages fills the air. The city of Noor brings people of all colors, ethnicities, and religions together and takes from them everything they do not always want to give. Fatima has seen people pay more for the city's grace than they ever thought they would have to.

She walks quickly, cleaving to the shadows, not wanting to be recognized by friends or drawn into conversations by acquaintances. Not that any friend of hers would be out on the streets at this time of the night. But just in case, she keeps her head down and her feet swift. She passes a group of boys returning home from praying Fajr at Jama Masjid, and her eyes snag on Bilal, the muezzin, whose voice is more familiar to her than her own.

Away from residential Northern Taaj Gul, the foot traffic

decreases, allowing Fatima to hasten her pace. She takes the Rootha Rasta and emerges onto a main road that connects Northern Taaj Gul to the more affluent areas of the city. A ride hitched on a mule-pulled cart deposits her by a line of beautiful houses that come complete with courtyards painted in pastel shades and paved with intricately decorated tiles. Fatima follows a haphazard path through the row of houses and ends up in Chameli Baag, named for the flowers that no longer grow there. It is not much of a garden; the land became desert a long time ago. A number of khejri trees still wage war with the elements, though, surviving one day to fight again the next.

Gardens on the forest side of Noor City are explosions of green, embarrassingly lush after the dearth of natural bounty on the desert side. Fatima has traveled to Southern Noor carrying messages or packages from one side of the city to the other. Sometimes she lingers over the rosebushes in the gardens there. At other times, her work takes her into courtyards spilling over with trailing vines and other wanton greenery.

Two distributaries of the River Rahat section Noor into three parts. Aftab Mahal, the palace shared by the royal family, the Emir, and the human and Djinn armies is located in the middle of the city on a tract of land separated from the rest of the city by the two distributaries.

It takes Fatima three-quarters of an hour to reach Neem Ghat, the riverside port in Northern Noor. She comes to an abrupt stop under the neem trees that grow in a line along the river a few meters from the steps leading down to the river's edge. Time is of the essence, yet Aftab Mahal, luminous in the waning darkness, commands her attention. Dawn has tender regard for the palace's domes and spires. The carved stonework on the palace walls is said to be exquisite—not that Fatima has ever had the pleasure of looking at them herself. A muted shout from a man piloting a wayward boat reminds Fatima of her errand. She takes one last glance at Aftab Mahal before hurrying down to the river's edge, where several boats laden with flowers are already in the process of docking.

A number of dockworkers walk around with lamps dangling from long sticks. Because it is Deepavali, the port is more crowded than usual. Fatima looks at the flowers on offer and is, as always, taken aback by the opulence of the blooms. There are coy nargis, delicate lilies, jewel-colored gladiolas, and haughty orchids. Vying for equal attention are irises, roses, poppies, buttercups, hollyhocks, and flowers whose names are mysteries to Fatima—mysteries she'd very much like to solve one day.

Fatima breathes deeply of the floral bouquet and looks around for a familiar face among the flower sellers. She finds him securing his boat on the far side of the port and hurries toward him. The flower seller, Niyamat Khan, has a kind face with eyes that shine with the smiles he has yet to give the world. Though he is in the twilight of his life, he has a wiry body and a thirst for life that is evident in the care he takes of the flowers he sells. The last time Fatima bought flowers, it was from him. She hadn't been able to afford many, so he had gathered the leftover and rejected flowers into a bouquet and presented it to her. Fatima smiles at the old man, at his blue cotton shalwar kameez that is not wrinkled even after a night on the River Rahat, and at the taqiyah that sits straight on his head. Niyamat Khan's face lights up when he catches sight of Fatima.

"Assalaam wa alaikum, baba," Fatima greets him. "It has been a while since I saw you."

"Wa alaikum ussalaam, beta," Niyamat Khan says, beaming.

She helps him unload his boat and waits patiently while he deals with the porter he contracts to transport his flowers to the market. Finally, he turns to her and smiles.

"Do you have them, baba?" Fatima asks.

As an answer, Niyamat Khan goes back into his boat and drags out a basket he kept separate from the rest. The basket is heavy with the blooms of damask roses in several colors: many shades of pink, red, yellow, white, and maroon. Fatima looks at the roses and, to her horror, feels her throat grow thick and her eyes sting. She swallows and blinks before taking out the money she has been saving for a month. She pays the flower seller, thanks him, and picks up the basket of flowers, flinching at the weight.

Carrying it all the way back to Northern Taaj Gul would usually be a daunting task for Fatima, but luck is on her side. She runs into Amrit, an acquaintance who raises camels for their milk, and begs a ride home on his cart. In return, she listens to him complain about the human servants in the mahal who take the milk he delivers daily without so much as a thank-you.

In about an hour, and before the clock is able to strike six, Fatima, with her precious basket of flowers held close, is carefully easing open the front door to her apartment.

CHAPTER 2

The air inside the apartment smells of dried marigold petals with notes of orange. Through the window on the wall opposite the front door, Fatima can see the morning sun assert a brilliant mien, a fitting prologue to what promises to be a blisteringly hot day. Incense sticks burn at Sunaina's altar to the goddess Lakshmi. A silver tray has been set in front of the altar next to the chest of drawers with offerings of mithai and flowers on it. Also on the silver tray is a clay diya with its wick still burning.

Sunaina is in the right-hand corner of the room, in the area designated as the kitchen. She sits on the floor in front of the chulha: a cooking stove with a pipe attached to the back that extends up the wall and through the window. The smoke from the wood and other fuel flows through this chimney of sorts so the air inside the apartment is breathable. A stack of rotis have been placed on a plate beside the chulha with the last roti still cooking on the tava. The room should smell of incense or roti or even the smoke, yet when Fatima takes a breath, all she smells are marigold petals and oranges.

Sunaina sees Fatima and abruptly removes the last roti from the tava, adding it to the stack, which she covers with a clean kitchen towel. She gets to her feet and brushes herself off. The tired red shalwar kameez she usually sleeps in has charcoal smudges from the chulha.

Fatima knows she is in trouble when Sunaina turns stormy eyes her way and stands with her arms crossed. Her short stature takes nothing away from her imposing presence. Fatima steps farther into the apartment and closes the door behind her. She takes off her shoes at the entrance, thinking fiercely about the best way to appease her sister. They are only five years apart in age, but the difference may as well be an eternity for the way Sunaina treats her. When their parents were alive, the spaces and the silences between them were full of warm memories, shared anecdotes, and a sisterhood that, though not borne of blood, was strong and resilient.

However, their parents are gone, and their relationship has been tainted by memories of blood, smoke, and the ways in which Fatima is different; the spaces between them are emptier and the silences longer.

Sunaina looks at the basket of flowers Fatima is holding. "You went to Neem Ghat," she says flatly.

"The damask roses are not available anywhere in the city. I promised Laali—"

"How much did you spend on them?" Sunaina cuts her off.

"I saved—"

"Your shoes are falling apart! And when was the last time you bought yourself new clothes?"

"The flowers are important to her, didi."

"The flowers will wilt and die before sunset tomorrow!" That the rebuke is whispered does little to lessen its intensity. The walls are thin.

Fatima places the basket of roses carefully on the lone chair in the room. She goes to the chest of drawers and opens the bottommost drawer and takes out a package wrapped in coarse brown paper before returning to stand in front of her sister. She holds out the package, and Sunaina, still frowning, takes it. Giving Fatima a suspicious look, she opens the package and freezes when she sees what it contains: a hair chotli Sunaina had admired at a jewelry store in Bijli Bazaar months ago. Gold-coated metal flower pins with garnet centers linked with delicate gold chains to attach to the long braid that is Sunaina's one vanity. Sunaina had walked away from the hair accessory, judging it too expensive, too frivolous, too everything that she couldn't have and shouldn't want.

"Shubh Deepavali, didi," Fatima says, and smiles. Two dimples pop into existence.

Her sister looks at her for one long, pregnant moment before bursting into tears. Fatima watches Sunaina sniff and wonders if she has weathered the bulk of the storm for today. "Is there any chai?" she risks asking.

Sunaina wipes her eyes with the edge of her sleeve and sniffs loudly. She stomps to a kettle on the counter, pours chai into a copper cup, and hands it to Fatima, who accepts it gratefully. Fatima glances at the clock on a wall and sits down cross-legged on a mat in the middle of the room, deciding she has time to enjoy her chai.

Sunaina glowers at Fatima but doesn't say another word. Instead, she busies herself dishing out jackfruit curry and roti on a plate. She presents the food to Fatima with another glower; Fatima accepts the plate meekly.

"Are you going to the mandir this evening?" Fatima asks between bites of roti wrapped around the jackfruit curry, enjoying each spicy mouthful.

"Yes. We'll come to the maidaan straight after. I had better see you there." Yet another glower punctuates her words. Sunaina buzzes around like a bee in a field of sunflowers; she washes dishes, packs food into a thali, and sweeps the room around Fatima. "Hurry up and eat. We need to give Laali the flowers you wasted money on before work."

"Work? But it's Deepavali!" Fatima protests. "You never work on Deepavali!"

"Sushila-ji is having a Deepavali party tonight. Gossip says Rajkumari Bhavya is going to make an appearance, so the household is in an uproar." Sunaina works as a maid in one of the more affluent houses in Northern Noor. "Sushila-ji says she will double the pay for whoever works today."

Fatima listens without comment. She wishes she could tell her sister that money is not important, but that would be a lie. Money *is* important, perhaps more to her sister than to her. She swallows the last morsel of food and asks instead, "Aren't you meeting Niral today?"

Sunaina flushes and turns her back on Fatima. "We are going to the mandir together," she mumbles.

"Ah," Fatima says noncommittally.

"What?" Sunaina whirls around, her eyes flashing. Fatima decides to keep her counsel to herself and shrugs.

"Are you finished?" At Fatima's nod, Sunaina grabs the empty plate and cup and washes them in the sink. While Sunaina changes her clothes, Fatima gets up and goes into the tiny bathroom to freshen up. She washes her face and blinks at herself in the cracked mirror on the wall. Next she retrieves an oud that is hanging from a nail on the wall in the bedroom. The oud is the only connection Fatima has to her birth family. Her adoptive father, Jagan, used to tell stories about finding her in the darkness in bloody clothes, hugging the oud like a mother. The instrument is old, but some strange enchantment keeps its strings fresh and tune clear.

"Let's go!" Sunaina calls. The day is heating up. Fatima rolls her shoulders, taking comfort in the oud she carries strapped over one shoulder. She observes the loose threads in Sunaina's sari and the way her hair is worn tightly in a bun without adornments. Surely

Sushila-ji can allow some festivity on Deepavali. They make their way silently down the stairs, as Laali lives in a room on the first floor of their building. The room had originally been used for storage until the building residents petitioned the landlord to allow Laali to live there. The landlord, as vulnerable to the demands of tradition as anyone else, agreed. He went one step further and had part of the room closed off to create a bathroom. The room was furnished with the bare necessities: a charpai and a chair. A mat was spread on the floor so visitors not lucky enough to get the chair had a place to sit. Many of the residents, including Fatima and Sunaina, would have happily kept Laali with them, but Laali insists on her independence.

The door to Laali's room is closed when they reach it. Sunaina reaches out and gives it a sharp rap.

"Come in," a quivery voice calls from within.

A little table near the front door of the room is already full of packages proving the sisters are not the first who have been to see Laali. Thalis full of food, prasad from Deepavali puja, and fragrant flowers make up for a portion of the bounty. Sunaina puts another thali on the table and beside it a lota full of some concoction. Once again, Fatima smells the scent of dried marigold petals infused with the fragrance of fresh oranges.

"It's something I made," Sunaina says in response to Fatima's questioning look. She turns to greet Laali, who is sitting in a rocking chair beside a window overlooking the busy street in front of their building.

Eight years ago, when Sunaina was fifteen and Fatima ten, the Shayateen attacked the city of Noor without warning or provocation. The humans living in Noor proved helpless against the Djinn, who had vaster strength and who seemed to have no goals but to create chaos. People fell like trees in a hurricane. No one was spared the Shayateen's blades and their particular brand of cruelty. The maharajah at the time had been left with no choice but to beg the Ifrit for their help in defeating the Shayateen.

After the final battle was fought, their Ifrit saviors collected the survivors and counted them. There weren't very many. Sunaina and Fatima were two, Laali was the other. She disappeared right before the Ifrit found them cowering under a table in their apartment and only reconnected with them years later when they came to rent an apartment in this building and found her already there. Where she went and how she managed are all mysteries that the old woman refuses to speak about.

She is a small woman, diminished by age. Life has embroidered all her experiences in the lines on her face. The wrinkles near her lips keep record of the smiles she gives generously while the lines on her forehead echo the worries she has battled. Deep grooves at the corners of her eyes lend weight to all the things she has seen in the years she has been alive—not that anyone is sure how many those are. However, though time has aged her, it has yet to defeat her. Apples still bloom in her cheeks; her gaze is as bright and inquisitive as a child's.

Laali welcomes Fatima and Sunaina into her room with a flush of pleasure. Sunaina kisses Laali's soft cheeks and squeezes her hands. Laali, as always, is beautifully dressed in a navy-and-gray sari with a matching blouse. She has bangles on her wrists and a nathni in her nose. A chain strand, which is pinned to her hair, extends from the nathni. Delicately peeking out from under her sari are her feet, adorned with silver anklets and matching toe rings.

"I got you some of the fresh marigold and orange potpourri I made. You said the smell of the street in your room bothered you?"

Sunaina says to Laali. "We'll go to the mandir in the evening at six. Anu said she will bring you there."

"Thank you, beta," Laali says with a smile. She turns to Fatima expectantly.

Without preamble, Fatima places the basket of damask roses on Laali's lap. For a moment, Laali appears frozen. Then she lifts a trembling hand and gathers a handful of the blooms. Bringing them up, she buries her face in the roses, breathing deep of their fragrance. Her eyes are wet when she raises her face, but her smile is incandescent.

"Udit used to give me a damask rose every single day when we were courting." Laali's voice is a whisper in the stillness. "When we got married, he promised me a bouquet every Friday. It was a promise he kept. These roses let him live again, if only in my memories. Thank you, child, I will never forget this kindness." She gives Fatima a teary hug.

They spend a few more minutes with Laali, fussing over the old woman, making her laugh, and plying her with Deepavali sweets. When the clock strikes seven, Fatima and Sunaina say their goodbyes.

Out on the street, Sunaina catches Fatima by the wrist. "I was wrong . . . about the flowers. They made her so happy."

Fatima grins at her sister. "They weren't much, but I am glad they let her remember him."

"Marigolds remind me of Amma," Sunaina confesses suddenly. She shakes herself. "Be safe today, all right? Don't take unnecessary risks."

"I won't," Fatima replies with a sigh, used to the warnings.

"Don't work too late. Don't agree to go to dangerous places!" Sunaina continues.

"I won't! Beeji wouldn't send us to anywhere she thinks is too dangerous!" Fatima protests.

"Wouldn't she?" Sunaina's lips twist a little. "I will see you in the maidaan tonight. If you don't come, I will be angry."

"I will be there, didi. I need to go now, or I'll be late." Fatima offers her sister one last smile before turning and walking off rapidly in the other direction.

CHAPTER 3

Fatima thinks about the women in her life as she walks the narrow streets to work. The women she loves, respects, and seeks to please: her sister, obviously, and Laali, their adopted grandmother, and her boss. Achal Kaur is a woman in her sixties, gruff until you prove yourself to her. Fatima remembers the first time she met the woman. Fatima was twelve, used to the streets on which she and her sister lived. Sometimes they spent nights in empty houses, sometimes in corners of Bijli Bazaar. They spoke the language of the streets: a language of desperation and survival. That day, Fatima was fleeing from bullies and not cognizant of anything except a desire to be safe.

She had bumped into Achal Kaur, and the woman had fallen. Horrified, Fatima had stared down at her, not knowing whether to stay and help the old woman up or to keep running. She had stayed and her life was changed.

Over the years, Fatima has learned much about the woman who has become so important to her. Achal Kaur fled terror, war, and cruelty with her extended family. In Noor, Achal Kaur lost her eldest son to Ghuls, her husband to illness, and her sleep to nightmares. In return, she grew a messenger business that found success beyond anything anyone had ever expected from her. She showed people that business acumen is not solely the purview of men. Achal Kaur employs both girls and boys, usually from the lower spectrum of society. She told Fatima once that she remembers hunger very well.

Fatima hastens her pace, calling out a greeting to the trash collectors. Achal Kaur's haveli is located in the Dewar District of Northern Noor. The haveli doubles as a residence for her extended family, who are scattered throughout the many rooms of the second and third floor. When Fatima enters through the front gate of the haveli, she spies Achal Kaur sweeping the area in front of the main entrance.

"Shubh Deepavali, Beeji," Fatima calls out with a cheerful smile. Achal Kaur is imposing in her magenta shalwar kameez with a sheer dupatta in the same shade covering her impressive bosom. Though Achal Kaur is flirting with seventy, no one who knows her would call her old.

"You too, chanda," Achal says fondly. "Make sure you go upstairs and get your share of the mithai. Rupi has a box ready for you."

"Will do." Fatima beams. The best part of Deepavali is the sweets. "Where am I delivering today?" Fatima asks.

Achal pauses and gives Fatima a long look before a smile lights up her plump face. "Bijli Bazaar." She knows how much Fatima adores the market. "We are done at twelve today, so you can go home and celebrate with your sister after."

"Thanks, Beeji." Fatima feels like if she smiles any wider, her lips will split.

Achal Kaur reaches out and pats her cheek. "Don't forget to get the mithai from upstairs. Go off, then."

Fatima keeps a calm face on the first floor, where her fellow messengers are finding out about their own routes, but she cannot quite suppress the skip in her step as she heads to collect her box of Deepavali sweets from Rupi, Achal's youngest granddaughter.

Bijli Bazaar is located in the center of Northern Noor and is pur-
ported to be the oldest market in the entire city. In fact, Fatima has
heard rumors contend that Noor was built around the market. The
name comes from an old lightning-struck tree in the middle of the
market that clings to life despite its age and the dust around it.
Initially the market was simply wooden beams driven in the ground
with sheets of tin as roofs to provide bare protection from the elements, but as the market grew, it gained walls and a wooden roof
with frequent gaps on the portions above corridors and walkways to
allow for light and air. The market expanded outward in twists and
turns until it resembled nothing so much as a rabbit warren. Mithai
stores with their mounds of laddoo, peda, barfi, jalebiyaan, and
other sweets do brisk business during festival times, as do stores
selling saris, shalwar kameez, and other fancier, more sparkly
sorts of clothing. Near the clothes stores are stores selling jewelry,
shoes, and other accessories. Henna artists are available in one
alley as are other beauticians who do everything from makeup to
hair styling and arrangement.

Deeper into the market are the more esoteric stores such as
apothecaries, chemists, candle makers, perfumeries, and rug sellers. Some vendors have closed off their wares with three walls;
others have laid out their choicest pieces in the open in the hopes of
attracting customers. The air smells like cardamom or cinnamon in
one alley, leather in another, and perfume in yet another. A hundred scents compete for attention, as interspersed among the stores
are food vendors who sell everything from kebabs to pani puri,
spicy noodles and fried dumplings, lassi and coconut milk.

To the outsider, Bijli Bazaar would be impossible to navigate.
The labyrinthine passages have the power to confuse even the most
directionally confident person, but Fatima survived her years on
the streets by running wild in the market. She makes deliveries to

various vendors in Bijli Bazaar before stopping at Mahmoud's, the baklava stall; he gives her a box for her final client, who is not located anywhere near Bijli Bazaar.

By the time Fatima finishes delivering all messages, it is nearly noon. Firdaus's bookstore is located on Kalandar Street, which is about three kilometers from Bijli Bazaar. She buys herself a glass of chilled coconut water from a store and settles down outside the bazaar under the shade of an awning to enjoy the drink. Once she is refreshed, she grabs the boxes of baklava and Deepavali mithai, adjusts the oud hanging from her shoulder, and sets out in the heat. Kalandar Street is full of booksellers and bookbinders. What sets Firdaus's bookstore apart from the rest of its ilk is its business practices. Firdaus does not seem at all inclined to sell any of his books—a fact that sits ill with his competitive neighbors who cannot understand how Firdaus can afford to make no sales and still remain in business. No, not only does he remain in business, the store is flourishing.

The first time Fatima found her way to the store with the dirty glass windows and the shelves full of books with faded pages, she had been thirteen and on her first outing as a messenger. The old man to whom she was delivering a book had appeared in front of her, and Fatima had immediately known that Firdaus was no man. She knew it the same way she had known her blood would repel the Shayateen eight years ago. Fatima identified the old man as one of the Ifrit, a member of the Djinn clan that had been saviors of Noor City eight years ago. What surprised her was the kinship she felt for the grumpy old Ifrit—that she still feels for him.

Firdaus taught her the pleasure of reading. First in Arabic, then in Hindi, and when she mastered Urdu, he taught her Qadr, the language of the Djinn. She learns mathematics and science from him; she reads histories and literature in the books he gives to her. When the heat is too intense for reading, she sits in a chair in the inner room surrounded by volumes of poetry and fiction, with a jug full of minty sharbat, and plays the oud. Usually Firdaus is content to listen to her playing, though occasionally he brings out the nay and they play a taqsim.

In all the time Fatima has been frequenting Firdaus's book-store, she has never seen a customer enter or leave the store. Today is no different. Fatima escapes the sun's persistent attention in the cool, if musty, confines of the bookstore, and slips into the back room, hoping to surprise Firdaus.

The Ifrit, who for all intents and purposes looks like a human man in his seventies, glances up from the book he is reading and smiles. "I thought I heard you."

"Assalaam wa alaikum, baba," Fatima says with a little chagrin.

"Wa alaikum ussalaam," Firdaus replies.

"Your baklava and a box of mithai from Beeji," Fatima says, putting the sweet boxes on Firdaus's desk.

"Shukraan." Firdaus opens the box containing the baklava. The aroma of sugar and butter fills the air. "Let's feast."

Ten minutes later, both boxes are empty and their fingers are sticky. Fatima washes her hand with water from an urn in a sink at the back of the room. Wiping her hands and lips with a hand-kerchief, she turns to a cart containing the newest books bought by the bookstore. She peruses the titles, picking up a book here and there to read more. Firdaus has returned to his book. All of a sudden he raises his head.

"It is time for Zohr." Before he finishes speaking, the azaan for Zohr sounds. After they pray, Firdaus beckons Fatima to the desk, and they go over Baheri, the language of the Bayars.

On a break, Fatima comments, "You got new books, baba."

"Yes. I got them for you, actually. Since you scorn the classics . . ."

"The classics are singular narratives focusing on those privileged enough to know how to read and write," Fatima retorts.

"But surely you cannot deny the beauty of the rhetoric?"

"I don't trust that beauty, baba," Fatima says, and directs her gaze at Firdaus. "*You* taught me not to trust that beauty."

"Indeed I did. But I did not intend for you to eschew the great literary works in favor of—"

"Works by the common people? These works may not have wondrous prose, baba, but the experiences they write about are theirs, which makes their stories so much better than those who live in gilded cages and write about the world outside. *These* writers don't have the luxury of ennui, you see."

"Ah." Firdaus puts his pen down and pulls on his white beard, as is his habit when he is thinking. His shaggy brows draw together as if captive to some particularly trenchant thought. Then he rises to his feet. "I have to see Mohiuddin about that edition of Ghalib's poetry that I am having him rebind. Will you stay here until I get back? We can continue our discussion then."

"Of course!" When Firdaus leaves, Fatima makes herself comfortable on the chair she usually sits on. It has been a long day, and fatigue demands recompense. After about fifteen minutes of reading, Fatima's eyes flutter closed and her head falls back.

She doesn't know how long she has been sleeping when her eyes snap open. A whisper of caution makes her sit up, and the book she was reading falls off her lap to the ground. Disquiet hisses in her ears and presses into her skin. Fatima looks around for the source of these feelings. When she identifies him, her breath escapes her all at once.

Standing in the doorway of the back room of the bookstore is an Ifrit. He, too, looks entirely human, but as with Firdaus, Fatima is able to identify his Djinn nature immediately. This Ifrit is dressed in a red vest that leaves most of his arms, chest, and abdomen bare. He wears black Patiala shalwar and what looks like a sheathed scimitar hangs at his hips. Fatima raises her eyes to his face and is captivated by the beauty of it.

A red turban is wound around his hair and his eyes are kohled, very much like Fatima's. He has high cheekbones, pursed lips, and gold eyes. These gold eyes are currently trained on Fatima.

He takes a step into the room, and Fatima jumps to her feet.

The temperature in the room rises; Fatima's breath gets shallower. Twin impulses pull her in opposite directions. The first one urges her to flee: some innate instinct warning her that this Ifrit has the ability to hurt her in ways people don't usually recover from. The other impulse urges her to stay. Staying would mean something she is not sure she has the words for right now. The Ifrit walks farther into the room, and Fatima tenses, her gaze unwillingly drawn to his face, to his hollow cheeks and his narrow forehead. She looks a minute too long at his high cheekbones and his full lips. Her eyes collide with his and finds in them curiosity and a surprised interest. A blush stains Fatima's cheeks. She immediately looks away.

"What impudence," the Ifrit says, his voice deep and slightly rough.

"Because I *looked* at you?" Fatima asks, her voice higher than usual.

The Ifrit looks startled at her response. His eyes narrow, and he takes a step closer. "Who are you, sayyida? What are you doing here?"

"I don't believe I have to answer your questions," Fatima

mumbles, trying to move past him. As she does, he rears back as if she has stung him. His hand is on his scimitar, and he is radiating a menace that was missing not a moment ago. He looks ready to cut her down. Fatima freezes, wondering if she has unwittingly broken some sacred Ifrit rule.

"Why do you smell of fire, human?" he growls.

"Fire?" she repeats, utterly confused.

"Zulfikar." The voice is calm, soft even, but the command in it is undeniable. The Ifrit looks at the door where Firdaus is standing with a vexed look on his face. When Fatima sees Firdaus, she sighs with relief; he will know how to make sense of this Ifrit's questions.

"Your business is with me. Let Fatima pass." At Firdaus's words, the Ifrit turns to look at her. He looks displeased by Firdaus's command. Fatima's cheeks heat again at his continuing regard; she ducks her head.

"Zulfikar," Firdaus says again. This time with a warning in his voice. The Ifrit—Zulfikar—relaxes his hold on his weapon, though the frown remains like a thundercloud on his eyebrows. Fatima moves past him, banging her hip on Firdaus's desk in her haste. She cries out in pain.

"Calm yourself, ya binti," Firdaus says. "You will be fine."

Fatima takes a deep breath and releases it. She will be fine. She *is* fine.

"You may go now." Firdaus passes Fatima the oud she had left on his desk and smiles. "I will see you soon."

"Allah hafiz, baba," Fatima says to Firdaus. With one last wondering look at the Ifrit, Fatima walks out of the room.

CHAPTER 4

The Ifrit, Zulfikar, watches the girl leave and fights the insane urge to chase her. To bring her back and make her answer all his questions.

"Why does she have Djinn fire, Firdaus? She's human, isn't she? Who is she?" he asks the older Ifrit, fighting the urge to shake the answers out of him.

"A messenger," Firdaus replies shortly. He pours tea from a copper teapot into two matching copper cups. He offers a cube of sugar to Zulfikar, who shakes his head.

"That is not what I meant, and you know it," Zulfikar says, his voice tightly controlled.

"But that is all I will tell you." Firdaus takes a sip of his tea, grimaces, and drops another sugar cube into it.

"You are protecting her!" Why this should surprise him so much, Zulfikar isn't sure, but it does. To think, the great Name Giver of the Ifrit would lower himself to protect humans.

"Astute of you to realize that." Firdaus smiles, though his eyes remain cool and watchful. "Now what business does the Emir of Noor City have with me? Don't you have half a city to run? No conflicts to resolve?"

At the question, Zulfikar's thoughts shift focus. There will be time enough later to think about human girls with Djinn fire. "The Raees plans to come to the human world."

Firdaus has lived long enough that the world rarely surprises him. This news, however, is unexpected and beyond anything he could have predicted. "Zafirah is coming to Noor City, you say? I haven't heard anything about this. The last time she crossed over was when the Wazir was injured in a fight with the Shayateen . . . How long ago was that?" He looks at the young soldier in front of him and frowns. "What are you not telling me?"

Zulfikar looks at the older Ifrit and wishes he didn't have to be the one to convey this news. The leader of the Ifrit and the Name Giver of the Ifrit have a long history. "She has been ill for a long time, sayyid. The healers say it is the taint."

The color drains from Firdaus's face. A full minute passes before he can give voice to his new question. "How?"

"We do not know yet," Zulfikar says tersely.

"She cannot stay in Tayneeb." Firdaus sits down abruptly on the chair behind his desk and steeples his hands to hide their shaking. "Staying in the city will present a danger to all."

"Yes. That is why she has decided to come to Noor . . . but, sayyid, there is a danger that Naming her will taint your fire too," Zulfikar tells Firdaus.

The room seems just a little darker than it was a few minutes ago. "True though that might be, Zafirah continuing to stay in Tayneeb . . . on Al-Naar is not a feasible option. If the taint spreads . . . Did they not teach you of the Horror of Zubed?" Zulfikar winces. Of course he was taught of the war started by the Ifrit man in whom the taint spread unchecked. Thousands died in that war. The city of Tayneeb was laid to waste.

Firdaus is looking at Zulfikar bleakly. "It is a risk I will have to take."

Zulfikar nods. He expected no other reply from the Name Giver.

"When does she plan to shift planes?" Firdaus asks abruptly.

"At noon, on Juma, two weeks from now."

"I will be ready," Firdaus says. He gets to his feet and walks over to a shelf, perusing the books on it as if in search for something in particular.

Zulfikar understands the dismissal and makes his farewell. His cup of unsweetened tea remains untouched.

The heat peaks at two p.m. on the desert side of the city of Noor. The afternoons offer relief to those who search for it under the shade of the infrequent khejri trees. The desert nights, however, are cold enough that scorpions burrow into the sand for heat left over from the day. When Zulfikar steps out of the Name Giver's bookstore, an indulgence of the older Ifrit's, the clock has just struck two in the afternoon. He pauses for a minute outside the bookstore's doors and puts a hand on his chest, wondering why his heart feels like it is readying itself for a race. He looks around; the street is deserted. Most humans avoid being out of doors at this time of the day. Zulfikar walks easily, at home with the heat; he is, after all, made of fire.

His subordinates, two from the Amir clan of the Djinn, await him at the junction of Kalandar and Main Streets. Among the six Djinn clans in existence, the Ifrit and the Amir clans are most closely allied, having the same desire for order. Their clans have close trade alliances in Al-Naar and the Djinn army in Qirat has several Amir soldiers. Zulfikar's subordinates don't know who he went to meet, though they know who the Name Giver is. They may even know what he looks like; the Name Giver is always present the first time a djinni shifts planes. The secrecy is necessary to keep the Name Giver safe; history boasts of several attempts made on his life. Zulfikar mounts his horse, and they ride through the city at a leisurely pace. The streets are mostly empty, but if you know where to look, there is a tremendous amount still to be seen.

His predecessor, a garrulous Ifrit named Nabil, had been the Emir of Noor City since the Raees signed a treaty with Maharajah Arjun of Qirat. All the desert cities in the half of Qirat ruled by the Ifrit have Emirs, administrators of the city who answer only to the leader of the Ifrit, the Raees. The Emirs ensure the safety of the citizens and the economic stability of the cities they administrate. They are helped in their tasks by their advisors, the Wazirs. The Emir of the city of Noor, however, has a far more sensitive role.

Nabil, the first Emir of Noor, along with Firdaus, saw the city in all its decimated glory before leading the first of what would be many restoration efforts. The debris had to be cleared before any rebuilding could take place. In the absence of human workers, Firdaus had to Name many Ifrit architects, craftspeople, and other artisans who lent their skills to the rebuilding of the city of Noor. The city's human population had been all but annihilated. If Zulfikar remembers correctly, only a woman and two girl children had survived the Shayateen attacks. Maharajah Arjun had relocated his entire extended family to a fortress in a jungle city some distance away before leading the last of his troops in an offensive against the Shayateen. Accompanying him had been his eldest son and heir. The maharajah had faced the Shayateen without knowing if the Ifrit would honor their promise of assistance. He had ridden to war, to his death, without wavering. He had sacrificed his eldest son and heir to the cause. Zulfikar respects that kind of courage.

He looks around at the stores he passes. Most of them have names written not just in Hindi and Urdu, the two languages primarily used in Qirat, but also in the language of the store owner, whatever it may be. Nabil and his army of Ifrit and Amir soldiers were able to wrest the city of Noor back from the Shayateen, but without humans to live in it, the city lay fallow, lacking songs, color, and laughter to give it life. The rest of Qirat feared to live in a city populated by ghosts, a city where even the stone buildings were soaked in sorrow and blood.

No one expected what happened next.

The first of them came in the darkness, under the shadow of midnight. When their presence went unremarked, word spread, and very soon, the city of Noor became the city of the displaced. People fleeing from terror, war, and persecution found houses in the empty buildings of the city and homes in one another. People who spoke different languages learned to understand one another. People of different faiths learned tolerance—and were sometimes taught it.

Zulfikar's reverie is interrupted by one of his soldiers.

"Sayyid." The Amir soldier reins his horse to a stop beside Zulfikar's mount.

Zulfikar turns a questioning gaze to the slimmer djinni.

"Akram just sent us word of a fight in the dyers' section of Northern Taaj Gul." Amirs are mentally linked to one another, which allows them to communicate telepathically.

"How many soldiers are already at the scene?"

"Three, sayyid."

"Is the situation contained?"

"They are working on it, sayyid. One of the assailants is particularly violent and is resisting all pacification efforts."

"You two go and provide assistance. I want a report as soon as possible."

The two Amir soldiers nod sharply, turn their horses around, and leave. Zulfikar digs his legs into the sides of his horse, and it breaks into a canter. He directs it across the bridge that connects to the road leading to Northern Aftab, the official term for the side of the palace the Djinn inhabit.

The grounds of the mahal begin from the river's edge on both sides and are immense, as they need to contain the barracks for the Ifrit army on the Djinn side and the human army on the human side. The grounds also contain stables for the horses and camels, and training spaces for the soldiers of both armies. Pavilions dot the landscape, and human gardeners busily tend to the flowers and other decorative foliage the human royals insist upon. Zulfikar won't ever confess this, but he secretly takes great pleasure in the gulmohar trees that stand in a line above the river's edge like sentinels, blocking the view of the mahal courtyards from the prying eyes of the world.

"Salaam, sayyid," a soldier calls when Zulfikar dismounts from his horse outside the stable. He hands the reins to a human stable boy and turns to face the soldier hailing him.

"Mansoor," he says, returning the greeting. "Are the soldiers prepared for patrol tonight?"

"Yes, sayyid. The Wazir has organized the patrols so that each group has an even mix of Amir and Ifrit soldiers," Mansoor, a lieutenant in the Ifrit army, answers. His human form is of a man in his early forties with a muscular physique and brutish face that serves him well in battles. "Speaking of the Wazir, sayyid, he just returned from Rahm and requested that you find him in the library."

Zulfikar dismisses the soldier and turns toward the entrance of the Aftab Mahal. When the new maharajah offered to build the Ifrit a residence fit for the protectors of Qirat, the Raees accepted readily.

Aftab Mahal is made up of two five-storied buildings joined by roofed corridors on both sides and separated by an inner courtyard in the middle. The mahal is made of white granite with copper domes that gather the sun's rays and reflect it with intensified brilliance. The facade of the mahal is decorated by exquisite carved stonework. Placed at intervals are stone latticed jharoka, which are decorated by floral parchin kari in bright colors. The stone inlays are works of art and were commissioned from artists all over Qirat. Four domed spires stand in the four corners of the extensive mahal grounds.

The interior of the mahal is every bit as luxurious as the exterior suggests. The mahal contains curved vaulted ceilings covered with the same exquisite parchin kari, living rooms that open into balconies enclosed by jali, plush rugs, rich decor, and human domestics carefully vetted by the Ifrit responsible for the household of the Emir of Noor City.

Zulfikar strides through the tiled corridors of the mahal, almost impatient with its beauty. The richness of his surroundings always makes him aware of the poverty in the streets of the city. Only two Ifrit currently occupy Northern Aftab. This, in Zulfikar's opinion, compounds the waste of resources required to maintain it. In fact, were it up to him, he would have joined his soldiers in the barracks, but Anwar, his Wazir, frequently reminds Zulfikar that appearances are everything to humans. Other Ifrit hold office as Emirs in the desert cities of Qirat, and according to Anwar, it matters little if they sleep in rich havelis or join the horses in the stable. Because, unlike Zulfikar, *they* do not have to contend with the maharajah of Qirat. Not that the maharajah has any authority over Zulfikar. The only one he and the rest of the Emirs answer to is their leader, the Raees.

Zulfikar, deep in thought, ascends four flights of stairs and walks to the library. He pushes open the doors and strides inside, marveling, as he always does, at the size of the room. One wall of the library is made entirely of casement windows, which are heavily curtained to prevent sunshine from wreaking havoc on the books. The other three walls have floor-to-ceiling shelves built on them. The books on the shelves of the mahal library all belong to the Name Giver, who, in Zulfikar's private opinion, has gone out of control where his book buying is concerned.

Anwar is currently lounging on a divan strategically placed near a partially opened window. A breeze plays with the edges of the brocade curtains, causing them to part so fingers of sunlight can reach in and bathe Anwar's face in soft light. While Zulfikar is dressed in the usual uniform of the soldiers, Anwar is dressed meticulously in a white sherwani with silver buttons running down the length of the kameez. The same silver decorates the edges of his collar and the bottom of his shalwar. His feet are encased in soft leather slippers. His beard and hair have been neatly groomed.

Zulfikar always feels underdressed when he is beside Anwar. Why this should be when he is the one dressed like the soldiers they both are is beyond him. He raises an eyebrow at the older Ifrit.

"And where have you been, Oh great protector of half of this city?" The mocking edge is present as always. Zulfikar carefully ignores it.

"I went to the Name Giver," he says, and his smile sharpens. "It is unfortunate, but he didn't send you his regards."

Anwar's face empties at Zulfikar's words. He sits up on the divan, his jaws clenched. "It is good of you to tell me," he grinds out to Zulfikar, who gives him the blandest smile he can muster.

"What do you deem so important that you summoned me? What news from Rahm?" Zulfikar takes a seat on a chair in front of a low table containing a tray with a jug of sharbat and two empty glasses on it. He pours himself a drink.

The Ifrit rule the desert half of Qirat—this was the payment they demanded from the late maharajah in exchange for helping the humans with the Shayateen. They rule the desert cities of Rahm, Sabr, Baaz, and Ummeed. The desert half of the city of Noor also belongs to them.

"There were Ghul attacks in Rahm," Anwar answers flatly. "Ten deaths, seventeen injuries. All human, of course. I will be leaving for Sabr within the hour. They should know too."

"Were the Ghul captured?" Zulfikar asks without expression.

"No. One of them was injured and bled to death, but the rest escaped," the Wazir reports. "I will take soldiers along and hunt them after I inform the Emir at Sabr."

"You do that." Zulfikar drains his glass of sharbat, wipes his lips, and gets to his feet. He leaves the library without another word and sends a message to the maharajah: the Emir of Noor City wishes to meet with him. The meeting will take place in half an hour. The maharajah is to present himself at the usual location for their rendezvous.

CHAPTER 5

Maharajah Aarush Radhesh Gandiva Mehra has been having a vexing Deepavali. He had to deal with members of his extended family, many of whom approached him with requests that he allow them to make this trade or introduce that law just so their pockets see more gold than they already do. As if that weren't enough, his advisors waylaid him right after he completed breakfast and for dessert, he heard, once again, about the rebellion fomenting in Eastern Qirat. Now, finally, when he has managed to steal some time out of the day to coax a few kisses from his wife, someone is knocking repeatedly on his pointedly closed door.

"It might be important," Maharani Aruna says, smoothing down the long tunic of the jama Aarush is wearing.

"It is always important," Aarush says darkly.

Aruna reaches up to straighten her husband's pagadi and takes the chance to press a kiss on his pouting lips. Aarush very much enjoys the unexpected kiss but teases his wife by raising an eyebrow. Aruna blushes and smiles shyly. Aarush pulls her closer and wonders if kings get days off.

Apparently not, for the knocking resumes with renewed vigor.

"Go." Aruna pulls away. Aarush sighs grumpily, and Aruna's eyes light up with mischief. "You wouldn't want Jayanti Bua to show up, would you?"

An expression of profound horror arrests Aarush's face. He gives Aruna one last peck before walking to the door and wrenching it open. His oldest and most trusted advisor, Janab Jamshid, almost falls into the room, his hand raised to knock again.

"What is so important that it could not wait five minutes, Jamshid Chacha?" Aarush asks, knowing he is being churlish but unable to help himself.

"I am sorry, Maharaj," Janab Jamshid says, looking anything but. "The Emir requests a meeting."

Aarush stops in his steps and sighs. He very much doubts the Emir *requested* anything. "When does he want to meet?" Aarush starts walking, crossing the length of his apartments and descending the staircase that connects the fifth floor to the fourth.

"In ten minutes, Maharaj." This time the advisor's tone is apologetic.

"At the usual pavilion, I presume?" The advisor nods. Aarush bursts out of the front door of the mahal, the advisor and his guards trailing him. In the front courtyard, shielded from public view by tall hedges, his mother, youngest sister, and several aunts are working on an intricate diya rangoli. They all straighten when they see him. His sister bounds over.

"Are you going to see him now?" Aarush needs no detective to deduce whom his sister is talking about. How she knows about the upcoming meeting, though, he would like to know.

"Indeed I am. So stop talking to me and let me go."

"Can I come with you?" Bhavya asks. The sincerity of her request shocks Aarush to a standstill. Her crush on the young Emir is not new; she has been unswerving in her desire for the Emir ever since he arrived to take over from his predecessor four years ago, but this is the first time she has made any effort to get closer to him.

"Bhavya"—Aarush gentles his tone with some effort—"I know you like him a lot, but a union between you two is impossible."

Bhavya's eyes flash. At twenty, she is eight years younger than him but old enough to know better than to cause a scene. "I don't *like* him, Bhaiya." Her bottom lip trembles, and her voice lowers. "I love him!"

"All right. I suppose you can love him. Do we really have to discuss this now? Here?" Aarush looks at Bhavya's resolute face and sighs. "Look, it is impossible between you two. You *know* that."

An odd expression passes lightning fast on his sister's face. Aarush couldn't read it before it was gone. Bhavya takes a deep breath, grimaces, and then wails while the maids, manservants, relatives, and the cat look on. Aarush feels the headache that has been threatening break over his head like storm clouds do on an unsuspecting day.

"Bhavya, you and the Emir are not even the same species. You do not follow the same religion." He looks at his sister. "Do you really want me to go on?"

Bhavya opens her mouth perhaps to retort. Aarush sends an imploring look toward his mother and pushes past Bhavya. He hastens his pace, wondering if he will make it on time. The stone pavilion is located on the grounds of the mahal, right on the border between the desert and the forest. It was built on a platform with stone steps leading up to it. A jali encloses the pavilion, ensuring the safety of those who use it from assassin archers.

As he walks, Aarush wonders what he would have done if the Emir reciprocated Bhavya's feelings. Blessed their union? Aarush shudders, imagining the chaos such a decision would rain down upon him. He thanks all the goddesses he can think of that the young Emir doesn't even seem to realize that Bhavya exists. Tragic for his sister, of course, but it makes Aarush's life immensely easier. Being related to the Ifrit, even if only through marriage, is not something he wants to think about.

His father's journals detail the first time he met an Ifrit. An old man appeared in Noor City one day and demanded an audience with the king of the country. All attempts to turn him away were unsuccessful. When Maharajah Arjun received news of him, he invited the old man, not thinking him anything other than human, to appear in front of him. His father wrote of the old man's disdain for his expectations of obeisance. The old man stood in front of him without bowing or showing any sign of the respect Maharajah Arjun expected from his subjects. He asked the king for his help. In return, the old man would owe him a debt. Maharajah Arjun was initially amused and a little skeptical, but then the old man showed the king his fire. That was all it took to convince him.

By the time Aarush reaches the pavilion, the Emir is already there. He is dressed like any other Ifrit soldier, but his power is pronounced in the breadth of his shoulders and the confidence in his posture. His power is also obvious in the wickedly sharp scimitar that hangs at his waist.

Aarush awkwardly clears his throat. He is never more aware of his humanness than he is during the moments he shares space with those who aren't human. The Emir turns toward him with the unsettlingly direct gaze common to all Ifrit. The old Emir would have made small talk, discussed the weather, food, or perhaps related an anecdote. Not the new Emir.

"We have received reports of Ghul in the city of Rahm. There have been some human casualties," the Emir says abruptly.

Aarush takes a breath. "You fear they will attack here?" he asks, grateful that his soldiers remained outside the pavilion as did his advisor. He does not wish them to see their king so unsettled.

The Emir nods, his eyes troubled. "Tonight's revelry may tempt them out from their usual haunts."

"Is Southern Noor at risk too?" Aarush asks, hoping his voice doesn't reveal any of the fear he feels.

"Ghul do not recognize borders, Rajah." The Emir's inflection is vaguely mocking, and Aarush flushes.

"What should I do?" Even to his ears, he sounds young and inexperienced. Both these things are true, but the Emir is as young, if not younger, and tenfold more confident and capable.

"Increase your patrols, particularly in areas where a lot of people will gather to celebrate. I will send you a number of my Ifrit soldiers. Their presence on the streets may act as a deterrent to any Ghul searching for succor among your people."

"Shouldn't I warn people?"

"Of attacks that may not happen? Your people guard their right to celebrate jealously. Don't give them a reason to resent you."

He has a point, but Aarush still thinks it would be better if people know and are prepared. "How do people fight Ghul?"

"People don't," the Emir replies, his face all hard lines. "The most people can do if captured by one is hope they die quickly."

Aarush blanches. "Thank you for telling me." He turns to go, but a thought occurs to him and he stops. "Did the old man ever find his daughter?"

"What?" Aarush has successfully disconcerted the Emir with his abrupt question.

"My father wrote of the first Ifrit he met, an old man named Firdaus. He came to Noor looking for his daughter. Did he ever find her?"

The Emir gives a sharp shake of his head, his lips drawn tight. "No, he didn't."

Aarush nods and leaves the pavilion.

Fatima is almost sure she is dead. Or perhaps she is dying. She is lying on the charpai, her wet hair hanging over its edges, feeling very much like her bones have been swapped for jelly. After her encounter with the Ifrit in Firdaus's bookstore, an event her brain has cataloged under Dangerous and refuses to examine in any great detail, Fatima felt the need to seek out Niruthan and ask for a lesson. She had forgotten how excessively enthusiastic Niruthan is about teaching.

Achal Kaur requires her messengers to be versed in one or more martial arts so they can protect or defend themselves should the need to do so arise. Among the teachers she employs is Niruthan, a kalaripayattu teacher, who fled his home and country with his sister, Luxmi, after his love affair with the village chief's son was discovered.

Learning the art of kalaripayattu requires commitment and desire, a fact that Niruthan has been trying to impress upon Fatima since he took her on as a student two years ago. Fatima has the commitment, but she lacked the desire to learn—until today, when that Ifrit impressed upon her the whole extent of her helplessness.

Fatima grimly endured every minute of the two hours of training, then limped home, where she took a shower, washed her hair, and climbed into bed for a nap, waking to pray Asr and then some hours later, Maghrib. She has just flopped down on her bed again when three sharp knocks sound on the door. Fatima briefly considers pretending she isn't at home.

"We know you are home," a sweet voice calls out. Fatima recognizes it as belonging to Azizah, the youngest of the Alif sisters.

"Anu saw you coming home." That is Amirah, the middle sister. Fatima thinks unsavory thoughts about Anu, the building's nosy neighbor who keeps account of the comings and goings of its residents.

"It will be less painful if you open the door yourself, you know," Adila, the oldest sister, adds. She is eighteen, Fatima's age, and, supposedly, her best friend. "Sunaina Baji left us a key. Don't make us use it."

Grumbling, Fatima drags herself to the door and pulls it open. She is greeted by three unrepentant smiles on three almost identical faces. The Alif sisters, so called because of the first letter of all their names, are Fatima's oldest and closest friends. Fatima looks them up and down, noting the different shades of the blue shalwar kameez they are wearing. They wear their dupatta around their heads with gold and silver jhumars pinned to the side to give them a celebratory sparkle. Amirah is wearing ring bracelets on both hands while Azizah has chunky silver bangles around her wrists. Adila, predictably enough, has a simple watch around one wrist while the other one remains unadorned.

Azizah, the youngest at sixteen and, in Fatima's opinion, the bossiest, sweeps into the apartment and looks Fatima over from head to toe. She turns to her sisters, who have followed her inside, and says, "I *told* you she wouldn't be ready!"

"It's only five o'clock!" Fatima protests weakly. She rubs her eyes and stifles a yawn.

"Only five o'clock, she says," Amirah mutters. She is seventeen and only a smidgen less bossy than Azizah. She, too, looks at Fatima, then sighs loudly.

"Now, now," Adila says in a conciliatory tone. She is used to keeping peace. She leads Fatima to the chair in the living room, pushes her down on it, and grabs one of the clean towels hanging on a rack in the washroom. "We have an hour yet," she says, and proceeds to give Fatima's hair a brisk rubbing.

Fatima resurfaces a few minutes later, bemused, and asks no one in particular, "One hour to do what?"

"Dress you up!" Amirah chirps, taking items out of the chest of drawers. "Sunaina Baji gave us permission to use her cosmetics."

"But *why* are you dressing me up?" Fatima asks, feeling a little desperate.

"Here, put on this petticoat and blouse," Azizah commands, pushing the clothes at her. Her tone brooks no argument.

Fatima obeys a little sulkily. Adila expertly dresses her in a pale gold sari. She folds the cotton material into pleats and tucks them into the front of the petticoat. The pallu she brings over Fatima's shoulder, drapes it over the front, and pins it into place. Fatima endures the ministrations quietly, bewildered by the suddenness of the storm that has descended upon her.

When she has been dressed in the sari, the sisters stand in front of her, arms crossed and lips pursed. Fatima fights the urge not to flinch under their stares.

"I will do her hair," Azizah says decidedly.

"Then I will do her makeup!" Amirah nods happily. "I love Sunaina Baji's concoctions. Do you think she'll make me some if I ask extra nicely?"

"You can try asking," Adila replies.

"Why are you doing this?" Fatima is almost teary now. She wouldn't have skipped out of going to the maidaan tonight, but she had envisioned going dressed in the most comfortable clothes she owns.

Adila takes pity on her best friend. "We have it on good authority that Bilal is going to be at the maidaan tonight."

"Since we are good Muslim girls, we will stare at him from afar and hope he stares back," Amirah continues.

"And to help him stare back at us, we are all going to sparkle!" Azizah concludes with a flourish.

"Wait, are we talking about Bilal the muezzin?" Fatima holds up a hand, thinking of the boy she saw earlier that morning.

"Yes! He can call me to prayer *anytime*!" Azizah says. The other three fall silent for a bit and stare at the youngest girl with varying degrees of amusement in their expressions.

"I am rather impressed by how illicit you made that sound," Adila says to her youngest sister. Fatima feels a grin tug at her mouth, the day's fatigue easing. She starts to learn forward, and Amirah raps her on the shoulder.

"Don't move!"

"But are we really dressing up for a *boy*?" Fatima doesn't like the idea.

"No, of course we aren't. We are just joking . . . well, Azizah wasn't. But we don't often get the chance to dress up, do we? And there is nothing wrong with a little halal romance." Adila smiles, her eyes bright with mischief.

"Halal romance, huh?" For some reason, Fatima thinks of the Ifrit and wonders if she needs to go see a healer. Something is obviously wrong with her if she associates romance with Ifrit men who are offended when you simply look at them. If Fatima had a face as pretty as his, she would *want* people to look at her. "I don't think I'd want to be present when a boy comes to ask Ali Abbu for your hand."

Adila, who is unsnarling chains in Fatima's box of costume jewelry, pauses for a minute and says, "I don't think Abbu would be too happy if a boy came for *you* either, you know. He likes you better than us anyway."

Fatima smiles, though Adila's assertion is blatantly false.

"Do you think this yellow eye shadow is more seductive or this orange one?" Amirah holds up two pots.

"The eye shadow has the most important job?" Adila asks Amirah, raising an eyebrow.

"Yes, since none of us has any idea how to seduce anything or anyone," Amirah replies.

"I'm pretty certain *I* could seduce a tree," Azizah says, giving Fatima's coiffure one last pat.

Once again they all look at her silently.

"What?" she asks.

"The yellow one, I think," Fatima says, thinking it easier to judge an eye shadow's seductive properties than make sense of Azizah's thoughts.

After ten more minutes of primping and refreshing, the Alif sisters are finally satisfied with how Fatima looks.

"Let's go!" Azizah commands.

The sisters look at Fatima expectantly.

"What?" Fatima asks a bit fearfully. "I'm going, aren't I?"

"No, you have to lead," Adila explains.

"And why is that?" Fatima demands, smiling a little. All of a sudden, the night feels brighter and full of possibilities.

"You are wearing yellow," Azizah says seriously.

"What does that have— Actually, I don't want to know." Fatima grins at the youngest Alif's pout. "Let's go!"

CHAPTER 6

The flames of tiny clay diya undulate on windowsills, doorsteps, footpaths, and storefronts. Wooden barges filled with lit diya and candles are pushed off into both the forest and the desert arms of the River Rahat. The air smells of smoke, ghee, and food. The aroma of hot jalebiyaan, halwa puri, ras malai, and various kinds of laddoo tantalizes the tongue.

In Southern and Northern Taaj Gul, the buildings are too close together and fire too dangerous a risk to allow for a proper expression, a full celebration, of Deepavali. For the poor who have no space, there are the maidaan. These are empty grounds that are usually venues for weekly vegetable markets. On occasions such as Eid and Deepavali, the maidaan transform into festival grounds where people gather and celebrate. There are two maidaan in Noor City: one in Northern Noor and the other in Southern Noor.

The affluent celebrate in courtyards lit by the flicker of diya placed in and around dry fountains. Candles placed on stone fences add sparkle and shine to a night rapidly losing its hold on darkness. The royalty celebrate with the grandeur expected of them. The maharajah's side of Aftab Mahal, Southern Aftab, is lit up like the day at noon. Multitudes of diya light the front courtyard. Out on the grounds, the fountains have been turned off and candles flicker like fireflies in the darkness.

Southern Aftab is a whirlwind of courtiers who arrive dressed in their most expensive clothes: silk and brocade saris and jewel-hued ghagra choli for the ladies, and sherwani or jama for the men. People from all sorts of backgrounds come to pay respect to the maharajah and his family during Deepavali; religious denomination means little during festivals, though economic status is of paramount importance.

Bhavya lingers in front of a mirror in her apartment on the fifth floor of Southern Aftab. She is dressed in a blue ghagra choli embroidered with pearls and gold thread. A matha patti sits regally on her head, a kamarband glimmers at her hips and a long pearl haar gleams around her neck. Even her hair dazzles with a gold hair chotli attached to the long braid that ends in the belled tassels of a paranda.

She takes a deep breath, musters her courage, and meets her eyes in the mirror. Immediately, she flinches and looks away. Why is it, she wonders, that no matter how much jewelry she puts on, she can never see the reflection she wants to so desperately? It is easy to love herself in parts: She likes her lips, her hands, and the daintiness of her feet. But she cannot meet her eyes in the mirror without feeling the weight of all she is supposed to be judging her for all she is not. She cannot look at her body without looking at her faults.

"Do I tell you that you look beautiful, or will prostrating myself in your shadow suffice?" A very dry voice comes from the doorway to her inner rooms.

Bhavya turns to face the owner of the voice.

"You're late," she says. She looks over at the girl standing in the doorway, noting her bright silk sari, jewelry, and the sweet-smelling gajra she wears in her hair. She is the kind of beautiful Bhavya hungers to be.

Ruchika shrugs and glides into the room. She is well acquainted with her grace and her every step is like poetry. She is the daughter of Sanchit Goundar, one of the leaders in the maharajah's government, and has been foisted on Bhavya for as long as she can remember. Bhavya doesn't even have the freedom to choose her friends.

"It takes time to get ready," Ruchika murmurs, looking around the room. Bhavya wonders if the canopied bed, thick rugs, and other items denoting wealth and luxury make for a fitting cage for a rajkumari of Qirat.

"Did my plan work?" Ruchika asks Bhavya abruptly.

Bhavya turns away, color flooding her cheeks when she remembers the fool she made of herself earlier that day. "This morning was mortifying."

"Come, now. If it leads you to a meeting with the Emir, surely the embarrassment of the morning will be inconsequential. You ought to thank me. It is my source in Northern Aftab who sends you a message every time the Emir asks to meet the maharajah," Ruchika says, patting her hair in the mirror.

"It is easy for you to be flippant. *You* weren't the recipient of the scolding my mother and aunt gave me," Bhavya replies, her lips thinning at the memory.

"It's done, so there is no point dwelling on it." Ruchika lowers her voice. "Sushila Mausi assured me that the Emir will be at her party. Do you really want to let the chance to meet him go to waste?"

"I have to go and talk to Amma first," Bhavya says. If she could only meet the Emir, if only he would look at her once, things would happen. Things would change. Bhavya knows it.

"Shall I accompany you, O grand and glorious rajkumari?" Ruchika makes a show of obeisance.

"That will not be necessary, Ruchika." Bhavya's smile is not kind. "The Rajmata does not meet with outsiders on Deepavali."

She leaves Ruchika with instructions to await her on the first floor and makes her way through the mahal to the Rajmata's apartments on the fourth floor in the right wing of Southern Aftab. She is conscious of the eyes on her, the way gazes linger on the swell of her hips and the shine of her lips. She is conscious of being consumed visually and fights, as usual, to keep her lips smiling, her eyes cast demurely down, and her pace sedate. The morning's hoyden was an exception and not the norm.

Bhavya stops outside her mother's rooms and waits for the guards standing outside to announce her. She is ushered inside to a living room by one of her mother's maids. Rajmata Ekta, dressed in a white brocade sari with her gray hair tied in a bun at the nape of her neck, is sitting on a divan. Seated beside her is Jayanti, her dead husband's elder sister. They are looking at what seems to be a letter in the Rajmata's hands.

"Amma," Bhavya says, smiling back at her mother. She turns to the other woman and her expression cools. "Bua."

"You look beautiful, beta," the Rajmata says, her eyes filling with sudden tears. Bhavya knows that Deepavali, ever since her father and brother died in the Shayateen Massacre eight years ago, is difficult for her.

"Indeed you do, niece," Jayanti says, smirking as though Bhavya's beauty is a personal triumph. "Sundar Singh, the son of Rathod Singh from Khair, expressed a desire to meet you—"

"Amma, I am going to attend Sushila Mausi's Deepavali party," Bhavya cuts off her aunt.

"Absolutely not!" Jayanti is on her feet and shaking her head. "What will people say if we send you out during Deepavali?"

"Amma." Bhavya kneels on the floor beside her mother's seat. She takes a deep breath and tells the truth. "I can't bear to stay here. Everyone's talking about this morning."

"And whose fault is that?" Jayanti sneers and seems poised to say more. The Rajmata glances at her, and the woman subsides into silence. Bhavya witnesses this little exchange avidly.

When she realizes that her mother is looking at her, Bhavya ducks her head, fresh embarrassment staining her cheeks. "I *am* sorry for behaving as I did, but, Amma, Baba taught me that you can't passively wait if you want something. You have to go and get it."

The Rajmata's face softens at the mention of her husband while Jayanti's face grows stonier.

"You blame your father for your disgraceful behavior?" her aunt hisses. "You thank him for his teachings by dragging his name through mud? You think your infatuation with the djinni is love?"

"Jayanti Bua," Bhavya says, her voice gentle, "only those who know passion, who have *felt* passion, can understand the degree to which it can drive their actions. Those who don't, those who haven't, can only wonder and judge."

"That's enough, Bhavya!" Ekta says sharply. "Jayanti, could you ask Roshni to send up some dahl chawal, please? I am a bit hungry."

The woman leaves the room, though reluctantly, and Bhavya sighs with relief. She cannot stand her aunt and her perpetual insistence on finding fault with everything Bhavya does and is.

"Bhavya, adab! How many times must I tell you to respect your elders?" Ekta says as soon as the door closes behind Jayanti.

"I apologize, Amma," Bhavya says, and she *is* sorry, not for what she said to her aunt but for losing control in front of her.

"We are the raj, Bhavya. People will always expect more from us than from others. We cannot ever let go of grace and behave commonly."

Bhavya hangs her head and accepts the scolding. "I am sorry, Amma. I really am. Please don't make me stay here among people who are laughing at me. People who are mocking me. I know I deserve it for the way I acted this morning. I know I was foolish." Bhavya's voice wobbles. "I won't ever do it again, Amma."

"All right," Ekta concedes with a sigh. "But you must be back in two hours and you have to take the guards assigned to you."

Bhavya's tears vanish and she beams. "Thank you!" She gives her mother a hug and turns to go, when a thought occurs to her. "Who is the letter from?" she asks, indicating the letter lying on the seat beside Ekta.

"Aaruv," the Rajmata says with a fond smile. "Your brother says that he will be back this Friday."

Bhavya pales at the news, wishing she hadn't asked.

"What is it?" her mother asks, and Bhavya shakes her head.

"Nothing, Amma. I'll be going now."

Twenty minutes later, she is in a richly outfitted carriage drawn by a team of thoroughbred horses and accompanied by four guards. The darkness inside the carriage is broken by an oil lamp placed in a corner.

"Akaash is madly in love with Hye Joo," Ruchika suddenly says, breaking the rather tense silence in the carriage.

Bhavya leans forward, inviting more tidbits.

"His mother is terrified she's going to end up with a foreign daughter-in-law." Ruchika giggles, pleased with the attention Bhavya makes a show of giving her.

She launches into a series of gossip that Bhavya feels safe tuning out except for the odd acknowledgment here and there. She directs most of her attention outside. Bhavya spends her life sequestered in the mahal, and on the rare occasion she is allowed out, she is accompanied by guards who are supposed to protect her life, but who, Bhavya thinks, are more concerned with keeping her chaste.

Every minute of her life is accounted for. What she eats, what she wears, even her friends are chosen by her mother. For a long time, Bhavya accepted this as her lot in life, but recently, her cage, for all that it is gilded, seems suffocating.

She watches the poor of Noor celebrating out on the streets. Dressed in their best clothes, they spill out of their houses and into the night. Girls gather in groups, bright as the colors of a peacock's tail, and boys, majnuns all of them, stare after them, entranced. A group of boys sitting on dusty steps play the dholak, the beat of the drums reminding people they are alive and breathing. Some girls dance to much laughter and catcalling. Bhavya wonders how these people who have so little look so much happier than she, who has so much more.

"Are you sure the Emir is going to be at Sushila Mausi's party?" she asks Ruchika, interrupting her unkind recounting of the events at a party the week past.

Ruchika gets an evasive look on her face, and Bhavya feels the first prickle of unease. But the other girl smiles brightly. "Sushila Mausi is an important person. Surely the Emir wouldn't refuse her invitation."

Bhavya reaches for all the power her royal lineage grants her and says softly, "For your sake, Ruchika, he had better not have." She looks away from the older girl and outside. The carriage is passing the maidaan where the poorest of Noor have gathered to celebrate.

The initial plan had been to walk to the maidaan, but the sari complicates things. Fortunately, there are many oxen-pulled carts doing brisk business ferrying people to and from the venue. Fatima and the Alif sisters find themselves deposited outside the western entrance of the maidaan after a particularly bumpy ride. They brush themselves off—the carts aren't particularly clean—and look around. This is not the first time they have been to the maidaan, obviously, but it *is* the first time they are here unaccompanied by an adult. Ali, the Alif sisters' father, is away with a caravan train transporting rice and other materials to an oasis in the desert. Their mother, Asma, is not feeling well; rather than make her daughters pay the cost for her ill health, she gave them permission to join the festivities under the condition they return home before ten.

"Do you think heaven looks something like this?" Azizah asks, her brown eyes full of wonder at the spectacle in front of them.

"No, I think heaven has more trees," Amirah replies. Her eyes are just as wide.

"Are you ladies going to continue gawking or shall we go in?" Adila smirks at their starstruck expressions.

Fatima, laughing at their blissful faces, leads them inside the space enclosed by a wooden fence. This year, Ifrit soldiers stand on either side of the entrance, their postures straight and their hands on their swords. Fatima gives them nervous looks, but the soldiers let them enter the maidaan without stopping them.

Once inside, they take a moment to look around. The maidaan is lit by torches and an array of lamps. Fires burning in carefully monitored pits all around the maidaan provide more light. Stalls, set up around the circumference of the maidaan, sell food and other items. On one side of the maidaan are places that sell firecrackers and on the other are stations for assembling paper lanterns that are usually used in the festivals of the Kinh and Han people but have slowly been adopted by the Hindu community in Noor to celebrate Deepavali. Benches and chairs have been placed in an area obviously designated for eating. On a sizable platform some distance from the eating area, a group of musicians are setting up their instruments. Yet another area has been cordoned off for anyone who wants to create rangoli.

"Obviously we are going to eat first, right?" Adila asks. She nudges Fatima, who nods emphatically.

"So obvious you don't need to ask," Azizah replies solemnly.

"That's like asking if it rains during monsoon," Amirah adds.

"Or if Azizah likes Bilal." Fatima grins.

"Hey! I resent that! I'm still somewhat mysterious about the direction in which my affections lie." Azizah finds herself under the censure of three pairs of eyes and amends her statement. "All right, maybe I'm not, but you could let me pretend!"

Fatima and the Alif sisters pool their resources and descend upon the food vendors. They return triumphant twenty minutes later, find an unoccupied slice of mat-covered ground, and claim it as theirs. Fatima wishes for the umpteenth time that she had insisted on wearing a shalwar kameez. Sitting on the ground in a sari is an art form she hasn't yet perfected. They spread their edible haul in the middle and take a moment to appreciate its splendor.

"I wish life was like jalebiyaan," Amirah says, picking up one piece of the dessert.

"You want a fried life?" Adila asks skeptically. She reaches for the box containing the samosas.

"No, I mean, if life was like a jalebi, I'd take one bite of it and sweetness would spill out." Amirah demonstrates.

"Only fresh jalebi spills sweetness, Api," Azizah says. "Stale jalebiyaan are soggy things that are simply sugary dough . . . hey, so maybe life is more like jalebiyaan than I thought!"

"She is sixteen and talking like a grandmother," Adila mutters, chewing her samosas.

Fatima listens to the sisters bantering and takes comfort in their undemanding company. The constant stream of people passing by their seats contains many familiar faces that Fatima acknowledges with a smile or a wave. More Ifrit soldiers than is normal are present in the crowd. What strikes Fatima as suspicious is the way they're dressed not in the uniform of Ifrit soldiers but in the tunic and shalwar common to the men of Taaj Gul. Fatima wonders if their disguise is to prevent anxiety among the humans. None of the other people apart from Fatima seem to be aware of the stronger Ifrit presence. It is like the Ifrit emit a heat that only she, among the humans, can feel, that only she can identify. To everyone else, the only Ifrit present are the soldiers in their uniforms.

Fatima turns her head and sees an unexpected sight. "Oh look, there's Bilal," she says to Azizah, who freezes, a skewer of kebab halfway to her mouth. Fatima smiles widely and takes a big bite of stir-fried noodles.

"Is . . . is . . ." Azizah squeaks.

"Attend to your sister, Adila. She may be broken," Fatima says, laughing merrily at Azizah's panic.

"No, he's not looking over, Azizah. I don't think he knows we exist. If you don't want that kebab, I'll eat it," Adila says calmly.

"Of *course* I will eat it," Azizah says with injured dignity. "I enjoy looking at Bilal, but his beauty won't fill my stomach. Api, will you stop eating the jalebiyaan! I want some too." Despite her words, she turns and looks at the young muezzin, who is standing with his friends some distance away. They seem to be conferring on something.

"I wonder what you see in him," Fatima muses.

"Apart from his excellent muezzin abilities, you mean?" Adila says.

"The symmetry of his face moves me." Azizah sniffs.

"I think she wrote a poem about it." Amirah giggles helplessly.

A half hour later, they are done eating and have thrown away the detritus of their meal. "What shall we do now?" Amirah asks, rubbing her stomach.

"Fatima, Sunaina Baji said she'd be at the eastern gate at half past seven," Adila says to Fatima, pulling on her arm. "I'm sorry I forgot to tell you."

"What time is it now?'"

"Quarter after."

"Why don't you stay here and enjoy the view?" Fatima smiles, and her dimples make an appearance. "I will go and bring Didi here."

"Shouldn't I come with you?" Adila looks unsure. They look at the younger girls, who are standing together, offering their best smiles to the night.

"Azizah will kick up a fuss if we move from here while she can still see Bilal. Besides, do you want to leave them by themselves?"

"No," Adila replies immediately.

Fatima laughs. "Don't worry. I will be back soon."

Fatima slips into the crowd, losing herself among the colorfully dressed inhabitants of the poorer bits of Noor. The sari should hinder her movements—indeed, only an hour or so earlier it did—but now it pronounces her grace. Fatima navigates a path that keeps her from getting too close to any Ifrit soldier whether in disguise or in uniform, wary of them after the incident at the bookstore. She finally reaches the eastern gate of the maidaan, which strangely enough seems to have less traffic through it than the western gate. When Fatima looks around, she cannot see Sunaina anywhere near or around the gate, and after a few minutes pass, she grows concerned. It finally occurs to her that Sunaina may be waiting outside with Niral, so she makes her way through the gate.

Fatima expects the gate to be guarded by more Ifrit soldiers, but none of them are around. She peers into the darkness that is broken at intervals by large oil lamps placed high on posts. Her efforts pay off when she spies her sister's two friends, Ruka, the daughter of a tea shop owner, and Anjum, a maid who works with Sunaina. They are gathered around a third figure, who seems to be crying. Fatima identifies her as Sunaina and walks forward, anxious to know why her sister is upset. Before she can reach Sunaina, however, she hears her name and stops in her tracks.

"Why don't you simply talk to Fatima?" Ruka is saying. "Surely if you tell her that Niral wants to marry you but cannot afford to keep both of you, she will find other lodgings."

"You don't understand," Fatima hears Sunaina saying. "I am all she has."

"So what? You are going to throw away your happiness for her? Look, you don't owe her anything, Sunaina. If anything, she owes you and your family for taking her in! If not for your father's generosity, she would have starved to death in the desert!" Anjum says hotly. Fatima doesn't know the girl at all, so the animosity surprises her. "Don't you *want* to marry Niral?"

"Of course I do!" Sunaina replies immediately. "And I would if only Fatima wasn't in the way! She is a burden I promised to bear!"

Fatima must have made some sound, a wordless protest, because the women turn. Sunaina's face drains of color while the other two look horrified.

Fatima takes a deep breath and then another. She remembers Firdaus and the sense of belonging she feels with him, the kinship. She thinks of the Alif sisters, who are more family than friends. She is not alone. She will be all right. Not right now but later, when it hurts a bit less, she will be all right.

At this moment, though, Fatima doesn't know what to do. Does she turn around and go find the Alif sisters? Or is she supposed to wait for her sister? Cry? Pretend that she didn't overhear that conversation? What do you do in situations like these where your heart and your mind are two separate things and both of them have been crushed?

Fatima makes up her mind to leave, when suddenly something moves in the darkness. She smells something foul, something *wrong*, senses it stir in the shadows just beyond the puddle of light in which Sunaina and her friends stand.

A growl, low and guttural, comes from the darkness and even those unaware of the malice freeze. Fear blooms fully on the faces of the people, including Sunaina and her friends, closest to the shadows.

CHAPTER 7

It rained the day the Shayateen massacred the city of Noor. Fatima remembers the strangely metallic smell of it. A smell filled with anticipation. Tense, as the air before a conversation. Fatima and her sister were home by themselves, waiting for their parents to return with food from the market. It was a Friday, and Fridays meant masala dosa from their favorite vendor in the market.

When someone banged on the door, Fatima and Sunaina looked at each other. Fatima remembers her sister squaring her shoulders, perhaps to convey her courage, and pulling the door open, not knowing who waited on the other side—their parents wouldn't have knocked.

They hadn't recognized the old woman standing on the doorstep. They hadn't known what to make of her wide eyes, wild hair, and dirty sari. The old woman hadn't waited for an invite, just barged into the house and slammed the door shut behind her.

When Sunaina protested, the old woman hissed, "Quiet, they're coming!"

Before they could ask who, the screaming started. Fatima has spent the last eight years trying to forget the screaming.

When their door was broken down, Fatima screamed too. The monster that came through the door was beautiful. He had lifted his sword, wet with someone's blood, and brought it down. Fatima, closest to the door, was attacked first. She protected her face instinctually, and her arms were sliced.

The monster had grabbed Fatima's arm and licked her blood. A minute later, he was ash. Another monster came after him and he, too, suffered the same fate. Fatima bled, so she, her sister, and the old woman they would later call Laali would be able to live. They spent hours, covered in her blood, listening to the screams of first the citizens of Noor and later of the Shayateen who had killed them and who, themselves, were killed by the Ifrit.

Eight years have passed since then. Eight long years full of nightmares and unexpected pockets of grief.

The growl sounds again, and a creature emerges from the darkness. Whatever this creature is, it is neither Ifrit nor Shayateen, as it is only vaguely human in appearance. It has a too-wide mouth full of sharp teeth, orange eyes full of flames, and hair matted with dirt and leaves. Tattered clothes hide its groin but little else. Claws extend from its triple-jointed fingers. The creature turns its head toward Sunaina and her friends, sniffs the air, and slobbers.

Fatima's heart thuds in her chest. Her breaths become shallow. Eight years have passed, and yet, it is as though someone has reached out and scrubbed them all away. She is in that house again, facing yet another monster.

"Ghul!" a man screams, and terror breaks upon the people in the maidaan. Fatima stands frozen for one second before instinct takes over. She rips out a pin from her hair and slices her right arm. Blood immediately wells, and the creature, its nose twitching, turns in her direction. Fatima's breath shudders out of her. She reaches for courage.

The creatures takes two steps in her direction before it stills, head suddenly tilted as if hearing a sound everyone is deaf to. It makes a sound of frustration and leaps off into the night. Not a moment later, the Ifrit who had terrorized Fatima in Firdaus's book-store earlier that day arrives on the back of a white horse. His gaze tangles with Fatima's, and she holds up a hand almost uncon-sciously, pointing in the direction in which the creature fled. He nods once and is gone.

The night explodes into sound and movement. Fatima stum-bles, and someone places an arm around her waist. Fatima turns her head to meet the muezzin's opaque eyes. He nods again and moves to give way to Adila, who wraps her arm around Fatima's shoulders, supporting her weight. Sunaina walks over with ashen cheeks and bright eyes.

Fatima looks unseeing at her. She cannot move out of that day eight years ago, cannot stop hearing those screams.

"You're bleeding," Sunaina says. Amirah and Azizah immedi-ately start taking off their dupatta to use as makeshift bandages. Fatima begins shaking. She cannot stop hearing the screams. She is conscious of the world around her, but the past overlays it. The screams. The blood. The bodies.

"Fatima!" Sunaina shakes her.

"They won't stop screaming, Adila," Fatima says to her friend. "They won't stop *screaming*!"

The Alif sisters gather Fatima close to them, and she closes her eyes and cries.

When the past finally loosens its hold on Fatima, she finds herself with the Alif sisters and Sunaina on the back of a cart on the way home. The night has lost its sparkle. The last time she had one of these fits had been more than a year ago. Adila had screamed at a spider in front of her and sent her spiraling into the past.

"We were on our way to the eastern gate to get you and Sunaina Baji because we wanted to buy paper lamps from the stalls there,"

Amirah says suddenly, her voice lacking its usual verve. "Api heard of the Ghul and wanted to leave us behind while she came to check on you." She sounds outraged at the idea.

"As if we would let her," Azizah grumbles.

Adila says nothing. She is holding on tightly to Fatima's uninjured arm. Sunaina has her arms wrapped around herself and sits quietly with her face averted from Fatima.

The driver of the cart drops them off at the front door, shaking away their attempts to pay him. They walk up the stairs in silence. Some of the apartment doors are open; the sound of voices talking and the smell of food cooking follow them up to the seventh floor. Adila sends Amirah and Azizah home; they live on the ninth floor. Sunaina unlocks the front door and the women enter the apartment.

Sunaina lights two lamps and a candle, and the apartment is illuminated in golden light.

An uncertain silence holds them in its thrall before Adila says briskly, "Let's get your arm bandaged."

Fatima feels her sister looking at her, but she keeps her face averted. Sunaina opens a drawer and pulls out a clean strip of cloth. Adila cleans the cut with cotton wool dipped in water while Fatima sits in a chair and allows Adila to fuss over her. When Sunaina tries to wrap the bandage around her arm, Fatima pulls away and stands up.

"Adila, can I spend the night at your place?" she asks, still not looking at her sister.

"Of course," Adila replies. She notices the flush in Sunaina's cheeks and the evenness of Fatima's voice and doesn't question further.

Sunaina opens her mouth as if to protest but ultimately chooses to retreat to the kitchen area. Fatima disappears inside the bedroom only to emerge a few minutes later dressed in a shalwar kameez with a change of clothes under one arm and her oud slung over her shoulder.

"Let's go." Without waiting for a response or saying a farewell, Fatima walks out of the apartment. Adila mutters a goodbye and follows her.

After Isha prayers, Adila and Fatima spread a mat out on the open roof and pile it with cushions. The sounds of revelry drift up to them; the people of Noor will wring all the celebration out of the night before they relegate it to the past. Fatima lies back on the cushions and stares up at the star-filled sky. The sharp scent of a mandarin fills the air. Adila pops a piece in her mouth and offers one to Fatima. The juice is both sweet and tart.

"What happened between you and Sunaina Baji?" Adila ventures after a moment. Fatima doesn't ever talk about what she lived through. She doesn't have words big enough to express the pain inside of her.

Fatima breathes out, suddenly so weary that even breathing hurts. She sits up and considers Adila's question. "Do you remember that time Ali Abbu took us to Tameez for the cotton harvest?"

Tameez is an oasis three hours away from Noor and home to the largest number of cotton trees in Qirat.

Adila nods. "We were fourteen." Her lips quirk. "Amirah and Azizah complained for days because they weren't allowed to come with us. Why?"

"Do you remember that little orphan girl we met there?"

"Fazilat? Yes. She had the longest eyelashes I have ever seen on anyone."

"Before we let her out, she stood in that shack with her face pressed to the window."

"I remember that. Why did they lock her in?"

"They thought losing her parents meant she had bad luck. They didn't want her and her bad luck to affect the harvest."

"Ah." Adila looks pensive. "But why bring up Fazilat all of a sudden?"

"Because today for the first time, I felt what she must have felt." Fatima looks out at the desert. Storm clouds are gathering on the horizon.

Zulfikar roams the mahal in the still hour of the morning just after Fajr. A scent of lightning charges the air, making it impossible for him to sleep. He walks to the kitchen on the first floor and makes a request to the staff already awake. Ten minutes later, the boy who usually serves him his food carries up a tray containing a copper pot of tea with a bowl of sugar cubes, a cup, and a plate of Zulfikar's favorite dessert, gulab jamun.

"If you want a more substantial meal, sahib, I can bring it for you." The boy places the tray on a small table near the open balcony doors and leaves. Sheer white curtains flutter in a breeze. Zulfikar's apartment in Northern Aftab looks out over the desert arm of the River Rahat.

Zulfikar stands outside on the balcony, dressed in a white tunic and shalwar, the attire he usually sleeps in. A feeling of unease skitters down his back, and he stalks into the room. He pours himself a cup of tea and drops two sugar cubes into the cup. He returns to the balcony with his cup of tea and the plate of gulab jamun. Setting down the plate on a table on the balcony, he leans against the railing and stares out at the city before him. The feeling of unease persists. The Ghul attack on the city the night before perturbs him. Ghul usually only attack traveling parties; they do not take risks, and they definitely do not escape without killing anyone. The night before, Zulfikar and his soldiers chased three of the creatures, but all three managed to escape. That isn't the strange part. What concerns him is that the Ghul didn't kill or even injure anyone. It was as though their only intent was to incite fear among the Noor citizens.

His thoughts return to only a few hours earlier, when his pursuit of the Ghul led him to the girl with the Djinn fire. Her existence vexes him; she feels like a puzzle he ought to solve. Why has Firdaus kept her a secret? Zulfikar pops a gulab jamun in his mouth and closes his eyes to properly savor the taste. Is she a threat to Firdaus's safety?

Life in Al-Naar is simpler, Zulfikar muses. The enemy is obvious and cannot take advantage of shadows to spread their malice because Al-Naar, and the city of Tayneeb in particular, does not allow for shadows. Zulfikar looks at the red-streaked skies; dawn is the closest Earth skies get to the sky in Al-Naar. Dawn is when Zulfikar feels homesick the most. He gets up abruptly and returns to his room, closing the balcony doors behind him.

When Sunaina wakes up the next morning, the first thing she notices is Fatima's absence. For someone who barely talks, who clings to silence like a lover, Fatima's absence is loud; the memory of her fills all the spaces in the apartment until Sunaina can barely stand it. She performs her morning ablutions and makes roti, spinach curry, and chai flavored with cardamom and cloves. She glances frequently at the front door, thinking she heard the key turning in the lock, the door being pushed open, and Fatima slipping in.

The minutes turn into an hour. The chai cools, as does the food. The door remains closed. Sunaina packs up the food to drop off to Laali—no sense in it going to waste—and changes into the clothes she wears to work. Her heart seems to beat too fast in her chest, and her throat is thick with regret. She thinks of the look on Fatima's face the night before and swallows.

Would an apology solve anything? What if she marched to the Alifs' apartment right now and demanded to speak to Fatima? What would she say? I'm sorry? Would that suffice? But what is she sorry for? Why is she sorry? That Fatima heard her feelings? That she has these feelings? Or that she discussed Fatima with her friends?

The silence feels too large, and the apartment too empty. Sunaina makes her way to work without paying any attention to the road she travels. She gets a ride from one of the many carts on the road and gets off one street before Sushila-ji's haveli. Lost in her thoughts, she doesn't even pause like she usually does to admire the grand havelis along the street. She nods absentmindedly to the gatekeeper and walks up the driveway and through the back door into the kitchen. There she finds all the house servants gathered around Anjum, who is regaling them with the tale of the Ghul from the night before.

"Look, here's Sunaina!" Anjum says when she sees her. "You can ask Sunaina if you don't believe me!"

Before they can, however, the housekeeper arrives and scatters the servants to their individual duties. Sushila-ji's grand house is a mess from the previous night's party, and its occupants are still abed. The housekeeper wants the haveli cleaned and tidied before they wake up.

Sunaina and Anjum are sent to clean the courtyard.

"Did you get home safely?" Anjum asks, picking up the charred pieces of spent fireworks. "I was so scared I couldn't sleep all night long! Is your sister all right? I have never seen anyone as brave as her!" The other woman keeps talking, but Sunaina stops listening.

"Sunaina?" Anjum shakes the girl, looking at her pale face in concern. Sunaina starts.

"Sorry." Sunaina rubs her eyes with her hand. "I'm just a bit tired."

"Sunaina!" a maid calls out to her from the upper verandah.

"What is it?" Sunaina says. The maid, Razeema, bounds over.

"Rajkumari Bhavya was here last night! Maya-ji wore that orange eye shadow you made for her, and the rajkumari loved it! Maya-ji told me the rajkumari wants you to make her some!"

"What?" Sunaina stares at the younger maid, not comprehending for a second. "Really?"

"Yes! Really!" Razeema nods enthusiastically.

Sunaina's eyes widen.

Fatima arrives at work with her cheeks flushed and her clothes wrinkled. She is wearing a pale green tunic with matching shalwar. Her deep blue turban is unraveling, and she hurriedly fixes it. She fell into a deep sleep after Fajr and woke only when Amirah stepped on her on the way to the bathroom. Then she discovered that she had slept on the clothes she intended to wear that day but didn't have time to grab new ones from her apartment. No carts were headed the way she was going, so Fatima ran all the way over to Achal Kaur's haveli.

Her haste has been for naught. All deliveries have been assigned, and the only one in the reception is Achal Kaur sipping on a pyali of chai.

"I was getting worried," Achal Kaur says, looking anything but. "Come here."

"I'm sorry, Beeji, I slept in." Fatima is desperately apologetic. She has never been late before.

"It is not to scold you that I call you nearer, chanda. Your arm, it is bleeding." Fatima looks down and grimaces. The bandage Adila had tied around her arm the night before is now wet with blood.

She bumped into a corner while running to work. The wound has a dull ache that Fatima feels only now.

"My sources told me you had a bit of excitement last night," Achal Kaur says, untying the bandage and looking at the cut with pursed lips.

"Some kind of creature . . ." Fatima trails off.

"It was a Ghul. A kind of Djinn. They don't usually attack in cities." Achal Kaur's eyes are sad, and Fatima remembers that her son had been killed by a Ghul. "Don't worry, the Emir will keep us safe."

"Do you know the Emir, Beeji?" Fatima asks curiously.

"He and I do the occasional business," the old woman says vaguely. She finishes her chai and gets to her feet. "Come."

She takes Fatima to the second floor, where a bevy of matrons fuss over her, plying her with food and redressing her cut. By the time they return downstairs, Fatima has regained her energy if not her spirits.

"Beeji," Fatima says, following Achal Kaur into a room full of cubbies where outgoing packages and letters are kept.

"Hmm?" Achal Kaur riffles through a stack of small packages.

"Do you know anyone renting out single rooms?"

Achal Kaur's eyes sharpen. She turns to face Fatima. "Don't you live with your sister?"

"She's getting married," Fatima replies, trying to look happier at the news but finding it beyond her.

Achal Kaur's expression clears. "I will ask around."

"Thank you, Beeji."

"Too early to thank me, chanda. Ah yes, here it is." Achal Kaur removes a small package from the stack. It is addressed to Firdaus. "Taufiq dropped this off for the old man."

"Another book?" Fatima looks at the package.

"What else could it be? The old man only ever receives books from the merchant." Achal Kaur frowns at Fatima. "Will you be all right today? If your arm hurts, you can take the day off."

"No, I will work," Fatima says firmly. She bids farewell to her boss and leaves the haveli, making her way to Kalandar Street as quickly as she can manage.

Fatima pauses outside the bookstore and takes a deep breath before pulling the door open. The sense of homecoming she feels when she enters Firdaus's bookstore is enough to send fresh tears to her eyes.

"I didn't expect you today," Firdaus says from the doorway to the inner room. At the sight of him, all of Fatima's defenses come crumbling down and the tears she has been suppressing since the night before escape. Firdaus leads her to her chair in the back room, gives her a cup of tea, and waits silently. When the torrent of tears finally abates, Fatima takes a shuddering breath and looks up to see Firdaus's bemused expression.

"May I ask what's wrong, ya binti?"

"It's a long story, baba." Fatima manages a smile. "One I would rather not give words."

Firdaus nods and gestures to the tea. "Drink. Rahmat delivered some kunafeh this morning. Eat." Firdaus returns to his work at his desk, giving Fatima space and time to regain her equilibrium.

"Baba." Fatima remembers the package. She removes it from her messenger bag and holds it out to Firdaus. "The merchant, Taufiq, delivered this to Beeji today. It's a book."

Firdaus eagerly takes the package. "I've been waiting for a volume of poetry written by an obscure Kmemu poet."

Firdaus rips open the brown paper wrapped around the book and makes a sound of pleasure when he discovers that the book is indeed the volume he was seeking. He flips open the book, running his fingers through the text. Fatima watches him, consoled by the pleasure he takes in the written word. He suddenly, unexpectedly, goes still, and the old Ifrit's face empties of expression.

"What is it, baba?" Fatima moves closer to Firdaus. Firdaus lowers the book, and Fatima sees a smudge of black on the edge of the paper. She watches that viscous blackness slither from the paper onto Firdaus's hand before being absorbed through his skin.

Firdaus's gold eyes flash black, and Fatima staggers back a step.

"The taint," Firdaus says through clenched teeth. Black veins appear on his skin and spread like the vines of a grape plant. Fatima watches helplessly.

"What do I do, baba? Who do I call?"

Firdaus's skin is sallow, and he is sweating profusely. He grips the edge of his desk tightly, keeping himself upright. The book has fallen unnoticed to the floor. "Listen, ya binti, listen." Fatima nods frantically. "You are a child of flesh and blood, and I am a being of fire and bone. Were I merciful, I would bid you run and end this tale here. But I am Ifrit and my stories are eternal even though I am not." Firdaus extends his trembling right hand to Fatima. "In return for the kindness I have shown you, will you become the ink that writes my tale?"

There never was a choice.

Fatima reaches out and grabs his right hand with both of hers.

CHAPTER 8

The clock strikes two. Two minutes later, the world falls apart.

Zulfikar is sitting in the library with Anwar conferring on some oblique details forwarded by the Emir of Rahm. The Wazir, who returned from Rahm not an hour ago, raises an intricately decorated blue-and-gold teacup to his lips. Then the first wave of heat washes over them, and they are conscious of nothing except each other and agony. The second wave of heat is lesser in intensity but longer in duration.

When Zulfikar regains his senses, he finds himself on his feet with his sword out. The teacup is in three pieces on the floor, and Anwar's usual serenity is nowhere in sight.

"What was that?" Zulfikar asks the elder Ifrit, bracing himself in case there's another wave.

Before Anwar can respond, a sharp rap sounds on the door. Immediately after, the door is pushed open, and Mansoor, one of the lieutenants in the army, strides in. Despite the show of poise, the Ifrit soldier's eyes are wild and his hands are shaking. "Sayyid, the soldiers are panicking. Will you— We *need* you to reassure them."

Zulfikar's eyes widen. He sheathes his sword and asks the soldier, "The soldiers felt the heat too?"

"All Djinn did, sayyid. The Ifrit soldiers patrolling the city returned panicked. They said the pain felt like someone trying to cleave their name from them."

At the soldier's words, Zulfikar blanches and turns on his heel. He marches down the flights of stairs until he is out of the mahal. A thick dread fills him. "The Wazir will talk to the soldiers," he tells Mansoor, who follows him as he stalks to the stables. He whistles sharply, and quickly a stable boy leads Zulfikar's horse out.

"And what, pray, am I supposed to tell the soldiers, Zulfikar?" Anwar says from behind them. The Wazir has regained his composure far quicker than anyone else.

"Lie, Wazir," Zulfikar replies, baring his teeth. "You do that so very well." He turns to Mansoor next. "Tell Khalid and Tariq"—the two Amir soldiers who usually accompany Zulfikar—"to follow me to Kalandar Street and wait for me at the junction."

Without another word, Zulfikar mounts his horse and tears away. The urgency he feels is compounded by a despair that whispers he is far too late. He spurs his horse on at a mad pace, hardly noticing the humans who scramble out of his way. He covers the distance that usually takes him half an hour in fifteen minutes. Every single minute weighs on him.

He dismounts his horse in front of the Name Giver's bookstore, and as there are no tethering posts nearby, he commands a human boy to look after his horse. The boy is on the verge of hotly refusing the terse request but another look at the Emir changes his mind. Zulfikar's djinni nature is very close to the surface. His eyes are one shade away from the orange of fire. Heat rises from his skin, making the air above it shimmer.

He approaches the closed door of the bookstore slowly. The doorknob is warm to the touch. A gust of heat escapes when Zulfikar pulls the door open. He steps inside and looks around.

The Name Giver tried to tame a tornado in his shop. Books that were on shelves are now on the floor, and the furniture has been upended or damaged beyond recognition. Ripped pages litter the floor. Zulfikar steps over the books on his way to the back room. A curious reluctance to go on presses against him, cajoling him to turn and leave.

The same tornado that visited the front room of the store made its round in the back room, but Zulfikar is conscious of nothing except the pile of ashes in front of the Name Giver's broken desk. He sinks to his knees beside of the ashes, unable, for a moment, to comprehend exactly what it is before him. Time gains an astringent quality; each passing second seems like an insult to all that is sacred.

Death is not uncommon to the Ifrit, and violent deaths are more frequent than they should be. However, the Name Giver's death has more consequences than the death of a common Ifrit soldier. Zulfikar feels detached from the scene, as if he is observing everything through some great distance. Though he did not know the Name Giver well—you cannot really know a pillar in your house—his importance, his wisdom, his grace are all things that Zulfikar aspires to. When such a man has been reduced to ashes, how do you grieve? When the pillar is broken, your house will fall.

He looks around the back room and makes note of the charred pages and the ruined books. A slim volume on the floor, notable for its pristine condition, catches his eye; the page it is open to is blank, apart from a smudge in the margin. It lies at a little distance from the pile of ashes. Zulfikar moves to pick it up, when an odd caution halts his movement. He peers closer at the smudge, then rears back when the smudge moves, as though conscious of his regard. Without thought, Zulfikar brings up his fire and burns the book, smudge and all. When it is nothing but ash, tears prickle his eyes.

There are things he needs to do, messages he has to send, people he needs to speak with, but at this moment, all he can think of is how the Name Giver was but isn't anymore. Had he insisted on moving the old man into Northern Aftab, he might yet have been alive. Grief, sudden and explosive, hits Zulfikar squarely in his chest, and he breathes in sharply. He gets up from the floor, unable to bear the atmosphere in the bookstore for another second.

As he turns to leave, his feet hit an oud, oddly undamaged, lying on the floor. He picks it up, and when he turns it over, he sees a stamp on it that identifies it as a creation of an old Ifrit master in Tayneeb. A faint scent of fire clings to the oud's surface.

He brings the oud closer and inhales deeply. His eyes flare when he identifies the scent. The human girl with the Djinn fire. Was she here when Firdaus turned his fire on himself? Does she know how he got the tainted book? Will she know who gave it to him? The bookstore contains no signs that anyone else was injured or killed in it apart from the Name Giver. The girl must still be alive. Zulfikar grasps the oud tighter. He will find her and, with her, answers.

The afternoon brings with it a release from the drudgery that is a housemaid's work. Sunaina fairly skips down Rootha Rasta on the way home. She pops into her favorite mithai store and has the mithai wallah pack up jalebiyaan, barfi, and, Fatima's favorite, peda. She also buys two motichoor laddoo, eating one and saving the other for Fatima. With a spring in her step, Sunaina resumes her walk home, contemplating the future if she manages to win Rajkumari Bhavya's favor. With the princess's patronage, Sunaina will be able to stop working as a housemaid and focus on making cosmetics. She will earn much more money than she is earning now, and perhaps in time, she can earn enough to buy a house somewhere that is not Taaj Gul.

Sunaina decides to check on Laali before heading upstairs. She finds the door to Laali's room ajar and the old woman sitting on the floor with her clothes disheveled and hair wild.

In a rush of concern, Sunaina runs to Laali, but the old woman waves her away. "I'm all right, child."

"What happened, Laali?" Sunaina helps the woman to her feet and guides her to the rocking chair. Laali sits down with a thump.

"Just a flush of heat," Laali replies, smoothing down her hair with shaking hands.

"Should I take you to a healer?" Sunaina asks, worried.

"No, it was a momentary thing." Laali shakes her head emphatically. "Have you seen Fatima today?"

Sunaina starts at the question. "No. She went to work early. She's probably at home right now!" She smiles brightly.

"Tell her to come see me as soon as she can," Laali says, her eyes looking distant.

"Is there something worrying you, Laali?" Sunaina asks, looking uneasy.

"Nothing to be concerned about, beta. Now go on home; you must be tired."

Sunaina takes her leave and walks up the stairs slowly, her earlier exuberance banked. She smiles at the children running in the corridors and playing on the stairwells. She even responds to the women who stand in patches of sunlight, gossiping over many pyali of chai and pakoray. She murmurs noncommittal answers to more invasive questions about her life; busybodies want to know if she has a beloved, when she's thinking about getting married, or if she needs the services of a matchmaker. When she finally reaches her front door, Sunaina is almost jittery with relief. She opens the door quietly, not wanting to disturb Fatima in case she is sleeping.

However, the apartment is dark, with no sign of Fatima anywhere. Whatever remained of Sunaina's good cheer drains away. She puts the box of mithai on the kitchen counter and checks the bathroom and the bedroom again, just in case.

Sunaina doesn't want to do this, but it appears that she has no choice if she wants her sister back. Resigned, she climbs the two flights of stairs to the Alif sisters' apartment with feet that suddenly seem leaden.

She knocks on the door louder than she intends to. When it is pulled open, Sunaina sees the youngest Alif sister regarding her quizzically.

"Will you tell Fatima that I would like to talk to her?" Sunaina says stiffly.

"Fatima?" Azizah repeats, frowning. She calls over her shoulder, "Api, did Fatima Api come back?"

Adila appears behind Azizah. "What's the matter, Baji?"

"Is Fatima not here?" A cold fear runs its fingers down Sunaina's back and gives color to her words. "Are you hiding her because she doesn't want to talk to me?"

"Please come in, baji." Adila pulls Sunaina inside and closes the door behind them. "Fatima really isn't here. Has she not come home yet?"

"No . . ." Sunaina trails off.

"What's happening here?" Asma, the Alif sisters' mother, asks. She must have been making rotis because her hands are covered with flour. She takes one look at Sunaina and takes charge of the situation.

"Azizah, make some chai. Adila, you and Sunaina come with me." The girls obey. Once they are seated in the living room, Asma, an expression of concern on her face, asks Sunaina, "Is Fatima usually this late?"

Sunaina shakes her head, feeling sick. "If she has a late delivery, she lets me know."

Asma thinks. "Adila, did Fatima say anything to you this morning?"

"No, Amma, she was gone before we woke up, remember?" Adila says.

Sunaina suddenly stands up. "I'm sure she will be back soon. I am probably being overprotective!" Sunaina laughs, and even she can hear the false note in her voice. "I will go wait at home. I'm sorry for bothering you."

Without giving Asma and Adila time to respond, Sunaina makes her escape. Once home, she sits on her charpai with her knees drawn up to her chest and waits.

Hours pass, and the shadows lengthen. Sunaina doesn't move from her spot, convinced that if she waits long enough, she will hear a key turn in the lock, a tread on the floor, and Fatima's voice calling for her. It is nine o'clock at night when instead of a key she hears a knock. Sunaina jumps off the bed and hits her toe on the bed leg. Not heeding the pain or bothering to turn on a lamp, she runs to the door and wrenches it open.

"Fatima?" The name tumbles out of her lips before she realizes it isn't her sister on the doorstep.

"Is she still not back?" Adila asks, looking scared.

At her question, the tears in Sunaina's eyes spill over and she shakes her head.

"My abbu is back. I will ask him to accompany me to Achal Kaur's haveli. Light the lamps, baji. Stay here and wait. Fatima will return when she sees the lights." Adila gives Sunaina a smile that doesn't quite reach her eyes and leaves.

Sunaina turns to the dark apartment, closes the door behind her, and lights all the lamps she can find.

PART TWO

PART TWO

A STATE OF BECOMING

Awhisper in the dark and the memory of a red sky. She clasped his hand in both of hers, and he set her on fire. He set her on fire, and yet *he* was the one who burned. He burned, and there was nothing she could do except bear witness. She bore witness to his pain until she felt it herself. And now she lies in the ruins of a maharajah's palace, knowing that she has a name but unable to remember what it is. If she remembers, the pain will return. If the pain returns, the loss will become real.

She feels unanchored from her physical body. The air is cold and smells of smoke. The ground is hard and maybe damp. She cannot see the stars.

The girl slips in and out of consciousness. Her skin flushes hot and then cold. The third time she wakes up, the walls are on fire. Or perhaps she is. Perhaps she is still sleeping. If everything is a dream, then maybe she is too. The hours stretch into night. The next time the girl finds consciousness, she sees a glimpse of gold, not outside but within. She turns her gaze inward and sees that persistent flash of gold. It blinks at the corner of her eyes, there until she turns and looks at it fully. The girl is conscious of two things at this moment: physical discomfort and, contradictorily, a disconnect from her physical self. Is she, or isn't she? She looks at the flash of gold again. If the gold flash is a thing, a word, a name, *the* name, that tethers her to the part of her that feels the disconnect, if it remains forgotten, what is she? What is she going to become?

Fatima. The name blooms suddenly in her mind. This name has shades of a prickly sister and a father who tickled her until she laughed because he liked her dimples. The name reminds her of a mother who left vases full of marigold blooms all over the house. Marigold blooms and oranges. Fatima is familiar; Fatima feels like hers. Yet it is no longer enough. Fatima is only half a name and describes only half a person. There, the flash of gold again. In this dark place, the girl who used to be Fatima extends a hand and, as though it has been waiting for her, the name drops on her upturned palm.

It is hot to the touch. In fact, it is on fire. Smokeless fire. Images of a desert, an oud, a caravan train destroyed, corpses on the ground, a child named Shuruq, and Baba with his slow smile and kind eyes. This name has sharp edges; it has known despair and pain. A shadow clings to this name; it used to belong to someone else. Fatima brings this name up and presses it into the skin above her heart. The name flares, lighting the darkness briefly before it is absorbed into her skin. *Ghazala*. It is hers now.

She sleeps.

CHAPTER 9

Zulfikar is out of Northern Aftab before the sun has the chance to sweep the shadows out of the morning. He spent the night sending and receiving messages from Tayneeb, the city of the Ifrit in Al-Naar. The Name Giver's death has to be kept secret; there are many who would try to take advantage of the vulnerable straits this leaves the Qirati Ifrit in. Zulfikar makes his way slowly through the streets of Northern Noor, carrying along with him the guilt that sprang up inside him as soon as he comprehended Firdaus's death.

His only hope is to find the girl. He spent hours the day before looking through the streets of Noor to no avail. Then he remembered Firdaus saying that the girl is a messenger. If she is a messenger, there is only person she could be working for.

By the time Zulfikar arrives at Achal Kaur's haveli, the sun is out in full force and the door to the building is open as messengers enter and exit. Zulfikar swings off his horse and stalks through the entrance. He spots the formidable woman immediately, standing in the middle of the room, berating a young boy who shares more than a few facial features with her.

His presence causes a murmur, and Achal Kaur looks up, her eyebrows drawing together when she sees him. She leads him to an office in a corner of the room, where they will be granted some privacy.

"To what do I owe the honor of your presence, boy?" Achal Kaur asks. "It is not yet time for me to send the month's reports to you, is it?"

It was Firdaus who suggested that the Emir use Achal Kaur's messengers to observe the city and her citizens. Each messenger writes a report containing their observations of the city. If anything is out of the ordinary, they report to their boss, who then reports to the Emir. Zulfikar has managed to keep peace in the city on many occasions due to timely reports from Achal Kaur.

"Was there a delivery for the old man yesterday?" Firdaus found Achal Kaur an invaluable resource in his book-collecting hobby. Instead of having books delivered to him and increasing the risk to his person, he let the books be delivered to the messenger service, which then passed them on to him. He had been using them without incident for the past seven years.

"Yes," Achal Kaur says. "A merchant, Taufiq Kadir by name, delivered a book for him the day before yesterday. Fatima delivered it to him yesterday."

"Taufiq Kadir," Zulfikar repeats.

"Yes, he trades along the Silk Road. He said he was leaving right after delivering the book." The woman peers at him, her face tense. "Something has happened."

"Where is the messenger who delivered the book?" Zulfikar asks instead of replying.

Achal Kaur looks hesitant. "She's missing."

"Are you lying to me, sayyida?" Zulfikar growls.

"Mind your tone, Emir. You're still a child." The reprimand is immediate. Zulfikar bows his head in apology. "She didn't return after delivering the package, and I received news late last night that she didn't return home either."

"Do you know where she would go?" Zulfikar asks.

"I have my children out looking for her," Achal Kaur says.

"Send me a message as soon as you get word of her where-abouts," Zulfikar says. He turns to go, when Achal Kaur stops him.

"Do you mean her harm?"

"I just want some answers, sayyida." He takes a breath and corrects himself. "I *need* some answers."

Fatima Ghazala opens her eyes to a world too full of light. She sits up gingerly, her body gradually realizing the hurts it has suffered. She takes a deep breath of air and coughs. Her mouth is dry, her throat drier. The weight of all the prayers she has missed is heavy on her shoulders. She looks around, wondering where she is, and is discomfited when she identifies her surroundings as the ruins of the palace the last maharajah called home. The only things that remain of what was once a majestic building are the walls and the skeleton of the major staircase. These, too, bear scorch marks. The Ifrit could have removed the ruins, but they chose to leave them there on a hill in Southern Noor so the citizens would see them and remember the war and the dead.

The cloth Fatima Ghazala usually wraps around her head is missing, as are her memories of how she got to the old mahal. Her shalwar is dirty, and her tunic is torn. Fatima Ghazala reaches for her oud and then realizes she doesn't have it. She gets to her feet, her heart racing, and wonders why she feels so strange. Her oud is at Baba's bookstore. She left it there when—

When. She left it there. Yesterday. No blood was spilled. Blood. Her head hurts. Whose blood? Why? Beautiful faces in snarls. Fatima Ghazala's hands shake, and she rubs her cheeks, wiping away sudden tears. She straightens her tunic, takes a breath, and exits the ruins, stumbling on a loose block and surprising a napping cat. Unconscious of the looks she is getting from fellow pedestrians, Fatima Ghazala walks through the city streets she knows intimately. She crosses bridges, cuts through gardens and courtyards until she has left the verdant streets of Southern Noor behind. When she crosses another bridge over the desert arm of the River Rahat, she is finally in Northern Noor, where the air is arid and the heat feels like home.

She walks all the way to Kalandar Street and finds her path barred by Ifrit soldiers who stand before Firdaus's bookstore and allow no entry. Fatima Ghazala stands before these soldiers wondering how she can convince them that it is imperative she speak to Firdaus. Suddenly, her vision darkens, and the two soldiers standing before her fade into shadowy outlines. Each of them has a golden name embedded in the skin above their hearts. Each name has a different meaning, a different shape. The soldier on the right, his name is Qais; firm, lonely, and loyal. The qualities that compose this Ifrit are in his name. The soldier on the left is Masrur: happy and carefree, content to let life lead him where it chooses. The names glint, and upon a closer look, Fatima realizes that hundreds of gold tensile strings extend from the names and appear to shape the Ifrit who are no longer shadowy outlines but man-shaped smokeless fire.

"Sayyida." Masrur steps forward, and Fatima Ghazala blinks. As soon as she does, the veil falls back in front of her eyes, and the two soldiers resolve into their human shapes. "By decree of the Emir, no one but he may enter this shop."

Fatima Ghazala looks at the soldier uneasily and wonders if she has always been able to see the names of the Djinn.

"Sayyida . . ." Masrur tries again.

Fatima Ghazala looks up at the soldiers, drawing upon her fire to give her authority. The fire, *her* fire, races under her skin; Fatima takes comfort in the heat. The soldiers' eyes widen, and they look down in deference. "Call this Emir of yours. Tell him that I need to speak to my baba."

Zulfikar arrives at Kalandar Street just in time to hear the girl's command. His eyebrows rise at her imperial tone.

"Sayyid," Qais says, looking relieved to see him.

The girl turns to see who the soldier is talking to and stops short. Her eyes become unfocused, and her fire brightens. Then she blinks and shrugs, as if she is emerging from a trance.

"Zulfikar," she says softly.

His name is not a secret, but on her lips it seems like one. Zulfikar's cheeks grow warm, and he frowns.

"Are you Fatima?" She both looks like the girl he saw in the bookstore the other day and does not. Zulfikar cannot quite articulate the difference, but it is there.

"Fatima Ghazala," the girl corrects him. She looks at the closed door. "Why have you made Baba a prisoner in the store?"

Zulfikar flinches, and Fatima Ghazala catches it. Her eyes are wounded things. "What has happened to him?"

The fear that directed the course of their first meeting is entirely absent. "That is a question I must ask *you*."

"I don't understand." The girl meets his eyes, and he sees that she really doesn't. "I need to see Baba."

"He is at Aftab Mahal," Zulfikar finally replies. He is not lying except by omission. Firdaus's ashes *are* at Aftab Mahal.

"Will you let me see him?" the girl says, her hand reaching for a strap on her shoulder that isn't there.

"Yes." Zulfikar keeps his tone even, but his expression betrays him when she walks closer to him. Her fire smells as strong as it would if she were of the Ifrit. "Come with me," he says curtly.

The girl gives him a look. Zulfikar is reminded of the many other times he has been the recipient of this look from his mother, his sisters, all the Ifrit women who are able to decimate a djinni with their eyes alone. "Will you please accompany me?" He amends his words and is rewarded with a regal nod.

The horses present a problem. She has never ridden one and professes no desire to do so. After a minute of looking suspiciously at the horse, she acquiesces to riding in front of Zulfikar.

Zulfikar steels himself against the proximity; her nearness magnifies the wrongness he feels. Even though she is not Ifrit and he is not taking liberties with her person, being so close that their bodies touch still feels like he is willfully breaking the rules. Zulfikar doesn't break the rules, willfully or otherwise.

They reach the mahal, and Zulfikar dismounts first. He waits while she finishes looking around with wide eyes.

"Those gulmohar trees must be beautiful when in bloom," she says, looking down at him.

"Indeed they are," he replies shortly. "Will you get down?"

The girl looks from him to the ground and back again. She shrugs and jumps, and it is all Zulfikar can do to catch her. The shock of the contact is enough to fluster him, and his arms tighten for a second before he lets go and steps back.

The girl follows him silently up the stairs to the library. Only when he opens the door to the room does her face light up with pleasure and she says, "What a beautiful room."

Zulfikar gestures to the seats in the middle of the room and motions for her to sit. The girl hesitates, looking around. "Where is Baba?"

"By 'Baba' you mean Firdaus the bookseller?" Zulfikar says. He watches her carefully.

"Well, he doesn't sell very many books." The girl has dimples. "But yes, I do mean him. Where is he? Is he not here? Did you lie to me?"

"I did not lie," Zulfikar says bleakly. "Though I wish I had."

The girl looks at him uncertainly. Finally Zulfikar yields to the question in her gaze. He nods at the urn standing on a low table in front of the seats. "That urn contains all that remains of Firdaus the bookseller."

The girl, Fatima Ghazala, stares at him blankly for a minute, as if she cannot comprehend his words. Then she backs away from him, shaking her head, denying his words. Her face twists in pain, and she claws at her head, her eyes tightly closed against whatever she is seeing. She screams, and her fire rises to the surface of her skin.

CHAPTER 10

ulfikar frowns, unsure what to do, how to respond. Ifrit soldiers who lose control of their fire lose control of their names and thus their forms. They automatically shift planes until they are in Al-Naar. Of course this happens infrequently and only in moments of extreme mental and emotional distress. But for all that she has the fire, Fatima Ghazala is not Ifrit. Zulfikar doesn't even know if she has a name to lose. If she loses control of her fire, she will most probably die.

"What is going on here?" Anwar stands in the doorway of the library with a strange expression on his face. He looks at Fatima Ghazala and then at Zulfikar. "What is the matter with her? Who is she? When did she cross over? Is she related to the Name Giver . . . ?"

"Call for a healer," Zulfikar replies, stepping closer to Fatima Ghazala, who has wrapped her arms around herself and is rocking back and forth. He doesn't like the look in Anwar's eyes. "Send word to the rajah's side. They house healers."

The Wazir looks reluctant, but Zulfikar's piercing stare gives him no choice.

Once he is gone, Zulfikar returns his attention to Fatima Ghazala. She is oblivious to the world, locked in some kind of mental anguish. Zulfikar looks at her shaking form for a moment with his jaw clenched. He hates feeling helpless, so disregarding all bounds of propriety, he pulls her into his arms and accepts her fire into himself. Her fire is foreign and stings, but he endures the discomfort as it sinks through his skin and bonds with his fire. When it does, he feels her presence in him increase and understands why a bond between two fires is restricted to those who are married. Zulfikar wonders, with some panic, if he has leaped blindly off a precipice. But how could he stand by and let her die? She trembles in his arms, and he tightens his arms around her.

He holds her until she stops keening, until her grief, having been expressed, becomes manageable. He is aware of the moment she stops holding herself and slips her arms around him. When she finally stops shaking, he pulls away from her.

She stands in front of him, a portrait of grief. Her eyes are shining, and her cheeks are damp. Tendrils of hair have escaped her braid.

"Have you remembered what happened at the bookstore?" Zulfikar asks, gentling his tone with some effort. His need to know grows with each second.

The girl looks at him silently for a moment. Then, as if gathering her thoughts, she speaks slowly. "In flashes. Glimmers. Moments of pain. I was with Baba—" She breaks off and frowns. "No, that wasn't me. I mean, that wasn't me as I am right now." She stops again, looking frustrated. "I don't know how to explain it to you. I was Fatima before."

"And you are not Fatima anymore?" Zulfikar doesn't understand what she is trying to say.

"I am not *just* Fatima anymore. I am Fatima Ghazala. I didn't know I had that name before."

A thought occurs to Zulfikar, and his eyes widen. Surely not. It cannot be possible. The Name Giver's daughter, who was also Named Ghazala, is dead. Has been dead for the past fourteen years.

Zulfikar has more questions, but before he can give voice to any of them, the door opens and the Wazir enters, this time with a healer in tow. The two men stop short at the sight of Fatima, standing calmly before the Emir.

"I am perfectly well—unless you cure grief too? No? I didn't think so." The girl shakes away the healer's ministrations. "Though I would appreciate food and lots of dessert."

Zulfikar dismisses the healer and steps out into the corridor to call for refreshments for Fatima Ghazala. When he returns to the library, Anwar is pressed facedown on the tile floor. Fatima Ghazala has her knee against his spine to hold him in place while she twists his hand behind his back.

Zulfikar opens his mouth, then closes it. "What is the meaning of this?" he manages.

"I don't like strange men touching me," the girl says, her eyes almost molten in their intensity.

"He touched you?" Zulfikar asks, looking at the Wazir's position.

"He *tried* to touch me," the girl corrects him. She lets the Wazir go and stands up, wiping her hands on her tunic.

The Wazir gets to his feet, his face tight with rage. Zulfikar looks at the older Ifrit and notes that for the first time since he has known him Anwar is ruffled. The Wazir's clothes are creased, and there is a tremor to his movements. "Explain yourself, Wazir." The offense is a serious one, and were they in Al-Naar, the Wazir would have been in chains.

"She has Ghazala's fire, Zulfikar!" Anwar bites out. "Why does she have Ghazala's fire? Where is Ghazala? Where *is* she?"

Zulfikar feels his breath rush out of him. His suspicions have been confirmed. He tilts his head and looks at the girl. She meets his eyes without flinching. Her brows are furrowed, and she is looking at the Wazir as if he is some new insect that has recently crawled into existence.

"Ask her name, Anwar," Zulfikar says to the Wazir, not anticipating the explosion to come when he finds out. Instead of providing answers, the girl is just increasing the questions that Zulfikar will need to resolve before he faces the Raees. Though when and how he will face the Raees are also questions he doesn't yet have answers for.

"Why would I want her name?" Anwar sneers. "I want to know where Ghazala is, not the name of some inconsequential human."

"Why would I want to give *him* my name?" Fatima Ghazala asks, and Zulfikar is forced to concede. There is no reason she would want to give the Wazir anything, not the way he is behaving.

A knock on the door interrupts them. The food is brought in and laid out. Fatima Ghazala fills her plate and eats with relish, savoring every morsel. Anwar does not take his eyes off her, but the girl doesn't give the older Ifrit man another look.

Once she has finished eating her meal and the five different kinds of dessert that accompanied it, Fatima Ghazala washes her hands with water in a basin provided for the purpose and wipes her lips. "Ask your questions now," she says. Zulfikar straightens, unconsciously reacting to the command in her voice.

Anwar immediately repeats his question. "Where is Ghazala?"

Fatima Ghazala does not give any indication that she has even heard the Wazir's question. "Well?" she says to Zulfikar.

"You dare ignore me?" the Wazir hisses. "Know your place, sayyida!"

"And what place is that?" The girl keeps her face averted from Anwar. Her loathing for the man is practically a scream. Zulfikar decides to maintain his silence and simply observe for the time being.

"You are human," Anwar says as if that explains everything.

"I didn't realize being human is a sin," Fatima Ghazala retorts.

"We are the saviors of your kind!" Anwar grinds out.

"I saved myself, sayyid. And two others besides me. To my knowledge, no other human in the city escaped alive. Tell me again who you saved."

"You— No, more importantly, why do you have Ghazala's fire? Where is she?"

"Who is this Ghazala he speaks of?" Fatima Ghazala asks Zulfikar.

"She was his wife . . . until she chose otherwise," Zulfikar replies as blandly as he can manage. He doesn't miss the poisonous look Anwar shoots him.

"I do not know who Ghazala is," she says, still looking at Zulfikar, "or was. I also do not know why I have her fire."

"Do you think I will believe you?" Anwar replies.

"I do not think of inconsequential things," Fatima Ghazala says. "Ask your questions."

Anwar stands up; violence a promise in the lines of his body. Zulfikar clears his throat, reminding the Wazir of his position and his presence.

"This is important, Wazir. If you cannot restrain yourself, perhaps you ought to absent yourself for the rest of this meeting." Anwar glares at both the Emir and the human and sits back down without another word. "Will you tell me what happened in the bookstore?" Zulfikar asks gently.

Fatima Ghazala's eyes become cold, and the spark that animated her features fades away. She takes a deep breath and releases it. "Fatima went to deliver a book to Baba. She gave him the book, and the book killed him. He gave her his hand, and he killed her. When I opened my eyes, I was in the old mahal. Fatima is a memory—no, that is incorrect. She is not dead. She is here. I am her, but I am *more*. I am Fatima Ghazala."

Zulfikar feels the pieces fall firmly into place. Things make much more sense now. The reason why Firdaus protected the girl, the reason why he was so attached to her. The old Name Giver had known the human girl carried his daughter's fire. Zulfikar looks at the girl and finds her looking back at him.

"What is it that you aren't telling me?" she asks him.

"Ghazala, my wife, was Firdaus's daughter. The Emir probably doesn't want to tell you that any grace the old Ifrit showed you is due to your having her fire," Anwar says with a malicious smile.

"Ah." Fatima Ghazala doesn't flinch. Without looking at him, she responds, "I don't mind if the only reason he was kind to me is because of the fire I unwittingly possess. What matters is the kindness itself—though it seems the concept of it is foreign to you."

"The book didn't kill Firdaus," Zulfikar says before Anwar and Fatima Ghazala descend into an argument. "He killed himself."

"No." Fatima Ghazala refuses to believe that.

"Did he say anything before he set himself on fire?"

"I said he didn't!" Fatima Ghazala insists hotly.

"Did he?" Zulfikar will not be moved.

"I can't remember."

"Try!"

"Enough!" Fatima Ghazala stands up. She raises a trembling hand to her eyes and wipes them roughly. "It's going to be Zohr soon. I need to take a bath and change my clothes. Please arrange it."

Zulfikar looks dissatisfied but nods. Anwar's eyes are narrowed in thought, and his attention remains focused on Fatima Ghazala, though she betrays not the slightest sign that she is aware of it.

CHAPTER 11

Eight years ago, Maharajah Arjun, in a desperate bid to save the city of Noor and thus the country of Qirat from the invading Shayateen, gathered the remaining soldiers of his mostly decimated army and met the Shayateen in battle in the desert outside Noor City. With him was Sandeep, his eldest son and heir. The king, the crown prince, and the soldiers were all killed.

The first emotion Aarush was cognizant of when he got the news of his father's and brother's deaths was not grief but fear. At twenty, he was neither desirous of nor ready for the responsibility and burden of the crown. However, he couldn't refuse what his father and brother had died to protect. How could he refuse when he was alive and they weren't? When they had fought, and died, for their country, their people, while he sat at home, the spare heir, the just-in-case son? Aarush had argued with his father; he'd wanted to accompany them to battle. Twenty was old enough to die. His father had refused him every single time.

The mantle of the maharajah is oppressive; the gazes of his subjects always ask him for things he will not be able to give them. Aarush tries to be just, tries to care, but there are days like today when he would much rather retreat from the world and the many people laying claim to his attention and spend it in silence. Once upon a time, he harbored dreams of becoming a celebrated poet. Once upon a time, he spent days stuck inside his compositions.

But poetry has no place in politics, and so his verses wilted.

Aarush sits in the throne room, a grand hall with lavishly appointed seats for the maharajah and the maharani at the front, divans on the sides for the royal family, their relatives, and favored courtiers, and space in front for the masses to stand while waiting to supplicate the maharajah for whatever boon they seek. The final supplicant has just left, and Aarush is eager to escape the entirely overwhelming room. He gets to his feet.

Bhavya bursts into the throne room as if she is being chased by bandits. Luckily the room is empty apart from the immediate members of the royal family and Sanchit Goundar, a landowner and Ruchika's father.

Aarush takes one look at his younger sister's face and grimaces. He knows that expression. His advisor, Janab Jamshid, is right behind her, looking more anxious than usual. Bhavya has a way of making people anxious. "To what do we owe the honor of your presence, Bhavya?" Aarush decides to yield to the inevitable and sits down again. He pulls on Aruna's arm, and she sinks back in her seat gracefully.

"Why did the Emir call for a human healer, bhaiya?" Bhavya asks him, as if he is the Emir's personal secretary. Feeling exasperated, Aarush glances at his mother, who is seated on the side with Jayanti Bua. He also glances at Sanchit Goundar, but the man's face is impassive.

"Come inside and close the door. You too, Jamshid Chacha." They obey. "Your spies told you about the healer?" he asks, and Bhavya nods, not bothering to deny that she has spies. Aarush turns to Janab Jamshid. "Is the healer back?"

"Yes, Maháraj. He reported that he was summoned to look over a girl who claimed better health when he got there and refused to be examined."

"Is this girl he was supposed to examine human?" Aarush asks with interest. From all reports, the Emir has no friends, no confidants among his people. For him to be with a *girl* is particularly interesting.

"The healer cannot tell, Maharaj. She's young, he said, younger than Rajkumari Bhavya, perhaps." When Aarush looks at Bhavya, she has a scowl on her face. She does not like this particular turn of events at all.

"No Ifrit woman has ever manifested here before," Aarush muses out loud.

"Do you think they're bringing more of their soldiers over without talking to you first?" the Rajmata says anxiously.

"The Emir wouldn't do such things without reason, Amma," Aarush reassures his mother.

"Beta," Jayanti says with a sorrowful look on her face. "You cannot trust things like *them*. Isn't it about time we reclaimed our country from those creatures?"

"Your aunt is absolutely right, Maharaj," Sanchit Goundar says. "Your people are not happy having these Djinn ruling half of Qirat. The rebellion—"

"And how do you propose we find protection from the Shayateen without the Ifrit?" Aarush cuts off the man, keeping his voice genial.

"It is quite probable, Maharaj, that they are no longer a threat!" The landowner leans forward, talking excitedly.

"So you would have us risk our lives, our people, our *country*, on mere suppositions, Sanchit Baba?" Aarush asks softly. The landowner seems to realize he has made a gaffe. "Tell me, Sanchit Baba, where were you during the last war with the Shayateen? My father and my brother put their lives on the line and died protecting not just Noor but all of Qirat. Tell me, where were you then? Safe in some forest haveli as far away from Noor as possible?" Aarush scoffs. "And yet you dare to stand here and trivialize the sacrifices my father and my brother made so *you* can live?"

The man bows his head and apologizes. Aarush ignores him and looks very deliberately at Jayanti. She blanches and immediately lowers her gaze. "Know this, where the Ifrit are concerned, my father's words hold true now and they will hold true in the future. Anyone who speaks against the Ifrit speaks against my father."

"Come. Let us not talk of these things right now," the Rajmata says in an attempt to defuse the situation. "Do look up, Sanchit. Aarush, it is past time for lunch. Aruna, it is time for Vihaan's meal too, isn't it? Come now, let us move."

Bhavya watches her family members disperse. Her brother still looks grim, but her bhabhi, the maharani, gives her a warm smile in passing. Bhavya is much too preoccupied with the question of the human girl in Northern Aftab to pay the rest of them much attention.

"Bhavya." Her mother's voice cuts into her thoughts. "You and I will talk. Follow me."

The clock has just struck two in the afternoon when there is a knock on the door to Zulfikar's room. He gets up from the desk, where he was recording his thoughts, and walks across the room to the door. Fatima Ghazala stands on the other side, clean and comfortable in the cotton shalwar kameez she borrowed from a domestic.

"You have my oud," she says to Zulfikar, and stretches out a hand.

"Ah. I do. Will you come—" Zulfikar stops, horrified at himself. It has been too long since he was in the company of women if he is forgetting the strict rules of propriety.

"Come inside?" Fatima Ghazala gives him a curious look. "All right." She steps over the threshold. Zulfikar halts her progress with a hand on her arm, feeling his cheeks flush.

"Stay here. I will get your oud for you." He grabs the instrument from a side table and returns to her.

"Is this where you sleep?" she asks him, looking around. Zulfikar immediately feels self-conscious of the space. When she looks at his room, in the space where he wears no masks, it feels like she is looking into his soul.

"Yes. Here." He hands the instrument over, and she takes it reverently.

"Thank you." She pats the oud affectionately before slinging it over her shoulder. "I'm going home now."

"Home?" Zulfikar frowns. He doesn't quite know how this human girl with fire fits into Firdaus's story—well, he sort of knows, but letting her leave is probably not a good idea.

"You are not going to tell me I can't leave, are you?" The girl looks at him. Her eyes have a challenge in them.

Zulfikar considers. He cannot tell her about the taint until his superiors in Al-Naar authorize him to do so. He can tell her she will be in danger if she leaves, but considering the level of animosity directed toward her by the Wazir, she'll be in far more danger if she stays.

"I'm not," he finally says. "But would you let me escort you back?" Fatima Ghazala shrugs as if she doesn't care either way.

Later, Zulfikar reflects that his offer to take Fatima Ghazala home is less goodwill on his part and more a desire to feel her close to him once again. Ever since he took her fire into him and it bonded to his, he feels prickly around her. But not in an unpleasant way. The bond insists that she is important—and perhaps she is—but not in the emotional way that the bond suggests. Zulfikar wonders if he hasn't made an irreparable mistake by accepting her fire. For her part, she seems entirely unaffected by him, but perhaps he ought to take heart in the fact that she has yet to fling him on the floor and threaten bodily harm for daring to touch her.

"I am finding it difficult to believe that you are letting me leave," Fatima Ghazala says. They are riding slowly through the mostly empty streets toward Northern Taaj Gul.

"Me too," Zulfikar admits in a mutter. She should be placed in protective custody, but, in their world, in Al-Naar, no one tells the women what to do. They're the ones who make the rules and the male Ifrit are the ones who enforce them.

"Because it is most certainly my fault Baba came to his end," the girl says, a sob in her voice.

"If you are determined to blame yourself, nothing I say will appease you," Zulfikar replies. The blame for the Name Giver's death falls squarely on him, the Emir of Noor City, who failed to protect the one person he most needed to. He wonders how the girl will react if he tells her this.

Fatima Ghazala shifts on her perch in front of Zulfikar, and he, aware of the girl in a way he wasn't before, feels uncomfortable. They ride through the streets with Fatima Ghazala directing him until they stop outside the building where she and her sister live. The front of the building is deserted, though the hum of voices coming from within is proof that it is inhabited. Zulfikar dismounts and helps Fatima Ghazala off the horse. He hands her the oud.

"Be careful. Tell no one of your fire, and if you feel danger at any time—"

Fatima Ghazala shrugs. "I can take care of myself."

"You may have the strength, but you are not infallible. Don't forget that," Zulfikar warns her.

The girl flexes her fingers, as if trying out the strength he mentioned. She beams at him suddenly, and Zulfikar blinks. "What is it?"

"I like being strong," she replies.

Zulfikar shakes his head and gets back on his horse. He looks down at her and suddenly finds himself unwilling to leave. It is not that he doubts her ability to keep herself safe—well, he does. She *is* human, but then again, she has the fire. He doesn't know how to quantify her. In the end, all he can do is tell her again to be careful before muttering a brusque goodbye and riding away.

Fatima Ghazala stands for a moment, watching the Emir's receding figure. She doesn't know what to make of him. His name shines in his chest, in the space above his heart. Zulfikar: bladed, brimming with heat, clean, and honest. She should be able to trust him, but Fatima Ghazala feels wary. When she cannot see him anymore, she takes a deep breath and turns to face the entrance to the building.

The pink dust on the stone steps leading to the doors is familiar. The air, smelling of heat, chai, and chaunk is familiar. Also familiar are the drawings on the staircase wall. Colorful stick figures rollicking on the landscape provided by the rose-colored wall; childhood leaves its calling cards in the most unexpected places. One little blue sandal sits on the fifth-floor landing, no sign of its mate. Fatima Ghazala walks slowly; each step feels like a revelation. She thinks of her baba, so recently the most important person in her world, and now, less than a memory. Whatever he did to her has changed her innately. Like two halves of one piece finally becoming whole. Like having a voice and finding a song to sing with it.

The girl she was before the change feels like a story Fatima Ghazala heard a long time ago. Fatima, who was, seems like a reflection observed through a smudged mirror: hazy and distorted.

On the seventh floor, Fatima Ghazala turns into the corridor and walks down to the apartment she shares with Sunaina. She stares at the beaten blue door and hesitates. She has no key. Will anyone be inside? Does she want someone to be inside? Fatima Ghazala knocks on the door, and not one second passes before it is wrenched open.

She looks at the woman who opened the door, notes the shadows under her eyes and the pallor of her face. Her sister is at once familiar and strange. Fatima Ghazala feels a surge of love for her, a love peppered by pain. She remembers herself as she was, in the maidaan not two days past, listening to Sunaina call her a burden, an obstacle to her sister's future happiness.

"Didi," Fatima Ghazala tries saying. Sunaina stands in the doorway, looking shocked. For one moment anyway. Then she throws her arms around Fatima Ghazala and weeps. "Where have you been? Are you hurt? Do you know how much I was worried? I thought you were dead!"

"I apologize for the worry my absence caused you," Fatima Ghazala says, and is conscious of the lie. She *wanted* this woman, her sister, to worry.

"What happened to you?" Sunaina asks, her hands clutching Fatima Ghazala's hand. She pulls her inside and closes the door behind them.

Fatima Ghazala looks around the room, reassured by its familiarity. She looks down at the hands holding her and frowns. "There is something I must tell you."

Sunaina, face filled with concern, sits down, and pats the space beside her. Fatima Ghazala stares down at her older sister and remembers the night in the maidaan, the thorny words. She puts some distance between them—not much, the room is too small. She notes the look of hurt on her sister's face and feels a moment of pleasure. Why should she be the only one in pain? Then she stops, realizing that Fatima would never have felt this way. However, Fatima no longer exists.

"I am Fatima Ghazala," she says to Sunaina, conscious of a sense of empowerment that comes with putting into words what has become her truth.

"What do you mean? Fatima Ghazala? Do you feel ill? Do you need a healer?" Sunaina gets to her feet as well.

"I will only respond when both my names are used," Fatima Ghazala says. "I cannot speak of why or how." To explain would require knowing what happened to her, and at this moment, Fatima Ghazala doesn't.

"I don't understand what you mean. Are you acting this way because of what happened? What I said?" Fresh tears spill out of Sunaina's eyes. Fatima Ghazala watches her sister cry, and her conscience pricks. She ignores it. "Fatima!" Sunaina implores.

"Please address me as Fatima Ghazala." If she were still Fatima, she would give in to her sister, just like she did every time they disagreed. Her temper stirs. "Yes, actually, I am still upset by what I heard, by what you said. I didn't know that my existence creates an obstacle for your happiness. You should have told me. I will move out as soon as I can." She takes a breath. "However, calling me by my name has nothing to do with how you think I am a burden. I simply want to be addressed as Fatima Ghazala."

Sunaina flinches as if the words physically hurt her, but Fatima Ghazala isn't done yet. "If only you had spoken to me about your dilemma before speaking to other people about it, things would have been resolved quicker. I know we are not related by blood, but I would have thought you'd have granted me that consideration if only for the sake of the memories we share." Fatima Ghazala finds that she wants to say more things. Her words want to sting and hurt, but she reins herself in.

"How can you say this after being missing all night? Do you know how much I worried?" Her sister's eyes have brimmed over.

Fatima Ghazala looks at the only family she has left in the world. Fatima would have retreated from this confrontation. Fatima Ghazala refuses to. "If not now, then when?" She sighs. "I love you, didi. Hearing myself spoken of in that manner hurt. I don't ever wish to experience that pain again."

She meets her sister's eyes, and it is Sunaina who looks away first. Finally, she says, "You are right. You are not Fatima. Fatima would never have said something like this."

"No," Fatima Ghazala agrees. "But, didi, she still would have felt these words. Is that any better?"

The Alif sisters take the news better than Fatima Ghazala thought they would. After the initial round of teary hugs and scolding from the Alif parents, the Alif sisters and Fatima Ghazala retreat to the relative privacy of the open roof. It is not entirely abandoned, but the hour of the day means that people are either out working or cooking their evening meal. The children are still in school.

They take refuge under a shelter constructed by four posts, the roof of which is gauzy white fabric. The overhanging edges of the fabric flutter feebly in the hot breeze. Amirah pours them sharbat, and they all take long drafts of it.

After wiping her lips daintily on her embroidered handkerchief, Azizah fixes a gimlet eye on Fatima Ghazala. "What happened to you? You seem different. I can tell because I'm a great observer of people."

"That's what she calls her stalking of Bilal," Amirah adds, and yelps when her younger sister nudges her none too gently.

Fatima Ghazala laughs out loud at this, delighting in the simple companionship the girls offer. Her smile dims when she meets Adila's sadder eyes. "What happened to you, habibi?" the oldest Alif sister asks.

Fatima Ghazala has no desire to revisit the events of the past day. However, some people deserve all the truths she can give them. "To be honest, I'm not sure." She takes a deep breath. "Firdaus Baba died." She releases the breath in a shudder. "Before he did, something happened to me. Don't ask me what, I do not know. But when I woke up, I was no longer Fatima but Fatima Ghazala. I have fire . . . Djinn fire."

"Djinni fire? Are you Ifrit?" The three girls scoot closer to Fatima Ghazala and lower their voices.

"I don't know," Fatima Ghazala replies. "I don't think so."

"So you are not Ifrit, but you are Fatima Ghazala," Adila says slowly.

Fatima Ghazala nods firmly.

"Well, that's a mouthful." Azizah grins.

"It's nothing we can't handle, though," Amirah says, reaching for more sharbat.

"I will have you know that Bilal is still in excellent form." Azizah changes the subject. "His azaan last Maghrib was particularly beautiful."

"And yet you still drag your feet when it's time to pray," Amirah retorts.

It is not that they aren't curious or don't want to know more, but the sheen in Fatima Ghazala's eyes and the tremble of her lips asks them to retreat, to save their questions for another time. Adila slips her hand into Fatima Ghazala's and holds on tight.

Zulfikar manages to avoid the Wazir until after Maghrib. He is sitting in front of the fire pit behind the barracks, looking into the flames and seeing nothing when the Wazir finds him.

"What have you done with the human?" Anwar demands.

"There are much more important matters to discuss at this time than a human girl," Zulfikar says softly. "Even one with Djinn fire." In the orange glow cast by the fire, he looks closer to his Ifrit form than he ever has while being in his human shape.

Zulfikar looks at the Wazir and sees a brief expression of unadulterated rage on the older Ifrit's face. "Did you get news from Tayneeb?"

Zulfikar struggles to maintain a calm expression even as panic threatens to engulf him. He remembers what he was taught before he assumed the position of Emir: He cannot evince any fear or panic to anyone, human or otherwise. Some burdens are his alone to carry.

"Well?" Anwar prompts.

"The Name Giver's power failed to manifest in any of the four apprentices." Zulfikar feels sick even saying these words. He looks around belatedly and sighs in relief at finding the area empty apart from himself and the Wazir.

Anwar's eyes widen at the news, and he sits down on the wooden bench beside Zulfikar. "What are the elders doing about this? What did the Raees say?"

"The academics and the mystics are investigating, but they are limited in what they can achieve. For a full investigation, they need access to the location of Firdaus's death. Which is where we come in. Have you tracked down the merchant who sourced the book for the Name Giver?"

"Not yet. I have sent some Amir soldiers after his caravan on the Silk Road. As soon as they locate him, I will go."

"We need a new Name Giver as soon as possible." Zulfikar gets up and paces. He doesn't understand why the power hasn't passed on to an apprentice yet. No precedence exists in any of the books in any of the libraries in Tayneeb where the Name Giver's power hasn't manifested in someone new after the previous Name Giver's death.

The Wazir shrugs. "There is no imperative need for the Name Giver at this moment. We have enough soldiers. No specific conflict simmers to warrant any increase in our need for them. I think we will be all right until they resolve the problem."

Anwar has not been told of the Raees's condition, of the taint that even now is trying to eat her sanity. The Raees cannot stay in Tayneeb or even Al-Naar. If her control ever slips— Zulfikar shies away from the thought. He needs to talk to Fatima Ghazala one more time.

"It is more important to know how the human girl got Ghazala's fire," the Wazir says suddenly. "You might be too busy in the next few months to give her your full attention. I would like to lay claim to her."

Zulfikar's eyes narrow. "She's not an object. Do not speak of her as such."

"It is within my right—" Anwar says hotly.

"And what right is it that you speak of?" Zulfikar cuts him off.

"Ghazala was my wife!"

Zulfikar gets to his feet, suddenly furious. "If the records are correct, she released herself from that bond and pursued no other relationship with you before her disappearance."

"Even so."

"I refuse your petition, Wazir. And I repeat, Fatima Ghazala is not an object to be claimed." Zulfikar's tone is as cold as his anger is hot.

The Wazir's jaw tightens, and he opens his mouth, presumably to argue.

Zulfikar preempts the older Ifrit's protest: "You do realize that Fatima Ghazala is not a reincarnation of Ghazala."

"She has her fire," Anwar repeats, refusing to be persuaded.

"But not her soul," Zulfikar says, and walks away.

CHAPTER 12

A landscape littered with the bodies of people she loved, people she knew, and people she greeted. A fire extinguishing whatever remained of hope. Faces, beautiful enough to pull poetry from mirrors, hiding monstrous selves. The River Rahat running red with the blood of the dead. Her sister bleeding, burning with a strange light. Her sister, whose blood kept them alive from those who killed everyone. Her sister gone. Ashes remain.

Sunaina's eyes snap open, and for a moment, she lies in bed, breathing hard. Her dream is fading quickly, but the fear that choreographed it remains. She turns her head to check on Fatima Ghazala and sits up with a gasp. Her sister's skin is covered by an orange-yellow glow that lights up the room. Fatima Ghazala is making sounds of distress, as if under the thrall of some nightmare. Sunaina gathers up her courage and climbs out of bed, her feet curling on the cold stone floor. She moves closer to Fatima Ghazala's bed and reaches out to shake her shoulder but yelps and moves back even before her fingers make contact. The orange-yellow glow burned her. Sunaina looks down at her fingers, and terror washes over her.

What does this mean? Has Fatima changed in ways Sunaina doesn't understand? Ways she doesn't *want* to understand. What if this Fatima Ghazala is not her sweet sister but a djinni? A Shaitan? The same kind of creature that killed her parents. What if this Fatima Ghazala is here to kill Sunaina? No . . . What would her death achieve? But then again, when have the Djinn ever done anything logically? Fatima Ghazala cries out suddenly, and Sunaina jumps, tripping in her haste to move away. Her heart pounds furiously, and her throat is parched. She moves to the kitchen and with shaking hands pours herself some water. Standing in the dark, she sips the water, trying to calm herself. She needs to sleep before that creature wakes up for Fajr. Sunaina finishes her drink, takes a deep breath, and slips back into the bedroom. She stands looking at the sleeping figure before climbing back into bed. Her heart pounds. Sleep will not be a possibility tonight, but she can pretend.

Fatima Ghazala wakes up with a gasp. She cannot remember her dream entirely, but glimmers of it linger. A young child, about three, maybe four, with big gold eyes and a solemn smile. One minute smiling, the next minute cold in her arms. Fatima Ghazala raises a hand to her eyes and finds them wet. This despair, this feeling of loss. This is the third time she has dreamed about the child. Shuruq, her name is. This knowledge is innate.

Her sister is already up and cooking if the sounds coming from the other room are any indication. Fatima Ghazala grabs a light blue tunic and shalwar, pairing them with a red rectangular cloth that she wraps around her head. She eschews the breast binding; her femininity is no longer a weakness she has to hide. She performs her ablutions in the rickety bathroom and gets ready for the day ahead. Fatima Ghazala feels a keen sense of anticipation, as if the day is a ripe fruit just waiting to be picked. It is a feeling she does not remember having before. Fatima was cautious of shadows and corners. She was scared of many things though she pretended not to be. Fatima Ghazala flexes her fingers, and once again feels the strength in her body. No, Fatima Ghazala isn't afraid.

Wiping her face on a threadbare towel, she finally ventures out onto the battlefield. Sunaina is, as is her practice, making rotis for their morning meal. She has some eggplants roasting in the chulha fire, which she will later use to make baingan bharta.

Fatima Ghazala pours herself a pyali of chai. "I won't need lunch today."

Sunaina gives her a guarded look. "And why is that?"

"I'm meeting Adila at Lazeez Muhalla for lunch." Fatima Ghazala sips her chai with pleasure.

Sunaina finishes making the last roti without responding, removes the eggplants from the flames, and quenches the fire. Her movements are jerky, and she keeps glancing at Fatima Ghazala.

Fatima Ghazala puts down her pyali of chai. "What is it, didi? What have I done wrong this time?"

"Last night," Sunaina begins, stops, and swallows. She tries again. "Last night I saw you . . ." She stops again and takes a deep breath. "You . . . you were covered with smokeless fire . . . why?"

"Ah," Fatima Ghazala says. It was inevitable. "I suppose wishing you wouldn't find out was too much to ask for."

"Find out what?" Sunaina's voice is shrill.

"To be honest, didi, I don't quite understand what has happened to me," Fatima Ghazala says. "In the simplest words, from what I understand, I have Djinn fire."

Sunaina rears back at Fatima Ghazala's words, her hand losing its grip on the plate she is holding. The roasted eggplants splatter on the floor.

"You are a djinni?" Sunaina says slowly, disbelievingly. "You are one of the creatures that killed Amma and Baba?"

Fatima Ghazala looks at her sister, and her anger stirs faintly. "I don't know if I am a djinni, didi. I suspect not. I am certain, however, that I am not a Shaitan. I wish you would not blame the entire species for the actions of a specific few."

Sunaina barks out a laugh. "Look how quickly you defend them. After all they did to us!" Her eyes flash. "This just proves you are not human!"

"And what right do you have to judge my humanity?" Fatima Ghazala says, truly angry now. "You who forget so easily the reason you are even alive right now."

"Oh? So you think you did me a favor by saving me from those monsters? I wish you had let me die! That way I wouldn't have had to see you turning into one now!" Her last words are a scream that echoes in the silence that immediately follows it.

"I am a monster?" Fatima Ghazala laughs. The alternative would be to cry, and she refuses to give her sister the satisfaction. "I understand. I won't come back here," Fatima Ghazala says, her hands squeezed into fists, her heart quite possibly entirely broken. She retrieves her oud from their bedroom, slings it over her shoulder, and leaves without once looking back.

The road to Achal Kaur's haveli is long, and at this time of the day, very few carts travel in that direction. Fatima Ghazala walks slowly, navigating the early morning crowds without much effort. A few angry tears escape her, and she brushes them away brusquely. She will be fine. Perhaps not right now, but eventually, she will be fine. She doesn't know what has happened to her, but Fatima Ghazala is certain of one thing: She feels more like herself than she ever has before. Whether that means her real self is a monster, she doesn't know.

Her stomach growls, and she thinks of the breakfast she didn't eat and the chai she left unfinished. She purchases a glass of chai from one of the many chai wallahs along the way, and two steamed buns, stuffed with red bean paste, from a cart at the end of Rootha Rasta.

When she finally reaches the haveli, her boss is standing outside talking anxiously to a messenger. Fatima Ghazala feels a wave of fondness for the matriarch. Adila told her how worried she had been. Would her boss consider her a monster too? Fatima Ghazala grimaces at her thoughts. She will be fine. Fixing a smile on her face, she walks forward.

"Good morning, Beeji. These are for you." Fatima Ghazala hands her boss a superbly straggly bunch of daffodils she bought from a little girl and marches inside. Achal Kaur follows as rapidly as her girth allows.

"Why the flowers?" Achal Kaur asks, blinking in the dimmer light inside.

"For two reasons. The first is to apologize for missing work yesterday and causing you unnecessary worry. The second is because we are both alive, and that is a splendid thing." Fatima Ghazala beams determinedly at Achal Kaur.

"What's wrong, puttar?" the matriarch asks, and Fatima Ghazala shakes her head, unable to keep her smile from wilting.

"The man who died . . ." Achal Kaur starts, and trails off when Fatima Ghazala stops resisting her tears. Without another word, Achal Kaur pulls her into a hug, and Fatima Ghazala allows herself to be enveloped in the affection and love she needs so desperately.

Sunaina is welcomed back to Sushila-ji's haveli with open arms and not a little relief. Rajkumari Bhavya is waiting for her cosmetics, and no one wants to keep the princess waiting too long. Sunaina is shown into a large dimly lit room at the back of the haveli. The room is located on the ground floor, and the tiny windows of the room look out into the narrow alley separating Sushila-ji's haveli from the one beside it. One large wooden table, empty but for knives and other essential utensils, takes central position in the room. In the cupboards and on counters that stand against the three walls of the room are all the ingredients Sunaina could ever need to create any and all the cosmetics she desires.

Buckets filled with different flowers—from the decadent saffron to the fragrant gardenia—fill the top of one cupboard. Packets of ginseng roots, bowls of red beans and green mung bean to make into facial scrubs are strewn over the top of another cupboard. Also present are fresh peonies to extract oil from. Another counter is piled with packets of coconut flakes, cocoa both fresh and crushed, dried lavender buds, beetroot powder, turmeric, honey, and fresh cinnamon sticks. A basket full of jasmine flowers teeters dangerously at the edge of yet another counter. The bounty in this room is easily worth more than what Sunaina would be able to earn even after working for a decade.

"We purchased everything you asked for," Maya, her employer's eldest daughter, says. "If there is anything else you need, let me know right away."

Sunaina nods, and the girl smiles brightly. "Thank you, Sunaina. Rajkumari Bhavya couldn't stop asking about my eye shadow. It felt nice to have something she didn't for once." When Sunaina doesn't respond, Maya looks at her worriedly. "Did your sister come back? I'm sorry, I should have asked about her first."

"Oh, no, Maya-ji." Sunaina shakes her head, her hands curling into fists. "You don't need to apologize to me. My . . . sister came back safely."

"I'm glad to hear that. I hope you scolded her for worrying you so much! Could you make some things quickly? My cousin and I are going to visit Aftab Mahal today, and we need something to present to the rajkumari."

Sunaina nods once again, and after thanking her, Maya leaves. Sunaina stands for a moment, overwhelmed by the room and the things it contains. The temptation to sink into her work and forget everything is immense, and she almost yields to it. However, in the fragrance of the flowers are the whispers of a sister she may have lost forever. Fatima of the flowers, their father used to call her. Sunaina had often resented the love her parents lavished on her adoptive sister. There were times when her jealousy made her exclude the younger Fatima, times when Sunaina felt secure being harsh, knowing her discordant words would be heard without consequence. Fatima never spoke back; she didn't know how.

Sunaina sits down at the table and with shaking fingers starts removing the orange stamens from the saffron flowers.

Her sister is gone, and in her place is this being, this Fatima Ghazala, who is made of fire and bladed words. Anyone would think her a monster, but only a sister would call her one. Alone in the room full of flowers, Sunaina rests her head on her arms and cries.

Lazeez Muhalla stretches all the way from Northern Noor to Southern Noor, though not always in a straight line. The street is full of food vendors, restaurants, teahouses, and other establishments concerned with food and eating. No carts, horses, or camels are permitted, to allow for better use of space. Tables and chairs are set out on the sidewalks, sometimes spilling over onto the road itself. Some restaurants have small tents in front of them with low tables and cushions on the floor to seat their customers. Teahouses are frequent, one of which belongs to Sunaina's friend Ruka's family. Fatima Ghazala arranged to meet Adila at one of the better-known teahouses at half past noon. She is late when she arrives, her face flushed from running the last mile. The proprietor of the teahouse, a pleasant-faced Han man, looks at her curiously. Fatima Ghazala mops her face with a handkerchief and returns the proprietor's look with a regal nod. She looks around the teahouse and sees Adila sitting at a table set against a wall fitted with unlit fluted lamps. She is immersed in a book and fails to notice Fatima Ghazala's approach. She looks up, startled, when Fatima Ghazala drops into the chair opposite her.

"Oh, thank goodness!" Adila says. "I was afraid you wouldn't come."

"I don't break promises," Fatima Ghazala says, a tad offended. Fatima would have laughed off Adila's comment, but to Fatima Ghazala, her word is her most important possession.

She notes the flutter of surprise that crosses Adila's face, but then the other girl laughs. "I know you don't, but things have been strange recently."

"That is true. What were you reading?" Fatima Ghazala gestures to the book Adila is returning to her bag.

"About Moinuddin Chishti," Adila replies.

"Ah, the Sufi saint?" Fatima Ghazala asks. Adila nods. "And so? Do you agree with his philosophy?"

"That God is in giving? That worship is best done by easing the pain of others less fortunate than you? Yes. Don't you?"

Fatima Ghazala shrugs and stands up. "I don't *not* agree."

They leave the teahouse and emerge into the busy street, blinking at the intensity of the heat outside. Fatima Ghazala breathes deep of the enticing aromas and announces, "I am starved, Adila."

Adila catches hold of Fatima Ghazala's sleeve. "You are behaving strangely."

"Because I am hungry?" Fatima Ghazala looks away from her friend's too-perceptive eyes and makes an attempt at levity. "Well, I *am* a different person now. I am no longer the Fatima you knew."

"You are still her. Just . . . more," Adila replies.

"Maybe I am a monster," Fatima Ghazala mutters, remembering Sunaina's words.

"Are you really all right?" Adila seems truly worried now.

Fatima Ghazala grimaces at the question. "Adila, you are so grown-up away from Azizah and Amirah."

The other girl seems to realize the futility of questioning Fatima Ghazala any further. "I should hope so," she answers tartly.

"Are Azizah and Amirah still at the madrasa?" Fatima Ghazala asks with a grin, imagining the outrage when they discover they missed out on this outing.

"They are if they know what's good for them," Adila says grimly.

"All right, I really am hungry. Can I choose where we eat today?" Fatima Ghazala asks, looking around in anticipation. When her friend agrees, Fatima Ghazala steers both the conversation and the direction they are moving. Lazeez Muhalla is always crowded, but during lunchtime it becomes especially congested. Fatima Ghazala is unaffected by the sheer number of people and easily slips between the crowds like water, pulling Adila in her wake.

They pass stalls selling jiaozi stuffed with beef and vegetables, a restaurant specializing in mahaberawi, several dosa places, a quaint little place selling sato, another serving tagine. Plates of polow tempt them, as do the bowls of laksa being slurped from little containers by the hungry of Noor City. They finally stop outside a worn restaurant with a sign peeling so badly that decoding it is impossible. The interior is just as shabby as the sign suggests. Fatima Ghazala and Adila seat themselves and await attention from the lone waiter currently serving the only other customers in the restaurant. Adila looks around dubiously.

"Don't worry! Mandeep, that's Achal Kaur's grandson, promised me this place has great food. The chef is from Kashgar, an Uyghur man."

Fatima Ghazala and Adila feast on hemek naan, sprinkled with sesame seeds and garlic, and topped with salty and sweet onion. Following that is laghman made with hand-pulled noodles and a ragout of peppers, onions, garlic, and eggplant. Accompanying the noodles are meat-stuffed samsa. Fatima Ghazala and Adila manage one of each before washing down the food with black tea flavored with cardamom and cinnamon.

"We ate like queens." Adila pats her tummy. "But why the sudden benevolence?" she asks Fatima Ghazala when the latter returns from paying the bill. They linger in the dim restaurant, loath to exchange its shabby but cool interior for the heat outside.

Fatima Ghazala shrugs. "I simply wanted to."

"So Fatima has become Fatima Ghazala?" Adila muses.

"Yes."

"How?"

"I don't know. Maybe I always was Fatima Ghazala and just didn't know it." Fatima Ghazala lifts a shoulder, feigning nonchalance.

Her friend isn't fooled. "Do you *feel* different?"

"I feel like I spent the last eighteen years of my life as a charcoal drawing. And then I was filled with color." Fatima Ghazala smiles fully for the first time. "I feel alive."

"Then I am glad you are Fatima Ghazala even though I loved Fatima well." Adila returns her smile. "Ah, Abba brought back a rishta for me."

Fatima Ghazala's eyes round. "Rishta? From who?"

"Someone in Khair," Adila says, naming a forest province in the east. "He was in Noor last Ramadan and saw me at an Iftar party. Apparently he liked me enough to want me as a wife for his eldest son. I said no, of course."

"Thank goodness!" Fatima Ghazala flops back in her chair. "I was terrified you would say you'd accepted!"

"I won't leave Noor, you know that. Everyone I love is here. Though, to be honest, I wouldn't mind my own house and a husband to snuggle with." Adila glances at Fatima Ghazala and catches her with a contemplative look on her face. She pauses and looks at her friend suspiciously. "What?"

"Is there anyone you want to marry?" Fatima Ghazala asks. She remembers harmless flirtations here and there but never anyone she thought she could spend her life with.

"No," Adila admits. "But I am leaving it to Abbu to find me someone I can live with. I trust his choice."

"Don't you want to choose your own husband?" Fatima Ghazala asks. She cannot imagine letting anyone else make the choice.

"Not particularly. I know you think that's weird. We've already had this conversation." Adila grins.

"Have we?" Fatima Ghazala frowns, searching through her memories. "I don't remember it at all."

"You didn't want to talk about boys at all. What has you so interested in husbands anyway?" Adila's smile turns sly. "Are *you* interested in anyone?"

Inexplicably, Fatima Ghazala thinks of the Emir. Her face flames. "No! Of course not!"

"Ooh, very suspicious, Fatima Ghazala. Will you tell me who it is, or will Azizah have to tickle it out of you?"

"There is no one, I promise. I am not exactly in a position to think about husbands anyway. Didi threw me out of the apartment today. She thinks I'm a monster," Fatima Ghazala confesses. Saying it out loud makes it real. It hurts.

The color drains from Adila's face. "Why have you waited so long to tell me?"

"It would have ruined our lunch! You look sick already. Calm down, I'm all right. I am sad, yes, but strangely enough, I am also relieved. I am *fiercely* relieved, you know. It's as if I have been trying to occupy a space I do not fit for so long; I have been trying to be someone I am not. Now I have no reason to contort myself, no reason to pretend. It is a glorious feeling actually." Her words sound hollow even to her.

"Baji loves you, Fatima Ghazala," Adila says, her eyes warm.

"Didi loves Fatima, yes, that is true. She loves the version of me *she* defines, Adila. When I draw my boundaries myself, she no longer recognizes me," Fatima Ghazala says flatly. "She called me a monster."

Adila looks troubled. "You are staying with us, then."

"I was thinking of sleeping on the roof."

"Absolutely not. Ammi would throw a fit, and I don't even want to know what Abbu would say to that. You are staying with us."

Fatima Ghazala smiles tremulously. "Thank you."

CHAPTER 13

The afternoon court gathers under the shade of several peepal trees located in a corner of the vast grounds of Southern Aftab Mahal. The Rajmata complained that she felt suffocated inside the mahal, so Maharani Aruna requested that arrangements be made to take tea outside. The courtiers sit on cushions scattered upon thick rugs placed on the grass under the trees. Birds are singing, and a gentle breeze makes merry with the leaves on the trees and the bright dupattas on the women. Chai, flavored with the Rajmata's favorite cardamom, is poured into china cups, another of the Rajmata's indulgences, while platters of delicacies are passed around by the maids. The conversations are pleasant, and during the lengthier pauses, someone sings beautifully.

Bhavya sits apart from the rest of the gathered people, her face frozen in a benign expression. She talks to no one, and no one dares to talk to her. She wishes she could rage like a hurricane and tear down this gathering composed of mockery and deceit. She would much rather be in her room. The scolding her mother gave her still stings, and she would much rather lick her wounds in peace. But not attending the tea is unheard of. She is the rajkumari of Qirat, and her latest infraction—daring to express an active interest in the Emir—has still not been forgiven or forgotten. Bhavya tries to unclench her hands, which have bunched up the skirt of her ghagra choli, but it's no use. She can feel people looking at her, whispering about her. Someone laughs, and Bhavya tenses even more. Were they in on the prank Ruchika played on her? Get the princess to humiliate herself as the first phase of a grand plan. The second phase would be luring the lovesick princess to a party with promises to see the object of her affections. Only he wasn't even invited to the party. Was it fun for them to witness her groveling? Did they laugh at her reaction when she found out about their prank?

Even the social currency afforded her as a sister to the maharajah failed to save her from their malice. She doesn't matter now that the youngest of her three—two—brothers has finally returned home. He spent the past six months in parts traveling Qirat and spending time on the estates of their many affluent relatives.

Bhavya knows that Aaruv is the Rajmata's favorite son. Just as she knows that Aarush is the maharajah only because he is the older than Aaruv by two years. Sometimes Bhavya wonders what her life would be like if their oldest brother, Sandeep, was still here. She had adored him. Now he is gone, and she cannot speak about him. None of them can. So he exists in all their silences.

Bhavya looks over at her family, sitting in the center of the gathering. The maharajah is joking with his brother while his wife and the Rajmata look on. Even Jayanti Bua has a smile on her usually dour face. Aaruv is fair-faced and golden-tongued. Bhavya wishes he had stayed away forever.

As if responding to her thoughts, Aaruv looks over at Bhavya and raises an eyebrow. "Why don't you smile, kaddu? Aren't you happy your favorite brother has returned? You look even uglier with that sour expression on your face."

The women titter. Bhavya's fingernails dig into her palm, the pain letting her maintain her composure. She has learned not to react to Aaruv. He made her childhood hell with the nicknames to mock her plump figure. He made sure she knew at every turn that she is not physically beautiful and, as she grew older, desirable.

"My favorite brother is dead," Bhavya replies with a sweet smile and is satisfied, briefly, by the abrupt silence that falls on the gathering.

"Bhavya!" Jayanti Bua, as usual, chastises her.

"What did I say that is so wrong, Bua? Why is mentioning Sandeep so wrong? Why do you act as though even his name is forbidden?" Bhavya says hotly, not caring that she is the subject of several displeased looks.

"You are right," Aarush says gently, successfully defusing the situation.

"I know I am," Bhavya mutters, deflating. Her elder brother always, *always*, does this. Agrees with her, trying to correct things but making them worse. She cannot even be angry at him because he means well.

Taking the maharajah's cue, the rest of the courtiers return to their pleasant conversations. Bhavya deliberately doesn't look her mother's way; she doesn't need to. She can feel her mother's glare. Instead she looks at Aaruv, who is perusing her with an inexplicable expression on his face.

"What?" Bhavya snaps, very close to her breaking point.

Aaruv is spared the necessity of answering by the arrival of Sanchit Goundar, his wife, daughter, and niece. The man apologizes for his tardiness, citing a collision between two carts on the road as the cause for it. Bhavya keeps her face turned away, refusing to give Ruchika even the dignity of her attention.

The Goundars greet the royal family, and civility forces Bhavya to accord them the minimum respect. She does so but with extreme ill grace.

"Rajkumari Bhavya, your attention, please."

Bhavya raises her eyebrows at the girl who approaches her. Maya, Sanchit Goundar's niece, to whose house Bhavya was lured with false expectation. "What is it?"

"You admired the cosmetics I wore at the Deepavali party," Maya says, and Bhavya flinches. "I brought a selection of some freshly made items for your pleasure."

Bhavya is interested in spite of herself. Plus, Maya has just offered her an escape from the disgustingly saccharine atmosphere pervading the gathering. She looks at Ruchika, who is hanging on to every word Aaruv is saying with a besotted look on her face.

"You may call Ruchika to accompany us," Bhavya says grandly, getting to her feet. She makes her excuses and walks to the mahal, leaving the girls to follow.

The call of the desert grows stronger every hour, and when the clock strikes four in the afternoon, Fatima Ghazala decides to stop resisting. After praying Asr in the women's section at Jama Masjid, she makes her way to the northern city gates. The flow of traffic is steady, and Fatima Ghazala is able to slip out of the city without being stopped by anyone, Ifrit or human. Her oud is a pleasant weight on her shoulder, and her grief is an uncomfortable burden on her heart. Finally outside, without the walls of the city hemming her in, Fatima Ghazala takes a deep breath. Freedom has a smell to it, a taste.

Turning off from the road used by the caravans and other travelers, Fatima Ghazala walks into the desert, thinking, at this moment, of nothing but the sand, the sky, and herself. She has always felt like the desert sings of loss, always loss, and if she stands quietly with her eyes closed, it will grieve her too. At this moment, she needs its consolation. She lost her baba. Now she has lost her sister and the place she called home.

Fatima Ghazala walks for about thirty minutes before choosing a dune at random. She climbs to the top and sits down cross-legged on the ground. She pulls her oud off her shoulder and holds it close for a moment; its weathered exterior feels like home. The only one she has left now. She caresses the strings before playing a taqsim. Her grief translates into the music, and the wind carries the notes away.

Zulfikar is on his way to see Fatima Ghazala when a sense of impending danger rocks him. His mouth grows dry, his hands grow cold, and he almost loses control of his horse. It takes him a moment to realize that the fear he feels is not his own. The fear travels to him through the bond he forged with Fatima Ghazala. Though he concentrates on the bond, Zulfikar cannot see or tell what the cause of this fear is. But he can feel her fire tugging at him. Zulfikar changes direction and rides toward the northern gates. Whether he will reach her in time is a question Zulfikar doesn't want to answer.

Fatima Ghazala becomes conscious of the Djinn only when she pauses to give her fingers a reprieve. There are three of them, and with symmetrical faces, black hair, and spotless white caftans, they are exceptionally beautiful. But the pupils of their eyes have flooded the white, so their beauty has the taste of a lie and the scent of the monstrous.

Fatima Ghazala slowly gets to her feet as fear, smoky and intrusive, threatens to swallow her. Right behind her fear, however, is defiance. Fatima was terrified of the Shayateen. Fatima Ghazala is not. She *is* wary, but she refuses to cower before them.

The three Shayateen move to surround her, and one of them, his human form a slender youth, speaks. "Come with us."

"No." The answer is far simpler than the question. More absolute too.

"Then die."

CHAPTER 14

Not today, I don't think so." Fatima Ghazala lowers herself into a defensive stance even as she wonders where her confidence stems from. It feels new, but at the same time, it feels as if it has always been a part of her. Just like it feels she has always been Fatima Ghazala whether she knew it or not.

"You cannot win," the Shaitan, apparently the spokesperson of the three, says.

Fatima Ghazala ignores him. She marks the positions of the Shayateen around her and notes their vulnerabilities. Ever since she woke up that day in the ruins, her body has felt like a new landscape she has to learn to traverse. Not on the outside but on the inside. Her strength aside, Fatima Ghazala is aware of a new sleekness to her body, a capacity to wield violence. Fatima Ghazala takes a breath to center herself, and then she *moves*. Quickly and precisely, she combines the martial arts of southern kalaripayattu Fatima learned along with the skill that seems to be in her fire. Her hands become weapons, connecting with nerves and pressure points until two of the three Shayateen fall. The third one stands in front of her, his sword drawn.

Fatima Ghazala stares at the Shaitan, and all of a sudden, she hears a scream. Her heart lurches, and she clenches her hands before she realizes that it is the past trying to make a claim on her. She doesn't move her eyes from the monster. Her vision grows cloudy, and once again, she sees a golden word shaping smokeless fire. This time, though, the golden word is corroded black. She cannot read the name as it is in a language she has never come across before. Fatima Ghazala hears the Shayateen approach, but her vision refuses to clear. In desperation, she reaches out and touches the corroded word in the Shaitan's chest. The Shaitan screams, an unexpectedly shrill sound. Fatima Ghazala is suddenly thrust into the past again, and it takes everything she is to retain her senses. She pulls the name from the Shaitan's chest. When her vision clears, a column of smokeless fire burns where the Shaitan used to be.

The other two Shayateen, though on their feet now, are frozen. They look from the place their companion used to stand to Fatima Ghazala, as if unable to comprehend what just happened. Fatima Ghazala wonders if they can see the name on the palm of her hand or the column of smokeless fire.

She looks at them and feels her vision begin to cloud again. The Shayateen, perhaps sensing this, flee. Fatima Ghazala, her heart beating furiously, looks at the corroded word in her hand, then at the smokeless fire. Her anger is molten, and she closes her hands around the word. It crumbles, like a leaf giving in to the urges of autumn.

The smokeless fire flares and, in a voice audible only to Fatima Ghazala, shrieks, a sound of terror and surprise. In the next moment, it blinks out of existence.

Fatima Ghazala stares at her hands; the heat that filled her only moments ago is suddenly absent. Instead, she feels a bone-deep sorrow. She took someone's life, and no matter how much she justifies it, she cannot change this fact. Before she can process this fully, a sound to her left makes her tense again, and she turns, prepared this time.

The Emir stands a distance away from her, breathing hard. His eyes are wide, and his face is flushed. They stare at each other for one charged moment before he takes three steps forward and pulls her into a rough hug. He is shaking. Fatima Ghazala freezes for a moment before she gives in to the embrace and slowly wraps her arms around the Ifrit. Being held by the Emir is . . . strange but not unpleasant. She smooths her hands down his back and feels him shudder as if the contact hurts him. The embrace lasts only a moment.

"Are you hurt?" he asks, turning away from her. His action is so at odds with the concern in his voice that Fatima Ghazala is nonplussed.

"Do I look hurt?" she asks, and the Emir faces her again. He has an inscrutable expression on his face.

"What happened? Why are you here? What did you do to them?" he asks all at once. He speaks quickly, and his cheeks are tinged with an uncharacteristic pink. Fatima Ghazala wonders if he is embarrassed about embracing her. If the act was going to shame him, why did he do it in the first place?

"The Shayateen attacked me. I thought that was obvious," she says over her shoulder as she walks to her oud, picking it up. She frowns, examining it for damage. "Initially, they asked me to accompany them somewhere. I refused, and they didn't like that."

"How did you defeat them?" the Emir asks next. He sounds cool now. Unaffected.

"Look, I don't much feel like answering questions at the moment." Fatima Ghazala abruptly sits down on the sand dune, her back to him. The Emir walks closer, and she senses him hesitating. Then he sits down on the sand next to her, maintaining a proper distance between them. He doesn't speak, and neither does she, and for a while they sit in silence.

"I am much stronger now than I was before. Physically, I mean. I discovered that today. Are all Ifrit women strong? Are they stronger than Ifrit men?" Fatima Ghazala asks. It occurs to her that she knows very little about the Ifrit.

"The men have greater physical strength, but the women have stronger fires," Zulfikar replies, but doesn't offer more information. "Our society is matriarchal."

"I see," Fatima Ghazala says. "Can I ask you something?"

The Emir gestures for her to go ahead. She narrows her eyes in thought before asking, "Why did the Ifrit agree to the late maharajah's terms?" When Zulfikar looks at her, Fatima Ghazala elaborates. "It strikes me as strange, you see? You are arguably the superior of the two species and need not concern yourself with human problems . . . so why? What do you get out of being here on earth?"

Fatima Ghazala remembers her past self asking Baba the same question once. He hadn't answered her. Would the Emir be the same? "I don't know how to explain it in a way that you will understand," he starts, "but if you'll humor me, I will try."

Fatima Ghazala nods.

"We are a people of order. For us, reason and order are akin to worship. I was young when our people first came to earth, a fledgling soldier, so I wasn't allowed to even entertain ideas of crossing over. You see, human beings exist in a state of chaos. You don't intentionally create chaos like the Shayateen. You . . . *are* chaos. Your short lives, your many relationships, desires, conflicts. For us, bringing peace to your chaos is a reward. It is our nature; we cannot deny it. At least that's the reason we came to Qirat. The reason we stay is because the desert cities have become our home. The sun has become our sun; its heat has become our heat."

Fatima Ghazala ponders over his answer for a while. "I see. Can I ask something else?"

"Can I stop you?" the Emir says resignedly.

Fatima Ghazala grins slightly. Then asks anyway, "What

happened to me? A week ago, I was Fatima. I didn't have Djinn fire. Now I'm . . . what am I? Ifrit? Human? Something in between?" A monster?

Fatima Ghazala feels the Emir's eyes on her and turns to meet his gaze. He looks at her as if trying to translate her into words of a language he does not yet speak fluently.

"I have only speculations to offer you," the Emir says softly.

"I will take them," Fatima Ghazala responds immediately. No one else is offering her any other explanations.

"Names are important to my people. Important in a way they aren't to humans." The Emir pauses as if gathering his thoughts. "Our names are the expressions of our best qualities and, on earth, our names are what literally shape us." Fatima Ghazala remembers the Ifrit soldiers in front of her baba's bookstore. She remembers their names and how they did exactly what the Emir is saying they do. She nods for the Emir to continue.

"Your name . . . you already know who Ghazala was." Fatima Ghazala turns to face the Emir at the past tense, her eyebrows raised in question. "If my speculations are correct, she sacrificed herself while transferring her fire and thus her Name to you."

"Why would she do that?" A thought occurs to Fatima Ghazala. "Was she my mother?"

"No, you would have had your own fire were you Ifrit," the Emir answers quickly. "I don't know what circumstances led her to that decision, but from what I have heard of her, Ghazala was not someone who made rash decisions."

"If she did as you said, would it affect my blood as well?" Fatima Ghazala remembers the incident eight years ago. "Is Ifrit blood poisonous to the Shayateen?"

"How do you know that?" The Emir is surprised now. Fatima Ghazala hears it in his voice.

"When I was attacked during the massacre, the Shaitan who touched my blood turned to ash."

"Did you tell anyone this? Any of the Ifrit, I mean?" the Emir asks, his eyebrows drawing together.

"Of course not. My sister and I didn't want any attention from the Djinn. *Any* kind of Djinn." Fatima Ghazala pulls up the right-hand sleeve of her tunic and shows Zulfikar a pale scar that runs from her elbow to halfway down her arm. The Emir's lips pull into a straight thin line. "But if I have had Ghazala's name and fire since I was little, why was I not . . ." Fatima Ghazala trails off when she suddenly remembers those moments in the dark between sleep and consciousness. In that time right after her baba died. She remembers the golden word; she remembers pushing the name into her chest, right above her heart.

Without realizing it, she reaches over and grabs the Emir's arm. It is warm under her touch. The Emir looks startled. "I think I Named myself."

His reaction is more extreme than she anticipated. His face abruptly drains of color. "What do you mean?"

"I remember seeing a golden word; I remember recognizing it as a name. I *remember* pushing it in this space here!" Fatima Ghazala shows him, tapping the area above her heart. "Can you see my Name?"

"No." Fatima Ghazala feels her enthusiasm dim at his response. Then the Emir asks, "Can you see mine?"

"Yes." Fatima Ghazala looks at the name lodged in the Emir's chest. "Zulfikar: bladed, brimming with heat, clean, and honest. It's a beautiful name."

"I see. Tell me, how did you defeat the Shayateen?" the Emir asks. The demand in his tone unsettles Fatima Ghazala.

"I am not bad at physical combat, you know. I think I could have disarmed them all eventually, but"—Fatima Ghazala swallows at the memory of the dead Shaitan—"I pulled the name out of one of the Shayateen. This scared the other two, and they fled. I crushed the Name of the Shaitan. I think that killed him."

"You crushed his Name?" Zulfikar's voice is startled.

"Yes. I realize that I ought not to have killed him, but how am I supposed to show compassion to someone who has none for me? Someone who may have killed everyone I knew? Maybe even my parents?" This does not alleviate the guilt Fatima Ghazala bears, but she feels better for admitting what she did.

"Tell me something, Fatima Ghazala," Zulfikar says, and she starts. Her name sounds like it doesn't belong to her when he says it. "Did Firdaus ever teach you anything?"

"He taught me many things: languages, literature, and philosophy. We debated on the economy and the arts. Sometimes we discussed God and religion. We even ventured occasionally into mathematics and science."

"Did he ever teach you anything about Names and Naming? About the Djinn and the Ifrit?" The urgency in Zulfikar's voice is at odds with his stillness.

Fatima Ghazala closes her eyes and thinks for a moment. "No, not that I can recall. Why?"

"Indulge me for a moment, please. Before he died, did Firdaus say anything to you?" Fatima Ghazala winces at the question and Zulfikar's face softens. "I wouldn't ask if it weren't important."

"I don't remember exactly what he said . . . just that he told me to write his tale and gave me his hand," Fatima Ghazala replies after a moment.

"Did you?"

"Of course. He is . . . was my baba. I took his hand, but I don't quite remember what happened next."

Zulfikar rubs a hand over his eyes and sighs. He rises to his feet, pulling Fatima Ghazala up along with him. "I'm going to tell you some things that you cannot ever repeat to anyone."

"Maybe you shouldn't tell me these things, then," Fatima replies warily.

Zulfikar shakes his head. "When you took Firdaus's hand, you took away any choice you may ever have had in this matter."

Fatima Ghazala pulls herself from Zulfikar's grasp and walks a few steps away from him. She gestures for him to continue. "The Djinn live in a world called Al-Naar. In this world, the Ifrit live in a city called Tayneeb. These are facts." He pauses to see if Fatima Ghazala is following. "We can exist on earth in two forms: as smokeless fire and in this human form. As fire, we can do nothing but exist. In human form, we can live full lives: We can eat, sweat, fight, *live*. To attain human form, we need to be Named. Firdaus, your baba, was the Name Giver. He Named us so we don't just exist on this plane, on earth, as smokeless fire, but live here in bodies, in solid form. Do you understand what I am saying?"

Fatima Ghazala closes her eyes and thinks of the Names she has seen, how they seem to contain the smokeless fire in a shape, a human shape. "How did he do that?"

"I don't know," Zulfikar says. She stares at him, and he shrugs. "Only Name Givers and their apprentices know the process."

"Are there other Name Givers?"

"No, there is only one at any time." Fatima Ghazala narrows her eyes at his tone.

"He gave me his Name Giving power," she says, slowly piecing things together. "That's why I see Djinn names. That's why I can feel my fire now?"

"Yes. The power of the Name Giver woke your fire and with it your Name, Ghazala." Zulfikar hesitates. "But a Name Giver doesn't have the power to destroy Names—this is not a documented power." He looks at her, and Fatima Ghazala feels like the monster he doesn't say she is. She swallows.

"Why would Baba give me this Name Giving power?" she asks, moving on with some effort.

"I don't know. There are fully trained apprentices in Tayneeb, and the power would have passed to the most capable one had he died without handing it over to you. The fact that Firdaus chose someone with no training, someone who is not even fully Ifrit, to receive the power is important."

"Didn't he just make a mistake?" Fatima Ghazala asks.

"The Name Giver wasn't the sort to make mistakes," Zulfikar says firmly. "Not even when he was dying."

"So what does it mean? If I have these Name Giving powers, do I have responsibilities that I will have to fulfill?" Fatima Ghazala thinks of her baba's last request. She gave him her word to write his tale, whatever that meant.

"I am not sure what happens next," Zulfikar says. "I need to report to my superiors. They will decide our next course of action."

"I don't like the sound of that," Fatima Ghazala mutters. She looks at the sun's descent in the horizon and shivers in the rapidly cooling air. "It's almost Maghrib."

"We need to be back within the city walls before night falls. I don't fancy our chances with the Ghul out here," Zulfikar says. A tad uncomfortably, he holds out his arms to Fatima Ghazala. "If you don't mind, I can have us back in Noor in a few minutes."

Fatima Ghazala gives him an uncertain look but then shrugs and steps into his arms. He hasn't yet given her reason not to trust him. Zulfikar tucks her in close to him and starts moving. Fatima Ghazala squeezes her eyes shut as they go from being stationary one second to traveling at about the speed of the wind during a desert storm the next. Less than a whole minute passes before Zulfikar stops outside the northern gates of Noor City. He moves away from Fatima Ghazala immediately.

"Wait here, I left my horse at the guardhouse," Zulfikar says. Fatima Ghazala considers walking away in the other direction, but her heart feels unsteady. All she can think about is the information thrust upon her in the past hour. Her sense of self feels shaken— more so than when she woke up as Fatima Ghazala. She rubs her forehead, entirely overwhelmed.

She is lost in her thoughts when Zulfikar returns. Soon they are on his horse, navigating the short distance to Taaj Gul. The streets are full of people returning home after a hard day's labor. Food vendors have set up stalls on the pavement, and the air is full of the smells of meat cooking on the rotisserie. Fatima Ghazala's stomach grumbles a complaint.

"I am going to check how safe your apartment is," Zulfikar says in Fatima Ghazala's ear, and she starts. She is sitting in front of him on the horse, his chest warm against her back.

"About that . . ." Fatima Ghazala tries to think of the best way to articulate her current state of homelessness. "My sister found out about my Djinn fire and . . . So I am currently . . . I mean, I'm staying with friends until my employer finds me a room to stay in."

When no response is forthcoming, Fatima Ghazala is glad she cannot see the Emir's face. She remembers his command not to tell anyone about her fire. Suddenly he sighs, and his arms slightly tighten around her.

"The fire manifested when I was sleeping. I had no control over it!" Fatima Ghazala tries to twist around to see Zulfikar, but his arms make it impossible.

"I am not angry. I'm just thinking about where to move you," he says.

"You don't need to move me anywhere. I will thank you to remember that I am not a sack of rice," Fatima Ghazala retorts. They arrive at Fatima Ghazala's apartment building, and she slides down from the horse without waiting for Zulfikar's help. He dismounts, putting a hand on her arm to halt her when she would have left.

"I apologize if you find me overbearing. I have never come across a situation like this, so I am as much at a loss as you are." Though his voice and tone are sincere, Fatima Ghazala is not convinced. He looks much too confident to be at a loss.

She looks at Zulfikar curiously. "How old are you?"

"Why is that important?" Zulfikar frowns. Fatima Ghazala shrugs. "In human years, twenty-five."

"And in Ifrit years?"

"Fifty."

"You are old," Fatima Ghazala says respectfully. The look Zulfikar sends her way expresses clearly what she can do with the sentiment. She grins, unrepentant.

"Come, grab your belongings. I will take you to a—"

"I told you I am not a sack of rice to be moved around," Fatima Ghazala says, her smile fading.

"You are not staying here." Zulfikar crosses his arms.

"I very well am." Fatima Ghazala crosses *her* arms too.

"It isn't safe here," Zulfikar insists.

"Look, you and I are the only ones who know about the Name Giving thing. I am not going to tell anyone. Are you?" Fatima Ghazala tries, even though it is growing more difficult by the second, to be reasonable.

"Yes. I have to report this latest development to the Raees." At Fatima Ghazala's look, he elaborates. "Our leader."

"You do that. I will stay here safely." Fatima Ghazala has just about reached the limits of her endurance. "Allah hafiz."

"Fine." Zulfikar concedes this battle. She ought to be safe for one more night. "Please do not go out by yourself. Actually, don't go out at all. I will come for you tomorrow."

"Don't." Fatima Ghazala turns to go, then relents at the look on his face. "All right. Fine. Come tomorrow. We will discuss things."

"If you sense any danger at all through the night—"

"Then I will defend myself. Sayyid, it's almost Maghrib. I need to do my ablutions and change before I pray. Please go away now."

"Tomorrow," Zulfikar says in lieu of a farewell. Fatima Ghazala turns to go inside and finds herself the focus of three pairs of wide eyes.

"Api, I believe you have some explaining to do," Azizah says. The Alif sisters cross their arms.

Reports of a hostage situation in Shams Gali, a neighborhood not too far from Taaj Gul, arrive as Zulfikar is unsaddling his horse on his return to Northern Aftab. Amir soldiers at the scene request assistance and advice; the hostages include children and the elderly. Zulfikar resaddles his horse and sets off immediately, accompanied by five of his Djinn soldiers.

The streets are bustling, but as Zulfikar and his men near Shams Gali, they begin to empty. The neighborhood is composed mostly of schools and the domiciles of teachers; the buildings are constructed of stone and wood and are painted in pastel colors. Early evening dusts the tops of the buildings and the palm trees dotting the landscape. Shadows made half of starlight try, and fail, to give a sinister mien to the place.

An Amir soldier is standing outside a building painted, perhaps, a light green—it is difficult to tell in the dark. Zulfikar reins in his horse outside the school and dismounts. Leaving his horse to one of the other soldiers, he follows the Amir soldier, a lanky man Named Ibrahim, up the path to the school doors. According to one of the teachers, a man had been loitering around the school for a couple of days, trying to recruit students to join some army. No one had paid him any heed, so today he barged into a classroom containing a teacher and five students who had stayed behind after classes for extra lessons. He barricaded the door of the classroom and prevented the students and teacher from leaving until they promised to join whatever army he was recruiting for.

"How long has it been?" Zulfikar asks, pausing at the entrance to the school. He looks around at the closed windows in the houses and buildings surrounding the school. Not even a flicker of a curtain gives away any observers. Foot traffic is entirely absent. A tense air of expectancy, like the air before a storm, encapsulates the area.

"An hour, sayyid. The teachers tried reasoning with him, until he hit a child and broke his leg," the Amir soldier says, his eyes shimmering orange.

"Has he made any other demands?"

"No, sayyid."

Zulfikar steps into the foyer of the school, a cheerful place if a little threadbare. The scent of jasmine is heavy in the air, cloying in its intensity. The soldier leads him to a room on the first floor. Three elderly men are clustered around the closed door of the room, and one woman, dressed in a black abaya, leans against a wall, weeping into her hands. They turn at Zulfikar's arrival, their faces brightening with relief. Zulfikar presses a finger to his lips, stopping them before they can speak. He puts his hand on the handle of the door, drawing on his fire. A second later, without warning or hesitation, he pulls it open. The children are huddled in a corner, their teacher shielding them from the swarthy man who looms over them, hand raised threateningly.

Zulfikar doesn't give the man a chance to react. He has him pinned against the wall in the time it takes a human being to blink. Zulfikar can hear his soldiers evacuate the children and the teacher from the room; the woman wails when she sees the injured child.

Zulfikar removes his hand from the man's neck, and he sags to the ground. The man's white shalwar is wet; he lost control of his bladder. Zulfikar goes down on his haunches and looks at the man. He is about forty years of age with an unkempt beard and bloodshot eyes; dirty and desperate.

"What army?" Zulfikar asks, the two words carrying the weight of the world.

The man's eyes widen at the question, and instead of answering, he grimaces as if biting down on something. A second later, his mouth foams and he slumps over, dead. Zulfikar leans forward and sniffs at the foam. Poison.

CHAPTER 15

Aarush's brother has only been back for a day and already concerned fathers are removing their daughters from the court. Aaruv is an unapologetic connoisseur of women, frequently leaving broken hearts in his wake. In a society where a woman's virtue is of paramount importance, he presents a distinct and immediate threat. Aarush has often brought up the subject of marriage to Aaruv, but his brother shies away from the commitment, preferring to live unhindered by a wife and the responsibilities that come with being a husband. There was once a time, Aarush muses, when he had similar sentiments as his younger brother, but all it took to change his mind was meeting his wife once.

"I should let you know, bhaiya, that you have a very disgusting look on your face," his sister tells him tartly. Bhavya is visiting Aruna and him in their apartments, mainly to play with his six-month-old son, Vihaan. She cuddles him as he lies on her lap while Aruna looks on with a smile.

Aarush stops smiling and sniffs at his sister. "There must be a rule somewhere that states you cannot speak to the maharajah in that manner."

"You may be the maharajah out there, but in here you are simply a baba and a husband." Bhavya hands Vihaan back to Aruna and adds slyly, "And, of course, a stinky brother."

"I assure you he is not stinky," Aruna says, tickling the baby's tummy. He chortles.

"I'm not inclined to believe you, bhabhi. You are so ridiculously in love with my brother you think the sun rises with him!" Bhavya smirks at him. Aarush fights the urge to flick her. He won't ever tell her, but he is grateful for the way she treats him, as if he is merely her brother and not the architect of their futures. He is lucky, Aarush thinks, looking at his family; he has people to anchor him.

"You mean it doesn't?" Aruna feigns surprise. His sister giggles, and Aarush finds himself smiling broadly, like he usually does when around his wife.

"Speaking of love," Aarush asks curiously, "what did Amma say to you?"

All mirth suddenly leaves his sister's face, and she slumps in her chair. "She told me that as a daughter of the royal family of Qirat, I have a certain reputation to uphold. She said that my actions paint me as wanton and cast doubts on my virtue."

Aarush winces. "That's a bit harsh, isn't it?" His mother has always been very concerned by how the world perceives the royal family, but these words seem uncharacteristic of her.

"She listened to Jayanti Bua. Amma would never say things like that without instigation." Bhavya looks grim. His sister still doesn't know their mother very well.

"Did she succeed in making you rethink your affection for the Emir?" Aruna asks, glancing at Aarush. She hands Vihaan to him, and he cuddles the baby, taking quiet pleasure in the child's sweet smell and the softness of his body. His son's complete trust in his abilities to protect him humbles Aarush. At the same time, it makes him aware of how great the consequences of his failure to be a good king would be.

"Of course not!" Bhavya sets her lips in that way Aarush is

familiar with. "If anything, she made me more determined to win his heart."

A knock sounds on the door, and the women hastily pull on their veils. A few minutes later, a maid shows in Aarush's much-beleaguered advisor, Janab Jamshid. "I apologize for disturbing you in your time of rest, huzoor. The Emir requests your presence at the usual meeting place."

"Do you know why?" Aarush gets up reluctantly. Why is it that the Emir always chooses the time when he is the most comfortable to summon him for meetings? Why can't he request for a meeting when Aarush is grappling with his ministers about budgets?

"No, huzoor." The old man bows deferentially. Aarush sighs, hands his son to Aruna, and follows his advisor out of his rooms. A dozen of his guards join him as he treks across the grounds of the mahal to the pavilion. The darkness is kept at bay by the lanterns his soldiers carry. The pavilion, too, is lit by torches and presents a beacon in the darkness. The Emir turns when Aarush walks up the steps and into the pavilion. Shadows cover the Ifrit's face, making him look far more sinister than Aarush has ever seen him before.

"I apologize for calling you in your time of repose," the Emir says, his voice sounding even more formal than usual.

"Is something the matter?" Aarush asks, uncertain he wants the answer to his question.

"I have a request and a report. Which would you like to hear first?" the Emir responds. He stops speaking, and the pause beats awkwardly.

"The request," Aarush says, wondering exactly what the Emir could want from him.

The Emir hesitates. "Would you be willing to accept a girl into the Southern Aftab and keep her protected while she resides there?" he finally asks.

"A human girl?" Aarush asks, and wonders if this girl is the same one Bhavya mentioned.

"Not entirely."

"She's Ifrit?" Aarush asks, a bit incredulously. The Ifrit society is a matriarchal one, and the greater number of soldiers in the Ifrit army are women. The majority of them stay in the Djinn world in the Ifrit city to defend it against the constant threat of the Shayateen. They are not as expendable as their male counterparts, who are sent to earth. This is one of the few tidbits of information available only to the maharajah.

"Not wholly. She is human with Djinn fire." The Emir walks closer to Aarush. The flames from the torch illuminate the Ifrit's face. "I tell you with confidence that this knowledge will remain between us."

Aarush nods. "Of course." It is his turn to pause now. "What is your relationship to the girl?"

Aarush's eyebrows rise at the expression on the Ifrit's face. "I'm not entirely sure," the Emir replies.

"And the report?" Arush asks. He listens, his face paling, as the Emir relates to him of the happenings in a Shams Gali school not an hour past.

"So that very beautiful person dropping you off on his horse and standing very close to you is an Emir?" Azizah repeats as if unable to believe it.

"Not just any Emir, Azizah. *The* Emir. The only one that matters here in Noor," Amirah adds in the same tone.

"His name is Zulfikar," Fatima Ghazala replies. When the two Alif sisters look at her, she blushes.

"Did you just blush?" Amirah demands.

"I am feeling shy." Fatima Ghazala clears her throat. She presses her hands to her cheeks, willing them to cool. She has no reason to be blushing because of the Emir. None at all. "All this attention makes me self-conscious." Azizah snorts.

The stars are out in full force—they usually are—but for some reason, they seem brighter tonight. The rooftop is comfortably crowded as families take some air before retiring to their apartments for the night. Fatima Ghazala, in a shalwar kameez she borrowed from Adila, sits on a bench on the rooftop with Azizah on one side of her and Amirah on the other. These moments of peace feel priceless after the day she just lived through.

"Ustaad Hakim talked to us about the growing momentum of the rebellion against the Djinn in the forest provinces of Qirat," Amirah says after a period of companionable silence. "They no longer want the Ifrit ruling half the country they don't live in."

"Why does it matter to them who rules in the cities they don't live in?" Azizah asks. "The natives of Qirat living in the desert cities seem content with their Ifrit Emirs."

"Did the Emir say anything to you about the rebellion?" Amirah asks Fatima Ghazala.

"No. I didn't think to ask him. How does your teacher know about the rebellion, Azizah?" Fatima Ghazala asks curiously. Rumors have filtered in from the many travelers to Noor City about the murmurings of the Qirati who want the country to be returned to them, but Fatima Ghazala had no idea that there was force behind these whispers.

"His brother arrived in Noor City from Khair the other day. Ustaad Hakim got the news from him directly," Azizah replies.

One of the women sitting near them, Anu, hears the subject of their discussion. "I heard there's going to be a war," she says. Other people, attracted by her words, drift closer, and soon everyone on the rooftop is discussing the probability of war. Fatima Ghazala recognizes the current of fear running underneath their words. The people of Noor are afraid that the lives they have rebuilt will once again prove fragile in the face of forces outside their control.

"War scares me, api," Azizah says softly, burrowing closer. Her eyes are full of shadows. "Will we have to run away again?"

Fatima Ghazala shakes her head but says nothing. How can she know what the future holds for any of them?

"We can't keep running away, daughter," an older woman says. Her name is Ling. She lives on the fifth floor with her husband. "There is only so much we can leave behind."

The mood on the rooftop grows somber, and soon people start dispersing. Even the stars seem subdued now.

"Well, that was fun, Azizah," Amirah grumbles. "Maybe next time you can keep your teacher's dire warnings to yourself."

"Adila's back," Fatima Ghazala says, and stands up. Adila is waiting for them at the entrance to the rooftop. The girls traipse down one flight of stairs and along the corridor to the Alif apartment. They pile inside, calling out greetings to the Alif parents, who are entertaining in the living room, before continuing to the large bedroom at the back of the apartment. This room is shared by the three sisters and now Fatima Ghazala.

Instead of beds, the Alif sisters sleep on futons—Azizah's idea. This leaves them with more space in the room for their miscellaneous belongings. Two large lamps illuminate the room.

"What did Sunaina Baji say?" Amirah asks Adila, her curiosity getting the better of her.

Adila shoots her sister a repressive look, but Fatima Ghazala shrugs, her heart pounding. "I want to know too."

"Nothing. She simply handed me that bag," Adila says, gesturing to a bulging cloth bag placed beside the door. "It's full of your stuff."

Fatima Ghazala feels her eyes prickle, and she swallows. "I see." An awkward pause lingers as she tries to compose herself.

"Well, I am hungry again." Azizah stands up all of a sudden. "Abbu bought steamed buns, and we need to eat all of them before they go bad. Right, api?"

Amirah nods decisively. "Let's go get some. We should also have some chai. You can never have enough chai."

The younger girls leave, and a pronounced melancholy slips into the room.

"She didn't ask about me, huh?" Fatima Ghazala says, her voice determinedly light. "Not even once?"

"I'm sorry, habibi," Adila replies, her dark eyes compassionate.

Fatima Ghazala shrugs. "I'm all right. I really am." She's not, but maybe if she pretends hard enough, she will be.

Zulfikar is acquainted with worry: how it worms itself into all your thoughts and flavors all your actions. He knows the ponderousness that accompanies fear: when a slew of misgivings paint the future red. What he was completely unprepared for is the ache that accompanies this particular separation.

He sends his reports to the Raees and her advisors through the fire burning in the pit behind the barracks. He tries, unsuccessfully, to locate the Wazir and later finds out the Ifrit left for his usual patrols of the desert earlier, taking with him two Ifrit soldiers. After dinner, he settles in to stare blankly at a page of the book he is pretending to read. Finally he sits outside on his balcony and contemplates the city.

The hours seem interminably long, and his worries deepen. What if the Shayateen attack again? What if Fatima Ghazala gets hurt? How will he get to her in time? Maybe he should have stayed near her apartment building. Of course, to a certain extent, Zulfikar is worried about Fatima Ghazala because she is the Name Giver and he owes her his protection. But the other reason he worries is one that he does not understand. No, that is not quite correct. He does understand what the feelings burgeoning within him are, but he doesn't know why or how he could feel this intensely for someone he barely knows. Zulfikar is not ready to trust his heart to anyone again. He may never be.

Fajr comes and passes, the sun rises, and at nine a.m. Zulfikar is on his horse racing the roads to Taaj Gul. It is a rest day, so the city is slower to rise, which suits Zulfikar fine. He tethers his horse to a post outside Fatima Ghazala's building and, trusting the pull of Fatima Ghazala's fire, makes his way up the flights of stairs until he reaches the apartment she is currently in.

He raps sharply on the door of the apartment, and it is pulled open by a sleepy-looking girl with a veil haphazardly wrapped around her head. She takes one look at him, her jaw drops open, and she slams the door shut. Zulfikar stares at the door, affronted. Beyond it, he hears a voice yell, "Api, the beautiful man you said is the Emir is at the door!"

Two minutes later, Fatima Ghazala opens the door. Her hair is unbound, and Zulfikar's breath hitches. She is wearing a pale pink shalwar kameez, her lips are pursed, and her eyes are full of exasperation. Exasperation and—Zulfikar smiles slightly—something else. "What are you doing here?" she asks him gruffly.

"I told you I would come get you today," Zulfikar replies. "Let's go."

"Do you think you can command me to come with you and I will happily oblige?" Fatima Ghazala asks as if genuinely curious.

"Well, actually, yes," Zulfikar replies. That is generally the way things work in the human world when you are the Emir.

"Is that how they usually do it in Al-Naar? Do men command and women rush to obey?" she asks next, and Zulfikar flushes. He imagines his sisters' responses to that question and shudders slightly.

"Not quite," he says, not meeting the new Name Giver's eyes.

"It doesn't work that way here either," Fatima Ghazala says. "Come in, Ali Abbu and Asma Ammi want to talk to you." Leaving the door open, she turns to go. "And take your shoes off at the entrance."

A bit bemused, Zulfikar follows Fatima Ghazala into the apartment, leaving his shoes at the door. She takes him to the living room, tells him to wait, and disappears. Zulfikar sits down on a chair beside a divan and waits. He looks around the small room. The furnishings are worn but clean and tidy. A small window looks out into the corridor outside and provides the main source of light. Little knickknacks placed on dust-free surfaces show the pride this family takes in their home.

A man and a woman, both in their forties, enter the room, and Zulfikar gets to his feet. "Assalaam wa alaikum," he greets them.

"Wa alaikum ussalaam," they both respond, and sit down in the settee opposite him. They look at him with piercing disregard, and Zulfikar looks down at his hands, his feet, the floor, and the wall. For a long while, they don't say a word. Zulfikar feels the walls press against him. Finally, just as he is about to beg for mercy, the man speaks. "So you are here for my Fatima?"

Zulfikar looks at the man in surprise. He didn't know Fatima Ghazala had parents. The man, Ali, interprets his look correctly. "Fatima might not be a daughter of my blood, but she *is* a daughter of my heart. Tell me, what are your intentions toward her?"

Fatima Ghazala pops her head into the room. "Abbu, our relationship isn't—"

The woman, Asma, cuts her off. "Fatima, don't interrupt your elders."

Chastened, Fatima Ghazala lowers her head in apology and disappears. Zulfikar swallows. "I understand your concern, sayyid, sayyida," he says in a conciliatory tone, "but I cannot divulge the reason why it is dangerous for Fatima Ghazala to remain here."

"I can protect my family," Ali says stubbornly.

"I am not saying you cannot, sayyid. However, again for reasons I cannot tell you, protecting her is *my* responsibility." Zulfikar adds heat to his words.

"I will protect myself, thank you very much." Fatima Ghazala marches inside the room and glares at Zulfikar.

"You will risk not just this family but all the families in this building if you insist on remaining here," Zulfikar replies evenly. "You may be able to battle the Shayateen, sayyida, but everyone else will be at their mercy. Surely you do not want that on your conscience?"

Fatima Ghazala blanches at his words. She looks at him angrily for one charged moment, and then her shoulders slump. "Fine. I give up. I will go with you."

Ali gets to his feet. "You don't have to leave, beta. We will find another way to protect ourselves."

"I cannot put any of you in any danger, Abbu. I could never do that. Besides, he"—she gestures to Zulfikar with her chin—"is annoyingly imperious but not entirely bad. He means me no harm."

Ali turns distrusting eyes to Zulfikar. It's clear that he neither likes nor approves of Zulfikar, but he keeps his peace while Fatima Ghazala makes her farewells. He tells her to return immediately if she doesn't like wherever Zulfikar is taking her. On his part, Zulfikar is introduced to the Alif sisters and forced to trail behind as they accompany Fatima Ghazala to the building entrance.

"I'll come see you soon," Fatima Ghazala promises them. After a few more weepy hugs, Zulfikar finally has Fatima Ghazala on the horse, riding toward Aftab Mahal. He feels like he has aged about a hundred years in the past hour.

He brings his horse to a walk as they attempt to navigate a road full of fruit-filled carts. The smells of guavas with pink flesh, several varieties of mangoes, ripe figs, and dates candy the air. Fatima Ghazala breathes in deeply.

"I am imperious?" Zulfikar asks, conscious of the way the Name Giver holds herself stiff and apart from him. He fights the urge to pull her closer.

"You remove me from the only home I know and pretend as if your word is law. Of course you are imperious," she replies stiffly.

Zulfikar wonders how to respond to that. "I do not intend to be," he finally says, but he can tell that she is not convinced.

They do not speak as they cross the bridge over the desert arm of the River Rahat and ride into the palace grounds. Zulfikar dismounts from his horse in front of the stables. Fatima Ghazala does not move from her perch on the horse.

"Surely you do not expect me to live with you in Aftab Mahal," she says, looking around uncertainly.

Zulfikar takes her oud out of the saddlebag and puts it aside. Next he reaches for her bag. Fatima Ghazala reads his intent moments before he can pluck her off the horse and dismounts before he can touch her. Stable boys peer out at her from the stable curiously while Ifrit soldiers arriving and leaving the grounds on various errands salute Zulfikar and pretend she is invisible.

"Follow me," Zulfikar says, and starts walking. It takes him a minute to realize she isn't. He stops and turns to see her standing by his horse with a mutinous expression on her face.

"I told you yesterday that I am not a sack of rice, didn't I?" The Name Giver, for all that she is mostly human, has an authority to her voice that Zulfikar finds difficult to not react to. "I am not asking you for the secrets of your existence, Emir. I just want to know where you are taking me. Is that too difficult a question for you?"

Zulfikar blinks, aware that he is being cruel. She is possibly afraid of what the future holds for her. Yet, being kind to her feels like he is giving in to his feelings, and Zulfikar will be damned if he allows that to happen again. "Among the Ifrit, it is best to obey without asking questions."

"I am not Ifrit, Emir. Nor do I want to be." The Name Giver lifts her chin and only the slight wobble of her voice gives her away. "Forget it, I'm going home."

Zulfikar catches her arm. "I'm sorry," he says, and he genuinely is. "I truly am. We are going to Southern Aftab. You will be staying with the maharajah's family." Zulfikar catches her gaze and holds it, trying to impress upon her his good intentions. Through the bond he can feel her distrust of him, and it hurts him. "I just want to keep you safe. Please?"

Fatima Ghazala finally nods and allows him to lead the way across the mahal grounds.

"There are things I must tell you that I don't yet know how to," Zulfikar says, knowing he sounds vague but unable to help it. "I know you have many questions—"

"How long do I have to stay here? When can I go back to being me instead of the Name Giver?" Fatima Ghazala asks. "I have been extremely patient, don't you think? Can't you tell me that at the very least?"

Zulfikar stops suddenly and stares down at Fatima Ghazala, confused. "Go back to being you?" he echoes her question, frowning.

"Yes?" the Name Giver says. "If I accomplish whatever Baba wanted me to, can't I return to my life? Go back to being a messenger?" She looks at Zulfikar, and her face pales when she reads the answer in his eyes.

CHAPTER 16

T here they are," Aruna says softly.

Aarush turns his attention away from his wife to look in the direction of her gaze. The Emir is talking—no, arguing with a girl who does not at all seem scared or overwhelmed by the Ifrit. They are too far away for Aruna and Aarush to hear the topic of the argument, but it is clear from the way the girl turns her body away from the Emir that no resolution was found.

They walk closer, and Aarush is struck by the unintentional synchronicity of their movements. The girl is willowy with dusky skin that shines with youth and vigor. She moves with a grace that reminds Aarush of a gazelle he saw once while on a hunt in the jungles of Asur. Her eyes are the same gold color as the Emir's, with the same startlingly direct gaze. Aruna walks forward with a smile when the two reach them, and Aarush realizes with a start that the girl is very young, perhaps younger than Bhavya. Her composure, however, gives her a depth that his sister currently lacks.

"Maharani, Maharajah, my greetings to you." The Emir inclines his head toward them.

The girl, perhaps realizing it is her turn to make some greetings, also inclines her head in a perfect echo of the Emir. This is all the deference she is going to show the royal couple. Aarush exchanges a smile with Aruna.

"This is Fatima Ghazala," the Emir says with a look at the girl. "Please take care of her."

The girl draws a breath as if to respond to the Emir's words but turns aside at the last minute, choosing to keep her words unspoken. Her eyes are bright and her lips are pulled tight, but she doesn't look once in the Emir's direction. Aarush feels a spurt of pity for the Ifrit.

"Aruna is going to take Fatima Ghazala on as a companion," Aarush says to the Emir.

The maharani smiles and, with exquisite grace, draws Fatima Ghazala away. "We will be leaving first," she says to Aarush and nods to the Emir. She gestures for a guard to take the bag Fatima Ghazala is carrying. Aarush waits for the girl to make a farewell of sorts to the Emir, but she leaves without another look at either man.

"You've made her angry," Aarush says to the Emir, whose eyes do not waver from the receding figure of the girl.

"I told her a truth she didn't want to hear," the Emir says quietly. Aarush feels his reality hiccup.

"Will that truth affect my people? My family?" he asks.

"*Her* truth won't." The Emir turns assessing eyes on Aarush. "As we spoke last night, the truth about the Qirati rebels might."

"Those are just rumors," Aarush immediately protests. He thought the entire night about the man who died in the school in Shams Gali.

"Can you really call them rumors? How do you explain the man who hurt the child last night? Was he just a rumor?" the Emir responds, almost disbelievingly.

"He was a man who had lost his hold on sanity. That is all. I spoke to my people in Khair, Emir. They assure me there is no army of rebels gathering in the province! If I react to these rumors, and let me assure you that is what they are, I will be giving them a credibility they don't deserve," Aarush says, avoiding the Emir's eyes.

He doesn't want the Ifrit reading the truth he is not yet ready to admit to.

"When do rumors become fact, Rajah? How much do you trust your people? I can tell you right now that the rebellion, whether you believe in it or not, is fueled by propaganda originating from Noor City." The Emir smiles thinly. "Someone in your government is unhappy with the way Qirat is ruled."

Aarush pales. The Emir continues. "You rule half a country, Maharajah, while I rule half a city. It is not my place to tell you how to do your job. However, since the humans have hurt those I have vowed to protect, I have no choice but to be prepared for all eventualities. If there is a war, know that we will fight."

Aarush lingers in the pavilion for a while after the Emir leaves. The idea that a traitor lurks somewhere close scares him far more than it ought to. What if he loses the kingdom? How is he supposed to figure out who he can trust? Who he can turn to? That old feeling, the feeling he hasn't had to battle in a while, resurges in him. He feels like he is in the mythical sea, trying to stay afloat so the country he is holding up in his elevated arms doesn't sink. But everyone knows what he is not allowed to admit: He does not know how to swim.

Forever tastes like ash on Fatima Ghazala's tongue. She didn't comprehend the immensity of the role thrust upon her until the mechanics of time were applied to it. How many mornings are there in forever? How many nights? What has she become?

Fatima Ghazala follows the maharani quietly, grateful that no one is demanding any conversation from her. She doesn't think she is capable of it at the moment. A group of ten women dressed in bright Banarasi saris with fragrant gajra in their hair join the maharani as soon they enter the mahal and leave the guards behind.

Fatima Ghazala becomes conscious of their eyes on her, aware that she sticks out like a sparrow among peacocks. Though no one dares to question the maharani about Fatima Ghazala's identity, the air is thick with curiosity. Fatima Ghazala holds on tightly to the bag the guard returned to her and takes comfort in the oud slung over her shoulder.

They meet no other royal family member as the maharani leads everyone up to the fifth floor. She opens the door to one of the empty suites and sweeps in. Following the companions into the room, Fatima Ghazala feels overwhelmed by the luxury of Southern Aftab. It is far more ostentatious than Northern Aftab, which, though richly decorated, lacks the vibrance of Southern Aftab. She feels alien in the midst of the rich decor, the exquisite architecture, and the people who have never wondered where they are going to sleep at night or known the thorny edges of hunger.

"Come here," the maharani says, holding out her hand to Fatima Ghazala, who moves to stand beside her. "This is Fatima Ghazala," the maharani tells her companions. "She is my guest and will remain in our company until necessary. You will treat her with respect. You will protect her as you do me." A murmur of assent goes up.

Fatima Ghazala looks at the women closer, observing their stiff postures and the way they hold themselves carefully. A part of her recognizes them for the warriors they are. She looks at the maharani with a question in her eyes.

"They are my guards, though the rest of the world thinks them merely companions. Very few people know the actual role my companions play. In fact, apart from those gathered here, the maharajah is the only other person who knows that my ladies are some of the deadliest fighters Qirat is fortunate to have."

"Can *you* fight? Are you dangerous?" a girl wearing a bright yellow sari asks.

"Dangerous?" Fatima Ghazala is startled by the question. It is the first time someone has asked her that. She thinks of the Shaitan, dead by her hand. She thinks of her capacity for violence, the potential to wreak destruction in the fire she now carries. "I can be," she tells the woman.

"That will do," the woman replies with a smile. "I'm Indra." After Indra, the other women introduce themselves. Fatima Ghazala does her best to memorize all the names and faces presented to her. She turns from the introductions to see the maharani looking at her speculatively.

"We must change your clothes . . . you probably do not have any clothes befitting one of my companions," the maharani says without rancor. "Indra, see to Fatima Ghazala's clothes, the rest of you come with me. The Rajmata wants to lunch together. We also have to see to the preparations for the puja next week." She turns again to Fatima Ghazala. "Please stay in these rooms until proper attire has been prepared for you. Then, if you wish, you may join me in my work."

With a kind smile, the maharani exits the room, her companions following. They leave behind the scent of the jasmine flowers the gajra are made of and a deafening silence. Fatima Ghazala looks around the living room that opens up to a balcony. Two closed doors get her attention; one of them leads to a bedroom and the other to a very large bathroom. Bigger than the apartment that used to be home not very many days ago.

Fatima Ghazala puts down her bag and embraces her oud, trying to fight off the homesickness that sweeps over her in tremors. She yearns for the practical and abrasive love of her sister and the complete acceptance of the Alif sisters. She forgets how annoyed she is with Zulfikar and wants him because he is familiar. Most of all, though, she longs for the gruff kindness of her baba, for the word-soaked home that was his bookstore, and for that unconditional sense of belonging she found with him.

She doesn't know how long she spends perched on a chair in that room dripping with splendor before the knock on the door. She opens the door to admit Indra of the yellow sari. The older girl bustles in hauling a pack containing a dozen Banarasi saris, some costume jewelry, and a fresh gajra. Without wasting time on conversation, she helps Fatima Ghazala put on a green sari with gold-and-red borders. Fatima Ghazala puts her hair up in a bun, and Indra arranges the gajra around it. A matha patti and a kamarband are the only pieces of jewelry Indra recommends. Once she has been changed and coiffed to Indra's satisfaction, they look in the mirror. Fatima Ghazala almost doesn't recognize herself.

"You are quite beautiful, which will only get you the wrong type of attention here," Indra says. She meets Fatima Ghazala's eyes. "Keep your head down, but always be aware. No one here is your friend. Try not to attract anyone's attention, but in the event you do, act demure—no matter how difficult that may be."

"What do the companions do?" Fatima Ghazala asks.

"Our primary task is to keep the maharani and her child safe. Our second task is to help her fulfill the tasks she has to tackle as the maharani." Indra puts her hand on the doorknob of the door leading out and says over her shoulder, "You will have to leave the oud here."

"Oh . . ." Fatima Ghazala wasn't even aware of slinging it over shoulder. She takes it off reluctantly and lays it out of sight behind an ornate table. "This room is safe, right?"

Indra smiles and tosses a key to Fatima Ghazala. "It's all yours."

Zulfikar is sitting alone in front of the fire pit behind the barracks, when he feels Fatima Ghazala's fire. Frowning, he gets to his feet, peering into the gloom beyond the fire burning in the pit. A minute later, she glides into the light, and another minute passes before Zulfikar remembers it is rude to stare. He sits down and coughs to cover his embarrassment. Smiling slightly, she sits down on the bench beside him. He shifts to maintain a distance between them.

"I look like a girl, don't I?" She grins at him. Zulfikar swallows. The firelight is kind to her.

"You have always looked like a girl. It's just that now you look like a woman," he says, turning away so he is not tempted to let his eyes linger on the curves the sari clings to so lovingly.

When she doesn't reply, he risks a look at her face and finds her blushing so hard an entire rose garden has bloomed in her cheeks.

"Weren't you too angry to even look at me?" he says, thinking back to the way they had parted earlier that day.

"I wasn't angry at you. I just needed someone to blame, and you were convenient. I'm sorry."

Zulfikar is startled by how much her simple apology affects him. He grips the edge of the bench with both his hands in case he gives in to his decidedly improper desire and takes her in his arms. "And so?" he asks more brusquely than he intends.

"So what?" she retorts.

"Is their security so lacking they let you out at night without guards?" Zulfikar wonders if he should have a word with the maharajah.

Fatima Ghazala's eyes brighten, and she moves nearer to Zulfikar. He nearly jumps but manages to restrain himself. He shifts away again. Fatima Ghazala looks at him with some exasperation but doesn't comment otherwise. "Did you know the maharani's companions are actually her guards?"

Zulfikar shakes his head. He has a bad feeling about this.

"Well, they are, and I am an honorary member." She beams at him, and just like that, he is persuaded. "One of the benefits to being the maharani's companion is that the soldiers on patrol do not stop you when you go out at night."

"Please don't go out at night. Coming to find me is fine, but don't go out into the city by yourself," Zulfikar says. Fatima Ghazala shrugs noncommittally, and he gives her a dark look. "Is everything else all right?"

"Yes. No." Fatima Ghazala sighs. "I miss home. What do I do?" Her earlier enthusiasm and cheer disappears. She sits with her shoulders drooping.

"Aren't you cold?" Zulfikar shrugs off the plain black shawl he had around his shoulders and wraps it around Fatima Ghazala.

"It smells like you," she says, drawing it close around her.

"I didn't need that observation," Zulfikar mutters.

"Thank you." She is quiet for a moment. "I suppose I can no longer work as a messenger."

"I'm sorry."

"I will tell Beeji myself."

Zulfikar nods. He is relieved that she is not resisting more.

"What else can't I do? Go back home?"

"Not right away."

"I can protect myself, you know."

"That is exactly what Firdaus said. He used the very same words." Zulfikar's voice breaks. He takes a deep breath.

"If anyone is to blame for Baba's death, it is me. I am the one who gave him the book. Right into his hands." Fatima Ghazala turns to Zulfikar, frowning. "You still haven't told me how the book killed him."

"It wasn't the book but what was in it that led to Firdaus's death," Zulfikar says, thinking of the dark thing he burned.

"And what was in it?"

"The taint—it is difficult to explain what the taint is. Bear with me." Zulfikar pauses. "Do you know that the Ifrit are but one clan of many among the Djinn?"

Fatima Ghazala nods.

"The Shayateen, as you know, are another. Our enmity is decreed by the divine. As the night cannot withstand the day, the Shayateen cannot withstand the Ifrit. They are chaos; we are order. Their affinity for chaos is not what makes them evil, mind. It is their complete disregard for good. You have seen the destruction they wrought when they murdered Noor and her people. They are what we fight against every day in our world."

"But why did they attack Noor?" Fatima Ghazala interrupts.

"They don't need reasons to do things," Zulfikar replies. "That is what makes them so difficult to understand and impossible to fight. They don't move with logic or order. Those are dirty words to them. Impulse and chaos are the things that rule them.

"But the Shayateen aren't entirely without limits. When their actions move against children, the innocent, and those without the ability to defend themselves, the Shayateen become tainted." Zulfikar glances at Fatima Ghazala to see if she understands and continues. "I spoke to you about the importance of names to the Djinn, do you remember?"

"Yes."

"When the Shayateen get tainted, their Names start corroding. We cannot exist without Names, not in Al-Naar and not on earth. Tainted Names mean death, slow deaths. A tainted Shaitan cannot access his or her fire. It is somewhat like being able to see the world but unable to feel the breeze on your skin or seeing the sun without also feeling the heat."

"But the taint only affects the Shayateen, right? Not the Ifrit?" Fatima Ghazala asks.

Zulfikar rubs his eyes tiredly. "I wish that were true. The blood of tainted Shayateen undoes the Ifrit it comes in contact with. Unlike the Shayateen, the Ifrit move toward order. Tainted blood undoes that. An Ifrit infected by the blood of a tainted Shaitan glories in chaos. Our history contains an Ifrit who got poisoned by tainted blood. Before he was caught, he burned cities and villages, killing thousands." Zulfikar hesitates. "Firdaus chose death over losing his goodness. He knew better than anyone the destruction he was capable of." Zulfikar stops speaking. The quiet feels full of holes. He glances at Fatima Ghazala and finds her frozen, her face a mask of anguish.

"Fatima . . ." he starts, but she shakes her head.

"I will be all right. It hurts, so I need a moment. Just give me one moment."

Zulfikar sits quietly and gives her the entire night.

CHAPTER 17

When Fatima Ghazala's eyes snap open, she realizes three things simultaneously: One, she is in a strange room; two, the azaan for Fajr has yet to sound; and three, she was dreaming about the child, Shuruq, again. She wipes her eyes and sits up. Though Fatima Ghazala slept on a mattress softer than any she has ever rested on in a room bigger than any she has ever been in, she feels exhausted. She gets up groggily, performs her ablutions in the bathroom, and settles in to wait for the azaan, which sounds five minutes later. The piercing call sounds as beautiful as it always does though the extra distance lessens the intensity of it. Fatima Ghazala thinks wistfully of the rooftop that belonged to her in the chill of the early dawn air; she thinks of the muezzin's call, so close once that it seemed like he was calling especially to her. She thinks of the charpai in the room she shared with Sunaina, and that sense of belonging she took for granted.

When Indra arrives at eight a.m. along with maids bearing trays full of food, Fatima Ghazala has dressed herself in a pale pink sari with a rose-gold border. She couldn't go back to sleep after Fajr, so she spent the time practicing putting on a sari. She tied her hair up in a bun and lined her eyes with kohl. Her lips she leaves bare in anticipation of breakfast. Indra knocks and enters, smiling approvingly when she finds Fatima Ghazala already dressed.

"Did you sleep well?" Indra asks, and smirks at the answering expression on Fatima Ghazala's face. All conversation is paused while the maids set out the food on a low table on the balcony that overlooks the courtyard between Northern Aftab and Southern Aftab. The maids leave, and Fatima Ghazala sits at the table perusing the food with silent appreciation. There is a lot to admire: little silver bowls containing crisply fried okra seasoned with spices and chili, leafy saijan cooked with roasted coconut flakes, and savory sambar. Accompanying all this is a separate dish full of freshly made rotis that are still warm to the touch along with a little cup full of seasoned yogurt. And of course, most importantly, a silver teapot filled with masala chai. For dessert, there is a platter of fruits with a creamy custard apple in the center.

"A feast," Fatima Ghazala whispers in awe.

Indra snickers, and Fatima Ghazala gets the sense that she has become a major source of entertainment for the older girl. "We usually eat together," Indra says, "but the maharani thought it would be better if you do not meet any other members of the royal family just yet. So I volunteered to eat with you."

Fatima Ghazala nods her thanks, already reaching for a roti. She tears off a piece and scoops up some saijan with it. She pops the morsel into her mouth and sighs with pleasure at the explosion of flavors.

Indra chews her own mouthful slowly, her gaze not moving from Fatima Ghazala, who catches her staring and raises an eyebrow in question. "Where did you go last night?" Indra asks casually.

Fatima Ghazala finishes chewing and swallows her second mouthful of food. "I had business to attend to."

"What kind of business?" With a practiced move, Indra pours chai into two cups and passes one to Fatima Ghazala.

"I needed to talk to the Emir," Fatima Ghazala says, taking the cup with a smile of thanks.

Indra whistles, surprising Fatima Ghazala. "The maharani told us that you are here at the Emir's request, but I didn't put weight to her words—she cannot always tell us the truth—but you actually do know him. Is that why we are supposed to keep you safe?"

"I can keep myself safe," Fatima Ghazala says irritably. She eats some okra with a piece of roti and feels better. "I just humor the Emir."

"You must be precious to him," Indra replies, and Fatima Ghazala makes a gagging face. Indra laughs loudly. Her expression grows somber, and after a moment's contemplation, she says, "Whatever your relationship is to the Emir, I advise you to conceal it from everyone. Rajkumari Bhavya fancies herself in love with the Emir, and she will make your life miserable if she considers you a rival for his affections."

Fatima Ghazala narrows her eyes.

"Do *not* consider it a challenge," Indra cautions. "And while I am on the topic of potential trouble, steer clear of Rajkumar Aaruv. He likes beautiful girls and has often tried his luck on us. If he does corner you, try not to hurt him too much."

"Thank you for the warnings."

Indra shrugs, and her grin turns wicked. "I will fight you for the custard apple."

Fatima Ghazala smiles back, just as wickedly. "I will win."

After the morning puja is finished and breakfast eaten, the men of Bhavya's family disperse: the rajkumar to find fitting entertainment, and the maharajah to tackle the weighty job of administrating half a country. The Rajmata and Jayanti Bua leave for their weekly session at an ashram just outside the city where they will feed the gathered poor and listen to the lectures of the many pujari who lecture there. Many of the court ladies, eager to be in their good graces, join the Rajmata and Jayanti at the ashram.

The women left in Southern Aftab are younger in age and seek more secular ways to spend their time. Bhavya is especially looking forward to the day, as Ruchika and her cousin, per her demands, will be bringing the cosmetics chemist to the mahal.

Bhavya strolls down to the first floor, trailed by her maid, and into a spacious receiving room, where the royal women usually entertain visitors. With the large windows open to let in the sunshine and whatever breeze there is, the room presents an inviting and cool place to while away the hours. Carefully groomed indoor plants decorate the room with trailing branches while fresh flowers, arranged artistically in ornate vases, sit atop the sideboards and side tables. On this day, the divans and other chairs have been removed from the center of the room, and rugs have been placed on the ground in their place. The removal of the furniture allows the room to admit a lot more people than it would otherwise. The only chair remaining is a divan at the very front for the rajkumari and the maharani. Bhavya, suddenly filled with good cheer, beams at the maids arranging things. They, in turn, look bemused by the unexpected sweetness.

"Are they here yet?" Bhavya asks her maid. The harried woman gives a quick shake of her head. "Go remind the maharani that she is expected," Bhavya orders. Without waiting to see if her maid obeys, she sits down on the divan. In front of her is a low table and beyond it the rug where other women interested in cosmetics will sit.

Bhavya waits and soon other women start arriving. Courtiers, cousins, all women born to wealth and boredom, all seeking ways to alleviate the unchanging panorama of their days. Ruchika and her cousin finally arrive and are shown into the room by Bhavya's maid. Accompanying the girls are servants loaded with various bags and containers. Also walking a few steps behind Ruchika and the cousin is a petite woman dressed beautifully in a modest sari that, though cheap, manages to convey both dignity and elegance. She has no jewelry on except for a nose ring that glints in the light. Her tikka is a small black dot, and her hair is a long braid down her back. She has the restrained sort of beauty that Bhavya often longs for.

Ruchika looks like she indulged in a few lemons before coming, and the cousin looks proud, being the employer of the cosmetics chemist who attracted the rajkumari's attention. The servants unload their burdens on the low table and disperse.

"We have been eagerly waiting to see what wonderful things you have brought us, Ruchika," Bhavya says, deliberately sounding as magnanimous as she can. Hot, sweet glee fills her at the wary look Ruchika sends her. "Do introduce me to the person who makes these amazing concoctions."

The cousin calls forward the woman dressed in the gray sari. "This is Sunaina." The woman brings her palms together.

"Namaste," she says respectfully.

Bhavya draws back, surprised. The woman's eyes are opaque, the emotion in them difficult to read. After being surrounded by obsequious courtiers, it is disconcerting to find someone who doesn't pretend to be impressed by her. Bhavya opens her mouth to interrogate the woman further, but at that moment, the maharani sweeps into the room followed by five of her companions. The women present immediately fall over themselves greeting the maharani, all except for the cosmetics chemist who stands frozen, her eyes unmoving from one of the maharani's companions.

Bhavya follows the woman's gaze and frowns at the new face. The girl the cosmetics chemist is looking at is exceedingly pretty, with eyes the same color as the Emir's. She is looking back at the cosmetics creator with such hurt in her eyes that Bhavya feels *her* eyes smart.

"Sunaina, you haven't greeted the maharani," Maya admonishes. The woman blinks and drags her gaze to the maharani, who sits beside Bhavya with her companions standing behind her.

"Namaste," Sunaina says again.

Aruna looks at her kindly. "I am quite anxious to see what you've brought for us today."

From the whispers filling the room, so are the other women. Sunaina gives a wan smile and kneels at the side of the low table that bears all the containers and bags the servants carried in. Bhavya doesn't miss the proprietary way the cousin looks at Sunaina. Bhavya's lips curl.

Sunaina uncovers little ceramic dishes, displaying the contents and explaining the use and ingredients of each. She shows facial scrubs made from ginseng root, red bean, green mung bean, and sponge gourd. Some of the dishes contain freshly concocted lotions made from cucumber or watermelon juices and infused with oil from scented plants to make them fragrant. There are little vials of cosmetics oils made from sunflower seeds or cabbage seeds or castor oil plants.

"Peony oil will make your hair shine." Sunaina demonstrates on her own hair.

Eye shadow made from beetroot powder is a particular favorite, as are the ones made from dried lavender buds. The orange eye shadow that initially attracted Bhavya's attention is shown to Aruna, who pronounces it an instant favorite. But the concoction that evokes the most excitement is the rouge made from saffron and honey with a small extract of orange peel to plump the lips.

Bhavya takes another look at the cosmetics chemist, who, having finished her explanation, sits with downcast eyes. The despair on the woman's face annoys her. "This is all very impressive. Where did you learn to make them?"

"My family spared no—" the cousin chimes in.

Bhavya cuts her off coldly. "I am asking Sunaina."

At her name, the woman looks up. Her gaze immediately goes to the companion before returning to Bhavya. "I had a Han friend, Jung Sori. Her mother taught me the recipes when she saw how interested I was in learning them. They returned to their country but left me a book containing the recipes."

"You know the Han language?" Aruna asks, and Sunaina answers in the affirmative.

"My father traded with the Han people quite extensively."

"Where are you originally from?" Bhavya asks, her curiosity piqued.

"I am from Noor City, Rajkumari." Sunaina smiles humorlessly. "I have lived my entire life there."

At her words, all voices stop, and people look closer at the woman.

"You mean you are one of the three survivors?" Aruna asks, sitting up at the unexpected revelation.

Something dark shifts in the woman's eyes. "I don't know if I would call it surviving, sahiba, but yes, I am."

Bhavya nods somberly. Now for the part she has been waiting for. "I have decided," she says, and turns to the maharani. Aruna inclines her head; the maharani will support the Bhavya's decision.

"Decided what?" Ruchika asks suspiciously, and Bhavya stifles a grin. Oh, this is fun.

"I will have Sunaina create her concoctions for the royal women first, the courtiers second, and the rest of the world third. She will work from Aftab Mahal," Bhavya announces with a flourish, and gives in to the urge to beam.

"But, Rajkumari Bhavya!" Maya stands up to protest.

"Tell me, Maya, did I sound like I was asking for your permission?" Bhavya says, her eyes bright with malice. The cousin blanches. "How much did you pay Sunaina for her creations?"

"W-w-well, we provided the materials . . ." the girl stammers.

"In other words, nothing." Bhavya shakes her head. "Tch, so cheap. I expected better from your cousin, Ruchika."

Ruchika goes scarlet, her embarrassment robbing her of speech.

"Sunaina, you will move into the mahal as soon as you can. Someone here will help you with the details," Bhavya says, waving her hand vaguely. Aruna nods at one of her companions, and the woman comes forward to talk to Sunaina.

"Go ahead and try the cosmetics," Bhavya urges the women present, and they surge forward, not needing any more encouragement.

Fatima Ghazala looks at her sister and wonders if she should try, once again, to approach her, but the hurt from their last confrontation still lingers. The word "monster" crawls under her skin, trying to make her into the thing she was accused of being. No, Fatima Ghazala decides, she will not be the one making conciliatory overtures. Not this time.

"Do you know the cosmetics chemist, Fatima Ghazala?" the maharani asks, and Fatima Ghazala realizes she hasn't been very circumspect with her expressions.

"She's my sister, sahiba," Fatima Ghazala says softly with a glance at Sunaina, who is answering questions from the court ladies. The admission costs nothing except a twinge in her heart.

The rajkumari turns and looks at Fatima Ghazala.

"Her parents adopted me and brought me up as Muslim," Fatima Ghazala elaborates at the look on the rajkumari's face.

"Does this mean you are a survivor too?" the rajkumari asks.

Fatima Ghazala feels her lips twist humorlessly at the word. Survival hardly encompasses the entirety of their experiences. What word should they use to describe nights full of nightmares? What words will properly articulate the feeling when you turn a corner in a neighborhood you have lived in your entire life and all you can see are the ghosts of people you used to know? "I guess you can call it surviving," she says to the rajkumari.

"What about the third person? Do you know her?" Aruna asks.

"Her name is Laali. Yes, she was with us at the time, sahiba," Fatima Ghazala answers. She feels a pang of guilt as she realizes that she left Taaj Gul without once visiting the grandmother she is so fond of.

A footman comes forward carrying a message for the maharani, and a cousin calls Bhavya to join the rest of the women trying out the cosmetics. The moment is broken, but the words spoken echo, weighting the atmosphere with a reminder of all they have lost.

The maharani gestures Fatima Ghazala closer. "The Emir asks that you attend him in Northern Aftab. Indra will show you how to leave without being seen," Aruna says in a low voice.

Fatima Ghazala nods and leaves the room with one last look at her sister. She follows Indra through large airy rooms and wide corridors and turns a corner only to almost bump into someone traveling at full speed in the opposite direction. She avoids him, neatly stepping aside at the last moment.

"Fatima Ghazala, hurry it up!" Indra calls sharply. Fatima Ghazala spares one look at the person she almost bumped into, nods her head at him, and runs after Indra.

Indra shows Fatima Ghazala a little dark room in the pantry where she can change into her usual uniform of tunic, shalwar, and turban, and walk out with no one giving her a second look. A half hour later from the time the Emir called for her, Fatima Ghazala makes her way to Northern Aftab through the corridor that connects the two palaces, wondering if she is supposed to simply march inside and demand to be taken to the Emir. It turns out she needn't have worried, as Zulfikar is waiting for her in the courtyard in front of the entrance. He smiles when he sees her, and Fatima Ghazala forgets to breathe. She had forgotten how beautiful he is. He is dressed in the usual Patiala pants and vest that is the uniform of the Ifrit soldiers. Fatima Ghazala lets her eyes linger on his bare arms and chest. She clears her throat and ducks her head, her cheeks hot.

"You asked for me?" she asks, deliberately keeping her eyes turned from him.

"I received word from my superiors earlier today. They told me that I may take you into confidence and ask for your help," Zulfikar says.

At his words, Fatima Ghazala immediately forgets her not-very-halal desires. "What kind of help?" she asks.

"We should probably talk about this in a more private place. Please follow me."

Fatima Ghazala hesitates. "The Wazir isn't around, is he?"

"No. The Wazir spends most of his time moving between the desert cities of Qirat that are ruled by the Ifrit. He also patrols the Silk Road to ensure the caravans can travel it without fear of attack from Shayateen and other less savory creatures," Zulfikar says.

"Right now he is tracking the merchant who delivered the book for Firdaus."

Fatima Ghazala follows Zulfikar to a small room on the third floor. Books and other paraphernalia are arranged on bookshelves that stand against one wall. In the middle of the room are three chairs arranged around a coffee table. This is the humblest room Fatima Ghazala has seen on either side of the mahal.

"Take a seat and give me a minute. I will be back." Zulfikar leaves, and Fatima Ghazala wanders around the room, peering at the books on the shelves. They all deal with military strategy. On the table is a shatranj game paused in mid-play. Fatima Ghazala is peering at the board, trying to make sense of it, when Zulfikar returns carrying a tray full of desserts and a coffeepot.

"Do you play?" he asks, shifting the game over and placing the tray on the table. Fatima Ghazala shakes her head. "I'll teach you someday," he says casually. Fatima Ghazala frowns. Does he envision them being in the kind of relationship where he would teach her things? Would Fatima Ghazala mind? No, she answers herself honestly, she wouldn't mind being taught things by the Emir.

"Dessert?" Fatima Ghazala says, looking at a plate piled with gulab jamun, kunafeh, and baklava.

"Don't you want any?" Zulfikar helps himself to a gulab jamun.

"I always have room for dessert," Fatima Ghazala says. She pours thick, bitter coffee from the coffeepot into a cup and adds two cubes of sugar to it. She hands it to Zulfikar. "But right now I am more interested in what you have to tell me."

"Ah." Zulfikar takes a sip of the coffee. "You may have heard me mention her before, but the Ifrit leader is called the Raees. She holds the position because she has the strongest fire of us all." Zulfikar takes a deep breath. "The Raees got infected by the taint and is, at this very moment, internally battling it as it tries to take over her fire. Firdaus was supposed to Name her into being this coming Juma. It is imperative that she leave Al-Naar."

"Otherwise she'll destroy your cities and kill your people? Like that other Ifrit did?" Fatima Ghazala asks.

"Yes. She will try to resist it, but you cannot hold back a mountain determined to fall."

"Won't the taint affect humans?"

"Not that we have seen. But we do not know. There might be effects that we have not foreseen."

"And you want me to Name the Raees into the human world?" Fatima Ghazala asks incredulously.

"Yes," the Emir says.

"But I don't know how." Fatima Ghazala is not sure she fully understands what Naming is either.

"We will tackle that problem later. I can only move forward if I have your agreement."

"I promised Baba that I would write his tale. If this is what he meant by that, I have to try, don't I? I gave him my word."

"It might be dangerous, so think twice."

"I am not afraid of dying, Emir." Fatima Ghazala looks at him and shrugs. "I have cheated death so many times I feel that if I die this time, it will be deserved."

"Don't say that. Don't think it. *I* am afraid of you dying." A moment arcs between them, electric and consuming. Confusing. The Emir looks away first.

"Sayyid!" An Amir soldier appears in the doorway. Fatima Ghazala breathes out, relieved by the interruption. The soldier looks at Fatima Ghazala, then walks over to Zulfikar and whispers urgently in his ear. Zulfikar is rising from his seat before the soldier finishes speaking.

"A Qareen haunts one of the apartments in Taaj Gul. I have to go and try to resolve the situation immediately."

"I'll go with you," Fatima Ghazala says promptly, not realizing the note of command in her voice.

"As you wish," the Emir says.

CHAPTER 18

Ten minutes later, Zulfikar, Fatima Ghazala, and six other Ifrit soldiers are making their way rapidly to Taaj Gul. It is a little after one in the afternoon, and the heat is gaining intensity. Their destination is an old apartment building that still bears scars from the Shayateen attacks. Zulfikar and Fatima Ghazala dismount from the horse as do the soldiers.

An atmosphere of gloom envelops the place, as if even the stones of the building have private sorrows. The surrounding buildings also seem abandoned, though Fatima Ghazala is sure they are fully inhabited. People of Noor City know very well how and when to disappear in the woodwork. The silence surrounding the entire area feels unnatural. Fatima Ghazala keeps thinking that it will be broken by a child's scream or laughter, but the quiet persists.

"The building has been evacuated, and the occupants moved to the maidaan to wait until the situation has been dealt with," an Ifrit soldiers says. His Name is Mansoor, Fatima Ghazala reads, of unswerving loyalty, humor, and luck. He gives her a look but does not comment on her presence.

"Get me all the information you can about whoever died in the apartment," Zulfikar says. Mansoor nods and moves to do his bidding.

"Qareen are a diminutive clan of Djinn. Every human has one bonded to them. Their express purpose is to record your deeds, good or bad," Zulfikar says, correctly reading the question in Fatima Ghazala's eyes.

"Every human does? Do I have one?"

"They only show themselves under extreme circumstances. Well, books contain reports of Qareen manifesting to their child hosts. I . . . don't know whether you have one or not, but since you are . . . I can't call you entirely human, can I now? I am not sure whether you do." Zulfikar grimaces through his explanation.

Mansoor returns with a couple following him. Both the man and woman have the glassy-eyed appearance of those whose emotions have been taxed two shades beyond endurance.

"A boy child died in the apartment late last night. These are his parents, Nazim Ali and Razia Buksh." Mansoor gestures to the couple.

"May Allah grant your child paradise," Zulfikar says, and Fatima Ghazala echoes the customary consolation.

The parents bow their heads silently. "Could you tell me exactly what happened?" Zulfikar asks gently.

"He has been sick his entire life," the mother says, and her voice breaks when she realizes that the present tense no longer applies to her child. "We thought he was getting better. Everyone says that, don't they? But we really did. He went outside and played. I made him chai and gulgula. He ate dinner. Told us he loved us. I should have known when he thanked us for being his parents. I should have known something was terribly wrong, but I thought he was just expressing his love. When I went to check on him during the night, he was gone." The woman breaks down and weeps. Her husband puts his arm around her, supporting her weight.

"We buried him this morning," the husband continues. "When we came home, the creature was in his bed. It looks so much like Imran that for a moment I thought I had been having a nightmare and my child had been returned to me. Then I looked into its eyes and saw a monster staring back at me."

Fatima Ghazala flinches at the word. Zulfikar thanks the parents, and they leave.

"Well, it is time for me to go face the Qareen," Zulfikar says heavily. "It's the most difficult when they take on the guise of children."

"Is it dangerous?" Fatima Ghazala asks. Her eyes are wet. She brushes away her tears quickly.

"No, right now the Qareen is most likely simply grieving. The attachment is strongest when the human is a child."

"Are Qareen hauntings common?"

"All Qareens are attached to their humans," Mansoor answers Fatima Ghazala, much to her surprise. The other soldiers pretend that she is invisible. "When their human dies, some cannot handle their grief and manifest themselves in the appearance of their humans. They are what humans usually call ghosts."

Fatima Ghazala nods a thank-you to the soldier for his explanation.

"Will you remain here?" Zulfikar asks Fatima Ghazala.

"Can I not come with you? I know a thing or two about grief. Maybe I could help?" Fatima Ghazala cannot explain the sudden compulsion that tells her she must see this incident through, but she is not about to question it.

Zulfikar gives in after a slight hesitation. "Very well. Mansoor, which apartment is the haunted one?"

"The first one on the third floor from the east, sayyid."

"Follow me with two soldiers. I do not expect violence, but nonetheless, be wary. Fatima Ghazala, stay with the soldiers, please."

Fatima Ghazala nods. The climb to the third floor is eerily

quiet. The sounds of their footsteps seem magnified. A light coating of pale pink dust covers all surfaces—and even in these circumstances, Fatima Ghazala feels a sense of home. As they get nearer to the apartment, the oppressive atmosphere of sadness grows stronger until Fatima Ghazala can barely breathe for the lump in her throat and the press of tears in her eyes.

Mansoor gestures to the apartment with the front door ajar. Zulfikar holds up a hand. He enters and gestures for them to stop at the doorway. Fatima Ghazala looks inside the apartment and reads of a life interrupted in the way a pile of laundry lies on a table, pieces of chalk are scattered on the floor, drawings are pasted on the wall.

Zulfikar takes a deep breath; in the next moment, his body is enveloped by his fire, an orange sheen rising from the surface of his skin. "Qareen," he commands, "show yourself!"

For a few moments, there is no response, but then comes the giggle of a child. Fatima Ghazala steels herself.

"Qareen, I command you on the ninety-nine names of our Creator, show yourself!" Zulfikar says, his voice thundering.

"I no longer believe in this Creator," a little boy's voice says. The creature that walks into the living room of the apartment has the appearance of a child not more than six years old. He has tousled curly hair and flushed, sunken cheeks. But his eyes—ah, his eyes are the dark of sorrow. A dark that Fatima Ghazala knows very well. "Why would He create me for this child and force me to witness his pain? Why would He leave me behind and take only the child? Why wasn't *I* given the same relief? What about *my* pain? What kind of Creator does that?"

"You have your own life to lead, Qareen. This is the way of your kind," Zulfikar says firmly though not unkindly.

"Life?" The Qareen gives a short bark of laughter. "I have spent all of my time tethered to Imran. I don't know what life is without him."

Fatima Ghazala stares at the creature, and her vision grows hazy. She sees silvery pieces glowing in the region of the Qareen's chest. They are like puzzle pieces, straining toward each other, trying to form a whole but being kept from unification by a viscous matter that to Fatima Ghazala's eyes looks very much like grief made tangible. Without considering the consequences, Fatima Ghazala reaches out and touches one of the silvery pieces.

The Qareen shudders, and his eyes flame blue. He turns to Fatima Ghazala and snarls.

CHAPTER 19

atima Ghazala's mother used to say that each moment is a universe, infinite in its possibilities. The moment the Qareen looks at Fatima Ghazala and realizes her presence in the doorway is one such moment, one such universe.

"You— What did you do to me?" The Qareen speaks in Qadr, the language of the Djinn. The words sound as if they were torn from his throat.

Fatima Ghazala remembers her dark days, remembers the time when the city died and echoes were all that was left. Echoes of footsteps, people, and peace. "It hurts, so you cry. You miss them, so you cry. You scream. Sometimes you bleed," she says to the Qareen, her voice a whisper. "You do not give in to the grief. You *never* give in to the grief. Doing so shames both you and your dead."

"What do *you* know of death? Of grief?" the Qareen hisses.

"I know better," Fatima Ghazala says coldly, "than to dress my grief up in tears and parade it around like a circus."

The Qareen's hold on his assumed appearance slips. He rapidly devolves into a coiling mass of blue flames. After some obvious effort, he regains a face, a shadow of the one he had previously assumed. He keens, a piercing sound that rattles the glass in the window and the cutlery in the kitchen cupboards. "Why will you not let me grieve?" he screams at the gathered Ifrit and Fatima Ghazala.

"It is not your grief we are asking you to keep contained, Qareen. It is your obsession," Zulfikar says, and Fatima Ghazala starts. With a jolt she realizes that she has been so immersed in looking at the silver pieces of the broken word in the Qareen's chest—or well, where his chest used to be—that she can't even remember stepping into the apartment. She retreats.

The Qareen seems unwilling to listen to any reason. He growls, and Fatima Ghazala's eyes slide back to the silver pieces. She watches the black matter grow and spread till it covers almost all the silver.

"Zulfikar," she warns, still in Qadr, "you are losing him."

The Qareen turns to Fatima Ghazala: another moment, another universe. Too late, Fatima Ghazala realizes that though she knows a lot about grieving, she knows almost nothing about comforting. Should she open her arms to the monster approaching her? Would the monster within her, the monster her sister is so convinced she is, consider it an invitation to step outside?

"Qareen, reconsider," Zulfikar says. He still maintains his calm though his control illustrates itself in the white-knuckled grip he has on his scimitar. "If you harm her, you will lose any chance of a life beyond your grief."

The Qareen relinquishes all attempts at a human appearance and becomes a small ball of roiling blue flame. Fatima Ghazala tenses as the flames approach; the heat rises exponentially. Before the Qareen can cause her any real damage, however, Zulfikar moves. He intones a few words, grabs the flames, tangible in his hands, and stuffs it into a glass jar. He closes the jar, screwing the lid on tightly, before handing it to Mansoor. The speed at which all this occurs leaves Fatima Ghazala feeling slightly dizzy.

"Keep it safe. We will search for the local population of liberated Qareen and hand them this one. They will know what to do with him. You may leave now," Zulfikar says to Mansoor, looking unruffled.

Mansoor takes the jar carefully, nods at Fatima Ghazala and Zulfikar, and leaves. The other two soldiers follow him. Fatima Ghazala sags against the door, feeling entirely drained of energy. She wishes she had eaten some of Zulfikar's desserts. She turns to him and finds him looking at her with a frown on his face. She flinches and turns away, presenting him with her back.

"I'm sorry. I thought I could do better," she says over her shoulder. "Instead, I provoked him. I . . . thought everyone felt grief the same way, grieved the same way. Arrogant of me, huh?" Fatima Ghazala wonders what expression the Emir has on his face, but she feels too nervous to check. The idea of disappointing him makes her feel like a road full of muddy puddles.

"Fatima Ghazala," he says, and she turns around miserably. She looks up unwillingly and is surprised by the expression on his face. He doesn't look angry. He looks . . . kind, which, in Fatima Ghazala's opinion, might be worse. "Will you show me around Northern Noor?"

Of all the things Fatima Ghazala expected the Emir to say, this was not one of them. "Now?"

"Unless you would rather return to Southern Aftab—" Fatima Ghazala is shaking her head before Zulfikar can complete the sentence.

"I need to go visit someone first. Is that all right? She lives in Taaj Gul, not far from here in fact." Zulfikar agrees readily enough.

A question occurs to Fatima Ghazala as they descend the stairs to the first floor. "What happens to the Qareen after their humans die? You said something about liberation?"

"They are long-lived; sometimes their lives span three times that of a human's. After their service is over, they are free to live as they please. They live a nomadic life in the desert," Zulfikar says over his shoulder.

"The Qareen just now has a name, you know." Fatima Ghazala thinks of the silver pieces. "I couldn't read it, though. If I hadn't been here, do you think you could have talked him out of haunting . . . ?"

"You can't talk someone out of grief." Zulfikar suddenly stops and turns around. Fatima Ghazala comes to a startled stop before she crashes into him.

"Ha. I should know that better than anyone." She bites her lip. She meets his eyes and looks away quickly. "I really am sorry for exacerbating the situation."

Zulfikar starts walking again. "I don't think you need to apologize. Not to me anyway."

Fatima Ghazala allows his words to make her feel slightly better as they emerge from the building. She waits while Zulfikar talks to his lieutenants, appreciating that he is taking time he doesn't have to be with her. Twenty minutes later, they are on their way.

"I need riding lessons," Fatima Ghazala says, patting Zulfikar's horse. "I don't like being carted around by you like that sack of rice you think I am."

"I don't know," Zulfikar says. "I have a feeling it will become impossible for you to remain in the mahal once you know how to ride and have access to horses."

"What if I promise to be good?" she answers him over her shoulder, and he makes a disbelieving sound. They are moving slowly through a busy road, and Fatima Ghazala takes in the cacophony of a thousand voices speaking perhaps as many languages with pleasure. Her good cheer begins to reassert itself as they get nearer to her building. She has Zulfikar stop at a mithai shop; no one ever visits anyone else in Noor City empty-handed.

Zulfikar remains outside with the horse while Fatima Ghazala goes to visit the Alif sisters, who aren't home, and then Laali. She pauses outside Laali's door and takes a deep breath. She hasn't seen her adopted grandmother since she became Fatima Ghazala. Will Laali be able to recognize Fatima Ghazala as a fundamentally different person from the one she knew?

She knocks, and a familiar, though more querulous, voice bids her enter. Fatima Ghazala knows something is wrong as soon as she enters Laali's room. For one thing, the curtains are drawn and the room is dark. For another, Laali is wearing an old nightdress and lying in bed. Fatima Ghazala cannot fathom how a woman so rigid about the way she dresses can endure being seen in this state of dishabille.

"Laali?" Fatima Ghazala touches the old woman's forehead gently with the back of her hand. She doesn't have a fever. Her skin is soft to the touch. Fatima Ghazala squints in the gloom of the room and frowns. Laali is glowing a faint blue. "Laali?" she says a bit more urgently. She reaches out to touch the old woman, scared suddenly, and the blue crackles. She retreats a step, thinking furiously. Is the blue Djinn fire? Why does Laali have fire?

The old woman opens her eyes and peers into the gloom. When she realizes it is Fatima Ghazala who stands above her, she struggles to a sitting position. "I told your sister quite a while ago to tell you to come see me," Laali complains agitatedly.

"She must have gotten busy and forgotten," Fatima Ghazala says with some discomfort. She doesn't want to speculate about Sunaina.

"It was important I talk to you," Laali frets, pulling at her uncombed hair.

Fatima Ghazala catches the woman's hands in her own, not caring that the blue flames sting her slightly. "I'm here now, Laali. You can talk to me now."

Laali suddenly wails and starts struggling. "I see blood, so much blood. Death and disaster. I see death!" she cries out.

"What do you mean, Laali?" Fatima Ghazala asks, and the woman grabs her hands tightly.

"The only reason I survived the Shayateen was because I knew you would keep us safe. I Saw it. So I came to find you."

"What do you mean you Saw it, Laali?" Fatima Ghazala frowns, sensing that her adopted grandmother is telling her something of significance but unable to quite understand.

"I should have told people to run. I should have. I did! No one listened, and they all died. Now it's my turn!" Laali starts crying loudly, rocking back and forth as if she is in great pain. Fatima Ghazala stands frozen, not knowing what to do.

"Is she at it again?" Laali's door opens, and Anu comes bustling in. "She has been wailing about death, dying, and blood these past few days." Anu clicks her tongue. "Poor dear is losing hold of reality. Run along, Fatima. I'll help her bathe and change her clothes. It's almost time for chai too."

Fatima Ghazala nods slowly, unable to take her eyes off the frail old woman. Her blue glow is faint but constant. She tries to tell Laali she is leaving, but the old woman has drifted too far into her nightmares to comprehend. Fatima Ghazala places a box of mithai on a table on her way out. The reality of Laali and the inevitability of the end weigh upon her shoulders. Her expression is somber when she returns to Zulfikar.

"Is everything all right?" he asks, helping her mount the horse.

Fatima Ghazala shakes her head. "No, but I don't want to talk about it." Why was Laali glowing blue? What does she mean, "Saw" it? What did she see? She glances at Zulfikar. What if Laali's glow means she is part djinni? Fatima Ghazala remembers the Wazir's assertion. What would he do to Laali? She's already so ill.

"Fair enough," the Emir says easily. "So now where will you take me?"

"First"—Fatima Ghazala looks at the remaining box of mithai in the bag she is carrying—"I need to go to Beeji's haveli."

Zulfikar obliges, and half an hour later, they are at Achal Kaur's haveli. After a teary meeting with the old matriarch that culminates in a long hug, Fatima Ghazala is finally ready to show Zulfikar the sides of Noor only she knows. She asks the Emir some questions as they ride away from Achal Kaur's haveli, their pace slow in the honeyed heat of the day. "How long have you been in Noor?"

"Four years," Zulfikar replies.

"Is it much different from . . . Do the Ifrit live in cities?" Fatima Ghazala could never get Firdaus to talk much about the Djinn.

"In Al-Naar, I lived in the city of Tayneeb." The Emir falls silent until Fatima Ghazala nudges him. "Sorry, I was just remembering. Tayneeb is . . ." He pauses again. "Different. Especially the architecture in the city. Our houses are made of marble. Sounds improbable, doesn't it? But in Tayneeb, every domicile is an expression of the matriarch's pride in her family, in her Name. People use only the best materials and the best architects to create their houses. We live in extended families of thirty to forty people, so imagine multiple buildings the size of Aftab Mahal. We do not have kings or queens but a Raees, the Ifrit with the strongest fire, and among us, that's always a woman."

"Why did you leave?" The longing for his home is apparent in the words the Emir speaks.

He is quiet for such a long while that Fatima Ghazala thinks the Emir is not going to answer. But finally, after a short laugh that has nothing to do with humor, he says, "I got my heart broken. It hurt too much to stay in the same city as her. To watch her create a life in which I would be less than a bystander. So I left. The farthest I could run to was here."

"I see." Fatima Ghazala mulls for a second. "Will you never go back?"

"I am scared to," the Emir confesses in a whisper. Fatima Ghazala twists in her seat in front of him and tries to look at him, but he makes her turn around again.

"So it still hurts." Fatima Ghazala feels a peculiar sting in her own chest at the thought. She wonders why people fall in love when all it ever ends in is pain.

"I suspect it always will." Zulfikar laughs again. Fatima Ghazala can tell he is embarrassed by all he has told her. "Where exactly are we going?"

"The public stables." At Zulfikar's expression of surprise, she elaborates, "The Noor I know, the Noor I want to show you, is not a city to be seen on a horse."

The Noor Fatima Ghazala knows is not one that is easily visible to those born in wealth and privilege. It never was. She remembers exploring the city with her adoptive father, her small hand held snugly in his much larger one. "Noor," Jagan told her, "means light. But not just any light. Noor means heavenly light. The kind of light you see in a mother's face the first time she sees her child."

The Noor Fatima Ghazala walks in now is vastly different from the Noor she grew up in. Firdaus taught her that no city is ever a simple sum of its streets and buildings. Neither is Noor. The city of Noor is a harmony of her people and her places; Fatima Ghazala intends to show the Emir this.

She takes him through colorful alleys composed of narrow walks and tiny shops selling everything from candles to jewelry made of blue beads and silver pieces. They walk through a street that is perfectly ordinary except for the rioting of hot-pink bougainvillea flowers on the walls between the houses and the sidewalk. Along the way she shows him the poetry, sometimes written, sometimes drawn, on doors and doorsteps, on the walls and in hidden alcoves. Love letters to the city from the people she shelters.

She takes him to a Buddhist temple on a leafy hill in Southern Noor where cats gather after dark. A grove of date palms in Northern Noor that yield the sweetest Medjool dates. They eat sugarcane and drink coconut milk. From a grizzly vendor wearing an ambi-patterned kurta, they buy naan stuffed with roasted meat and vegetables, which they wash down with glasses of sikhye they purchase from a Han vendor.

Their final stop is Bijli Bazaar.

"This is my favorite place in Noor City," Fatima Ghazala tells the Emir as they stand in front of one of the many entrances to the market. "Do you have a place similar to this in Tayneeb?"

"We do have markets, but nothing this chaotic." He grins. "Is there a reason this place is so special to you?"

Fatima Ghazala leads him inside, breathing deep of the air that is scented with ittar and spices. As it is late in the afternoon, the market isn't too crowded. It will close its doors at eight in the evening. "For six months after the massacre, my sister and I lived in a shelter provided by the Emir at the time. We were too shattered to care for ourselves." Fatima Ghazala shudders slightly, remembering. "But as time lessened the intensity of our losses, my sister decided we could no longer accept the charity of the Djinn. We didn't have anywhere to go, so we took to the streets. It was okay. Noor had people again. It was no longer a graveyard."

They start walking down an alley populated by spice vendors. Barrels of black, green, and red chili powder, nutmeg, ginger

powder, star anise, cardamom, turmeric, and many other spices
vie for their attention. Fatima Ghazala feels like she is in heaven.
"We spent our nights at several places: the masjid, synagogue, mandir, gurdwara, wherever we could be safe. But sometimes we would
secretly spend the night locked in here. I would explore while my
sister slept. I would peer into the stores and make up wild stories
about the merchants and the merchandise they sell. I spent a lot of
time running around this place, tiring myself so I could sleep even
when I was hungry." She smiles at the Emir. "The bazaar with its
twists and turns became a place to call home."

When they finally retrieve Zulfikar's horse and return to Aftab
Mahal, it is late in the evening. Fatima Ghazala is exhausted and
wondering if she can make it to Southern Aftab without succumb-
ing to the demands of sleep.

"Thank you," the Emir says before they part.

"I should be the one thanking you," Fatima Ghazala replies.
"This was your way of distracting me from the incident with the
Qareen, was it not?"

The Emir looks away but not before Fatima Ghazala sees his
smile. She stands transfixed, her heart a bit wobbly. Then she
shakes herself free and takes her leave of him.

Fatima Ghazala makes her way to the dark room in Southern
Aftab where she swiftly changes clothes. The kitchen is deserted, as
are the hallways. Fatima Ghazala assumes that the majority of the
mahal inhabitants have retired for the night. No sooner does she
have the thought than someone steps directly in her path. Fatima
Ghazala moves aside very quickly, avoiding collision at the last
minute.

"You really do have excellent reflexes," the man who stepped in
front of her says.

Fatima Ghazala turns to look at him. His likeness to the maharajah is such that Fatima Ghazala can only conclude that the man before her is Rajkumar Aaruv, the man Indra warned her about. He is currently evaluating Fatima Ghazala much like one would livestock; his eyes linger on her lips, her chest, before traveling down. His very gaze is a violation. Fatima Ghazala stiffens, gives him the barest of nods, and starts walking away.

"I haven't given you leave to go yet," the rajkumar says.

"I do not answer to you, Rajkumar Aaruv," Fatima Ghazala replies as calmly as she can.

"It is not fair that you know my name and I do not know yours," the rajkumar says, falling into step with her.

"Life's not fair. Shouldn't you know that by now?" Without waiting for an answer, Fatima Ghazala hastens her pace and walks away, leaving the rajkumar staring after her.

CHAPTER 20

Dust motes float in a ray of sunlight that has slipped through a crack in the shutters sealed over the windows in the bookstore that used to belong to Firdaus. Now it has no owner and is, to Zulfikar at least, just the scene of a tragedy that he will hold close all his life. The air inside the bookstore smells musty and, if sorrow has a smell, sad. Zulfikar asks a soldier to light a lamp and the answering illumination reveals the chaos in the bookstore clearly. Zulfikar sifts methodically through the books; though a large number of them are beyond repair, some of them may yet be salvageable. He wonders if Fatima Ghazala would be interested in the task.

It has been two days since he accompanied Fatima Ghazala around the city, seeing Noor through her eyes. Thanks to her, his appreciation of the city and her people has increased. Zulfikar hasn't been able to stop thinking about the new Name Giver, remembering suddenly the shine in her eyes when she talked about living on the streets, her infectious enthusiasm for mangoes, and the way she ate that made him hungry for whatever she was enjoying. Zulfikar recognizes the feelings unfurling within him. He has felt them before, and he'll be damned if he yields to them this time. There are no other worlds he can run to anymore.

Today, after resolving a conflict between the shopkeepers' union and some Silk Road merchants, Zulfikar was readying to go back to the mahal, when it occurred to him that he had not yet been back to Firdaus's bookstore. If the Name Giver had any writings pertaining to the Naming process, they would be at the bookstore. So here he is, neck-deep in books. Zulfikar spies a stack of books pinned underneath the Name Giver's desk and pulls them out. He recognizes the writing on the first page of the topmost book; in fact, he feels the recognition like a blow to his stomach. The old man and Zulfikar had never had much of a relationship beyond what their respective positions obligated them to, but the Name Giver was the Name Giver. You do not need to make friends with the walls around you to know that they are there.

The memory of the old man is so strong that it feels like he has left an indentation of himself carved in the air. Zulfikar looks through the book at the very top of the stack and realizes that it is Firdaus's journal. In fact, all the books in the stack are journals Firdaus kept. Zulfikar closes the journal and absently rubs the cover with his fingers. A scent of mitti ittar fills the air; the scent Firdaus used to wear. Zulfikar picks up the pile of journals and strides to the door. Fatima Ghazala has more right than he to read the old man's words.

When Zulfikar gets to Northern Aftab, the Wazir is waiting for him right in front of the entrance. Zulfikar moves past the Ifrit without speaking a word to him. That does not deter Anwar, who simply follows Zulfikar all the way up to the library. Zulfikar places the stack of journals on a table, sits down on a chair, and gestures to the Wazir to sit. "When did you return?"

Anwar sits in the indicated chair; his face is tense, but his expression is a shade smug. Zulfikar raises his eyebrow at his so-called advisor. "An hour ago. I traveled to Baaz"—the Wazir names another desert city—"and apparently it, too, suffered from Ghul attacks."

"I see." Zulfikar frowns. The Ghul have not returned to Noor, and Zulfikar doesn't know what to make of their attacks. "What about the merchant who supplied Firdaus with the tainted book?"

"I haven't had any reports from the soldiers I set on his trail. I'm going to give them another two days before I go after them," the Wazir replies a bit too neatly.

"We also have to look for the tainted Shayateen. I have had Mansoor prepare blooded blades for the soldiers," Zulfikar says, mentioning the tradition of covering sword blades with Ifrit blood so any Shaitan struck with one would immediately burn. "And the man who held the children hostage? You said you were looking into him?"

"He hails from Khair. He arrived in Noor last week and immediately made his way to the schools. From what I learned, he was tasked with recruiting fifty new soldiers for the rebel army." Anwar smiles slightly. "What did the rajah say when you told him about the man and the army he was recruiting for?"

"He doesn't believe in the rebellion," Zulfikar replies tightly. "He thinks it is a rumor."

"Let it be, then. You cannot make him believe what he doesn't want to. If war comes, and it will, we will be there spilling the first blood."

Zulfikar looks sharply at the Wazir, disturbed by the eagerness in the Ifrit's voice.

"I have a question for you, Emir," Anwar says, abruptly changing expression.

"What is it?" Zulfikar replies warily.

"Do you know how Fatima Ghazala survived the Shayateen attacks? Oh, I see by your face that you do. Does she have Ifrit blood?" The Wazir leans forward, his glee apparent.

"I am not sure. Perhaps she does. What does it matter?" Retaining a veneer of measured calm is becoming difficult, but Zulfikar manages.

"What do you think the Raees will say when I tell her that her favored Emir is harboring an abomination?" Anwar sneers, his mask slipping slightly. Zulfikar sees the Ifrit's true feelings glance out at him.

"I don't think she is going to say or do anything at all, Wazir," he replies slowly. "At least nothing like what you are expecting her to."

"And how can you be so sure of that?" Anwar demands.

"You haven't asked me who the new Name Giver is, Wazir," Zulfikar says pleasantly.

The blood drains from Anwar's face. "Impossible," he whispers.

"Not at all, as Fatima Ghazala has readily proved with her powers." Zulfikar rises to his feet. "Even the Raees will hesitate to execute a Name Giver, don't you think?"

Anwar responds by leaving the room, slamming the door on his way out. When he is gone, Zulfikar broods. While it is true that the Raees needs Fatima Ghazala right now, what happens when that need has been fulfilled and Fatima Ghazala is no longer essential? Will her life be forfeit then? And what about the Wazir? Zulfikar does not foresee the Ifrit ceasing in his attempts to gain control of Fatima Ghazala. If what he saw in the Wazir's face is any indication of the strength of his obsession with the Name Giver, the greatest danger to Fatima Ghazala will be from him. Zulfikar gets to his feet. He has things he must do.

After breakfast with the other companions, Indra, the unofficial leader of Maharani Aruna's companions, leads half the ladies to guard the maharani while she breaks her fast with the rest of the royal family. Fatima Ghazala would have asked to remain with the half left to run errands, but Indra refuses to hear of any alternatives. They stand on one side of a dining room fairly dripping with wealth and splendor. The maharajah's guards line up on the other side. Still, the situation wouldn't have been unendurable except for the fact that every time Fatima Ghazala looks up, Rajkumar Aaruv is staring at her. Fatima Ghazala keeps her face blank and her gaze on the floor to mask her growing irritation.

The conversation among the royal family isn't scintillating, so Fatima Ghazala allows her mind to wander. A particular thought makes her look up, and as usual, the rajkumar has his eyes on her. She immediately averts her gaze.

"Bhabhi, who is this new face among your companions?" the rajkumar asks suddenly. The Rajmata and Jayanti also turn to look at Fatima Ghazala.

"She is one of the survivors of the Shayateen attacks," the maharani says sweetly. "Her name is Fatima Ghazala."

At the maharani's words, all attention falls, like a hoe on a clod of earth, on Fatima Ghazala. She forces herself to look up. The Rajmata, imperious in her white sari, examines Fatima Ghazala and clearly finds her wanting. Jayanti, the late king's sister, keeps her emotions cloaked. The rajkumar is clearly pleased that Fatima Ghazala has no choice but to keep looking up. Only the rajkumari seems uninterested in all that's happening. She is poking at her food without actually eating any of it.

Then she perks up as if a thought has just occurred to her. "Bhabhi, will you lend me Fatima Ghazala just for today? Her sister, remember the cosmetics chemist? She is moving in today. Fatima Ghazala can help her settle in."

"Fatima Ghazala is not an object to be lent or borrowed, Bhavya," the maharani chastises gently. "You can ask her directly if she wants to help."

Bhavya raises an eyebrow at Fatima Ghazala. "Well?"

Fatima Ghazala wants to say no. She wants to be left to her own devices. Why would she want to see someone who called her a monster? But the truth is, Fatima Ghazala is not her sister. *She* cannot suddenly stop caring about someone she thought of as family. "Yes," she finally replies to the rajkumari. "I will help."

"Count me in too, kaddu," the rajkumar says a beat later. "I am mightily curious to meet this cosmetics chemist you talk so much about."

Sunaina's life is a glory of ghosts. Her dreams are haunted, the streets she walks on are haunted, and now her apartment is newly blessed with her sister's ghost. Not that her sister is dead, but she might as well be. Sunaina shocks herself with that thought. She is standing outside the apartment building waiting for a carriage from the mahal to pick her up.

Does she really think Fatima Ghazala would be better off dead? A horror awakens in the pit of her stomach. What is she turning into? When she saw her sister in the mahal, Sunaina felt actual pain—can grief hurt like a wound? Of course it can. Hasn't Sunaina felt this hurt before?

The carriage finally arrives. Sunaina climbs into it, and they set off. She doesn't look back, not once, as the carriage trundles away. She doesn't want to say goodbye to anyone; she doesn't want to tell anyone she is leaving. Sunaina knows better than to form attachments to people anymore. Her life has more than enough ghosts in it. Breaking up with the man she had almost married relieved her. While walking away from him, leaving him coated in the brief twilight, she had finally conceded, though begrudgingly, that Fatima Ghazala had been right. She had never wanted to marry him.

The carriage deposits her at the entrance of Southern Aftab, and a servant shows Sunaina to a suite of rooms on the first floor very near the kitchens. Rajkumari Bhavya is standing outside the rooms along with someone who has enough familial resemblance to Bhavya to be her brother. Sunaina's expression falls when she sees the other person with them—Fatima Ghazala. She manages to compose herself before her discomfort becomes apparent. She keeps her gaze firmly on the rajkumari though she glances at the rajkumar once in a while.

"Strange, I thought you would be more pleased to see your sister," Bhavya comments while unlocking the door to the rooms. They enter the first room, and Sunaina is saved from having to respond. She does glance at Fatima Ghazala and finds her face shuttered. No emotion in her eyes or smile on her lips. The girl who used to be her sister has retreated somewhere inside herself. In her place is a person, a creature, Sunaina doesn't recognize.

The room they are in is empty except for one large worktable; the setup is almost identical to Sunaina's previous workshop. The familiarity makes her feel more at ease.

"Make a list of all you need, and I will have everything purchased for you. Furniture as well," Bhavya says. She casts a critical eye over Sunaina's clothes. "You will also need a new wardrobe."

Sunaina's lips thin at the rajkumari's presumption. "I like my clothes," she says stiffly.

"Ooh, look, kaddu, your cosmetics chemist actually talks," the rajkumar says. Sunaina flushes and dares a glance at Fatima Ghazala again. However, Fatima Ghazala is now standing with her face turned away from all of them.

"I don't want Ruchika to imply that I can't keep you in fashion," Bhavya, ignoring her brother, says to Sunaina.

"She's your employee. You are her employer. She is not an object in your possession," Fatima Ghazala says in a low voice.

Sunaina refuses to feel gratified for the defense and looks, instead, at the rajkumar. She finds him looking at Fatima Ghazala with a repulsive degree of lust in his eyes. Against her own wishes, Sunaina finds herself getting bristly for her sister. She has seen other men stare at her sister in that way. She has been on the receiving end of such looks. She knows how disgusting it feels to be objectified.

"I know that!" Bhavya says hotly. "I just mean that as my *employee* she needs to have a certain appearance. Anyway, Sunaina, I will have the tailor over in a couple of days, and she will take your measurements for blouses and the like. I have some saris that will look perfect on you."

Sunaina nods. What else can she do?

"Your monetary compensation will be . . ." Bhavya names an amount that raises Sunaina's eyebrows. "You can also keep whatever money you make selling your products to the other court women."

"Is there anything you need me here for?" Fatima Ghazala asks suddenly.

"No . . . I just thought you might like to spend time with your sister . . ." Bhavya says with some confusion.

"I appreciate your thoughtfulness, but as we are currently estranged, it is rather uncomfortable being here. I will be leaving first." Sunaina grimaces at her words and pretends a fascination with her hands.

The rajkumar moves to intercept Fatima Ghazala. "Oh, come now, you cannot simply leave, not after I made the time to be here."

Sunaina notices Fatima Ghazala tense. The rajkumar continues. "I am especially interested in your views on the Djinn." The question is abrupt and completely unexpected, but it doesn't make it any less dangerous.

The tension in the room rises, as if the very walls are holding their breath.

"Do you not hate the Ifrit? How can you not after being through the attacks?" Aaruv says. His tone is sympathetic. "In fact, I would be surprised if you *didn't* hate them."

"I will be leaving, then," Fatima Ghazala says, and leaves the room without even looking at the prince.

"What is wrong with you, Aaruv? Can't you stop spewing hate every chance you get? Why would Fatima Ghazala hate the Ifrit?" Bhavya rages. "Your logic is skewed—the Ifrit were the ones who saved Noor City. They are the heroes!"

"They are Djinn," Aaruv says as if that is enough. "I have neither the time nor the desire to discuss this matter with a superficial fool like you." The rajkumar stalks out of the room.

"I hate him," Bhavya mutters. She glances at Sunaina. "I hope you do not share my idiot brother's narrow-minded opinions."

"They *are* Djinn," Sunaina says carefully.

Bhavya exhales. "Listen, Sunaina, if we follow Aaruv's reasoning, we would have to execute an entire city just because one among their number is a murderer. Does that sound right to you?"

"You weren't there during the attacks, Rajkumari Bhavya. You don't know what it was like. I lost everything. Everyone," Sunaina says flatly. She knows she should not be speaking out of turn. That she should pretend not to even have opinions, but she can't. Not on this matter. She cannot keep her silence.

"You have your sister, don't you?" Bhavya asks. "You have your life."

"You do not understand." Sunaina shakes her head. What could a spoiled princess like Bhavya know about grief? About terror? She has spent her entire life being cosseted.

"My brother came home in pieces—at least we think the pieces were our brother. My father didn't come home at all, not even in pieces." Bhavya's voice is hard. "I am certain I do understand."

Sunaina looks at the rajkumari, feeling tears threaten.

"You can't judge an entire population of a people by the actions of a select few. You can't use your grief and your sorrow to justify your hate and your discrimination. My father taught me that. Didn't yours?"

Sunaina has no response to that question.

CHAPTER 21

*H*er rage demands a reckoning, but Fatima Ghazala forces herself to walk away. The rajkumar's gaze lingers like a particularly repugnant aftertaste, making her feel dirty. The way he looks at her makes her feel like a stranger in her own body. The rage persists even when she prays Zohr; she pours her heart out to her Creator and yet . . .

Does the rajkumar think she ought to feel flattered by his attentions? Or does he think she will automatically reciprocate his dubious affections? Because he is the rajkumar and she a mere servant, does he think he has the right to treat her without the respect that is her due as a woman, as a citizen of the country his family rules? How many others has he pursued to this point? Does he think submission to his attentions the only viable action available to her?

Fatima Ghazala's rage becomes complex; it develops layers and depth. Deciding she cannot stand to be in her room one more second, she changes into a pink tunic embroidered with green and blue flowers and a matching shalwar and dupatta and steps out of the room, only to bump into Indra, who was coming by to get her for lunch.

"I don't want food," Fatima Ghazala tells the older girl. She can feel her fire react to her rage, simmering under the surface of her skin. "Is there a place I can . . . I don't know, hit things?"

"You want to hit someone?" The maharani's companion looks contemplative.

"Not just anyone. The rajkumar. I want to hit him rather badly, but I gather that won't be too acceptable to your employers," Fatima Ghazala says seriously.

"Come with me," Indra says. She leads Fatima Ghazala across the mahal grounds and through a narrow path between two bushes lush with purple bougainvillea until they emerge into an open space containing a wooden building. Female guards wearing wicked scimitars stand at the entrance to this building. Indra nods at them, and they move aside to let Fatima Ghazala and her pass.

The building is one large hall, sparsely furnished. Wooden floors with some mats for meditation purposes are spread out on the sides. Some of those mats are occupied. Faces Fatima Ghazala recognizes as fellow companions are crowded around one man who is also familiar to her.

"Niruthan?" Fatima Ghazala says, and the man looks up at her. He immediately breaks into a beaming smile and walks over.

"You know our asaan?" Indra asks.

"Yes, he is my asaan too. I have been learning from him for the last two years. Does he teach you kalaripayattu too?" Fatima Ghazala asks. Nirthan is a muscled but slender man a few years older than Fatima Ghazala. The kindness in his face and eyes are at odds with the brutal precision with which he practices his martial arts.

"I teach them silambam too," Niruthan says, hearing Fatima Ghazala's question. He gives her a hug and a smile. "Why haven't you been back to the practice hall, Fatima?"

"It's Fatima Ghazala now, Asaan. Many things happened. Life got complicated." Fatima Ghazala shrugs. "How's Luxmi?"

"Eh, my sister, you know how she is. Busy as always. She and Jun are expecting a child," Niruthan says with a fond smile.

"Give her my congratulations," Fatima Ghazala replies, beaming at the news.

"Do you want to spar with me?" Indra asks Fatima Ghazala.

Fatima Ghazala agrees immediately.

Niruthan shakes his head. "Fatima Ghazala is still a beginner. She will be too easy to defeat for you, Indra. You need more of a challenge."

"I think I am offended," Fatima Ghazala grumbles. "You will be so surprised when I defeat Indra."

"You? Defeat *me*?" Indra snorts.

Fatima Ghazala glances at Niruthan. "She's been practicing a decade longer than you, Fatima Ghazala. I wouldn't advise sparring with her," he says.

Fatima Ghazala grins wickedly. "Let's fight, Indra."

Rather than using kalaripayattu to fight, they decide to use silambam; stick fighting that both Fatima Ghazala and Indra are somewhat good at. Kalaripayattu, at least the sort they are trained in, uses marma adi, the art of striking at pressure points to effectively disarm and disable the opponent, sometimes fatally. Niruthan hands a bamboo staff, the usual weapon of choice, to each of them. Indra, who has changed into a tunic and shalwar, and Fatima Ghazala take their positions in the center of the now-empty room. The high ceiling means they can wield their weapons without hitting any obstacles. People gather around the room, a safe distance away from them, in anticipation of the fight. Fatima Ghazala is sure bets are being made with the odds stacked against her.

She rolls her shoulders, stretching to warm up. Indra does the same.

"To win, disarm your opponent," Niruthan says from the side of the room. He will be refereeing the fight.

"Scared?" Indra taunts.

Fatima Ghazala smiles. A strange peace fills her, as if she has been at the start of a fight many times before. This moment of calm just before the storm hits is dear to her. No, not to *her*, but to Ghazala. Suddenly, Fatima Ghazala feels the Name hot in its place above her heart. She breathes in deeply.

Fatima Ghazala and Indra circle each other, whirling their staffs, gauging the other. Indra attacks first; Fatima Ghazala reads her intent in the sudden stiffening of her shoulders. She defends herself, pulling up her staff, hitting back but not with her entire strength. Soon, the only noises in the practice hall are the hiss of the air as the bamboo staffs cut it and the slap the staffs make on contact. Fatima Ghazala springs closer and tries to jab at Indra but is driven back by the other girl. They are moving at an incredible speed; approach, jab, retreat, and repeat. Fatima Ghazala feels flushed with life and happiness. She could probably fight at this speed and intensity for hours. Indra, on the other hand, is flagging; she is an extremely skilled fighter, but she's a human one. Fatima Ghazala feigns a move, pointing her staff toward Indra's abdomen. Indra spins to avoid the hit, and Fatima Ghazala uses the moment to hit Indra's staff, this time without holding back on her strength. The staff falls from Indra's hand and onto the floor with a loud clatter. Indra stops moving, looking from her empty hands to her staff with a bewildered expression on her face.

"What was that?" she exclaims. "How did you move so fast?"

Fatima Ghazala shrugs. She is not even breathing hard. How else has the Djinn fire changed her? "I guess I am better at fighting than the asaan gives me credit for," she says with a grin. "That was fun. Let's do it again soon."

"We certainly will! I am not resting until I beat you!" Indra huffs.

Other companions converge on them, asking Fatima Ghazala to demonstrate moves she isn't even sure she made. Fatima Ghazala glances toward Niruthan and finds him looking at her with a puzzled look on his face. Fatima Ghazala's euphoria dims. She remembers Sunaina's accusation; the word "monster" stirs in her consciousness. As soon as she can, she extracts herself from the company of the women and makes her way to Northern Aftab.

When Zulfikar returns from a meeting with the lieutenants of the Ifrit army, he finds Anwar waiting for him in the small room he uses as an office. The rage that animated the Wazir's face the last time Zulfikar saw him is not evident. Instead an atmosphere of gloom envelops the Ifrit. Zulfikar settles down in the chair in front of the standing Wazir and prepares himself.

"The soldiers found Taufiq Kadir . . . or what remains of him," Anwar says. Zulfikar rises to his feet in shock.

"What exactly do you mean by that?" he demands.

"They found the remains of his caravan and his body a little ways from the Silk Road near Sabr," Anwar says. "I traveled to the scene myself before coming here, and indeed, there is little left of the man."

"I have to examine the scene as well," Zulfikar says. It is his right as Emir.

"Do you not trust my words, cousin?" Anwar says softly. Zulfikar narrows his eyes. The Wazir has never evoked their kinship before.

"No," Zulfikar replies. "In case you have forgotten, Wazir, your word has no meaning anymore."

The Ifrit's face shutters. "I'm afraid the man's remains have already been removed. It is apparent that he was killed by a Shaitan. I will be returning to the desert to continue my search for the Shayateen responsible for the Name Giver's death." He turns and leaves without another word.

The front of Northern Aftab is deserted so Fatima Ghazala decides to try her luck in the mahal. She walks into the entry hall only to be faced with Anwar, who to all appearances is getting ready to go out. She immediately averts her eyes from him, but that's not enough. He affects her to such a degree that she cannot endure being in the same space as him. It feels like her aversion to the Wazir is increasing each day she spends as . . . whatever she is.

Fatima Ghazala attempts to walk past the Ifrit without paying any attention to him, but he stops her with a hand on her arm. She flings his arm away, shuddering at the contact. A sudden memory assails her: the Wazir holding a child. Shuruq. Fatima Ghazala frowns; this memory is not hers. If Ghazala was Shuruq's mother that means . . . Fatima Ghazala recoils. "Don't touch me. Don't speak to me. Don't even look at me," she tells the Wazir over her shoulder.

"I know Ghazala is somewhere in you. I am very patient, sayyida. I will get her. One way or another." The threat in the Wazir's voice should have terrified Fatima Ghazala, but instead it angers her. She turns around and meets the Ifrit's eyes.

"You know, Wazir, I have nightmares. Ever since I can remember, I have dreamed of blood, fire, and sometimes, if I am lucky, the desert. But ever since I became Fatima Ghazala, I dream of a girl child. She has round cheeks, brown hair, and, when they are open, gold eyes, like yours, like mine. Sometimes in my dreams she is alive, but mostly she is dead. Her name is . . . was? . . . Shuruq. Do you remember her?"

"What do *you* know about Shuruq?" Anwar demands an answer from Fatima Ghazala. A pulse beats furiously in his throat, and his eyes shine.

"Nothing . . . except her name and that *you* killed her." Fatima Ghazala turns her back on the Wazir once again, unable to endure seeing his face. "If the fire I call my own is indeed Ghazala's, then the pockets of memories she has left in them will eventually be mine. What will these memories reveal, I wonder?" Fatima Ghazala leaves the Wazir standing at the entrance and makes her way to what she privately thinks of as the Emir's office.

She finds Zulfikar there, brooding. When she knocks on the open door, he looks up. The smile with which he welcomes her unsettles her so she is gruff with her greetings. "Is anything the matter?" the Emir asks her, waving her to a seat.

"Ghazala and the Wazir were married, yes? They had a child, Shuruq, yes?" Fatima Ghazala asks without hesitating.

In the gloom of the room, she sees the Emir flinch at the questions. "How do you know Shuruq?"

"I dream about her," Fatima Ghazala replies. "I always have nightmares, Zulfikar. I can't remember one night I haven't had one since the massacre. Before I used to dream about the Shayateen and the screaming; now I dream about a sweet Ifrit child dying. I know her name is Shuruq. I know she is dead." Her eyes sting so she squeezes them shut. Tears escape anyway. "And every morning when I open my eyes, I realize the truth of her death over and over again. What happened to her?"

Zulfikar takes a deep breath and rubs his forehead. "I was young when this happened, so I am not certain of the details." He frowns as though trying to find words. "From what I have heard and been told, the Wazir was . . . his love for his wife bordered on obsession. He even begrudged his child the attention his wife lavished on her. I think people indulged it, thinking him devoted, but his devotion was dark. He took Shuruq, their child, out, saying he was going to take her for a walk, but they ended up in the desert, where they were attacked by a band of Shayateen. Later he would tell his wife that the Shayateen were present in too great numbers for him to attempt fighting them." Zulfikar stops and swallows. "Shuruq was killed by the Shayateen. The Wazir escaped unscathed.

"Even though the Wazir denied that he had planned to leave Shuruq to the mercy of the Shayateen, the circumstances were suspicious . . . and there was a witness. A camel herder who got hurt trying to save Shuruq and ultimately perished. The Wazir was acquitted, but he lost Ghazala, who would never look at him the same way again. She divorced him and then, some months later, disappeared. That is Ghazala's story."

"A tragedy," Fatima Ghazala whispers.

"That remains to be seen," Zulfikar replies.

CHAPTER 22

The sun is out, and the birds are singing. His wife is wonderful, and their son is a miracle. Aarush is relatively sure he is going to have a wonderful day. Of course this feeling lasts only until he steps into his office and is told of the meetings and responsibilities that await him. He has lunch with foreign dignitaries from Darsala, the country they share borders with on the eastern front of Qirat and also the country that Maharani Aruna was born in.

Among these dignitaries is a woman his mother's age who is present as the queen of Darsala's representative. Aarush finds the woman a bit intimidating; he doesn't think she has ever forgiven him for marrying the wrong princess.

"Maharajah Aarush, we may as well get to the reason for our presence here," the woman says as soon as the meal is concluded.

"Surely it can wait until we move to a more private place?" Janab Jamshid says, but the woman gives a stern shake of her head.

"We do not have the time to linger here any longer than necessary." At her words, Aarush sucks in a breath and wishes he hadn't eaten so much of the dahl makhani.

"Let us wait until the dishes are cleared at least," he says politely. The servants move quickly, and soon the table is empty.

"We have heard that Qirat plans to oust the Ifrit presence from her soil," the woman says without preamble. "Our queen wants to know the truth of this and asks that you consider how this move will affect Qirat's alliance with Darsala and other countries. You also know that doing this will make Qirat vulnerable to the Angrez."

Aarush listens, trying not to betray the slightest emotion on his face. He knows it is useless; he has never been able to hide his emotions. When the Ifrit answered his father's call for help, Qirat did not just gain powerful allies that saved her from the Shayateen but also recognition from other sovereign countries for the strength of its two armies. Countries that would have otherwise overlooked Qirat sent dignitaries in order to form alliances. The countries they had enmity with, the countries in the West, tried to sign peace treaties. Rumors of a civil war in Qirat will gain attention from far and wide. If the Ifrit leave, those in power will see Qirat as a country vulnerable to invasion and exploitation. Aarush knows all of this.

After the woman has finished talking, Aarush clears his throat. "I appreciate you traveling all the way here to bring me your queen's message. I am sure the journey was difficult. But I am afraid it was also an unwarranted one. Qirat, at this point in time, indeed as long as I am alive, has no plans to cease our alliance with the Ifrit."

The woman frowns, and then her expression shifts to something close to pity. "I don't know what is happening with your intelligence gatherers, Maharajah, but apparently they haven't been giving you the latest reports. Word among the soldiers along the border on our side is that there is a mass recruitment taking place: Qirati men are being asked to fight for their country."

Aarush's heart quakes at the woman's words. He regains his composure, but it is too late. The dignitaries have all seen his reaction to the news. He manages to get through the rest of the meeting with some effort, assuring the dignitaries that he has no plans to sweep his country into some long-drawn civil war. Aarush doesn't know if he convinces them, or if they leave pitying him for his rapidly unraveling rule.

As soon as he emerges from the extended luncheon, Janab Jamshid tells him that the representatives of the five forest provinces of Qirat request a private audience with him.

White-lipped with anger, Aarush responds shortly, "Tell the representatives that I will grant them an audience in the grand hall in ten minutes." He is in no mood to indulge anyone.

The five men who enter the grand hall, where Aarush hears all petitions, are all rich men. They have always been rich men; their families have owned the most lands in their provinces for centuries. They also all look distinctly displeased. Some of them are staring at him disapprovingly. Aarush narrows his eyes and leans back on the throne, waiting for them to speak. Earlier today, he would have been tripping all over himself to keep these men happy. Earlier today, he hadn't tasted the salt of desperation.

"Maharaj, we come to bring your attention to the rebellion gaining momentum in the forest provinces of Qirat. We think the rebels have credible grievances, and we would like you to pay attention to them," the oldest man, Rathod Singh of Khair, says.

Aarush smiles, and the entire assembly takes a startled breath. No one has seen the young maharajah smile this way ever before. His eyes are hard, and his face, once the smile fades, is furious. "Tell me about these rebels since you know so much about them."

"They are all working men, men of Qirat. They want to see Qirat returned to them," Malhotra of Asur, another rich man, says.

"And you all presume to speak for these working men?" Aarush keeps his voice light. He keeps his anger reined in. "Tell me, these working men you speak about, these rebels, are they all from the forest provinces of Qirat?"

"What does that matter, Maharaj?" Rathod says loudly, as if the volume of his voice will make up for the shoddiness of his reply.

"Have any of you been to the desert cities? Have you been to Rahm? Sabr? Baaz? Perhaps some of you went to Ummeed? Did you ask the working men in the desert cities of Qirat whether they want Qirat back? Have you asked the working women? Surely the working women in this country get a voice too. Do they want Qirat back as well?"

"Huzoor, you are deliberately muddying the issue," Rathod says.

"When was Qirat taken from these working men you speak so admiringly about? I don't recall any of them being dragged off their lands and out of their houses. Ah, we did have more than eight hundred thousand people in Noor dead when the Shayateen attacked. Was it then that Qirat was taken from these working men?"

"You gave half our country to those creatures, and you dare question us when we demand it back?" Rathod roars. The man must have realized the gravity of his actions because he hasn't even finished speaking before he starts backing away.

"You *dare* stand here and speak against your king? Against my father?" Aarush's voice slips down an octave. "Tell me, Rathod Singh of Khair, when did you find out about the gold mines in the desert city of Sabr? Oh, I knew when the gold was discovered; the Emir himself told me about them. Offered to share the wealth, but I said no. We are blessed with the diamond mines, our agriculture, and so much more. We can give them the gold. Did you find out before or after the fever of patriotism burned in you?"

Aarush pauses and looks at each man in turn. All of them avoid his gaze.

"Do you know the consequences of treason, my friends?" Aarush asks, his voice barely a whisper. Silence slams down in the grand hall. "Perhaps I should refresh your memories. Your families will be stripped of their lands and their riches. They will be stripped of their names and their histories. They will be exiled from Qirat, never to cross any of its borders again. You, however, will be too dead to witness any of this. Small blessings, I suppose."

The five men are all suddenly very pale, their bluster from earlier lost in the pallor of their skin.

"I want you to consider very carefully who you are, who I am, and what you are telling me to do." Aarush looks around the room and addresses everyone present. "I may not have spilled blood yet, but I do know how to wield a sword."

The old man falls to his knees in front of the throne, as do the other four; they beg his forgiveness. Aarush leaves them kneeling there.

People, Firdaus told Fatima Ghazala, are afraid of death for two very different reasons. The first one is obvious: They do not know what, if anything, lies beyond the veil. That is a matter of faith. The second reason is also obvious: People are being afraid of being forgotten. They live their lives carving themselves spaces in time and history only to be forgotten anyway. Even those who gain fame or notoriety fall victim to time; what people remember are not the individuals directly but as they were experienced by the people who knew them. A person's truth, a person's essence, fades with a person's death. That is simply the way of life.

Fatima Ghazala picks up the journal on top of the stack she received from Zulfikar. Her baba's journals are simple notebooks, worn and well-used. She presses the cover to her face, and the elusive scent of mitti ittar—ittar that smells like the scent of the rain as it falls on parched earth—assails her. This was Firdaus's favored scent. She breathes in deeply, and for a moment, just for a tiny moment, thinks she can feel him in the room with her.

The grief she so carefully packaged away rises to the surface, and for a while, Fatima Ghazala can't see the pages through tears that fall fast and hard. Firdaus knew many languages, but he chose to write his deepest thoughts in Qadr, the language he called his own. Fatima Ghazala wonders if the reason he insisted on teaching her this language was because he intended to give her these journals someday.

She will never know.

She locks the door of her room in Southern Aftab against the distractions of the world outside and starts reading. She pauses only to pray or when her hunger demands fulfillment. Through Firdaus's eyes, she sees the red-streaked skies of Al-Naar, the red sands of the deserts in Tayneeb and the grand estate he had a room in. Through his words she experiences his grief at losing his wife to the Shayateen and the wonder he felt every time he looked at his daughter, Ghazala.

A fair number of the journals are a devoted father's records of a daughter he adores. The only time Firdaus falters is when he writes his concern that the Ifrit his daughter has chosen to marry is not worthy of her. In her father's eyes, Ghazala was a tempest, unexpectedly softhearted, and vulnerable to those she gave her heart. She loved Anwar, but Firdaus writes of meetings after her marriage in which she confessed to her father her deep unease about her husband's possessiveness and love that strayed too deep in dark places. How she felt suffocated by his attention. Soon, her only solace was her child, Shuruq, on whom she lavished attention and love.

As Fatima Ghazala reads about her, the Ifrit woman who gave up her name and her fire for her sake becomes real. She gains flesh, blood, and fire. She becomes the heat Fatima Ghazala feels in the fire that burns underneath her skin.

When she disappeared, Firdaus looked for his daughter. While following her trail, he came to the human world and met with

Maharajah Arjun. Firdaus writes of meeting the king and asking his help in locating Ghazala. In return for the king's aid, Firdaus gave his word to provide assistance one time. That occasion came seven years later, when the king sent him a message through a fire asking for assistance against the Shayateen attacking Noor. But Maharajah Arjun asked too late; by the time Firdaus Named the Ifrit army, almost everyone in Noor was dead.

The sun is rising when Fatima Ghazala finally finishes reading the journals. She succumbs to her exhaustion and sleeps.

Zulfikar is going through the reports sent to him by the emirs of Sabr and Baaz when he feels Fatima Ghazala's fire approach. He gets to his feet and walks to the open door of his office without realizing he is doing so. The strength of his feelings for the Name Giver flusters him. He forces himself to return to his seat, not at all desiring to present himself as an overeager swain. In fact, he has no intention of acting on these feelings because he knows they are not his. These feelings, these entirely inappropriate feelings he doesn't want to give a name to, are a result of the bond between his fire and hers. A bond forged without proper thought.

Still, Zulfikar knows the exact moment she stops in front of his door. He knows she is tired, happy, sad, a mix of feelings, before he looks up and sees the smile she seems to have only for him. One that tells him he is not a stranger but not exactly a friend. One that both pulls at him and holds him at bay. The bond tattles on her freely. Zulfikar knows that the liberty the bond affords him to see and feel into Fatima Ghazala's emotions is a violation, but try as he might, he cannot stop himself from doing these things. The only one who can break this bond is the Raees.

"Assalaam wa alaikum," she greets him, and Zulfikar replies, doing his best to keep his face as bland as possible. She is wearing her favored mint-green tunic and shalwar. Her turban is blue today.

"So? Have you read the journals?" Zulfikar asks, and she nods, placing the stack she has been carrying on his desk. "Did you learn anything about the Naming process?"

Fatima Ghazala sits down in the chair opposite him and pulls up her legs. Zulfikar wonders when she became so comfortable in his presence. As if she reads his mind, she smiles apologetically. "I am sorry, I read all through the night and lack sleep." Zulfikar pours her a cup of coffee from the pot he usually keeps on his desk. She takes it gratefully. He drags his attention back to his reports while waiting for her to speak, but he can't help sneaking glances at her. His traitorous heart whispers that having her beside him just like this is the forever he is looking for. He stanches the thought immediately.

"All right. I think I have regained enough of my wits," Fatima Ghazala says, cutting into his thoughts. Zulfikar inclines his head and gestures for her to continue. "I told you the Qareen we saw has a name, didn't I? As I saw it, his name was in pieces, trying to join together. The grief he felt prevented the pieces from uniting." Her voice warms. "Do you think that because the Qareen are present on earth since inception, they don't need Name Givers to Name them? The pieces of their names unify automatically once their service is completed? Do all Djinn, apart from the Qareen, have Name Givers? What about the Shayateen?"

"The Shayateen have Name Givers, but I'm not sure about the rest of the clans. The Si'lat, a clan of shape-shifting Djinn, might but they are very secretive, so we don't have much interaction with them. They keep entirely to themselves and do not have relation-ships with anyone outside their own clan—or at least that's what we think. Everything we know about them comes from the few books that exist about them in Tayneeb. I have never heard of the Qareen having names either." Zulfikar thinks. "It makes sense, however, that they would function on the same basic principle as the rest of us."

"Exactly. So I wondered if the disparity between Qareen names and Ifrit names is that the former unifies automatically while the latter requires a Name Giver. My theory was somewhat confirmed by Baba, though he discusses Naming far less in the journals than you would assume," Fatima Ghazala says, blushing. Zulfikar watches in fascination as her entire face is suffused by a rosy-pink color.

"What *does* he discuss?" Zulfikar asks. What could the old man have written to provoke such a reaction?

"He talks about his daughter and . . . he talked about me." Fatima Ghazala ducks her head shyly. "My learning abilities. He is quite effusive in his praise in his journals, though he never said more than 'good job' to me during our lessons. Anyway"—she clears her throat—"I feel like I have the theory of Naming understood. The power is instinctual."

"Only if the Ifrit you are Naming isn't tainted," Zulfikar confesses. But Fatima Ghazala's reaction is unexpected.

She looks contemplative. "You said that a tainted Shaitan will have a corrupted Name? Sort of like a rusted—no, more like a decayed Name?"

"I suppose? I can't see Names, remember?" Zulfikar says.

"The Shayateen in the desert, the ones that attacked me. They had tainted Names. Well, the one that I killed had a tainted Name."

Zulfikar tenses. "You held a tainted Name?"

"Yes. It didn't affect me." Her eyes are clear and fearless.

"Are you sure?" Zulfikar is not certain he can believe her.

"Well, would I know if my Name got corrupted?" she asks.

"Yes, definitely."

"Then yes, I am sure." The Name Giver frowns. "The taint that killed Baba, how was it transferred?"

"Through a tainted Shaitan's blood," Zulfikar replies.

"Why would they attack Baba specifically? How did they know where he was? What he was?"

Zulfikar grows grim at the questions. They are ones he has been constantly asking himself.

"I don't yet know." He is failing Firdaus, even in death. He shakes the thought away with some difficulty. "Do you want to try Naming someone? Obviously not the Raees, but someone with weaker fire. Just to see if you can work out the mechanics of the process."

Fatima Ghazala thinks, and Zulfikar waits. They don't have much time, but he does not want to push her into anything she is not ready for. Finally, she nods. "I will try."

"I will contact the elders, my superiors, in Al-Naar, and they will send someone you can Name." Zulfikar is pleased. Perhaps not everything is as bleak as he thinks it is.

The Name Giver nods again and rises, as if to leave. Then she pauses as if something has occurred to her. "If Ifrit have to be Named to gain form on earth, why was Ghazala able to be here without being Named?"

"Firdaus handed his power to her before she passed on. It's how we knew she had died, actually. The only reason the power would return to Firdaus is if Ghazala had died."

"I thought the power could only be passed over if the original holder died," Fatima Ghazala asks.

"Only if the power passes to a different family line. It is possible to pass the power to your direct heir as Firdaus did."

The Name Giver nods slowly, as if some great curiosity of hers has been satisfied. She looks up suddenly, and Zulfikar freezes, wondering if the grin on his face is going to give him away. But thankfully, she seems distracted by her thoughts.

"I will send you a message when I have something more concrete to report. I may receive word from Al-Naar this afternoon or by tomorrow morning by the latest." Zulfikar stands up, too, intending to escort her to the door, but the Name Giver waves him away. She mumbles a goodbye and, stifling a yawn, walks away. The room seems too empty without her in it. Zulfikar feels the need to spar.

It is a little after seven in the evening and the lower levels of Southern Aftab are mostly deserted. Sunaina has just finished her day's work and is cleaning up. She leaves the door to her rooms open to let some of the heat out. A pleasant ache, the sign of work well done, has her rolling her shoulders.

The work is fulfilling; creating cosmetics makes her happy. Being at the mahal while doing this work that she loves makes her happier. Or it should. There is no reason for her to be sad. Her hours are full, and she sleeps through the night . . . mostly. So she has nightmares. Who doesn't? So she misses her sister. Why can't she? It would be strange if she didn't. Lost in her thoughts, she sinks down in a chair.

Sunaina hasn't seen Fatima Ghazala ever since her first day at the mahal. She doesn't know what Fatima Ghazala does at the mahal, where she goes, and whom she spends her time with. And that is just fine, Sunaina tells herself. Fatima Ghazala can take care of herself. But then she remembers the filthy eyes with which the rajkumar was looking at her sister, and she worries.

Just then, as if someone has carved her right out of her thoughts, Fatima Ghazala walks past the open doors of Sunaina's room. Sunaina jumps to her feet. A few seconds later, Rajkumar Aaruv follows in Fatima Ghazala's footsteps. Sunaina runs to her open doors and peeks out. The corridor outside is enveloped in shadows. No one apart from the servants uses this corridor. And the servants have all retired for the night. Sunaina watches the rajkumar stalk her sister, who walks ahead, seemingly oblivious to the danger. She watches the rajkumar lift a hand, perhaps to grab her sister's shoulder.

"Fatima Ghazala!" Sunaina is unaware of speaking out until her exclamation splinters the silence.

Fatima Ghazala whirls around. Upon seeing the rajkumar so close to her, her eyes widen. The rajkumar turns and gives Sunaina an annoyed look before he continues walking. Fatima Ghazala turns and watches the prince walk away.

"Fatima . . . Ghazala, come here!" Sunaina commands.

The reluctance on her sister's face hurts Sunaina. But really, how could she expect anything different? "I have somewhere I need to be."

"You will come here right now." Sunaina's tone brooks no dis-obedience. Fatima Ghazala, scowling, stomps her way into Sunaina's room. She folds her arms and stands right in front of the doors, her face mutinous.

"Sit," Sunaina says.

"No," Fatima Ghazala replies. Sunaina's heart lurches at the emptiness in her sister's eyes. Did she put it there? "If this is about the rajkumar, you needn't worry. I would have handled him."

"How? He's the prince. We are lower than the dirt on his shoes." Her sister refuses to see anyone in the way society dictates they should be seen. For her, everyone is equal.

"Have you forgotten, didi? I am a monster," Fatima Ghazala bites out. "If he had touched me, he would have regretted it."

"Can you handle the consequences of harming the rajkumar of Qirat?" Sunaina asks.

"Listen, didi— Ah, my apologies, I can't call you that, can I? Not anymore. You do not need to pretend to care about me. In fact, please don't. I will try not to burden you with my monstrous presence." Fatima Ghazala turns to leave.

"I'm sorry!" The apology bursts out from Sunaina's lips.

Fatima Ghazala turns around, a wary look on her face. "Sorry for what?"

"Sorry for calling you a monster. Sorry for making you leave . . . I'm just sorry. I was—am—scared. Of the Djinn. And the idea that you are one terrifies me. But you are the best person I know. And you may be a djinni . . . I am not making much sense, I know. I'm just sorry." Sunaina winces her way through her apology, aware that she sounds inept but unable to help herself. "Will you forgive me?"

"I don't know," Fatima Ghazala says. Her eyes are very large on her face. "I will try." She leaves.

When Fatima Ghazala returns to Northern Aftab, it is close to eight; she is an hour early. Zulfikar sent her a message late in the afternoon. His superiors from Al-Naar are going to send someone she can Name. Fatima Ghazala is shown to the library, where she finds the Emir absorbed in reading reports. On the desk in front of him are a cup of coffee and a plate of gulab jamun. Fatima Ghazala greets him, steals some of the dessert, and takes a seat on a divan by the window. She brings her knees to her chest and rests her head on them, staring down at the river outside. She should be thinking about the upcoming Naming, but she keeps on reliving her meeting with her sister. Sunaina's apology confuses her. Does it mean that her sister no longer considers her a monster? Does her not thinking of Fatima Ghazala as a monster make her any less of one? If she forgives Sunaina, does that mean she's only making herself vulnerable to hurt the next time her sister gets angry?

What about the rajkumar? How far does he intend to take things? Is he doing this because he likes her? Do romantic feelings make his actions acceptable? A wave of revulsion sweeps over Fatima Ghazala, and she shudders. No, they most certainly don't. What the prince is doing is not an expression of romance but rather an attempt at control. Fresh anger has Fatima Ghazala clenching her fists. She looks up to find the Emir observing her with an inscrutable expression on his face.

"What are you thinking so hard about?" he asks curiously.

"Nothing I want to talk about," Fatima Ghazala replies, flushing. She can hardly tell the Emir she is currently entertaining thoughts about murdering the rajkumar.

"Very well. Give me just a minute and I will be with you," the Emir says. Fatima Ghazala nods. She observes the Emir while he reads. Some may find his physical presence intimidating, but she likes how solid he is. She likes his longish curly black hair, his eyes framed with long eyelashes that curl slightly at the tip. The way his lips purse when he is concentrating. The way he listens with all his attention. His inability to refuse gulab jamun. Everything Fatima Ghazala learns about the Emir feels like the pieces to a puzzle she could enjoy putting together.

"What do you think about love?" the Emir asks, suddenly looking up. His cheeks are red, as if he knows what Fatima Ghazala is thinking about.

"Love?" she echoes. There is no way he has access to her thoughts, she tells herself. But the question is a strange one.

"Yes. Why do you think people fall in love?" Zulfikar comes to sit in the chair in front of the divan.

"You will have to ask people that," Fatima Ghazala replies carefully.

"Have you never fallen in love?" The Emir seems more interested in the answer than she would have thought.

"No." Fatima Ghazala thinks. "At least I don't think so."

"Not even once?" the Emir persists.

"What does it matter?" Fatima Ghazala frowns.

"It doesn't but . . ." The Emir sighs. "Listen. I have a confession to make."

Fatima Ghazala straightens, prickles of unease marching down her shoulders.

"When . . . the first time we met, you lost control of your fire, so I absorbed some of it. All I intended was to keep you from hurting yourself. But your fire bonded with mine."

"What does that mean?" Fatima Ghazala asks, not liking the look on the Emir's face or the tone of his voice.

"This bond . . . among the Ifrit, this bond only exists between married couples and for good reason." The Emir rubs his cheeks, which are redder than Fatima Ghazala has ever seen them. "Through the bond I can feel what you feel, know where you are. It may cause me to behave like I am in love with you."

"How do we break it?" Fatima Ghazala asks immediately.

"We can't. Only the Raees can." The Emir won't meet her eyes.

"You didn't need to tell me any of this. You could have kept quiet, and I wouldn't be any wiser. Why did you confess?" The answer is obvious. "Ah, so I don't misunderstand? So I don't think that you . . . love me." A thought occurs to her, and Fatima Ghazala takes a deep breath. "So all your kindnesses, all your words, were because of the bond? That time we spent in Noor." She laughs slightly. "What did I think? Why would the great Emir spend time with me unless compelled to by a bond?"

"That is not true," Zulfikar protests.

"No, it is quite fine. You do not need to say anything more. I appreciate that you told me before I made a fool of myself. More than I already have, I mean." Fatima Ghazala's eyes smart. Her face feels hot, and the last place she wants to be is here before him. "Please excuse me for a bit."

The Naming is to be conducted in front of the fire pits behind the barracks—Zulfikar usually sends and receives messages from Al-Naar through the fire there. At a quarter to nine, Zulfikar and Fatima Ghazala have made themselves comfortable on the wooden benches in front of the fire. The soldiers are either sleeping or on patrol. The Wazir hasn't returned since the afternoon. A silence— thick and new—makes its place between Fatima Ghazala and Zulfikar. It is full of the things neither of them wants to talk about.

Fatima Ghazala takes a deep breath and empties her mind—she would much rather think of anything else right now than how much she embarrassed herself in front of the Emir. She looks into the fire burning in the pit and sees within it the promise of a city. Her consciousness expands until she can feel the night beat like a pulse in her throat. Suddenly she feels a tickle in her mind. It is quite possibly the most loathsome sensation in the entire world. Shuddering, Fatima Ghazala turns, her vision blurring as she stares into the darkness. She sees before her a column of smokeless orange-red flame, and within its depths, the golden pieces of a name. These pieces are in motion but still as if sensing her attention when she looks at them. Then, as if taunting her, they begin to move at a greater frequency, almost in a frenzy, within the boundary presented by the column of orange flames.

Firdaus taught her that in the natural order of things, the world moves toward entropy, toward chaos. Order and structure are unnatural so it makes sense that the golden pieces do not want to connect. Fatima Ghazala plunges her hands into the fire and struggles to catch the golden pieces. The fire stings, but it doesn't burn her. As she comes into contact with the pieces, their meaning becomes clear to her. The first piece means ambition, and connected to this piece is a flurry of memories; the second piece means pride, and once again Fatima Ghazala is treated to memories that are associated with this word. She sees Tayneeb in all its glory in the memories of the Ifrit woman she is Naming. She sees the Ifrit who look much like they do in their human forms but more perfect somehow, more defined; their flaws reduced. The final piece of the name is the most elusive. Fatima Ghazala struggles to grasp it. The heat of the flame is hungry and snaps at her.

When she finally catches hold of the last piece, she is so surprised by the memories associated with it that she nearly lets go of it again. The piece means desire and the memories of the Ifrit woman that describe this word all feature Zulfikar in some way. He is laughing, running, talking, fighting. He is the Emir in a way Fatima Ghazala has never seen him; Zulfikar with all his soft sides revealed, his face unguarded and affectionate. Whoever this Ifrit woman is, she means a lot to him.

Fatima Ghazala brings the three golden pieces of the Name together and joins them as one would a jigsaw puzzle. They fit together easily. Once joined, the golden pieces read Tali, the name of the Ifrit woman. Fatima Ghazala takes the Name, presses it into the column of the flame, in the region of the heart, and steps back. Her vision returns to normal, and she immediately turns to the Emir. But he is not looking at her. He is gazing at the Ifrit woman with a look of pure wonder and delight.

Fatima Ghazala turns around and starts walking away. Her steps are shaky, but she is determined. For reasons she doesn't want to think of too closely, she does not want to stay and watch the two Ifrit reunite. Dimly she hears Zulfikar calling her name, but Fatima Ghazala doesn't stop. If dignity is all she has left, she will cling to it with everything she is.

CHAPTER 23

The chai is extra sweet today. Bhavya takes a sip and feels it warm her all the way through. Breakfast with her family in the ostentatious dining room is always a stilted affair. Being the only meal the family eats together, conversation is expected. However, more often than not, the only people talking are Jayanti and the Rajmata. Today is no exception.

"You are a fool, Aarush. You had no reason to alienate the landowners," the Rajmata is saying. "You need to indulge—"

Her brother puts down the cup he was holding, and the Rajmata stutters to a stop. Though she is his mother, calling the maharajah a fool in front of the guards and other servants who will hear and gossip is not done. Even Bhavya knows this.

"Amma, I appreciate your concern and am, as always, thankful for your advice," her brother says, even though it is clear he is not at all thankful. Aarush has dark circles under his eyes and a stiffness to his movements that are worrying. Bhavya loses the little appetite she had and pushes away her plate. Her brother continues. "However, you and the landowners seem to forget one pertinent thing: My father, Maharajah Arjun, was the one who signed the deal with the Ifrit. By advocating for those who want the Ifrit gone, you effectively make his word false.

"I refuse to indulge rich men who foment rebellion in order to add to their already overflowing coffers. Amma, you are asking me to topple this country into war. A war we might never recover from. A war we might not live to see through. I shouldn't have to spell these things out." Bhavya watches her brother drink some water and wipe his lips on a napkin. He stands, squeezing his wife's shoulder. She smiles up at him. "If you will excuse me, I have half a country to run."

The maharajah leaves a strained silence behind him. Bhavya is much too scared to glance at her mother. This is the first time Aarush has spoken back to the Rajmata, and Bhavya does not want to attract her attention and ire.

"Bhabhi, I haven't seen your new companion around recently," Aaruv says, breaking the silence.

Aruna looks surprised by the question. "She has been a bit unwell."

"Oh, I am sorry to hear that." Bhavya can hardly believe her ears. For Aaruv to express concern for anyone other than himself is deeply suspicious. She glances at him, but he has a benign smile on his face. What is he planning?

"Bhavya, your aunt and I have been talking, and I think that she is correct," the Rajmata says. "It is about time you get married. From now on I will be considering all the rishtay I get for you more seriously."

Bhavya looks at her mother, the wind knocked out of her sails. Of all the things she expected at breakfast, the announcement of a lifetime of punishment was definitely not it.

"What if I don't want to marry? You can't simply make me wed someone I don't want to." Her voice trembles, and Bhavya feels panic threaten to override her senses.

"You are a rajkumari of Qirat. You have duties and responsibili-ties." Marriage is a duty?

"What else are you good for but marriage, kaddu? Don't worry, we will find you someone who doesn't mind your ugly face." Aaruv snickers.

Bhavya waits for her mother to remonstrate Aaruv for his words, for Jayanti Bua to scold him. When it becomes apparent that neither of them is going to say a word, Bhavya gets to her feet and leaves the breakfast room. She walks slowly, taking deep breaths as she does, reminding herself that she is a rajkumari and rajkumaris don't cry in public. Somehow Bhavya manages to reach Sunaina's workshop on the first floor; it has become her refuge of late. She pushes open the door and enters.

"You wouldn't believe . . ." Bhavya trails off when she realizes Sunaina is not alone. "Aren't you supposed to be sick?" she asks Fatima Ghazala, who is curled up in a chair, pulling the petals off different types of roses.

Fatima Ghazala glances up from her work, gives Bhavya a blank look, and returns to her task. "I'm visiting my sister."

"Weren't you estranged?" Bhavya looks to Sunaina for confirmation.

"We are in the process of reconciling," Sunaina replies shortly.

Bhavya frowns; she feels like her only haven has been invaded. "You are not welcome here during working hours."

Fatima Ghazala puts down the rose she had just picked up. "All right."

"You don't have to go, Fatima . . . Ghazala," Sunaina says. "Rajkumari Bhavya, I trust that you will understand when I say that I cannot work in an environment where someone else dictates who I can and cannot welcome in my own space."

"I'm your employer!" Bhavya protests.

"Which is why I'm being polite," Sunaina replies evenly.

"It's fine, didi." Fatima Ghazala gets up and pushes her chair back. "I wanted to go see Laali anyway."

"What's wrong with Laali?" Sunaina asks, frowning.

"Didn't you visit her before you left?" Sunaina shakes her head, looking guilty. "She was sick when I visited her about five days ago." Fatima Ghazala picks up her oud.

"Wait, I will go with you," Sunaina says, pulling off her apron.

"Hold on a minute!" Bhavya holds up her hands, trying to gain control of a situation that's rapidly moving beyond her. There is something unbearable about feeling like you are on the outside looking in. The two turn to face her with the same questioning expression on their faces. "I will come with you," Bhavya mumbles.

"No way." Fatima Ghazala immediately rejects her. "You are a rajkumari."

"Thank you, I had no idea," Bhavya says. "Look, I feel like there's a caged bird inside my chest. If I don't get out of the mahal, I'm going to go mad."

Sunaina and Fatima Ghazala exchange a long look. Just when Bhavya is afraid they're going to leave her behind, Sunaina turns to her and says, "We'll take you with us, but you will need to wear one of my saris."

"What? No way!"

"Then you can stay behind," Sunaina says. "We can't take you to Taaj Gul dressed as you are. You would stick out like a . . ."

"Laddoo on a plate of pedas," Fatima Ghazala finishes. The other two stare at her. She shrugs. "I might be hungry."

"So will you change?" Sunaina turns back to Bhavya.

Bhavya bites her lip and then, after a minute, nods.

She changes into a rather shabby brown sari with a matching blouse and does her hair into a simple braid without dressing it up in any accessories. As a result, she walks out of Southern Aftab without attracting a single glance from either the courtiers or the mahal guards. Bhavya wonders if being a rajkumari of Qirat is a performance with the appropriate costumes and lines. What if she stops performing? Will she no longer be a princess expected to behave in a certain manner and do certain things? If she is not a princess, then what is she?

She notices that people, men and women both, turn to look at Fatima Ghazala, whose manly getup attracts attention rather than deflects it. The contrast of her startling gold eyes against her dusky skin is compelling enough, but pairing it with the almost liquid way in which she moves—as if each step she takes is a dance move— makes her more beautiful than a symmetrical face would. Fatima Ghazala could wear a sack or the most opulent clothing and people would look at her the same. Does that mean she is not performing her role? Or is it that her beauty defines her?

Fatima Ghazala notices her staring and raises an eyebrow in question.

"Is your beauty a burden?" Bhavya asks her.

"You think I'm beautiful?" the girl asks, surprised.

Bhavya frowns. "You don't have to pretend to be modest," she bites off, turning away.

"She's not." Sunaina comes to her sister's defense. "Fatima Ghazala doesn't look in the mirror unless absolutely necessary. It is very irritating."

"There are so many other things to look at, didi. I already know what my face looks like. It's not like looking in a mirror will change it," Fatima Ghazala tells Sunaina. Bhavya hears the echoes of an old argument in those words. She wonders how it feels to not care what you look like.

"If we walk fast enough, we'll be in Taaj Gul in about two hours," Sunaina says over her shoulder a few minutes later.

"Wait a minute." Bhavya is certain she heard wrong. "What do you mean walk?"

By this time they have reached the bridge that connects Northern Aftab to Northern Noor. They keep their heads down and walk swiftly over the bridge. It is a busy area with Neem Ghat and the flower market located not very far away. Carts trundle past on the road, and the sidewalk is crowded with pedestrians lugging bags and other burdens. Bhavya hastens her pace and tries to keep up with the sisters, but they are moving too quickly. Finally, she comes to a stop. "Wait for me!" she calls loudly. People look at her, and belatedly, Bhavya remembers that she is in the middle of an escape attempt.

The sisters stop and wait until Bhavya reaches them, panting slightly. Fatima Ghazala takes one look at her and pulls them off the sidewalk and into an alley where they can stand and talk without presenting an obstacle to anyone.

"Look, if we walk at the pace you do, it will take us forever to reach Taaj Gul," Fatima Ghazala tells Bhavya not unkindly. "Maybe you should return to the mahal."

"No!" Bhavya feels tears prick at the idea of returning home. She looks imploringly at Sunaina.

"Do you think we'll be accused of kidnapping her?" Sunaina asks Fatima Ghazala, not paying attention to Bhavya.

"Can't be kidnapping if she came with us willingly and without any coercion," Fatima Ghazala points out.

"You know rich people. It will be easier for them to claim we kidnapped her than admit that she ran away," Sunaina says darkly.

"I am right here," Bhavya says as haughtily as she can manage under the circumstances.

"Indeed, you are," Sunaina placates.

Fatima Ghazala grins and looks toward the street. Her expression perks up. "Oh. You are lucky, Rajkumari." She lets out a piercing whistle and attracts the attention of a cart driver. Soon, Bhavya is sitting on the back of an ox-driven cart for the very first time in her life. Sunaina has the dubious pleasure of being the one in the middle. Their feet dangle over the edge of the cart. Bhavya peers at the ground, pales, and clutches the side of the cart desperately. A hundred different scenarios, all of which involve her falling and dying in the most painful ways, play out in her head.

"How do you know this man?" Bhavya asks Fatima Ghazala when they have been riding for about ten minutes.

"I delivered some milk for him once. It was cheaper for him to hire us to do his deliveries than to hire employees," Fatima Ghazala replies.

"I see," Bhavya says, though she truly doesn't. Fatima Ghazala's life sounds foreign to her. She cannot imagine what it means to be able to plan your own days and decide your own movements. A life where your every action is not commented on and either praised or censured. A life where you can be anyone you want to be. Bhavya looks at the passing scenery avidly, paying particular attention to the people. Even though she has been living in Noor all her life, she doesn't get to venture into the city on her own like this, so everything feels new to her. People wear different styles of clothing but almost always in bright, bold colors. She catches snippets of a hundred different languages, which adds to the cacophony and charm of the city. A trepidatious feeling sprouts in her, however, as the cart treads the road to the poorer parts of Northern Noor.

The streets get busier, and Bhavya's discomfort rises. When the cart shudders to a stop, Fatima Ghazala jumps off, helps Sunaina get off, and turns to Bhavya expectantly. Bhavya hesitates, looking around the street.

"What? Too poor for the rajkumari?" Fatima Ghazala quips. Bhavya bristles and jumps off. She miscalculates the distance to the ground and stumbles. Sunaina steadies her with a hand on her arm.

Fatima Ghazala thanks the cart driver, and they set off, plunging into the busy streets. Sunaina warns Bhavya not to dawdle, but she can't help it and keeps stopping to stare at one spectacle after another: trick-performing monkeys, snake charmers, bangle sellers, and many more. Finally, exasperated, Sunaina grabs Bhavya by the arm and forces her to walk faster. When they reach the apartment building, Bhavya comes to a complete standstill. She gapes at the building, twin feelings of pity and shame filling her. Pity because she cannot imagine anyone being happy living in such a squalid place. The shame is secondhand because she thinks that the sisters can't be anything but ashamed of showing her the place they used to call home.

Fatima Ghazala and Sunaina, however, betray no shame when they realize that the rajkumari has stopped walking.

"Will you hurry up?" Fatima Ghazala growls.

Bhavya starts and reluctantly follows them up the stairs and through the entrance of the building, fearing, as she does, that the building will succumb to its mortality and collapse while she is still inside it. A film of rose-pink dust covers everything, the walls are filthy with handprints and other stains, and Bhavya doesn't even want to look at the floor of the building. She hears a dozen voices arguing, screaming, whispering, and talking behind closed doors. Different smells waft from up and down the corridor—not all of them palatable. Bhavya hangs back when the sisters go to visit the old grandma they call Laali; there is no way she's stepping into a room in this place. Luckily they exit quickly; the grandma is not lucid and cannot recognize either of them. Fatima Ghazala bounds up the stairs to the ninth floor to see if her friends are home. Sunaina and Bhavya wait in the foyer at the entrance.

"How did you live here?" Bhavya finally asks.

"What do you mean?" Sunaina frowns at the question.

"It's filthy and small. It stinks and is noisy. How can anyone live here?" Bhavya knows she's being rude, but she can't help it.

"Is that how you see this place?" Sunaina says, and lets out a huff of breath. "I suppose that's to be expected. Did you think, Rajkumari, that we all lived in gilded palaces?"

Bhavya remains silent.

"Do you know where Fatima Ghazala and I lived before we moved here?" Sunaina doesn't wait for an answer. "On the streets. We couldn't afford anything else and were too young and too proud to accept charity. When it rained, we stayed in the masjid, the mandir, the gurdwara—any safe place that had room for us. We huddled in the darkest corners at night so we wouldn't be prey to those who thought us tender morsels. This building and the four walls it gave us are infinitely more precious to us than Southern Aftab is to you." Sunaina swallows. "The money we poor people spend is ours. We have earned it through our own sweat and hard work unlike the landowners who live on the blood of their workers. We have more right to our humble comforts, Rajkumari, than you do to your luxuries."

A moment, ponderous in its silence, passes.

"I apologize. I got carried away. I forgot that I am not supposed to have opinions," Sunaina says, and retreats into an icy silence.

To Bhavya's complete mortification, the tail end of Sunaina's speech was heard by Fatima Ghazala and the three girls who accompany her. The girls all have dupattas around their heads and glee in their eyes.

"Rajkumari, this is Adila, Amirah, and Azizah, also known as the Alif sisters." Fatima Ghazala makes the introductions without commenting on, or acknowledging, the excoriation Bhavya just received from Sunaina. "Ladies, this is Rajkumari Bhavya from Southern Aftab."

Bhavya finds herself the subject of an intense stare from the youngest Alif sister.

"Azizah, stop staring at her!" the oldest sister reprimands.

"I can't help it! I've never seen an actual live rajkumari before!"

"Have you seen many dead ones?"

"That's disgusting, Amirah! You make me sound like I go peering into coffins all the time!"

"No, but you did it once."

"I was five!" Azizah says huffily.

"What is the rajkumari doing with you?" the oldest one asks Fatima Ghazala in a loud whisper.

"She ran away from home," Fatima Ghazala replies in a louder whisper. Bhavya glares at her.

"Why would she do that?" The middle sister joins the conversation.

"She heard rumors of Bilal's beauty," Fatima Ghazala says completely seriously.

The youngest girl's mouth drops open. Bhavya wonders who Bilal is.

"She's just joking, Azizah. Calm down." Adila elbows Fatima Ghazala.

"Didi, the Alif sisters and I are off to see a nautanki. A troupe from Bharat is in Noor for only a week, and they're holding performances in the maidaan. Are you going to go back to the mahal, or will you come with us?" Fatima Ghazala links arms with Adila, looking happier in this moment than Bhavya has ever seen her.

"Coming with you!" Bhavya says eagerly. She has never been to a nautanki before, though she has heard much about their wonders.

The nautanki begins with the wail of a sitar and continues with skits, songs, music, and dialogue. The costumes are glorious and colorful. The characters feature handsome monsters and pretty princesses with hidden depths. Bhavya laughs, cries, and gasps. By the time the performance is over, she is seriously considering running away to join the troupe. But reality objects immediately when Fatima Ghazala and Sunaina look at each other and decide in silent accord that it is time to return to the mahal. Fatima Ghazala insists on escorting the Alif sisters home. They are lucky enough to hitch a ride on a cart in Taaj Gul that delivers them very close to the Northern Aftab. The plan is to return to Southern Aftab through Northern Aftab without, hopefully, rousing any suspicion from anyone.

However, when they cross the bridge and step into the driveway leading up to Northern Aftab, a small commotion breaks out among a group of Ifrit soldiers gathered in front of the mahal. Bhavya keeps her head down as Fatima Ghazala leads them quickly up the driveway. They are almost at the corridor connecting the two sides of the mahal, when, all of a sudden, a horse blocks their path. Bhavya looks up and sees the Emir glaring down at them. She forgets to breathe for a moment. The Emir is furious; his eyes are narrowed, his lips are thinned, and his jaw is clenched. Bhavya thinks that he looks beautiful. He dismounts from his horse and strides over to them. Bhavya wonders if he is finally going to speak to her.

Instead, he walks to Fatima Ghazala and grabs her by the shoulders. Sunaina makes a sound of protest.

"Where have you been?" the Emir says in a low voice, practically seething with the force of his anger.

"I believe you are overstepping your boundaries, Emir." Fatima Ghazala extricates herself from his grasp. The Emir sucks in a breath at her words like they have hurt him.

"Let's go," Fatima Ghazala says. Bhavya follows her and Sunaina but keeps looking back at the Emir, not that he even glances at her.

CHAPTER 24

*Z*ulfikar clenches his fists and watches Fatima Ghazala walk away from him. He has no right to feel hurt by her coldness. None at all. Not when he practically courted it, but at this moment, *particularly* at this moment, his heart is a wounded thing. Conscious of the bemused glances his soldiers are giving him, he retreats to the library. The moment Zulfikar realized he couldn't feel Fatima Ghazala's fire in Southern Aftab had been a terrifying one. Firdaus died all over again in his memory.

He slumps down in a chair, aware that his misery is of his own making but piqued anyway. The idea that Fatima Ghazala's elusive smiles with the flash of those dimples will never again be directed his way makes him mournful. He felt her hurt at his words the night before, felt her surprised embarrassment and a deeper pain that made him hurt too. But he cannot let the bond between their fires link them any further than this. He will not risk his heart again.

"What have you done to anger the little Name Giver so?" a husky voice asks from the doorway.

Zulfikar stiffens. He had been so deeply immersed in his thoughts that he did not hear the door open. The scent of desert roses announces the owner of the voice. Once upon a time, Zulfikar would have been able to identify the Ifrit woman by her footsteps alone. The night before, when Fatima Ghazala Named this Ifrit woman into the human world, into human form, that one brief moment before memory tainted everything between them, Zulfikar had felt an intense unadulterated joy at her presence. But that moment was a firefly blinking out. Now, every time he looks at her, all he can remember is her betrayal and the way it undid him.

"I got tired of awaiting your summons, Emir," says Tali, Firdaus's primary apprentice and the Ifrit who used to be Zulfikar's beloved. She is wearing a red tunic and a white shalwar. Her hair is in a braid down her back, and a pale pink dupatta is wrapped around her head. She looks at Zulfikar and smiles slightly. "Are you not going to answer my question?"

Zulfikar can feel himself returning to the hurt he had thought was a thing of the past. "My affairs with the Name Giver are my own and none of your concern, sayyida."

Tali's face, beautiful if a bit too narrow, freezes for an instant, before her features ease into a smile. "Come now, you do not need to make me feel like an outsider."

"Will you train the Name Giver?" Zulfikar changes the subject. He will not be drawn into a discussion. It is difficult enough to share space with her.

"As much as is possible. But, Zulfikar"—Tali comes and sits down beside him—"training your Name Giver is my secondary purpose."

Zulfikar gets to his feet and moves away. He pretends not to see the hurt in Tali's eyes. He doesn't want to know the reason she is here. He wills her not to say it.

"Even if you don't ask, I will tell you," Tali says with a smile Zulfikar used to know well. "I am here for you. I am here to reclaim you."

Zulfikar looks at the Ifrit woman he spent his entire life loving until that one afternoon now carved into his memories. That afternoon when she took him aside in the garden and told him she was in love with someone else. That he was too safe, too easy. She needed the danger he couldn't provide.

Their parents had been inside talking about their engagement. Zulfikar remembers the exact moment his heart broke. He remembers the shadows on the garden walls, the heat of the midday sun, that moment.

"Am I some sort of land or object for you to reclaim?" he says to her now, conscious of how his voice breaks.

"Of course not! That is not what I meant!" A plea resides in her voice.

"What has happened to your great love? Did you think I do not know who your heart wandered to?"

"It was a momentary madness! You and I grew up together, Zulfikar. Our lives entwined long before either of us knew what love meant. I was scared that I was settling. That I was confusing friendship for love."

"Was that why it was so easy for you to toss me aside?" Zulfikar takes a deep breath and is grateful his voice doesn't wobble. Small mercies.

"You know that's not true."

"What you did, Tali, what you said, unmade me. You were the standard by which I measured myself. You were both my road and my destination. I didn't know who I was without you. I had to leave Al-Naar to find myself again." He pauses. "In this world, I am beginning to know who I am, and who I am is not the boy you knew. I will never be that boy again."

"I will learn you once more!"

"Do you think I can just forgive and forget? Fine, maybe I can forgive, but I will never forget. I cannot wipe the slate clean."

"You can try!" Her eyes are full of tears she is too proud to shed. Her voice trembles, and she is taking quick little breaths that announce her distress. Zulfikar observes her as if from a distance.

"I don't want to," he says, and watches as her control crumples. He wonders if he'd say the same thing if Fatima Ghazala weren't around, if their bond didn't exist. But that's a moot question because she is and Zulfikar will ensure that she remains that way.

"Are you in a relationship with the Name Giver, Zulfikar? I ask as Firdaus's apprentice," Tali says, wiping her tears away brusquely.

"No," Zulfikar replies shortly. "You will be given a week to make the Name Giver familiar with the theory of Naming."

"She's not strong enough," Tali says, all evidence of her earlier distress absent.

"What exactly do you mean?"

"She barely Named me. I am not at all confident she will be able to name the Raees. The Raees's fire will kill her." Tali gets to her feet. "The Name Giver's physical strength is considerable, but her fire is weak. Too weak perhaps. I will have more to report once I meet with her tonight." She leaves Zulfikar sitting in the library with a stricken look on his face.

The air is fragrant with the scent of night-blooming jasmine. Fatima Ghazala prays Isha, wraps a shawl around herself, and sets off for her appointment with the apprentice. The Ifrit woman has a Name—no one knows that better than Fatima Ghazala—but Fatima Ghazala is loath to use it. As she navigates the darkness and draws closer to the fire pit behind the barracks, the scent of the air changes slightly. The air still smells of the jasmine, but now it has smoky notes Fatima Ghazala associates with the Ifrit. Zulfikar is present when she reaches her destination, standing stiffly beside the apprentice. He sees her, and a yearning blooms on his face. Fatima

Ghazala looks away from him, telling herself that he presents a lie. She cannot yield to the softness in his smiles, especially not when he has warned her not to.

"Name Giver," the Emir says, "I present to you, Tali, a soldier in the Ifrit army and Firdaus's primary apprentice. She will instruct you as much as she can." Contrary to the expression on his face, his voice is cool and impersonal. Fatima Ghazala clenches her fists and tells herself that this distance is for the best. "If you need me for anything, I will be in the mahal." With a nod, he leaves. When Fatima turns to the apprentice, she finds the Ifrit woman staring after Zulfikar's retreating back with a longing look on her face. Fatima Ghazala clears her throat.

"I am not at all sure what to teach you," the apprentice says, seeming unconcerned that her feelings for the Emir are so apparent. She is a tall, striking woman with high cheekbones, gold eyes, and long black hair. She wears a dupatta around her head and a pale green shalwar kameez.

"How do I control my fire?" Fatima Ghazala asks. "It flares sometimes when I am scared or angry."

"Did Zulfikar not teach you those things? Did he not discuss with you what Djinn fire is?" The apprentice frowns. "If what I was told is correct, then you were born human but something happened that led to Ghazala transferring her fire and her Name to you. Which means that until recently you had no idea about Names and fire. Am I correct?"

Fatima Ghazala nods. "The knowledge of fire is there, perhaps in the fire itself. What it is, what it means. I don't know how it feels to you, but the fire feels like an innate part of me. Not like a limb but like my strength. It's there when I need it and absent when I don't."

The apprentice looks thoughtful at the comment. "I can teach you the things we learned as Ifrit children. How to control our fire in times of emotional upheaval. How to mask it when we want to hide. Things like that. I can also teach you the theory of Name Giving since that's all I ever learned."

"I would appreciate that." Fatima Ghazala's lips quirk in a half smile. "Talking to you is an interesting feeling. You are a stranger, but because I Named you, I know all your secrets."

"So you already know how I feel about the Emir," the apprentice says softly.

"I don't think I would need to look into your memories to know that," Fatima Ghazala replies.

"I thought that if I came here, he would look at me again. That he would forgive me." The Ifrit woman grimaces as if in pain. "I was such a fool . . ."

There is nothing Fatima Ghazala can say to that, so she says nothing at all.

After a minute, the apprentice takes a breath and says, "Shall we begin, then?"

And so begins a long week of training. Fatima Ghazala spends the afternoons and a major portion of the evenings with Tali. She learns how to control her fire, how to wield it like a blade, how to intensify its heat. She learns about Names; the golden pieces of a Name reflect the kind of person the Ifrit is. She soaks up the knowledge.

After breakfast with Sunaina, she spends time in the practice hall, where teachers skilled in various fighting disciplines regularly make appearances to train and teach willing students. Fatima Ghazala sees Zulfikar everywhere, but he doesn't approach her, nor does he try to get her attention in any way. Of the Wazir there is no sign and no one seems particularly anxious for his company.

On the seventh day of training, Fatima Ghazala finds herself, suddenly, in Zulfikar's path. She is entering Northern Aftab as he is leaving it. She bumps into him, and he catches hold of her arms when she would have fallen. The moment is unexpected and all the more bittersweet for it. Fatima Ghazala makes to move away, and Zulfikar tightens his grip. She raises an eyebrow at him.

"If you think you are ready, the Raees wishes to be Named today," he says, sounding oddly stilted, as if he no longer knows how to speak to her.

"I don't know that I will ever be ready," Fatima Ghazala replies, not meeting his eyes, "but I am willing to try."

Zulfikar nods politely to her and continues on his way. Fatima Ghazala looks up to see that Tali has been observing their interaction from the second floor.

Later, after the training, the apprentice sits beside Fatima Ghazala in a wide airy room and asks, "Do you have him in your heart?"

"The Emir?" Fatima Ghazala does not want to have this conversation.

"Coyness doesn't become you, Name Giver."

Fatima Ghazala wonders how the apprentice can say that with any authority, considering she has known her for less than a week at this point.

"If you are talking about the Emir, I . . . Do we really have to talk about this? I confess you are not the person I would choose to be my confidante," Fatima Ghazala tells the apprentice.

"Because of my history with him?" Tali replies.

"Because you do not consider it *history*," Fatima Ghazala corrects her.

"I asked him to come back to me. To return to Al-Naar with me," the Ifrit woman confesses entirely without warning.

Fatima Ghazala steels herself. "Are congratulations in order?"

"No. Not yet."

"Why are you telling me this?"

"Perhaps it is a warning. I do not intend to let him go so easily."

"Your intentions are not the problem, though. His are," Fatima Ghazala points out.

Tali looks as if she is going to speak. Fatima Ghazala stands up, no longer wanting to be physically part of this conversation. "I apologize. I spoke out of turn. I know nothing about the Emir, let alone what his intentions are. You do not need to worry on my account. I am not going to confess my feelings, whatever they are, to him. Excuse me."

After the week of training, on a Monday morning, Tali pronounces Fatima Ghazala ready to name the Raees. When the night has settled in, they gather in front of the now-familiar fire pit behind the barracks. Fatima Ghazala is conscious of the world around her in a way she has never been before. Not even when she was Naming Tali. She closes her eyes and takes deep measured breaths. Tali stands on one side of her and Zulfikar on the other. Fatima Ghazala feels their Names tug at her. Not urgently, just little pulls to make her aware of their existence. If she concentrates, she can feel the Names of all the Ifrit soldiers sleeping in the barracks.

The fire in the pit is blazing. It keeps the cold at bay and anticipates the Raees's arrival. If she doesn't fail. If she is strong enough. Fatima Ghazala feels like a string taut with possibilities and little else. She sneaks a look at Zulfikar and finds him looking at her, a worried frown tangling his eyebrows. He meets her gaze and holds it without smiling. The moment stretches. Fatima Ghazala turns away, her breath short and her cheeks hot.

"I'm ready," she says, aware that her voice is not at all convincing.

The two Ifrit nod and step back. Fatima Ghazala lets her consciousness expand, opening entirely to the world around her, an invitation of sorts. A tickle in her mind makes her turn, and for a moment, she forgets to breathe. A column of fire, easily as tall as one of the mahal's spires, undulates in front of her. Fear slams into her, and she has to force herself not to flee at the sight. She can barely see the pieces of the Name she is supposed to be joining together.

Fatima Ghazala forces herself to take one step closer and nearly recoils at the heat emanating from the fire. She squares her shoulders and takes another step. The heat is so intense that she is surprised she is not on fire already. She is not going to survive this Naming. But she gave her word to her baba. Death has been dogging her heels for so long now she may as well give in. Fatima Ghazala wonders how badly dying will hurt. She decides to find out and raises a hand to plunge into the column of smokeless fire.

Before she can do so, however, someone pulls her back and away. She finds herself cradled against the Emir's chest. His heart is racing. Or maybe it's hers. Fatima Ghazala can't tell. She tries to pull away, but she is trembling so hard she finds herself unable to. A few minutes later, she finally finds enough strength to step out of his arms.

She looks at the Emir, but he is looking at Tali defiantly.

"I will not stand by and watch her die, Tali. I will find another way," he says to the Ifrit woman.

CHAPTER 25

*S*unaina looks in consternation first at her sister and then at the rajkumari. She has to prepare a big batch of various cosmetics for a visiting merchant's wife. In order to have everything prepared in time, she needs to work without distractions or interruptions. Fatima Ghazala and Bhavya are both distracting her from her work and interrupting it. They are sitting opposite each other at the worktable, hostility thick in the air between them.

"What is your relationship to the Emir?" Bhavya demands.

Fatima Ghazala's eyebrows rise at the rajkumari's tone. "I suppose I am a citizen of the half of the Noor City he administrates. What relationship does a citizen have with the leader of the city?"

"You are lying to me," Bhavya says. Her calmness is worrying. "I will ask you again. What is your relationship to the Emir?"

"I cannot tell you." Fatima Ghazala frowns. A little impatiently. "But let me reassure you, the Emir and I are not in a romantic relationship."

"Am I supposed to take your word for it?" the rajkumari says coldly.

"Whether you do or don't is not my concern, rajkumari." Sunaina watches her sister's eyes flicker and tenses.

"Have you forgotten who I am?" the rajkumari asks. Her voice is low and filled with an emotion Sunaina cannot identify.

"Why do you think your social status has any bearing on me? Am I supposed to give you respect simply because of the family you were born in?" Fatima Ghazala leans back in her chair and folds her arms.

Bhavya breathes in sharply. "How dare you?"

"Are you never tired of being judged for what you are instead of who you are? Don't you wish to be more than a title? Ah, but we were not talking about this, were we?" Fatima Ghazala gets to her feet. Sunaina meets her eyes across the room and gives a quick shake of her head. The younger girl sighs. "Listen, I do not know what monsters chase you, but you can rest assured on this one point. The Emir—whatever he feels for me isn't love. He told me so himself."

She leaves the room without another word. Sunaina stares after her and frowns. Does this mean that Fatima Ghazala has feelings for the Emir? Her sister has never previously expressed any interest in romance. The Emir . . . there was more than anger in his eyes when they saw him yesterday. Sunaina shakes her head. She does not want the Emir for a brother-in-law.

"Here." Sunaina hands Bhavya a mortar and pestle along with a bag of dried marigold petals. "Grind this for me."

The rajkumari accepts the proffered items without protest. After a moment of silence, Sunaina cautiously ventures, "Are you in love with the Emir?"

The rajkumari doesn't reply. Sunaina chooses to take her silence as an admission.

She moves around briskly, stirring a potion here and sifting a mix there. "Why do you love him?"

"Why does anyone love anybody?" Bhavya finally responds.

"I don't know. I haven't loved anyone before," Sunaina confesses, looking at the rajkumari's bowed head.

"He is an escape," Bhavya finally says in a small voice. "Being with him would mean no one would push me around to behave in a certain manner or be a certain way."

"Does it need to be the Emir? I mean, wouldn't anyone do if he lets you escape tradition?" Sunaina speaks carefully.

"You have no idea what you are talking about!" Bhavya stops grinding. Her face is flushed, and she looks panicked.

Sunaina sighs deeply. "The thing is . . . I do. I'm only saying what I am because I see myself in you. Does that seem presumptuous of me?" The rajkumari's silence encourages her to continue. "I was with a man simply because I was expected to be in some sort of relationship with one. I suppose I still am. I just don't care about expectations anymore."

Sunaina grimaces, remembering the last time she saw Niral. "I didn't want to marry him, so I told people Fatima was an obstacle to the wedded bliss I didn't really want. In the end, I hurt Fatima Ghazala and I hurt Niral both by clinging to and fighting against what was expected of me."

Sunaina looks to see if she has the rajkumari's attention. She does.

"I thought that if I tried hard enough, I would be able to love him. If I pretended hard enough, I would." Sunaina smiles slightly. "I *wanted* to love him. Being with him felt normal. It felt like the natural progression in my life, in any woman's life. You grow up a daughter to become a wife and later a mother. That was all I knew. But . . . I couldn't accept it in the end. I couldn't accept him or the idea of marriage. I felt suffocated when I thought about marrying him. He felt wrong. All men do."

"But you are not a rajkumari. You decided not to marry, so you didn't. I don't have that luxury." Angry tears escape the rajkumari's eyes. Sunaina looks away. She is uncomfortable with excess emotion. "Having the Emir on my side would mean freedom. A limited sort of freedom but freedom anyway. I wish I wasn't a girl. I wish I had been born a boy. Then no one would have been able to force me to do things I don't want to do." The rajkumari gets up. The chair she was sitting on falls to the ground. She leaves without another word.

Tali's silence follows Zulfikar into Noor in the early morning and throughout the day as he meets with various petitioners, has meetings, and goes through reports from Achal Kaur's messengers. He can hear everything she doesn't say. He feels judged. Or maybe he is judging himself. Should he have let Fatima Ghazala proceed to her death? How could he?

He is weary of the tension when they finally return to Northern Aftab around noon. He heads into the mahal followed closely by Tali. They end up in a room on the first floor.

"I wish you would speak your mind," he says to her as soon as the door closes behind them.

"Have you found a way?" Tali replies. At Zulfikar's puzzled look, she elaborates, "To strengthen the Name Giver's fire."

"You already know the answer to that."

"Why aren't you discussing this with the Wazir? Why haven't I seen Anwar anywhere?" Tali crosses her arms. Though this is her first time in the human world, she is well aware of the hierarchy in the Ifrit-controlled cities of Qirat.

"He spends the majority of his time traveling between the desert cities and patrolling the Silk Road. We have found that the less we are in each other's presence, the better our relationship is. Besides, he isn't exactly rational where Fatima Ghazala is concerned," Zulfikar replies.

Tali looks at him sharply.

"He thinks Fatima Ghazala belongs to him because she has Ghazala's fire."

The Ifrit woman winces. She drops down on a chair and looks

up at Zulfikar. "I have a suggestion, though I would rather not make it."

Zulfikar raises an eyebrow.

"I really am not as selfless as this will imply." Tali scrunches up her face. "It is a matter of survival, however . . ."

"Get to the point, Tali."

"Marry the Name Giver," she says in a rush.

"Are you out of your mind?" Zulfikar gapes at her.

"If her fire bonds to yours, her fire will increase in strength," Tali says unhappily. "The increase in fire strength between married couples is documented."

Zulfikar stares at the Ifrit woman. She meets his gaze calmly. "Do you think I want you to do this? Do you think I'm taking pleasure in telling you this?" Tali asks. "I came here to convince you of my heart, not encourage you into someone else's! But I am a soldier, Zulfikar. I know about the Raees's condition. I know that she can't remain in Al-Naar."

"Your plan is a mad one," Zulfikar says. The idea of marrying Fatima Ghazala terrifies him, mostly because of how much he wants to.

"It needn't be a true marriage, Zulfikar. It needn't be forever."

"If I marry her, it will be forever, Tali. I'm not going to use her for our convenience," he tells her, and watches as tears fill the woman's eyes.

"So be it," Tali mutters.

At four in the afternoon, the royal family, including the maharajah and other courtiers, make their way to a baag located on the outer edges of the mahal grounds. The baag's main attraction is a line of gulmohar trees that are currently in bloom. Fatima Ghazala accompanies the rest of the companions because she can never deny herself a chance to be near flowers, and the gulmohar flowers, especially, are glorious.

The retinue moves slowly due to the Rajmata's mincing gait. Fatima Ghazala hangs in the back, not wanting to gain anyone's attention—especially the rajkumari's. Suddenly, someone wraps an arm around her waist. Fatima Ghazala twists away and turns to see Aaruv grinning at her. He seems unconcerned that people are taking note of the attention he is giving her.

"Don't touch me," Fatima Ghazala tells him in a voice danger-ous for its lack of inflection. Indra and the rest of the companions are too far away to provide distraction or aid.

"The fun is just beginning," Aaruv replies, unrepentant, and moves away. For the entirety of the time they spend in the baag, no matter where Fatima Ghazala is, Aaruv is always in her line of sight. He looks at her as though she is his, and people begin to whisper. Some titter in amusement, and others look at Fatima Ghazala with different gazes. Even the maharajah looks upon Aaruv's actions with an indulgent eye. The maharani looks trou-bled but doesn't speak up. Fatima Ghazala tries to stay with the rest of the companions, but that doesn't deter the rajkumar from look-ing at her boldly. His very gaze is a violation. Fatima Ghazala's anger grows steadily; her eyes become molten and her skin flushes.

The party wraps up when the skies are streaked orange. Fatima Ghazala lags behind, watching the members of the royal family go first, making their slow way to the mahal. She tries to help the ser-vants tidy up the detritus left behind but is shooed away. Finally, she joins the very end of the group of people walking slowly so as not to outpace the Rajmata.

"Do I not deserve at least a smile?" Aaruv says suddenly in

Fatima Ghazala's ear. She moves away from the rajkumar and is about to leave the group when Aaruv, taking advantage of the falling darkness, grabs her shoulder.

Fatima Ghazala stops and turns around. She feels her control snap, feels her fire ready. "I believe I told you not to touch me," she says in a clear, carrying voice.

The rest of the party turns to see what is happening. Aarush and Aruna exchange panicked glances.

Aaruv, conscious of the eyes on him, puts on a bored expression. "I am a rajkumar; you should be honored I even look at you."

Fatima Ghazala doesn't blink at his words. She says in the same even tone, "Do not touch me again."

"And if I do?" Aaruv grabs Fatima Ghazala's arm. "Like this. What will you do? What *can* you do?"

"Aaruv!" the maharajah says, moving toward them.

For a moment, Fatima Ghazala's expression remains unchanged. Then her eyes flicker orange, and a smell of burning flesh fills the air. Aaruv screams and flings Fatima Ghazala's arm away. He looks down at his hand, a disbelieving expression on his face, before he looks at Fatima Ghazala again. He staggers back a few steps.

Fatima Ghazala feels her fire cover her skin. She looks at the faces around her, lit by the orange glow of her fire, before her gaze finally stops on Aaruv. "Consider this one consequence," she says to him. She turns and walks away. No one dares to stop her.

CHAPTER 26

Flames flutter in fluted glass lamps, illuminating rich rugs, fine silks, and the kind of grandeur that most people cannot even imagine. Present in the room, small by the standards set by others, are the royal family excluding Bhavya.

The maharajah glances at his brother; Aaruv stands turned away from the rest of them, his face in shadow. A familiar exasperation fills Aarush. This time, though, the exasperation is spiced liberally with anger. He had thought his brother a harmless flirt, but what he witnessed in the garden seems a lot more sinister and concerning.

Predictably, it is his mother who speaks first. "How long have you been harboring that creature in our midst?"

Not so predictably, it is his wife who responds to the Rajmata. "I appreciate your concern for your son, Amma, but Fatima Ghazala's presence in the mahal is not up for discussion right now. The issue at hand is that your son, my husband's brother, Rajkumar Aaruv, made unwanted advances on a woman."

"Do you have any idea who she is?" Aarush says, if only to deflect some of the anger directed at Aruna by his mother and aunt.

"It doesn't matter who she is!" Aruna says, turning to Aarush. She is truly, spectacularly angry, angrier than Aarush has ever seen her. "She could be a beggar on the streets, and it would not excuse what the rajkumar did. A woman's body is her own, and no one has the right to touch it without her permission. It doesn't matter if you are a rajkumar or the maharajah, if a woman doesn't welcome your advances, don't make them!" Aruna looks at the rajkumar, who still won't look them in the eyes. "I am ashamed of you, Aaruv. I expected so much better from you."

"Aruna!" the Rajmata says sharply. "Do you forget who you are talking to?"

"It is precisely because I know who I am speaking to that I speak thusly, Amma. As a rajkumar of Qirat, Aaruv has the responsibility to behave in a manner befitting his position. You are always concerned that Bhavya behave properly; should this concern not extend also to your son? My companions have long complained about his unwelcome attentions, and I, instead of speaking to the rajkumar, told them to avoid him. I thought that his brother, his mother, or even his aunt would and should speak to him about his proclivities." She skewers them all with a look. "Clearly, I thought wrong. The fault is as much mine as it is yours, Maharaj."

Aarush feels Aruna's disappointment in him keenly. He turns to his mother. "She is the Emir's charge, Amma. He requested that we keep her among us temporarily. If Aaruv has managed to malign her in any way, he will find the war he is courting on our doorstep." Aaruv finally turns to them; his face is pale, but his expression is defiant.

"Do not think Fatima Ghazala's strength is limited only to that extent," Aruna warns, gesturing to Aaruv's bandaged hands. "If she desired to, she could have set you on fire, Aaruv . . ." She pauses and looks at her brother-in-law for a second before adding, "And you would have deserved it."

The Rajmata's expression grows stormier. Before she has the chance to say anything however, Aarush does. "I apologize, Aruna. I ought to have spoken to Aaruv. I didn't see his actions as particularly wrong or needing correction. I was wrong." He looks at his brother, but the rajkumar still won't meet his eyes. Aarush's lips thin, and he fights the urge to shake his brother.

A knock sounds on the closed door before it opens. Janab Jamshid appears in the doorway. He bows to Aarush and says the one thing the maharajah wished he wouldn't. "Maharaj, the Emir is here and awaiting your presence."

The moon is a sliver, and the shadows are malevolent. Fatima Ghazala walked away from Southern Aftab without giving any thought to where she was going. She found herself near a madrasa and, because her sari was inappropriate to wear during a prayer, borrowed an abaya from a sister and prayed Maghrib. She sat with her hands lifted in dua for half an hour or so, but no immediate solution seemed visible. Now she sits on the steps of the madrasa and considers her options. She can go to Achal Kaur or to the Alifs, but those are the first places Zulfikar will look. Why Fatima Ghazala is so certain Zulfikar will look for her, she doesn't know. It is as though she feels his attention on her like one would feel a breeze on their skin. Even when he is not present, she can feel him thinking of her. She hasn't seen him since she failed . . . No, he pulled her away from the fire, so it isn't as though she failed. But she did, didn't she? She should have just gone through with the Naming. If she had died, the Name Giving power would have gone to someone more able. Fatima Ghazala takes a deep breath. She doesn't want to face Zulfikar at all. She remembers Tali teaching her to cloak her fire and decides a practical application of the theory is in order.

The imam of the madrasa comes out and asks her kindly if she needs a place to stay or help of a more delicate sort. Fatima Ghazala thanks him for his concern and gets up to leave. As she steps out onto the pavement, a light rain begins to fall. Fatima Ghazala looks in wonder at the raindrops; she cannot remember the last time it rained in Northern Noor. The rain fades away, leaving a glow to the night and a scent that reminds her of Firdaus. Fatima Ghazala walks the streets of Southern Noor, with lush bougainvillea climbing over walls and the intoxicating fragrances of night jasmine and frangipani. She follows her hunger to a small market set up in the southern maidaan.

The night is suddenly alive with song, laughter, and voices. Fatima Ghazala lets go of her mental hold on her fire and breathes easily for the first time in hours. Her problems still concern her. The rajkumar whose gaze makes her want to pluck out his eyes—will she have to face him again? Will she be punished for burning his hands? What about Zulfikar? How long is she going to deny herself his smiles?

Deciding not to think about them, she checks the pouch at her hips for money and is pleased to find enough for a meal. The sari she is wearing is a pale yellow with wide red borders. The material is fine, and though the jewelry she wears is costume, they are well-crafted pieces. Fatima Ghazala wonders why she has been able to walk around without being hassled by men who seem to think all women are fair game. In fact, no one gives her even a second look.

She spies a pani puri seller doing excellent business in one corner of the maidaan and lines up behind two matronly women, one from Nippon and the other Qirati. They are gossiping about their daughters-in-law. Fatima Ghazala amuses herself by eavesdropping unashamedly. Twenty minutes later, she walks away holding a paper tray filled with fifteen crispy little puris filled with potato curry, topped with fresh onion, and dipped in tamarind chutney. She finds a mostly dry wooden stump to sit on and proceeds to inhale her food.

As she is licking her fingers and wishing she had more pani puri, Fatima Ghazala feels a prickle on her shoulder. She looks up and sees Zulfikar standing a fair distance away. He walks toward her without once looking away. People move to clear his path, and Fatima Ghazala feels a spurt of annoyance at how easily he parts the crowds. When he is ten steps away, Fatima Ghazala decides that she would rather not talk to him after all.

Fatima Ghazala gets up and, without looking at the approaching Emir, plunges into the throngs. He may be able to part crowds, but Fatima Ghazala can move through them. She leads him on a merry chase. There are times when she thinks she has lost him only to have him reappear at the last minute. Finally, she leads him to Chandani Baag, which has rows of night-blooming jasmine and little else. The garden isn't entirely deserted; a few couples sit in shadows enjoying the darkness, the fragrance of the jasmine, and each other. Fatima Ghazala chooses to sit on a bench underneath a lamppost by a rather large jasmine bush and waits for Zulfikar to reach her.

He appears a little later, panting slightly, a light sheen of sweat over his chest and arms. He drops down on the bench, the scimitar he is wearing banging against the wooden surface.

"Your eyes are glowing orange" is the first thing he says before wiping his face with a handkerchief.

Oh. Fatima Ghazala suddenly understands how she, a woman dressed in relatively expensive clothes, has been able to walk the streets without being harassed. She didn't have to be scared of monsters; she just had to become one herself. Fatima Ghazala focuses her thoughts on her fire and, as Tali has taught her, imagines she is taking a step back from it.

"Better?" she asks Zulfikar. He nods. The darkness, aided by the jasmine, suddenly feels soft and pliant. "I suppose you heard what happened."

"Yes," Zulfikar says. "I'm surprised by how restrained you were. He has only light burns."

"Well, I wasn't sure whether I would be punished for hurting him." Fatima Ghazala lets out a short, brittle laugh. "What a strange world we live in. *He* attacked me, and yet *I* am the one worrying about being punished."

"You seem remarkably calm about this entire situation."

"He was never more than an annoying gnat to me. Were I simply human, I would have tasted an entirely different flavor of weakness."

"He didn't hurt you?"

"Not physically, no. But the way he looked at me made me feel dirty. Like he was undressing me." Fatima Ghazala shudders, remembering.

"You should have broken his arms and legs. You were too restrained," Zulfikar says, and Fatima Ghazala hears the skein of barely repressed anger in his voice.

"I think so too. I'm regretting not doing so right now."

"Fatima Ghazala . . ." Zulfikar says, and she looks at him. "Why were you running away from me?"

Fatima Ghazala wishes the night wasn't so kind to Zulfikar. She would have a much easier time resisting him then. "I failed to Name the Raees. I failed you and I failed Baba. How am I supposed to face you?"

"You didn't fail me!" Zulfikar replies fiercely. "You didn't fail Firdaus! You cannot ask a boulder to be a mountain."

"If you had let me make the attempt, I would have died. Then the Name Giving power would have gone to someone else, maybe even to your beloved Tali. Did you pull me back because of the bond?" Fatima Ghazala asks the question she most wants to know the answer to.

"Of course not," the Zulfikar replies immediately.

"I don't believe you." Fatima Ghazala is sitting so close to the Emir she can feel his warmth in the cool night air. But emotionally she feels miles away. "What do we do now? The Raees cannot stay in Al-Naar."

Zulfikar shifts even closer to Fatima Ghazala, and she freezes. She takes a deep breath and wills her heart to calm down. "Will you marry me?" he asks in such a low voice that she has to lean forward in order to hear him. At first she is certain she misheard.

"What did you just say?" The Emir's face is mostly in shadow, but Fatima Ghazala is sure his cheeks are red. "Did you just ask me to marry you? Why?"

"To strengthen your fire so you can Name the Raees," he explains in a rush. Fatima Ghazala's world screeches to a halt. Hurt crystallizes in her chest before splintering into pain.

"I would much rather die," she tells him succinctly, and gets up to go. The Emir moves fast. He grabs her hand and moves them farther into the shadows of a Palash tree. His arms are locked around her, making it impossible for her to move away from him. The darkness knows no light, and Fatima Ghazala cannot see the Emir's face at all.

"Do not speak of dying so easily," the Emir hisses at her. Fatima Ghazala feels her anger spark in turn.

"Let me go, Zulfikar. I cannot fathom what made you think asking me to make a mockery of marriage was a good idea, but if you let me go now, I will pretend it didn't happen." If he lets her go now, she will be able to walk away without crying.

"Yes, the reason I want to marry you is for my people. Yes, I wouldn't have considered marrying you except as a last resort. But, Fatima Ghazala, it wouldn't be a marriage in name alone. We would be truly wedded." Fatima Ghazala can feel the Emir's heart pounding, and for a moment, she is convinced. Then she wrenches out of his embrace.

"You cannot even be sure that your feelings for me are your own. What you feel for me may be a creation of the bond between your fire and mine," she bursts out.

"I don't care." He really doesn't, Fatima Ghazala realizes. "And truly, I am willing to seize the least excuse to have you. I have been trying to distance myself from you. I have been trying to pretend I don't care, and it has been hell. I don't want to do that anymore. I refuse to do that anymore. So if strengthening your fire is the excuse I can give to have you, I will take it thankfully."

Fatima Ghazala wishes she could see the Emir's face. Read his expression. "What about Tali? Don't you love her?"

"The boy I was loved her. He no longer exists. The person I am right now can see no one else other than you. Will you have me, Fatima Ghazala? Will you allow me into your heart?"

The new day has a pearly glow to it; Fatima Ghazala sits on the wall surrounding the open roof of the apartment building in Taaj Gul and watches the early morning greet the citizens of Northern Noor awake. She refused to return to Aftab Mahal the night before and insisted on coming to the Alif family.

From her perch, Fatima Ghazala can see the milkman making the rounds on his cart; the shops have been open since before dawn, but it is only now that shop boys and girls emerge from their depths to sweep the entrances clean. From all appearances, today is going to be like any other, perhaps with a little more heat. And yet, Fatima Ghazala's life is going to change forever. She doesn't quite know what to think of that. On the one hand, her life has been a madcap adventure ever since Firdaus was killed; she changed personalities, homes, and employment. But somehow, ludicrously enough, those changes seem far easier to handle than this future change. The other things simply happened to her; they were all things she had little choice over. Marrying Zulfikar is something she has decided all on her own. This makes the change weightier. Scarier.

"What are you doing up here?" Adila asks from behind her.

"Wondering if I'm making a mistake." Adila is the only one Fatima Ghazala has told about Zulfikar's proposal. The other two are sure to go into paroxysms of either joy or disbelief, and Fatima Ghazala is not sure she has the mental wherewithal to deal with that at the moment.

"Abbu hasn't even given his permission yet and you already have cold feet?" Adila grins, coming to sit beside her. "Do you love him?"

"Not yet. If he walks away from me right now, it will hurt, but it will be nothing I won't recover from. If I marry him, I will have to trust him with not just my body but also my heart. That scares me more than the Shayateen do."

"Am I supposed to have answers for you?" Adila pokes Fatima Ghazala.

Fatima Ghazala grins. "Is that your way of telling me I have to decide this all on my own?"

"Yes. But no matter what you decide, I'm here for you."

Fatima Ghazala lays her head on Adila's shoulder. "Thanks, Adila."

"You are welcome." They sit in silence for a few minutes. "By the way," Adila says suddenly, "I told Azizah that you are getting married to the Emir. When I left, she was planning your wedding."

Fatima Ghazala gives Adila a look of abject horror and leaps off the wall. "How could you?" she wails, and takes off running.

Adila smiles serenely and turns to the view of the city.

CHAPTER 27

ulfikar is somewhat prepared for this meeting. He didn't eat breakfast so he won't have the temptation to throw it all up. He also knows to refuse refreshments for the same reason. If he were in Al-Naar, his parents would have arranged everything, but here, he is the architect of his own fate. Zulfikar wonders when he should tell his parents about their new daughter-in-law. If he tells them before the wedding, he will have to deal with a lot of correspondence; his mother and sisters will want to cross over, and that's definitely not feasible at this point. No, he will tell them when it's too late for them to object or interrupt.

Zulfikar realizes he has been standing in front of the Alifs' door for a while. Flushing, he raises his hand and knocks firmly. The door is immediately opened by Fatima Ghazala. Zulfikar feels his edges grow soft at the sight of her in a simple blush-pink embroidered shalwar kameez. He hands over her oud; Fatima Ghazala's belongings were moved to Northern Aftab early this morning.

She looks at him without smiling, and he returns her gaze equally seriously. "Have you changed your mind?" He wouldn't blame her if she has, but he wishes fiercely that she hasn't.

She shakes her head once, definitively, and Zulfikar exhales. He knows it is a bit too early to feel relief, but as long as he is reassured of her consent, he can face the grumpy bear who functions as her father.

"I've battled monsters, you know. Faced the enemy in wars.

Defended my country and life against seemingly insurmountable odds. However, I have never been as terrified as I am right now." Zulfikar confesses in a low whisper. Fatima Ghazala reaches out and, after a slight hesitation, pats his cheek.

"Fatima, what are you doing? Bring the Emir here," Asma's stern voice calls from the living room.

Zulfikar follows Fatima Ghazala to the living room, pausing to smile at the Alif sisters, who are poking their heads out from a room at the end of the corridor. Then he takes a deep breath and enters the living room, faltering when Ali gives him a distinctly unfriendly look.

Asma and a woman Zulfikar recognizes as Fatima Ghazala's sister sit on either side of Ali. They all look at Zulfikar as if they'd much rather he wasn't there. Zulfikar swallows. Exchanging greetings, they sit: Fatima Ghazala and Zulfikar on one side of the room, the Alif parents and Sunaina on the other.

"You are here again," Ali says. "And this time my daughter tells me you have something to ask me." Yes, definitely unfriendly.

"I do, sayyid, sayyida." Zulfikar nods at both women. He stops, his throat dry.

"Fatima, bring the Emir some sharbat," Asma commands. Fatima Ghazala leaves, and Zulfikar immediately feels abandoned. She returns a little later carrying a jug of sharbat and some glasses. Zulfikar drinks the sharbat gratefully.

He tries again. "I am here to request your permission to marry Fatima Ghazala."

The couple exchanges looks while Sunaina narrows her eyes. Fatima Ghazala remains silent beside him. He is going to get no help from her.

"Why would the Emir of Noor want to marry a simple girl from Qirat?" Asma asks.

That is the question they most want answered and the one question Zulfikar cannot give them an answer to. He turns to Fatima Ghazala, and she shrugs. She won't help him out of this one. In fact, Zulfikar wonders if she isn't taking some pleasure at seeing him flounder.

"Is the question that difficult to answer?" Sunaina asks, her tone hostile.

"I apologize. I don't know how to talk about these things." He clears his throat. "I want to marry Fatima Ghazala because she is the only one in either world that I want to spend my life with," Zulfikar says, and looks down to hide his hot cheeks. At this point, that is the truth. Whether this truth will change, he doesn't know. What he is sure of is that even if there were a choice, he would still choose her.

"And you, child, are you sure you want to marry the Emir?" Ali asks Fatima Ghazala.

Fatima Ghazala turns and looks at Zulfikar for a long moment. "Yes." It is a sad admission, lacking the exuberance one would expect in someone madly in love. Sunaina frowns, and Zulfikar looks down at his hands.

The Alif parents exchange another look. Finally, Ali turns to Fatima Ghazala and Zulfikar. "If you really want to marry him, Fatima, you have our blessings."

"Thank you, Ammi and Abbu. Didi?" Fatima Ghazala looks at Sunaina.

"If he makes you happy, then I, too, have no objections." The permission is grudgingly given.

Zulfikar looks from the Alif parents to Fatima Ghazala to Sunaina and back again. "Does this mean my suit has been accepted?"

"You won't try to take her away, will you?" Amirah asks from the doorway.

"What about your parents? Will they mistreat her?" Adila asks.

"Of course not! To all of your questions!"

"It will take about three months to plan a wedding," Azizah announces.

Zulfikar feels as if he has walked into a whirlwind. "I'm afraid we have to marry within a week. Before next Juma to be precise," he tells the youngest Alif.

Azizah shrieks, an earsplitting sound. Everyone starts talking at once.

Since no one answered his question, Zulfikar assumes he has been given permission. He grabs Fatima Ghazala's hand and weaves his fingers through hers.

One week is not enough to prepare for a party let alone a wedding, as Azizah complains loudly to anyone who will listen. However, she is a general in the making and more than willing to take on the challenge. As the ceremony is going to be discreet, it will be held in Northern Aftab, eliminating the tradition of a baraat. Amirah is miffed because she, as she confides to Fatima Ghazala later, had expectations of a grand procession with dancers and musicians. However, the delicate nature of the agreement between Fatima Ghazala and Zulfikar is not exactly conducive to public celebration. Rather than being a community celebration, the wedding feels like an exclusive event only a few have been chosen to attend.

Azizah, with the Emir's blessing, and with her father as a chaperone, works with the domestic staff of Northern Noor to organize the food and venue for the wedding. Fatima Ghazala's previous boss and adopted grandmother, Achal Kaur, insists on purchasing for Fatima Ghazala a wedding outfit she would never have chosen for herself. A wedding gift Achal Kaur insists on and one Fatima Ghazala accepts with tears in her eyes.

"A bride must shine, chanda," Achal Kaur says. "Shine so even the stars take notice."

Four days before the wedding, Fatima Ghazala finds herself receiving a visitor she never would have expected. The maharani, clad in a rich silk sari in green and gold and a haar that would have ransomed a sheikh, is wildly out of place in the Alifs' living room. Accompanying the maharani are five of her companions, Indra among them. The living room is crowded with the maharani sitting and her companions arranged like a peacock's tail behind her. Fatima Ghazala sits opposite the maharani with a table between them.

"First, I must beg your forgiveness and extend the same plea on behalf of my husband. We gave our word to protect you, and we failed." The maharani's words are heartfelt, and all Fatima Ghazala can do is nod an acceptance. It is not them she blames for her experience with the rajkumar. "Second, I offer my congratulations on your upcoming wedding to the Emir." Aruna nods at her companions. They each pick up a box they brought with them and place it on the table. The boxes are opened, and Fatima Ghazala's jaw drops open. Jewelry of all kinds, made with precious gems and gold and silver, entice from the velvet boxes. "Please accept these," the maharani says.

"Sahiba, I like shiny things as much as any other woman, but surely you understand why I can't accept these. If you mean them as a way to assuage your conscience, please, you do not need to bother. I hold neither you nor the maharajah responsible for the rajkumar's actions," Fatima Ghazala says.

"Can I tell you a story?" the maharani says, seeming unmoved by Fatima Ghazala's protestations. Fatima Ghazala gestures for her to go ahead. "This is not common knowledge in Qirat, but I grew up in a place much like this one. In Darsala, the city of my birth, the slums are made of wood, and every few years, a fire swallows them whole. We always build anew. I was the king's concubine's child and a girl at that. When he died, my mother and I were cast out of the palace without a penny. The rani hated us both and with good reason perhaps; I, too, wouldn't want to share my husband with any other woman." Neither, Fatima Ghazala thinks, would she.

The maharani continues. "The slums weren't pretty or comfortable like the mahal I grew up in, but goodness, they were liberating. We no longer needed to watch our words and our actions. We were hungry sometimes, but even that is easier to endure when you have your dignity."

She pauses and smiles, her eyes misty with memories. "I met Aarush when he came to my country, to my city, to marry one of my half sisters. He got lost wandering around the city, and I was walking home from the seamstress's shop where I worked. All it took was one look into his eyes. Anyway"—the maharani clears her throat, her cheeks pink—"he was determined to marry me, and as you can see, he succeeded. I had no money to buy myself any jewelry, and there was no way I was going to take his. The night before my wedding, my father's wife, the rani, visited me just as I am visiting you. She told me that she didn't like me and she never would because I was the physical proof of her husband's infidelity but as a woman, as the rani of Darsala, she had certain obligations. One of which was this." The maharani gestures to the jewelry. "She gave them to me just as I am giving them to you. Maybe someday you can pass them on to someone else." The maharani gets to her feet, and Fatima Ghazala stands up too.

"Do not refuse me in this, please." The maharani smiles sweetly. She takes her leave a little later, and Fatima Ghazala, bemused, finally understands why the maharajah is so devoted to his wife.

Two days before the wedding, Sunaina and Fatima Ghazala go out and visit their favorite places in Noor City. Things between them have changed, irrevocably perhaps. The bond remains, but the strength of it has changed. Sunaina is particularly aware of her sister as someone who is more than the sum of her experiences. Her sister is a universe, one of those ephemeral moments; she is both a choice and the consequence of a choice.

They smell the flowers in Jalandar Baag, shop at Bijli Bazaar, and eat gyozas on Lazeez street. After getting mithai from their favorite store, Fatima Ghazala insists on taking Sunaina to a new shop she claims to have discovered earlier that year. Sunaina goes along, though not without protestations. She is battling the unwelcome realization that her sister will no longer be hers alone.

Fatima Ghazala takes Sunaina to an apothecary called Jung's. The store sells mostly herbal medicine, but a corner of it is devoted to cosmetics. Tending the corner is a young woman around the same age as Sunaina.

Sunaina's eyes widen when she sees the woman. "Is that . . . ?"

"Yes, your friend Jung Sori. I was going to tell you about her, but everything happened and she slipped my mind. I only remembered her when you mentioned her in Southern Aftab that day," Fatima Ghazala explains. "I recognized her immediately when I saw her. She hasn't changed much, has she?"

The Han woman looks over at that moment, and her face creases in a frown when she sees Sunaina. It has been a long time since they saw each other so Sunaina doesn't think Sori will recognize her. However, recognition lights up her features, and the woman steps forward with a cry. Sunaina takes Sori's hand and realizes that her cheeks are wet. She had thought she would never see her friend again.

Later, as they are walking home to Taaj Gul, Sunaina takes out a paper bag and hands it to Fatima Ghazala. Fatima Ghazala looks inside and finds two vials of ittar. She throws Sunaina a questioning look before uncapping one and sniffing at the contents.

"Gulmohar ittar. It's your favorite flower, isn't it? Since the flower is in season right now, I made you a batch. One is for the Emir if he cares for it."

"Thank you, didi."

"I love you, you know," Sunaina mumbles to cover her embarrassment.

Fatima Ghazala's smile is gentle. "I know you do. Even when you try very hard not to, you do. I love you too." They walk in silence for a few minutes.

"The men following us are soldiers, right?"

"Yes. Zulfikar thinks I need men to keep me safe," Fatima Ghazala says with some disgust.

"He is silly over you," Sunaina admits, and watches as her sister's smile turns sad. She frowns. "You don't think so?"

"No, I think he truly does feel something for me."

"Isn't that supposed to make you happy? Don't you want him to love you? Don't you love him?" Sunaina demands.

"Ah, I don't love him right now. But I will love him soon. That's what scares me."

"Fatima—"

"I also don't know what to say to the rajkumari, didi," Fatima Ghazala confesses. "After all I said to convince her, how do I tell her that I'm marrying the Emir?"

When Bhavya receives a message from Sunaina asking her to meet her in the workroom, she is pleased. She has questions she wants answered. For instance, she wants to know how and where Fatima Ghazala is. Is Sunaina's sister an Ifrit? If not, how does she have

fire? She didn't seem more than human all the times Bhavya inter-
acted with her. Bhavya also wants to thank Fatima Ghazala for
humiliating Aaruv. Seeing her brother reduced was a pleasure.

Bhavya pulls the door to the workroom open and sails in only
to stop short when she realizes Sunaina is not alone. Fatima Ghazala
stands beside her sister, sniffing a perfume Sunaina distilled. They
both glance up at her entrance. Bhavya looks at the younger girl
closely, wondering if she can sense some difference that gives away
her otherness, but there is nothing.

"I am so glad to see you!" Bhavya says, knowing she is being
uncharacteristically warm but unable to help herself. Anyone who
hates her brother is a friend.

"Rajkumari," Fatima Ghazala says softly. She clutches Sunaina's
hand briefly before turning to face Bhavya.

"What is it?" Bhavya smiles brightly.

"Look, I'm sorry. Before I say anything else, please know that I
wish things were different."

"You don't have to apologize for burning my brother. If
anything, I think you were too light on him!"

"I'm not talking about your brother." Fatima Ghazala swallows,
as if the words she wants to say are stuck in her throat. "I'm marrying the Emir in two days."

The smile on Bhavya's lips wilts. There is a roaring in her ears.
She feels a flash of pain so intense that she half expects to find herself bleeding. "What? You said that you and the Emir don't have
that sort of relationship."

"We don't. We didn't." Fatima Ghazala's eyes are full of tears.

Bhavya considers. She can give in to the tantrum she feels simmering beneath her skin or she can gather what remains of her dignity. She chooses the latter and reminds herself that the rajkumari
of Qirat doesn't cry in public. She affixes a bright and obviously

false smile on her face. "I see. Should I say congratulations?" She laughs. Fatima Ghazala winces. "Congratulations. Thank you for letting me know." The smile still glittering on her lips, she turns around jerkily and walks all the way back to her room.

She feels like a fool. Did they laugh at her? Of course they must have. No . . . the Emir isn't even aware of her existence. How could he laugh at someone he doesn't know? She was the only one wearing her heart out for the entire world to see and mock. Would it hurt less if the Emir at least knew her name? Would it hurt more?

Bhavya becomes conscious of crying in the middle of a sob. What grieves her most, if she is honest, is not the Emir's wedding but what it means for her hope of escaping the fate her mother seems determined to consign her to. His marriage makes the bars of her impending prison more visible. If she had been the Emir's bride, she could have easily forged a new destiny for herself. A thousand different destinies.

The scent of jasmine reaches her, and Bhavya raises her head to see her sister-in-law looking at her with compassion in her eyes. Bhavya cries harder. Aruna slips her arms around Bhavya, holding her as she weeps.

The night before the wedding, the Alif family plus Fatima Ghazala eat an early dinner. After Maghrib, Asma Ammi and Adila lead Fatima Ghazala to the rooftop, which has been decorated with candles, diya, and shimmering dupatta. They have arranged a henna night for her. All the ladies in the building are invited, though none of them are explicitly told about the upcoming wedding. Some may have guessed, but all of them have tasted enough of life not to ask questions when celebrations are offered. Even Laali is having a rare lucid day. She is wrapped in blankets and placed in a chair with the women feeding her mithai and otherwise cosseting her.

Someone plays a dholak, and someone else sings. Someone dances while someone pretends to grab the stars from the sky and lay them at Fatima Ghazala's feet. Anu puts henna on Fatima Ghazala's hands and arms first and then on her feet up till just past her ankles. She makes intricate designs, delicate as filigree, and much later when Fatima Ghazala washes the henna off, she finds that rich orange red has bloomed underneath.

Asma Ammi does not allow the festivities to continue for too long so they're all in bed and asleep long before midnight arrives to bid them good night. When Fatima Ghazala's eyes open just before Fajr the next morning, she finds herself alone in the room she shares with the Alif sisters. The lamps are all alight. She can hear Ali Abbu reciting the Quran in the living room, the Alif sisters and Asma in the kitchen. She sits up and is rubbing her eyes when Adila walks into the room.

"Oh, you're finally up," her friend says. She has a pile of folded laundry in her hands. She pulls open a drawer from a chest in the corner of the room and starts fitting the clothes in.

"Adila," Fatima Ghazala says a bit anxiously.

"Hmm?" Adila replies without looking over.

"I'm getting married today, aren't I?" Fatima Ghazala whispers.

The eldest Alif turns. "Do you want to make a run for it? Just say the word."

Fatima Ghazala wonders if she dares. The idea is more than tempting when she thinks of the rajkumari's shattered face. But then she remembers her baba and her vow to him. She sighs and shakes her head. "No, I'll go through with it. I'll marry the Emir."

CHAPTER 28

Zulfikar stands on the marble steps of the entrance of Northern Aftab and breathes deep of the morning air. A peculiar sense of an ending fills him. It is not exactly a poignant feeling, just one akin to finishing a particularly lengthy book. The soft morning light infuses everything with a glow; the world at this moment is awash with possibilities.

He hears the sound of footsteps and turns to see Tali emerging from the mahal dressed in the white caftan and trousers she crossed over in. He walks over to her and greets her. He even manages a smile.

"She will never understand what it means to be Ifrit, you know," Tali says without preamble. It is obvious who she is talking about. And why.

"I will never understand what it means to be human," Zulfikar replies easily.

"I would have loved you. Made you happy."

"I know that," Zulfikar says. He knows he should leave things be at this point, but he cannot resist. "You were young back then, but so was I. Why didn't you tell me about your insecurities?"

"Would it have made a difference?" she asks.

"We will never know," Zulfikar replies. He doesn't feel regret. How can he? It is his wedding day. But that sense of ending resonates deeply.

"I am returning to Tayneeb, Zulfikar. I cannot remain here and witness you becoming someone else's," Tali says, her tone shifting to something more formal. "I will report to the Raees if she is able and to her advisors if she isn't. I sincerely hope the fire bond makes the Name Giver stronger. Do not forget the reason you are marrying her."

"I am not marrying her because of the Raees, Tali. I am using the Raees as a reason to marry her. There is a difference," Zulfikar corrects her, and the Ifrit woman flinches.

"I will be going now," she says brusquely.

"Safe travels, Tali," Zulfikar says as she begins to walk away.

She stops and speaks to him over her shoulder. "I cannot wish you happiness, Zulfikar, not when it comes at the expense of mine. Forgive me. I will not see you again." She walks away and Zulfikar watches as her form shimmers and disappears.

A little later, he walks over to the barracks, thinking to look in on the soldiers still abed. Those not on patrol duties have been invited to attend his wedding.

"Sayyid, should you not be preparing for the wedding?" a young soldier calls cheekily when Zulfikar enters the barracks.

Zulfikar gives him a mock glare before his smile slips out. "Has anyone seen the Wazir?"

"Not since yesterday, sayyid," a soldier named Hamid replies. "I saw him in Southern Noor late in the evening."

Late evening . . . so that means right after the Wazir confronted him. Zulfikar nods his thanks to the soldier, distracted by the memories of the previous day.

He had been rubbing his horse down just outside the stables when Anwar appeared out of nowhere. The older Ifrit had grasped him by the shoulder and pulled him around. The violence of his action had taken Zulfikar by surprise, and he had withdrawn his scimitar in response.

Anwar was breathing hard. "I hear you are getting married," he spat out when he regained a measure of control.

"I am," Zulfikar replied, much more coolly than the situation warranted.

"To my wife!" The Wazir's eyes bled orange. Zulfikar's grasp on his scimitar tightened.

"Ghazala bint Firdaus divorced you, Wazir. She was no longer your wife when she died, and before you protest, she *is* dead." Zulfikar's voice lowered. "Fatima Ghazala is not your wife. She has never been and never will be your wife."

"She has Ghazala's fire! By rights she belongs to me!"

"She is not a thing!" Zulfikar rarely raised his voice, but when he did, everyone took notice. "She is not an object to be claimed or owned. Do not make me tell you this again."

The Wazir stared at Zulfikar for a long moment without speaking. Then he released a breath, and his features eased into a somewhat artificial expression of sheepish affability. "Forgive my outburst. I have been searching for Ghazala ever since she disappeared. I still have the fire bond, you know. It didn't fade, so I thought she wasn't dead. I have spent years in this human world searching for her. Only to find that she gave her fire away to a human."

"Stop lying, Wazir. Your fire bond was removed when Ghazala won her petition for a divorce from you. The Raees removed both your bonds," Zulfikar said flatly. "It wouldn't be a divorce otherwise."

"I AM NOT LYING!" the older Ifrit screamed. His voice was thin and hysterical. Ifrit soldiers had poured out from the barracks, all of them poised to defend the Emir. The Wazir noticed them and calmed himself with some visible effort.

"I am sure you will understand if I don't stay for your wedding ceremony. Or offer you congratulations," the Wazir said. He turned around and left as swiftly as he had arrived. Only when Zulfikar was sure he was gone did he loosen his grip on his sword.

In the present, Zulfikar grins at the good-natured teasing from the soldiers. Anwar is a problem Zulfikar needs to solve. Especially if he expects Fatima Ghazala to live under the same roof as him. Maybe he will let the Raees do the honors. Anwar is, after all, her son.

He ducks out of the barracks to return to Aftab mahal. The clatter in the driveway warns him to hurry. The bride and her family have arrived.

Fatima Ghazala and her companions, the Alif sisters and Sunaina, stand in front of the bridal outfit provided by Achal Kaur. They are in a suite of rooms requisitioned for the express purpose of readying the bride for her nikah ceremony. Fatima Ghazala has showered and moisturized. The next step requires her to change into the bridal outfit—the outfit that she and her companions are staring at with various expressions of awe.

Achal Kaur has excellent but extravagant taste in clothes. The outfit she chose for Fatima Ghazala is a pale gold lehenga choli featuring extensive zardozi embroidery and stone work in gold and silver. The skirt flares slightly. The long sleeves of the choli are made of fine diaphanous material, as is the dupatta.

"Put it on," Azizah commands.

Fatima Ghazala is somewhat tempted to recant at this late hour but grits her teeth and puts on the outfit with some help from her companions. Then she is pricked and prodded. Sheer gold powder is spread all over her eyelids while rouge brightens her lips and cheeks. Her eyes are kohled; she is perfumed at her wrists, throat, and behind her ears. Her hair is tied up in a bun and accessorized with jewels.

Then the jewelry is piled on: a glittering matha patti, a nathni, earrings, gold bangles, rings, haars around her neck, gold anklets around her ankles, toe rings. As a final touch, the dupatta is placed on her head and fixed into place with a small arsenal of pins.

Fatima Ghazala looks at her reflection in the mirror and doesn't recognize herself. She has seen other brides dressed in the same splendor, and even thought that one day she would be among their ranks, but now that the moment has arrived, she is terrified. Is marrying the Emir the right thing to do? Would Firdaus want her to do this? She doesn't know. She doesn't even know what will happen to their marriage once the Raees has been Named.

Just as she is considering calling the entire thing off, a summons comes for the bride. It takes Fatima Ghazala a moment to realize that she is the one being called. Taking a deep breath, she gets to her feet, holds her head high, and pretends she isn't trembling.

The large airy hall has been partitioned into two sections by a purdah made of swathes of dupatta. A light breeze drifting in from doors leading outside in the men's section has the purdah fluttering. Fatima Ghazala stops to take in the absurd number of vases full of different kinds of flowers sitting on every available surface around the hall. She beams a thank-you at Azizah.

Her guests, though not many, straighten when they see her. Achal Kaur weeps busily while the maharani smiles brightly. Fatima Ghazala tries to peer through the purdah, but though the barrier is not as opaque as prescribed, she cannot see much through it. She sits down in a chair at the head of their little group and her companions arrange themselves around her. As soon as she is seated, the imam from Jama Masjid, here to officiate the marriage, starts speaking. He welcomes everyone to the wedding of the Emir of Noor City to Fatima Ghazala, daughter and sister. Immediately after, Ali Abbu and two witnesses come over to the women's section to ask the bride if she will accept Zulfikar as her husband.

Azizah gasps loudly when she sees the third witness. The young muezzin keeps his eyes cast down, though a smile lingers around his lips.

"Shh!" Adila hushes Azizah, giving her a look that quiets her immediately.

"Do you, Fatima Ghazala, daughter of Jagan and Sangeeta, sister of Sunaina, accept Zulfikar bin Daud as your husband with the maher set at one tune on the oud?" Ali asks Fatima Ghazala. Usually, the maher, an obligatory gift from the groom to the bride, is money or jewelry, but Fatima Ghazala has no need of those things.

"Let me hear the tune first," she says clearly.

There is a pause, and then from the other side of the purdah comes the sound of the oud. The three witnesses from the men's side try to maintain straight faces, but the Alif sisters do not even bother. Azizah is snickering while Adila has buried her face in her hands, though her shaking shoulders give away her mirth. Amirah has stuck her fingers into her ears. The Emir's oud playing is that atrocious. Fatima Ghazala, however, looks delighted.

Thankfully, the piece the Emir is butchering is a short one and over fairly quickly. Ali repeats his question.

"I do," Fatima Ghazala replies loudly. The question is repeated two more times, and Fatima Ghazala answers in the affirmative two more times.

The witnesses return and tell the imam the bride has accepted the groom.

After a short sermon in which he speaks about marriage and happiness, the imam asks the groom, three times, whether he accepts Fatima Ghazala as his wife. Fatima Ghazala hears Zulfikar accept her loudly three times.

Thus, they are married. The imam makes a short dua where he prays for the couple's happiness and leaves as he has another wedding to officiate. To Azizah's eternal sorrow, he takes Bilal with him.

The ceremony concluded, it is now time for celebration. The domestic staff is setting up food on tables lined near the entrance to the hall. The soldiers who attended the wedding fill their plates with food and return to the barracks. As the only people remaining are family, the purdah is pulled aside, and Fatima Ghazala gets her first glimpse of Zulfikar. He is dressed in a cream sherwani with a matching turban. His cheeks are a bit red, perhaps from playing her oud, which rests on the divan beside him. He is talking to Mansoor but pauses in his conversation as if he feels Fatima Ghazala's eyes on him. They look at each other. Fatima Ghazala feels her doubts rise to the surface.

Zulfikar gets to his feet without taking his eyes off her, clearly intent on coming to her side, but he is waylaid by Ali Abbu, who demands his attention. He is forced to postpone his plans, whatever they were, and entertain his guests. Fatima Ghazala is a bit relieved not to have to face Zulfikar just yet and surrenders herself to the attentions of her guests.

They feast, talk, and laugh until it is time for dessert. Azizah reveals her surprise for the newly married couple: two tables packed with a dizzying array of desserts. From laddoo to jalebiyaan to kunafe to halva to baklava, the table has them all; there is even a tray of beautiful wagashi. Zulfikar and Fatima Ghazala stare at the tables with stunned expressions before they both reach for the same piece of gulab jamun. Their fingers tangle, and they look at each other once again.

At this point, the maharani and the maharajah take their leave. Sunaina, too, says she has things to do but promises to come by and see Fatima Ghazala the next day. Achal Kaur's grandson arrives to take her home, and she offers to drop the Alif family home on the way. Ali Abbu grumbles about wanting to stay longer, but Asma Ammi bundles him out the door, barely giving him a chance to say goodbye. Fatima Ghazala clings to the Alif sisters before they, too, are gone and she is left, alone, with her new husband.

Husband. Fatima Ghazala sneaks a look at Zulfikar and finds him looking at her. Embarrassed, she whirls around, presenting him with her back.

"Hey," he protests. "Let me look at you."

Fatima Ghazala turns around warily. "A bit too much, isn't it? How do brides dress up in Al-Naar?" she asks.

"Similarly, I suppose. I didn't pay them much attention." He smiles at her. Fatima Ghazala swallows and turns away. It is not like she doesn't know him, so why does he feel like a stranger right now? Is it because their relationship has so obviously changed? What if she lets herself be persuaded by his sweetness? He is her husband, whatever that means. What if she gives in to her feelings? But what happens when the Raees is here and Zulfikar no longer needs her help with the Ifrit?

"The fire bonding ritual? Do we do that here?" Fatima Ghazala gestures to the empty hall around them. Zulfikar looks startled by the stiffness in her voice, and a perplexed expression settles on his face.

"No, the human servants are around, and while the ritual is no secret, I would rather not shock them with any displays of fire," he says a little formally. "Let's go up to our room."

Our room? Fatima Ghazala's eyes widen. She is going to share the same room as the Emir? She knows that normal couples do, but . . . are they a normal couple? Northern Aftab is full of empty rooms, so wouldn't it better if she had one of those? Fatima Ghazala is not sure she can endure sharing space with someone who is not her sister or the Alifs. Zulfikar notices her hesitation.

"Do you not want to share a room, Fatima Ghazala?" he asks softly.

Fatima Ghazala looks at him and takes a deep breath, wishing she could stop being nervous. "Can I ask you something?"

"Anything," Zulfikar replies.

"We didn't get married because we love each other. Will our marriage, our relationship, be a true one?" Fatima Ghazala keeps her eyes downcast. Her face is hot as she asks her questions.

"Do you want it to be a true one?" Zulfikar asks in return. "I do, of course I do, but if you don't, I will respect your wishes."

"How do you know if it is truly what *you* want and not what the bond you have with my fire wants?"

"I don't," Zulfikar admits. "I no longer care. Our marriage does not have a time limit. I won't abandon you when the Raees gets here or petition her to dissolve the fire bond. You are the only one I want."

Fatima Ghazala abruptly feels too hot. If she blushes any more, she is going to catch fire. "All right. Stop. My heart can't take much more of your words, Zulfikar," she says, and his lips quirk. "I am willing to give this . . . us . . . a chance."

Zulfikar moves toward her then, his intention obvious on his face. Her pulls her into his arms and crushes her to him, jewelry and all. "Thank you."

"It is too early to thank me. I have never even been in a relationship, and I suddenly have a husband. You will have reason to regret in the coming days, I am sure." Fatima Ghazala's voice is muffled, squashed as she is against his chest. She pushes away from him. "Let's go up to . . . our room?"

Zulfikar leads her up the fifth floor, where the rooms he uses are located. Fatima Ghazala has seen his room, though she didn't enter it the last time she was there. Zulfikar pulls her over the threshold and closes the door behind them. Fatima Ghazala looks around. The door leads into a sitting room, which leads into the bedroom. A gauzy curtain separates the living room from the bedroom. She moves into the bedroom and is enchanted immediately by the attached balcony. Two closed doors connect other rooms to the bedroom. One of them, Fatima Ghazala is sure, is the bathroom but the other one is a mystery. Zulfikar's presence is dominant here. His books, his clothes, his scent. Fatima Ghazala wonders if, as the days pass, the room will come to reflect her existence as well.

"Will this suffice?" Zulfikar asks, more self-consciously than Fatima Ghazala expected him to. She nods and his face eases into a pleased smile.

"Let's do the fire bond ritual now," she says. She wants to get it over and done with. Mostly so, if she is honest with herself, she can change her clothes. Fatima Ghazala wonders where her belongings are. She looks around the room once more but cannot see them.

Zulfikar and Fatima Ghazala stand in the middle of the room, facing each other.

"Hold up your hands as if in prayer," Zulfikar instructs. Fatima Ghazala complies. Flames appear in his hands. He pours the flames into Fatima Ghazala's cupped hands. She braces herself, but Zulfikar's fire doesn't burn her. "Breathe it in," he says, and once again Fatima Ghazala complies. Zulfikar's fire prickles inside her. She feels the moment his fire comes in contact with hers. Feels the moment it bonds with hers.

Her consciousness expands to include the Emir. She can feel his heart racing. She can feel his desire, a fever simmering under her skin. Fatima Ghazala stumbles, assailed by emotions, both his and hers. Zulfikar doesn't move to help her though she can feel him wanting to.

"It will be worse if I touch you right now," he says. He retreats from her to sit in a chair across the room, though his eyes do not leave her for a second. Fatima Ghazala shudders. Even his gaze feels like a caress. Abruptly her eyes fill with tears. If this is how he felt when her fire bonded with his, how could he resist wanting her? His desire is false, called into existence by that bond. His love is false. Fatima Ghazala looks at him, sitting still, cognizant of the conflict within her. He doesn't say a word, but then, he no longer needs to. She can feel his anxiety, trembling like butterfly wings against her skin, his fear that she'll turn him away. She should. She should set boundaries, protect her heart, but how can she? How can she deny herself his heat?

She doesn't want to. The admission costs her, and Fatima Ghazala ducks her head, wanting to escape Zulfikar's gaze. This bond makes her feel both strong and vulnerable. Her fire feels fuller; it echoes the strength of Zulfikar's fire. She doesn't want him to know that the bond he didn't want is one she welcomes. While his feelings are constructed of Djinn fire and magic, hers were born through conversation and curiosity.

"I would like to change clothes," she tells him, deliberately changing the subject.

Zulfikar gets to his feet uncertainly. He can sense her emotions, but he can't read her mind. "Your dressing room," he says, opening one of the closed doors.

Fatima Ghazala follows him into the room and is taken aback at the opulence of the clothes neatly arranged in there. One side has the Emir's clothes, the other hers. A vanity table with a mirror leans against one wall and a sideboard full of jewelry occupies the middle.

"This . . . ?" Fatima Ghazala looks at Zulfikar.

"Your friend Azizah told me you needed a new wardrobe to suit your new status." He grins slightly. "She said you couldn't be trusted to get your own clothes, so she got them for you."

"Ah." Fatima Ghazala reminds herself to thank the younger girl even though she had gone overboard with her purchases. She chooses a relatively simple shalwar kameez made of soft pale green cotton to change into, then makes the unwelcome discovery that she will need help to get out of her wedding outfit. She looks at Zulfikar, who is looking at her expectantly, having discerned her conundrum.

"Will you help me?" she asks, her cheeks hot.

"Turn around." Zulfikar helps her remove her dupatta first, all the pins accumulating in a little ceramic bowl on the vanity table. The jewelry comes off next. He catches her hennaed hands in his and makes an expression of pleasure at the intricate designs. Then he turns her around again and unfastens the hooks holding her choli together. His fingers are cool against her bare skin.

"You can do the rest," he says, just a bit hoarsely. Fatima Ghazala turns to him, sure her heart is going to explode.

Their gazes collide. She thinks of something to say, but before she can, he leans down and captures her lips with his. His lips are soft, and the kiss initially gentle. She slips her arms around his neck, wanting more. Zulfikar coaxes her lips open and deepens the kiss. Fatima Ghazala squeezes her eyes shut and concentrates on the kiss, the slide of his tongue against hers, the sweetness and the bite of his fire. She is breathing hard when he finally lifts his head, her hands clutching his shirt.

Before she can react, he kisses her again. A shorter kiss, no less intense for its brevity, before he pulls away reluctantly. He caresses her cheek once before leaving the room.

CHAPTER 29

The Emir doesn't get a day off, not even on his wedding day. His presence is required at the merchant guild for a meeting that stretches well into the afternoon. After that he has to go broker peace between two Bedouin clans who both want the other to stop trading with Noor City. It's a delicate and lengthy process requiring multiple cups of hot, sweet cardamom-flavored tea and nutty baklava as they talk around a fire pit just outside the northern city gates. By the time Zulfikar returns to Northern Aftab, the clock hands have crept past ten in their pursuit of midnight. He walks up the many stairs, wondering if Fatima Ghazala is angry with him for being late, wondering what she will make him do before she forgives him. Mostly, he is wondering if he can coax more kisses from her.

Zulfikar lets himself into the room quietly. Two candles burn on the table by the bed; the rest of the room is dark. He moves to the bed, and there she is, sleeping deeply, with her arms around a pillow. Her hair is unbound; it is the second time Zulfikar has seen it this way, and unable to help himself, he picks up a lock of her hair. She stirs at his touch, and her eyes open. She sits up. Their eyes meet. She smiles at him. Zulfikar surrenders to himself and kisses her. He cups her face with his hands and loses himself to her taste. She touches him cautiously; he feels her fingers skim his face as if scared to touch him properly, so he catches hold of her hand and kisses each finger, assuring her of her right to him.

"I'm sorry I'm late," he says softly.

"You don't have to apologize. I understand that you have a lot to do as the Emir," she says, her voice colored with sleep. "Have you eaten?"

Before Zulfikar can reply, a knock sounds on their door: an unwelcome and insistent sound. Zulfikar looks down at Fatima Ghazala's face, soft in the candlelight, and kisses the tip of her nose before leaving to see who would dare disturb the Emir on his wedding night.

Mansoor is at the door with an apologetic look on his face. Zulfikar knows before he speaks what the soldier's words are going to be. He hears him through and closes the door, wishing he could bar it against the world. But alas, he can't. He returns to his bride to find her waiting for the news with a pensive look on her face.

"The Raees demands to cross over now. She doesn't know if she can resist the taint much longer. It's no longer safe for her to be in Tayneeb. If she loses control, she will lay waste to the city," Zulfikar says. He hates the thought of asking her to risk herself in this way. But there is no other choice left to him. How can he justify his selfishness when his people, his very world, is at risk? Fatima Ghazala must sense the conflict within him because she lays a hand on his arm.

"You do not need to feel responsible for any of this, Zulfikar. I gave my word to my baba that I will do what it takes for his story to continue. I would Name the Raees whether you were here or not," she says. "More importantly, do you think the bond will have affected my fire already?" Fatima Ghazala gets up from the bed and disappears into the dressing room, leaving the door open so they can converse.

"I don't know," Zulfikar says, hating that he doesn't.

She is silent; he can feel her thinking. She's not scared—no, that's the wrong word. She is resigned. She appears in the doorway of the dressing room, dressed in a long-sleeved purple tunic and matching shalwar, a pale yellow dupatta around her head.

"This is not something I can walk away from so whether I face it now or a week from now makes little difference. And, if this doesn't end well, maybe it *will* make a difference? I don't know. The point is, we don't have a choice." She smiles slightly, and Zulfikar is tempted to flee into the night with her, leaving behind both their responsibilities. She must have read his thoughts because her smile deepens into a grin.

"Fatima Ghazala, I . . ." Zulfikar starts to say but trails off. What can he say? How can he reassure her of his love when he isn't sure of it himself?

"It is all right. I understand," she tells him, straightening her shoulders. "Let's go."

No clouds obstruct the night sky, which is crushed full of stars gathered, Fatima Ghazala tells herself, to see her succeed. Or fail. The stars aren't very particular as long as they get to witness a spectacle. She walks beside Zulfikar silently. They stopped by the kitchen before continuing to the fire pit behind the barracks. Fatima Ghazala indulged in a plate full of leftover wedding mithai. The sugar helps.

It is almost midnight. Three Ifrit soldiers, including Mansoor, stand on the far side of the fire pit. Their faces, lit by the flames, paint them as the otherworldly beings they are.

Fatima Ghazala turns to Zulfikar. "I need to do this alone."

His lips part to protest, but he stops before speaking. He nods once and moves to stand with the soldiers. Not that the distance between them makes any difference. She can feel his presence through the fire bond. What will happen to Zulfikar, Fatima Ghazala wonders, if she does not make it through this Naming? Widowed on his wedding day. How will death feel? Her palms are slick with salt. If only Firdaus were here, she wouldn't need to be.

Without hesitating any longer, Fatima Ghazala sends a quick prayer to the Creator and opens her mind to possibilities and infinities. She is ready when the tickle in her mind announces the Raees's presence and turns to face the tall column of smokeless fire. Her heart thunders at the sight, and fear almost steals the ground from her feet. Then she feels Zulfikar's fire tug at hers, and suddenly he is next to her, if not in flesh then in mind. His strength bolsters hers.

Fatima Ghazala walks closer to the column of fire and plunges both hands into its depths without giving herself time to consider the fallacies of her actions. The heat hits her immediately, and she feels her fire resist, barely, the urge to burn. She tries to coax the pieces of the Raees's name to her, but they resist too. For a moment, she despairs, but then a sudden and strange knowing, a power both old and new, fills her. Zulfikar's fire gives hers the strength it was lacking. She commands the pieces of the Name to her, and they, newly biddable, obey.

The Raees's Name is in five pieces, and all of these are almost entirely covered by the same slimy black substance that the Shayateen Names Fatima Ghazala saw in the desert were covered with. She grabs one piece, illegible for the taint covering it. In her hands, the blackness changes texture and flakes off. Fatima Ghazala cleans the pieces as much as she can. She works quickly, aware that the heat may consume her before she can finish. The Raees's memories are complex and fascinating, but Fatima Ghazala cannot afford to linger; she is almost past the point of her endurance. Mostly clean, the pieces read mother, leader, honor, pride, and family. Together, these pieces form the Name Zafirah. Fatima Ghazala takes this Name, rises on her toes, and pushes it into the region of the heart in the column of the smokeless fire. Done, she retreats three steps and becomes aware of the excruciating pain in her burnt and blistered hands. The pain is a relief; it reassures her that she is still alive.

Someone's eyes are on her. When she looks up, she sees an Ifrit woman where the column of smokeless fire used to be. The Ifrit woman has a thin face and a glowering expression. Fatima Ghazala is thinking that the Raees would look much better with a smile, when the stars blink out and her world goes dark.

CHAPTER 30

*T*he walls of Bhavya's room are a cocoon, keeping her safe from those who have been waiting to cut her down. Bhavya thinks about Ruchika, who must be beside herself with glee at the fool the rajkumari turned out to be. She is curled up on a chair on her balcony, sipping extra-sweet chai and looking out at the view of Southern Noor gleaming in the afternoon sunshine. Her hair hasn't seen a comb in three days, and she is wearing the same shalwar kameez the second day in a row. All the mirrors in her rooms have been covered with a sheet. Bhavya refuses to look at any reflective surface.

She leans back in her chair with a sigh and wonders how many other walls exist in her future. Pleading illness, she has stayed in her room since that meeting with Fatima Ghazala, but Bhavya knows she will have to face people eventually. How should she behave when she does? Should she act unaffected or mournful? Does it matter how she behaves? Everyone will laugh at her anyway.

A knock on the door makes her stiffen. Her maid bustles into her bedroom a moment later to tell her she has a visitor. Bhavya is about to tell her to send whoever it is away, when her maid tells her the identity of her visitor. Bhavya stands up frowning and moves into the attached sitting room to greet Sunaina.

The cosmetics chemist is standing, ill at ease, in the middle of the room. Bhavya gestures for her to sit and takes a seat opposite her.

"What is it?" she asks bluntly, in no mood for niceties.

"Am I being relieved of my position?" Sunaina asks with equal frankness.

"What makes you say that?" Surely the woman doesn't think Bhavya is so petty that she'll fire her just because her sister married the Emir.

"I have heard things . . ." Sunaina trails off, looking uncomfortable.

"What things? From whom? Where?" Bhavya leans forward, abruptly furious. Has she already become a laughingstock? Are people laughing at her in the open?

"From the servants. In the kitchen. In the corridor in front of my room. They talk without worrying about being overheard." Sunaina hesitates. "They said you are getting married."

"What? To whom?" Bhavya demands.

"Someone named Sundar Singh." Sunaina meets her eyes. "Is that true?"

Sundar Singh. The name sounds familiar. Bhavya thinks for a second until a leering face with an abrasive personality attaches itself to the name. One of Aaruv's friends. Bhavya's looks at Sunaina in horror.

"What is it, sahiba?" Sunaina asks gently.

"They must be arranging my marriage—" Panic steals her breath, and Bhavya gasps. "My bua. My mother."

"Calm down," Sunaina says, moving to sit beside her.

"How?" Bhavya flails. Sunaina grabs her hands and holds them. "I can't marry him. I won't!" Bahvya's cheeks are wet.

Bhavya's maid enters the room, looking apologetic. "The Rajmata is calling for you."

Bhavya stills at the maid's words. She stands up slowly. Surely there is some sort of misunderstanding. Her mother wouldn't arrange her wedding without talking to her about it. Surely not. She turns to Sunaina. "Will you help me get ready?"

The woman nods.

Twenty minutes later, Bhavya makes her way to a meeting room on the third floor of Southern Aftab. From her maid, she learned that the Rajmata summoned the entire family, apart from Aaruv, who has gone hunting with his friends. Her composure is a shaky thing, and every time Bhavya speculates about the reason for the summons, tears threaten. When Bhavya reaches the room, she finds the rest of her family already there. Aarush and Aruna sit on one side on a settee and the Rajmata and Jayanti Bua on the other. She wonders when Jayanti Bua turned into her mother's closest confidante.

"Have a seat, Bhavya," the Rajmata says abruptly. "I have something to say."

Bhavya sits beside Aruna and Aarush and trembles.

"You have been the subject of a lot of gossip these past few days. I have come to realize that I was too lenient with you and excused your infatuation with the Emir as I ought not to have." The Rajmata pauses, and Bhavya holds her breath. "Rathod Singh of Khair brought a rishta for you. I have decided to accept it. His son's name is Sundar Singh," she adds as an afterthought.

For a second, Bhavya stares at her mother. Then the enormity of her mother's words slams into her, and she jumps to her feet to scream and protest. But Aruna catches her hand and shakes her head. Bhavya looks at her brother; he nods.

"Tell me, Amma, is this the same Rathod who begged me for mercy the other day?" Aarush asks more politely than Bhavya would have managed in the same situation. She sits beside Aruna, trying to stay quiet, trying to stay within the boundaries drawn for her.

"They are a moneyed family. Their lineage is exemplary. Sundar

Singh will make a fine husband," the Rajmata says a bit defensively. Is that all it takes to sell a daughter? Money and lineage?

"Has it not occurred to you that she may be mistreated, being the sister of the maharajah who cast aspersions on the honor of the patriarch of their family?" Aarush continues in the same polite tone. "Or is she to be a guarantee that their future sins will go unpunished? For surely the maharajah won't punish his sister's husband's family."

"I have been assured that they will treat Bhavya like a queen!"

"And who exactly has been reassuring you?" Aarush looks at his aunt, and the woman pales. "Listen, Amma, I will not marry my sister to the son of a man who moves so blatantly against the raj. I will not foist an unwanted husband on my sister."

"She is a rajkumari of Qirat. Marrying who she is told to is her duty!" Her mother says once more what Bhavya has been hearing all her life.

"What alliances are you making with Rathod that you need to solidify the bond by selling your daughter to him as security?" Aarush asks, and everyone in the room freezes.

"How dare you?" The Rajmata's voice is shrill.

"I am the maharajah, Amma. I dare much," Aarush says softly.

"I am your mother!" the Rajmata says, rising to her feet furiously. "I only want what's good for my children."

"So you keep saying, Amma, and yet you continue letting both Bhavya and me down with your refusal to see the true colors of the people you surround yourself with." Aarush is angrier than Bhavya has ever seen him. "I will say this again for the very last time: I will not condemn my sister to a life of misery. She will not be used as a pawn in any game." He gets to his feet. "Let's go, Bhavya. Aruna." Without another word he walks away. Bhavya follows him, not daring to look back.

CHAPTER 31

The night brings with it a false sense of peace. Quiet settles in the corners where the lamps have been extinguished. The inhabitants of Southern Aftab, the royalty, and the people who tend to them have all slipped into bed either alone or with a beloved. Everyone, that is, apart from the maharajah, who wishes for nothing more than the warm comfort of his wife in bed. Unfortunately, he has to sit in his well-lit office on the fourth floor and read a report that illustrates, in detail, just how much of a complacent fool he has been. When Janab Jamshid handed him the report hours earlier, his demeanor had been subdued but nothing that indicated the explosive nature of the words in the report.

Heeding his oldest advisor, Aarush had hired independent investigators to ferret out the identities of those behind the propaganda currently inciting hatred between the Qirati and their Ifrit saviors. The investigators uncovered a conspiracy that Aarush would never have considered possible. He has been a fool, thinking that a fair king would mean a peaceful rule. He has trusted the wrong people, been betrayed in the cruelest ways. Aarush gets up from his desk and burns the report on the silver tray until all that remains of it are ashes. He doesn't yet know what to do, so he must keep up all appearances of ignorance.

A step outside his door has him stiffening; his hand goes to his sword. Someone knocks on his door before pushing it open. It is his younger brother. Aarush's hand doesn't move from his sword.

"I have been sent to call for a truce between you and Amma, Bhaiya." Aaruv leans against the doorframe.

"What terms does she offer?"

"You let her go ahead with Bhavya's wedding and she will forget that you ever tried to go against her," Aaruv recites.

"Rejected," Aarush says tightly. His mother thinks that's a compromise?

"Come on, Bhai, do you really want to feud with Amma over Bhavya?" Aaruv's tone suggests that the idea is preposterous.

"The fact that you have to ask me this is ridiculous," Aarush snaps. "Bhavya is my responsibility. Baba and Bhai left her protection to me. I will do my duty even if it means going against the whole world to do it."

"She needs to get married. Why not to Sundar?"

"I didn't realize Sundar Singh is such a close friend of yours, Aaruv." Aarush looks at his brother. "A woman does not *have* to get married, and if she does, she has the right to choose who she wants to spend her life with. I know that some men are in the habit of using women as objects to be traded or as a mode of currency. I am not one of them." Aarush smiles. "Baba taught me better than that."

Aaruv flushes at the veiled insult.

"I do find it strange," Aarush continues, "that for all this talk of matrimony, neither Amma nor you has mentioned your upcoming nuptials to Sanchit Goundar's daughter. I had to find out from the pundit."

"I . . . It's still being planned," Aaruv flounders.

"And is my opinion worth so little that you wouldn't ask for it? I am your brother, Aaruv." The hurt Aarush feels is intense, and a smidgen of it escapes in his words. His brother looks surprised and opens his mouth to say something, but Aarush doesn't give him a chance. "Do you want to be maharajah, Aaruv?"

The younger man's eyes widen. "What are you saying, Bhai?"

"What would you do differently from me?" Aarush keeps his tone casual.

His brother frowns. "I would break the deal with the Ifrit and ask them to return Qirat to us. If asking failed, I would go to war and reclaim what is ours."

"What guarantee do you have of success? Hm, all right, let's say you are successful and the Ifrit are defeated, what about the lives lost in the process of reclaiming Qirat? How are you going to answer for them?" Aarush watches his brother frown. "Once the Ifrit protection has been removed, how do you propose to protect Qirat from invasion by the Angrez? Our armies are far less able compared to theirs."

His brother swallows, and Aarush feels a surge of satisfaction. "No answers for me? I guess that's why I am the maharajah and you aren't." Aarush gestures to the door in clear dismissal. Aaruv, fairly quivering with anger, turns on his heel and is gone.

A piercing hunger wakes Fatima Ghazala. She sits up gingerly, conscious of a bone-deep weariness and the now-familiar remnants of the nightmare that are the memories stored in her fire. She is in an unfamiliar bed in an unfamiliar room. Ah, Zulfikar's—no, *her* new room that she just happens to share with the Emir. Her hunger will not be denied, so she tries to get out of bed but her body is unwilling to cooperate. She sits back down when her legs refuse to support her. Her hands are swathed in bandages, and her skin feels scorched like she got entirely too close to an inferno.

Fatima Ghazala considers her options. She is not used to feeling so helpless, so weak. She thinks about Zulfikar and feels, curiously, along the bond, wondering where he is and what is happening with the Raees. How long has she been asleep? Frustrated, Fatima

Ghazala yanks along the bond, wishing she could magic the Emir in front of her. Much to her surprise, she feels his response to her mental yanking. She feels his worry and his relief when he realizes her presence.

Not ten minutes have passed when the door flies open. Zulfikar comes stalking in. He is breathing hard, his eyes are bloodshot, and he looks more bedraggled than Fatima Ghazala has ever seen him. He is looking at her as though for the very first time. A few seconds later, he strides forward, sits on the bed, and wraps his arms around her, holding her tightly. Fatima Ghazala can feel his heart pounding. He kisses the hollow of her neck, and she breathes in sharply. She slips her arms around him and hugs him back, cautiously, before trying to pull away.

"Wait," Zulfikar says, his arms tightening. "Open your mind to me."

"What?" Fatima Ghazala wonders if she heard wrong.

"Open your mind, your consciousness, to me," Zulfikar replies. "Please?"

It is the "please" that does it. Plus, she doesn't have the strength to resist. Fatima Ghazala rests her head on Zulfikar's shoulder and empties her mind, letting thoughts of the Emir fill her. A moment later, she breathes in and a feeling of well-being fills her. Underneath the bandages, her hands seem to heal, and the weariness in her bones fades. Fatima Ghazala pulls away from the Emir.

"What did you do to me?" she demands.

Zulfikar's arms remain loosely around her, as if he can't bear to let go. "I shared my strength with you. The Raees taught me how. It is one of the advantages of being bonded."

"Ah. Thank you." Fatima Ghazala ducks her head, suddenly aware of how close they are to each other. Her heart is racing, and her cheeks are warm. She reminds herself that it is not the time to act like a shy maiden. "How is the Raees? How long have I been asleep? I'm hungry."

Zulfikar tucks a curl of her hair behind her ear and answers, "She is far better than any of us expected. Did you do something to the taint? She says she feels like she can breathe easily for the first time in months."

"I cleaned her Name somewhat. Not entirely, mind you. I wonder if I can clean her Name completely. Maybe I can try."

"First you need to recover. You've been sleeping for two days. The Ifrit healer said you may not wake up. Your body almost failed you during the Naming." There are shadows under his eyes. "I called for food."

Fatima Ghazala frowns. Zulfikar is working hard to remain cheerful, but there is something worrying him. She can *feel* his anxiety nibbling on his thoughts. "What is the matter, Zulfikar?" When she sees that he will dismiss her question, she interrupts him, "I know you are not telling me something."

The Emir looks reluctant but finally confesses, "Shayateen were sighted at the northern gates. We are currently searching for them."

The world falls away at his words, and Fatima Ghazala is on her feet ready to rush away. She needs to collect her family: the Alifs, Sunaina, Achal Kaur, Laali. She needs to keep them safe. What if the screaming begins again? What will she do?

"Listen to me!" Zulfikar grabs her shoulders, and with a start, Fatima Ghazala realizes he has been talking to her. "We are looking for them. The Shayateen may—"

A knock on the door interrupts Zulfikar, and he immediately moves to answer it. A moment later, he returns to the bedroom. "They have picked up the trail. I need to go. I have posted extra guards around the mahal, so please, habibti, be safe." He presses a kiss on her lips and is gone.

Fatima Ghazala, with help from a maid, takes the bandages off her hands. She finds her burns healed though her skin is tender. She looks down at the scars on her hands and wonders how she will explain them to her family. After a meal and a shower, she makes up the prayers she has missed. Finally, there is nothing left to do but greet the thin-faced Raees she Named two days ago. She makes her way to the west wing on the second floor of the Northern Aftab, where the Raees is staying. The mahal is oddly silent; none of the domestic staff sing as they clean. The few maids she does see are walking with their heads lowered. Fatima Ghazala knocks on the closed door to the Raees's rooms, and a gruff voice bids her enter. Before she can pull the door open, though, someone screams her name from the entrance of the mahal. Fatima Ghazala turns around and runs to the staircase that leads to the first floor. She knows this voice.

Azizah, with her dupatta missing, her face ravaged by tearstains, is standing at the entrance, trembling violently. Fatima Ghazala runs to her and hears the sentence the youngest Alif is repeating.

"They killed Laali."

CHAPTER 32

Fatima Ghazala reaches out and grabs Azizah's hand. The youngest Alif takes a shuddering breath. "Azizah, meethi, I'm here. Tell me what has happened."

Between sobs, Azizah relates the events that have led her to Northern Aftab. A few hours ago, Adila took Laali her lunch and was sitting with her while she ate. When Adila didn't return in an hour, Azizah, who was waiting for her, went to look for her. She found Laali on the floor, dead, and Adila bleeding beside her. Fatima Ghazala listens to Azizah without speaking, afraid that if she speaks, she will fall apart, and if she falls apart, she will be in too many pieces to ever be whole again. She cannot fall apart. Not just yet.

"Here is what we will do," Fatima Ghazala says, holding on tight to Azizah's hand. "I will call the best healer in the city for Adila. She will be all right." No other alternative is acceptable. Fatima Ghazala beckons to a maid and asks her to take a message to Sunaina. She sends an Ifrit soldier hovering nearby to bring a healer to the Taaj Gul apartment building with as much haste as possible. After her sister, pale and shocked, arrives ten minutes later, they pile into a carriage that conveys them to Taaj Gul. Fatima Ghazala doesn't speak; she's not certain she can. She has retreated into that deepest part of herself, where all emotions are filtered through her thickest defenses. The distance allows her calm. It gives her sanity.

It takes them three-quarters of an hour to reach Taaj Gul. A small crowd of people are gathered outside the apartment building. They move toward the entrance of the building followed by three Ifrit soldiers who seem to be Fatima Ghazala's personal guards. At the entrance, Fatima Ghazala suddenly falters. Fear, like a hurricane, threatens to sweep her off her feet and blow her off course. Sunaina, perhaps sensing this, grips her arm tighter, and Azizah squeezes her hand.

In the foyer, Azizah averts her eyes from the corridor leading to Laali's room and tells them that she'll wait for them upstairs. Sunaina and Fatima Ghazala are left frozen in the corridor, which is suddenly teeming with Ifrit soldiers. Fatima Ghazala gathers all her courage and moves toward the room, only to stop short when Zulfikar emerges from within it.

He walks over. "I just sent a soldier with a message."

"Azizah came to get me," Fatima Ghazala replies. Her voice seems to come from far away. "Can we see Laali?"

Fatima Ghazala meets the Emir's eyes and sees the compassion in them. She grips her sister's hand tighter, aware of a rending deep within her.

"Come this way," Zulfikar says, leading them to the room.

Fatima Ghazala and Sunaina walk forward, almost as one. They pause at the door before going in. Laali's room is in shambles: the windows are damaged, the furniture destroyed. Blood splatters the wall. Laali, sweet Laali, on the floor. Broken. Her frail body still, a slash across her face. Fatima Ghazala hears someone keening, then realizes the sound is coming from her. The pain seems too big for her body. Sunaina gathers her in her arms. All at once they are back in that moment eight years ago, trying to identify their parents' bodies. The sight of the blood, the smell of the blood, the same broken song once again.

A minute later, when she is able to breathe without sobbing, she turns to Zulfikar. "Who did this to Laali? Why? Was it the Shayateen? Were they the ones who killed Laali?"

The Emir takes a deep breath. "From her wounds, it seems likely. We are waiting to question Adila."

Fatima Ghazala remembers her friend, and she stumbles. Zulfikar catches her arm and pulls her to stand beside him. "Don't panic, habibti. She is not as badly hurt as we feared, though she has yet to regain consciousness."

"Didi . . ." Fatima Ghazala pauses and swallows. She is so afraid to see Adila. What will she do if another person is taken away from her?

"Let's go see her now." Her sister takes her hand.

The door to the Alif apartment is open, and Ali Abbu is standing outside it talking to a woman Fatima Ghazala doesn't recognize. They look up as she and Sunaina approach. Ali Abbu's face is gray with anxiety, though he still manages a smile when he sees them. Fatima Ghazala greets him and the woman who can only be the healer.

"How is she?" Sunaina asks for both of them.

"Her wounds are not serious. The cuts have not affected any of her internal organs, though I imagine the pain is intense. With rest and a lot of care, along with good nutrition, your sister should recover completely." The healer smiles gently at them.

"Your payment," Ali Abbu begins.

"The Emir took care of the compensation, sahib. Do not worry. Be with your daughters. I will be back tomorrow morning." The healer excuses herself.

"Thank you for coming, Sunaina," Ali says. "Come along, Fatima Ghazala, the girls will be happy to see you."

The atmosphere inside the apartment is subdued. Fatima Ghazala breaks away from the other two and makes her way to the room at the end of the corridor. Asma Ammi, Azizah, and Amirah are standing at the door. They pull Fatima Ghazala into an embrace before they let her into the room. Adila is lying on a futon, her skin ashen and her eyes closed. Fatima Ghazala sits down on the floor beside the futon and picks up Adila's hand; it is warm to the touch.

Fatima Ghazala does not know how much time passes. She is not aware of Sunaina looking in or the Alif family bringing her food or coming by frequently to simply check in on them. Even Zulfikar is there once though all he does is look in. The only time Fatima Ghazala rouses is in response to the azaan. She prays for Adila, for mercy, and for hope.

The day submits to the night. The stars parlay with the sky. Lamps are lit, concerned neighbors drop by with food and affection. Finally, Adila's fingers twitch. Fatima Ghazala waits, hardly daring to hope. Adila's eyes snap open, and she screams, a sound of pure panic. Everyone in the apartment rushes to the room, reassuring her of her safety. Adila looks around the room, her eyes stopping on each face, as if evaluating their well-being and reassuring herself of their continued existence.

"Laali," she says, closing her eyes and lying back in exhaustion. Helpless tears escape her. "They killed Laali."

"Call the Emir," Ali suddenly says. Fatima Ghazala starts, surprised. She thought Zulfikar had left. "He will want to know who the perpetrators are."

Zulfikar arrives and is shown into the room once again. He kneels beside the futon. "Please tell me everything you can remember," he asks Adila gently.

She opens her eyes and looks at him, her eyes fierce. "They appeared suddenly. Opened the door and entered as if they had all the right to. Two of them, male, so beautiful. Yet there was no life in their eyes, no whites, just black. They called Laali an abomination, a Si'lat mongrel. I moved to defend her, but the one with the knife"—Adila swallows—"he would have killed me, but the other one said they would be discovered if they lingered. So they left. I tried to scream, but I couldn't. I tried to help Laali, but I couldn't. I . . ." Adila cries.

Zulfikar narrows his eyes, his jaw tense. "Thank you, sayyida. Please rest. I apologize for my failure in keeping you and the elder safe." He gets to his feet and leaves the room. Fatima Ghazala squeezes Adila's hand and follows Zulfikar out.

He leads them into the empty living room. "Shayateen?" Fatima Ghazala asks, her heart noisy.

Zulfikar nods, looking frustrated. "I don't know how they could simply waltz in without regard for the danger they put themselves in. The Shayateen are usually not this foolhardy."

Fatima Ghazala wraps her arms around herself. She feels ill. Her earlier strength is a thing of the past. "Are you well, Fatima Ghazala?" Zulfikar asks, his voice gentle.

She shakes her head, almost crying again. "Come home with me," he says.

"I need to stay here." How can she leave her family now? "I will be all right."

"Go with him, beta," Asma says from the entrance to the living room. Her eyes are tired, and new lines have embroidered today's experiences on her face. "Adila may be the wounded one, but it is you who looks sick and"—she gives Zulfikar a narrow look—"I will find out why as soon as I can."

"Ammi," Fatima Ghazala says in protest.

"Tomorrow is Laali's funeral. It will demand a lot from you.

Stay over tomorrow if you have to, but go home today." Asma Ammi leaves, confident of obedience.

While Zulfikar waits for her downstairs, Fatima Ghazala finds Sunaina at a neighbor's apartment to tell her that she is returning to Aftab Mahal for the night. To her surprise, Sunaina gives her an unexpected hug. "The Emir told me you were ill when I came to see you the day after the wedding. What's going on?"

"Didi . . ." Fatima Ghazala's eyes fill with tears.

"You can't tell me?" Her usually stoic sister is weeping silently. "Please look after yourself. What will I do if something happens to you?"

Fatima Ghazala clings to her sister for a minute. Sunaina is the first to pull away.

"The soldiers have released Laali's body. I'll stay with the Alifs tonight. Anu and the others will help me prepare Laali for the funeral." Sunaina pats Fatima Ghazala's cheeks.

"I will help too."

"No, Fatima, it is not yet your turn to do these things. Go. I will see you tomorrow early."

Fatima Ghazala looks in on Adila; she's sleeping more peacefully than before. After assuring Azizah and Amirah that she'll be back the next day, she makes her way downstairs to where Zulfikar is waiting.

They don't talk as Zulfikar mounts his horse and pulls Fatima Ghazala up in front of him. She leans against him, savoring his warmth. The city is still full of life, still full of beauty, but all Fatima Ghazala can see is the cruelty inherent in the actions that stole Laali. Laali who was in the gloaming of her life anyway.

By the time they reach the mahal, Fatima Ghazala has a raging headache and all she wants to do is crawl into bed. But the day isn't over. As soon as they step inside, an Amir soldier standing guard at the bottom of the staircase tells them that the Raees has commanded their presence as soon as they return. So they make their way to the Raees's suite, knock, and are admitted. Fatima Ghazala stops on the threshold of the room when she sees Anwar.

"I refuse to be in the same room as the Wazir." Fatima Ghazala addresses the imperious Ifrit woman sitting on a chair in the center of the room, which has been stripped of most of its luxurious trimmings. The Raees is flinty-eyed, tall even while sitting, and dressed in a plain white tunic and shalwar. Her hair is bound in a turban, and her eyes are kohled. Her skin looks gray, and her face is gaunt.

"He is my son, Name Giver," the Raees, her voice raspy. A disbelieving laugh escapes Fatima Ghazala. She turns to Zulfikar, and he makes an apologetic face.

"Is that supposed to exonerate his crimes? He killed Shuruq, Raees. Your grandchild, in case you have forgotten," she tells the leader of the Ifrit. Fatima Ghazala feels none of the qualms she thought she would when meeting the Raees. Just a weary defiance.

The Raees bows her head. "You may leave, Anwar." Fatima Ghazala does not watch the Wazir leave. She feels him glance at her, a whiff of something toxic. And then he is gone, and she is able to breathe again.

Fatima Ghazala glances at Zulfikar. "Is there anything else you haven't told me?"

He looks chagrined. "I might have forgotten to mention that the Raees is my mother's oldest sister, which makes her my aunt."

Fatima Ghazala briefly closes her eyes. "And my mother-in-law of sorts?"

"I suppose?" Zulfikar has the grace to look apologetic, but Fatima Ghazala doesn't think she is going to forgive him too easily.

"I wonder what it is about you that caused my normally stoic nephew to lose his head and my daughter-in-law to sacrifice her life," the Raees says. "We don't know who your family is, what kind of people you originated from. We may never know." As Name Giver, Fatima Ghazala knows she is almost equal in status to the Raees. The fact that she is an outsider with little knowledge of Ifrit tradition must grate on the older woman.

"Today I lost an adopted grandmother, Raees. She presented a bridge we could cross freely to learn of the people we were, to the histories we could claim. Without her, we may as well have no history. You are right. I may never know who my parents were and why they died. But, Raees, in Noor City, you are not limited to those who share your blood when creating a family. I may not know who or what kind of people I come from, but the family I have currently, the people I belong to, and the people who belong to me, if even a smidgen of their goodness has rubbed off on me, I deserve everything you say you wonder about."

"Is that so?" To Fatima Ghazala's surprise, the Raees smiles.

"Yes."

"I'm glad to hear that." The older woman spasms suddenly, her palm flat on her chest where her Name is. Fatima Ghazala lets her vision darken and watches as the taint spreads on the Name, trying to change what it says. Her eyebrows draw together, and without realizing she is doing so, she steps forward and coaxes the Name forward, not removing it from Raees and freeing her fire but bringing it to the surface. She scratches at the taint and like before, it flakes away. However, the process takes a lot of energy and she is still weak, so she is not able to remove as much taint as she wants to before she has to stop.

The Raees looks much better than she did before, breathing far more easily now than she had not five minutes ago.

"What did you do?" the leader of the Ifrit demands.

"I removed some of the taint," Fatima Ghazala replies wearily. She would like nothing more than to close her eyes. "Did it help?"

"How can you do that?" The Raees turns to Zulfikar. "Did you know she could do that?"

"No, Raees. Neither of us had any idea."

The older woman looks contemplative before her features sharpen. "What's the report, Emir? What is happening in Noor City?"

Zulfikar stands at attention. In a voice devoid of emotion, he describes being called to the scene of the murder, what he saw, and Adila's statement.

"Shayateen, then," the Raees says with a shudder. "They called her an abomination. Did she have fire?"

"I am uncertain," Zulfikar admits. "They called her a Si'lat mongrel, but I didn't meet her before she was killed, so I am not certain of the veracity of that statement."

"She was glowing blue last time I saw her. She spoke about Seeing things before they happened," Fatima Ghazala says. The Raees and Zulfikar exchange glances.

"Si'lat they said?" The Raees has a frown on her face. "I have never heard of a child of a human and a Si'lat."

"Si'lat?" Fatima Ghazala asks.

"They are a clan of Djinn known for their reticence to socialize with anyone other than those who belong to their clan. Even we, who live in the same world they do, know little about them. The idea that one or more of them came to earth and, what's more, had relations with a human that led to a mixed child is surprising," the Raees replies.

"Do you kill those born of human and Djinn?" Fatima Ghazala asks.

"No. But we do isolate them. Their potential to cause harm has been documented extensively. In your case, you were born human, so I suspect you will not develop the same symptoms. I suppose we will find out."

"How can you know that?"

"I am the Raees, Name Giver. That much I can tell. Your human origin is probably the reason the taint doesn't affect the Name you carry." The older woman looks her over, as if noticing Fatima Ghazala's fatigue for the first time. "Leave me now. I will rest."

"If you asked, would the Raees remove the fire bond you have with me?" Fatima Ghazala asks suddenly. It is an hour after their meeting with the leader of the Ifrit. They are in their room in Northern Aftab; Fatima Ghazala has taken a shower and changed into the loose white shalwar kameez she sleeps in.

Zulfikar freezes at her words. He puts down a report he was reading and turns to face Fatima Ghazala. "I won't ask her," he says very firmly.

"But if you did, would she?" Fatima Ghazala persists. Zulfikar can see that his answer is important to her.

"If she judges my reasons for asking for the removal valid, she would," he finally says.

Fatima Ghazala nods slowly. "I see."

"What exactly do you see?" Zulfikar asks. A foreboding skitters down his spine.

"If our fire bond is gone, does that mean our marriage is dissolved?" Fatima Ghazala asks instead.

Zulfikar walks over to his wife and takes her hands into his. He pulls her down to sit on the bed beside him. "Do you no longer want to be married to me?"

Fatima Ghazala shakes her hand and pulls her hands from his.

She wraps her arms around herself, withdrawing from Zulfikar. "My life is mired in losses. I just want to be prepared for the next one." She draws a ragged breath. "I didn't tell Laali goodbye. I thought I would have a chance before she left. How could I have been such a fool? I *know* better than that."

Zulfikar pulls her into his arms and holds her as she cries. A little later, her breathing evens out, and he lays her on the bed, noting with concern the paleness of her cheeks and the tremor of her lips. He presses a kiss on her forehead and turns to look at the report he was reading. With another look at his Name Giver, Zulfikar leaves the room. The night is passing quickly, and the Emir of Noor City has much to do.

CHAPTER 33

The stars glitter, smug in the security of their existence. Aarush considers the heavens with an envious gaze, wishing he, too, had the luxury of distance from earth and its humans and all the convolutions they are capable of. He shifts on his seat at a bench on the far side of the fire pit behind the barracks of the Ifrit army, aware that by venturing into Northern Aftab he has diverged from the accord agreed upon eight years back, but such is the time and such is his need.

"What brings you here, Rajah? And at this time of the night?" The Emir emerges from the darkness, and Aarush starts. He gets to his feet warily as the Ifrit comes closer.

"Was it the Shayateen?" he asks the Emir abruptly. He doesn't need to specify what he is talking about. There is little else being discussed everywhere in Noor. The Ifrit's jaw clenches, and what warmth had remained in his eyes disappears.

"Yes," he replies, and Aarush sags. "That is not all. Spies, either in the Ifrit army or the human, have leaked the details of the incident, and my sources tell me that someone is going around questioning the necessity or usefulness of the Ifrit when we apparently cannot even save an old woman from the dreaded Shayateen."

Aarush meets the Emir's eyes. "The same people behind the rebels in the forest provinces?"

"Indeed. So, Rajah, what are you going to do about your group of traitors and the army they are gathering?" the Emir asks.

"I don't know what to do," Aarush admits quietly.

"Of course you do," the Emir replies. "The question is, do you have the strength to do it?"

"You chose to be the Emir. I didn't choose to be the maharajah. It was a role foisted upon me. I do not want it. I have never wanted it," Aarush snaps, annoyed at the Ifrit.

"Then walk away. What is stopping you? What point is duty if your heart is not in it?"

"I am the king of this country. I cannot simply walk away!" Aarush hisses, keeping his voice down with some effort.

"Then behave like a king instead of a boy pretending to be one," the Emir replies, entirely without mercy. "I will bid you farewell here. I must join my soldiers on their patrols." The Ifrit returns to the darkness from which he emerged, and Aarush is left listening to the crackles of the flames in the fire pit.

In the city of Noor, Sunaina observes, death is not treated like a stranger that, in the depths of the night, steals that which is not his. No, death is very much a family member, granted the same respect and ritual that life is, a seat at the same table that life sits at. So when death comes calling, no matter what shape he takes, people have rituals to fall back upon while their emotions process the loss and label it grief.

Laali's body is washed by the women who took turns caring for her when she was alive. It is then wrapped gently in a shroud. Sunaina makes her a garland of sweet-smelling chameli and marigold. Anu plucks some tulsi from the little plant she grows in a pot in her kitchen and tucks it into the casket. And so, Sunaina's adopted grandmother, the woman whose sudden appearance in their lives perhaps saved them, is readied for her final journey.

The funeral procession moves from Taaj Gul to the cremation

grounds late in the morning, and despite the growing heat of the day, thousands of people line the streets to witness the passing of the casket. Sunaina looks at the people as she walks; all faces are somber and some are visibly scared. Some people are even crying though Sunaina cannot remember seeing them before.

The many pallbearers take turns carrying Laali's body to the cremation grounds located just outside the southern gates. The funeral procession moves slowly, according respect to the more infirm who insist on accompanying the casket. A sizable crowd gathers at the cremation grounds. Bhavya is present, along with the maharani, the maharajah, and their many guards. The Emir, along with his soldiers, stands at the back, guarding against possible Shayateen attacks.

Sunaina looks around the crowd and is thankful that she somehow persuaded Fatima Ghazala to remain and guard the Alifs instead of forcing herself to attend. Though her sister's color looks better today, there's a new frailty to her that worries Sunaina.

She is roused from her thoughts when the pundit asks who the karta is. She steps forward, accepting the duty as one of the two people Laali was closest to after the massacre. Laali's body is placed carefully on the pyre, her head to the north and her feet facing the south. Sunaina did not get to complete the funeral rites for her parents; they were impossible to identify. So though it is Laali's body lying on the pyre, she is not the only one being released in Sunaina's mind.

As karta, Sunaina walks counterclockwise around the pyre three times; with every turn she lets go of her pain. The next step is to sprinkle holy water on the pyre and on Laali's body. The final step is to touch the torch to the pyre, and Sunaina does, crying when the flames take Laali. She cries for her parents, for her city, and for the life that was taken from her.

CHAPTER 34

Fatima Ghazala allowed Sunaina to persuade her to stay behind. A feeling, a foreboding deep within her, tells her that something is going to happen while everyone else is distracted by the funeral. Ifrit soldiers are stationed outside and inside the building to provide a modicum of safety, and the Alif parents, at least, are reassured. Fatima Ghazala, though, feels danger approach with the passing of every single second. When the knock sounds on the door, they are all crammed into the room Adila is resting in.

"I will go see who it is," Ali Abbu says, but Fatima Ghazala shakes her head. That feeling of danger has now bloomed into certainty. Whoever waits on the other side of the closed door is no friend.

"Let me, Abbu. I am probably the strongest of us." She smiles at the stern-faced man. "I need you to protect your ladies. Unless I explicitly say so, please do not come out of the room."

"Api . . . ?" Azizah says uncertainly.

Fatima Ghazala pats her head on her way out. It is with a sense of inevitability that she opens the door and finds the fair-faced Shaitan standing outside. Fatima Ghazala looks him over for a minute, then steps across the threshold, and pulls the apartment door closed behind her.

Her nightmare has reneged on the treaty between day and night and spilled into reality.

Fatima Ghazala stares at the Shaitan, intensely aware of the distance at which he stands from her, the space he occupies, and his capacity for violence. She is the only one standing between the Shaitan and the Alifs. Fatima Ghazala will be damned before she lets any harm come to them. She'll bleed first.

"I have a proposition for you," the Shaitan says suddenly. The disparity between the beauty of his face and the malice emanating from him is pronounced in the fear that suddenly shocks her. Through the fire bond she can feel Zulfikar's concern, so she tamps down her emotions, cognizant, on some level, that her reaction could mean the difference between a bloodbath and a conversation.

"Go on," Fatima Ghazala says more coolly than she expected. Her new courage comes from her fire, of course. She *knows* she is no longer as helpless as she used to be. She knows exactly how she will disarm and possibly kill this Shaitan should he make a move toward violence.

But he disappoints her. "It is dangerous to talk here. Follow me." The Shaitan abruptly whirls around and walks down the corridor. Fatima Ghazala stares after him for a long minute before she decides to trust her fate to her Creator.

They end up on the roof. The sun is relentless, but she barely feels the heat. The Shaitan seems just as unaffected.

"Come with me to where our leader is, and we will let the people you protect live," the Shaitan says in a flat voice devoid of all emotion.

"Do you think that we are entirely without power?" Fatima Ghazala barely stops herself from showing her teeth. "We can protect our own."

"We won't be the only ones striking the matches in the upcoming war," the Shaitan replies, unaffected by her venom.

"What do you mean, war?" Fatima Ghazala demands. She thinks desperately of the on-goings in the city but can think of no specific event that augurs war. "Why would there be a war?"

"Humans always make war, Name Giver. Their reasons are scarcely important. But this is the first time that we have allied ourselves with humans . . . or the rebels, as they call themselves."

The world comes to a screeching halt. All of Fatima Ghazala's attention hones in on what the Shaitan said. Rebels. She thinks back to the conversation on the rooftop, what seems like an age ago. The rebels are the natives of Qirat who want the Ifrit to surrender their half of the country and leave. Why would the Shayateen ally themselves with humans? And more importantly . . .

"You are willing to betray your alliance with the humans. Why?"

"You will have to come with me to find out." The Shaitan curls his lip. "The choice is yours."

How can she not go when staying would mean the possible death of the city? Can she trust Zulfikar to catch the Shayateen before they kill anyone? What would Firdaus have done? Can she take the risk that everything will work out for the best? And if it doesn't, how will she live with herself? It isn't a choice. It *never* is a choice. "I will go with you."

The Shaitan bares his teeth in a semblance of a smile. "You chose well. Let us leave."

"Not right now. If I leave now, the Emir will tear the city apart searching for me. Come for me at midnight. Right here."

The Shaitan nods, and Fatima Ghazala leaves, thinking about the lies she will need to tell everyone.

Hours later, Zulfikar arrives in Taaj Gul to check in with Fatima Ghazala. She is waiting for him in front of the entrance, wearing a white shalwar kameez and a slight smile that battles against the weariness that threatens to overpower her expression. Zulfikar feels his breath hitch, and he wonders if there will ever be a time when seeing her will no longer feel like a gift. He grimaces at his thoughts and is glad no one can witness his extreme lovesickness. Getting off his horse in one easy movement, he walks over to the Name Giver and barely stops himself from pulling her into his arms for a hug he so desperately wants to give her.

"You were scared during the day?" He settles for grabbing her hand, allowing her to pull him into the relative privacy of the stairway. At this time of the day, it is all but deserted.

"Just grieving," she replies softly, resting her head on his shoulder. Zulfikar gives in and slips his arms around her. "I'm going to stay the night with the Alifs," she tells him.

"Are you sure you're well enough?" Zulfikar pulls away from her and looks into her face, wishing he could demand that she go home with him.

"Physically, there's nothing wrong with me," Fatima Ghazala says. "Emotionally . . ." She shrugs. "I just need to be with my family for a bit. I will come back."

"Of course you will. I am only sharing you for one night," Zulfikar mutters, and is relieved to see her grin at his words.

Her smile fades, however, and she considers him with an expression he cannot read, even through their bond. "I want you to know that even though we began our lives together for reasons other than love, I could have loved you."

"Could have? Do you not intend to any longer?" Zulfikar demands.

"No, I just mean we do not know what turns our lives will take, and whether we will have the chance to love. Laali's death has taught me not to leave things unsaid," Fatima Ghazala replies.

"In that case, let me tell you that *I* love you. It is a fiery kind of love that I didn't know I was capable of, but I am. I want to possess all of you: your heart, mind, and body. I want you to be mine just as much as I want to be yours. I do not know if it is the fire bond that led me to feeling this way, but if it is, then I am glad because I don't think I can be myself without you." Zulfikar feels his cheeks heat as he finishes his short impassioned speech and is glad for the falling darkness that hides them.

As a reply, Fatima Ghazala rises on her toes and presses a soft kiss to his lips, surprising him. He deepens the short kiss, grateful that she allowed him the contact, fleeting though it is.

"I will send you a carriage at midday tomorrow," he says, his arms still around her, loath to be apart.

"All right," she replies.

"I suppose I should go now. Mansoor is waiting for me to join him for a patrol." Zulfikar is reluctant.

Fatima Ghazala nods. She offers him a smile, a softening of the darkness, and he embraces her once again. He presses a final kiss on her lips and gestures for her to return upstairs. Once he is certain she is safe with the Alifs, he leaves.

A strange morning dawns, lighting the spires of Aftab Mahal, making them transcendent, not that Sunaina's workshop shows it, shrouded as it is in shadows. She returned to Southern Aftab late the night before, weary and wanting nothing else but the quiet. She spent the time since lying in bed trying to sleep and, when that failed, out in the workroom in her favorite chair with a cup of chai she brewed. She left the door to the workroom slightly ajar so she can see who walks past in the corridor outside.

Laali's death, a tragedy though it was, has left Sunaina feeling strangely untethered. Fatima Ghazala is married and her own person, her parents are gone, and Sunaina no longer has obligations to Laali. The walls of Noor City are suddenly suffocating, and her workroom, once a beloved space of her own, feels like a prison.

Sunaina doesn't know how to bear these feelings, so she sits still and quiet in the darkness, hoping they will pass.

Two voices outside her room interrupt her reverie, two voices Sunaina recognizes quite well. The women these voices belong to are the Rajmata's maids. At first, Sunaina is uninterested in their gossip and thinks she will clear her throat to alert them to her presence, but then she hears the content of their whispers, and all such thoughts cease.

"Is your man really going forward with it?" one of the women whispers, her voice threaded with fear.

"Yes! I tried to dissuade him, but he says it is his duty as a Qirati! When the maharajah is at breakfast today with his family, they are going to attack," the other woman replies.

"They will kill the baby too?" The disbelief in the woman's voice is stark.

"Rajkumar Aaruv has ordered him to do so," the woman says, and weeps. "What will happen to my children, didi?"

Sunaina wrenches the door to her workroom open, and the women scream their surprise. Their faces drain of color when they see her, and they flee down the corridor without giving her a chance to ask more questions. Sunaina glances at a clock in the workroom. All she knows is that the royal family has breakfast at eight in the morning and it is now ten minutes to the hour. The only person she can think of who will be able to protect the maharajah and his family is the Emir. Sunaina takes a deep breath and runs, praying that her brother-in-law is home.

The royal family no longer breakfasts together. All pretensions of unity have been abandoned, and Bhavya, for one, is glad she no longer has to countenance Jayanti Bua's sour face in the mornings. The change was abrupt. The Rajmata sent her excuses via a maid a day ago and has since taken all her meals in her room. Jayanti Bua, of course, goes only where their mother does. Aaruv of late has taken to spending most of his time at Sanchit Goundar's house. Regardless, he is rarely even awake in time for breakfast.

Bhavya looks over the feast spread out in front of her and sighs her pleasure. Breaking fast away from her mother and aunt has done wonders for her appetite. She tears a piece of a potato paratha and dips it into a little bowl of dahl and pops the morsel into her mouth. Chewing with relish, she looks at her brother, whose face is very grim for a pretty morning.

"Is anything the matter, Bhaiya?" Bhavya asks him. The maharani, too, has a troubled expression and her movements, though competent, are listless. Four of the maharajah's guards stand behind his chair and four of the maharani's companions stand behind hers. Bhavya wonders if she should get her own retinue.

"Nothing that you need to worry about, choti," Aarush says, and Bhavya frowns. Her brother doesn't use the endearment for her unless he is trying to distract her.

"Something's going on, isn't it?" Bhavya says, her appetite suddenly gone. She pushes her plate away. "You just don't want to tell me."

"You don't want to know, trust me," Aarush says. He, too, pushes his plate away.

"Bhabhi?" Bhavya says uncertainly, her unease deepening when the maharani doesn't smile and reassure her.

"I believe we are done with breakfast now," Aarush says decisively. He gets up from his chair, and that is when things fall apart.

Bhavya experiences the next few minutes as if in a dream. As her brother gets up from his chair, one of his guards pulls his sword out of its scabbard and pushes forward. The maharani screams as the sword sinks into the maharajah's side, and pandemonium breaks loose. The maharani's companions transform from demure maids into ruthless warriors as all four of the maharajah's guards attack. Bhavya sits frozen through the clash of the swords, her eyes not moving from her brother, who lies on the ground bleeding. Her bhabhi covers his body with her own while her companions fight to keep the king's guards from murdering both of them.

The doors burst open, and the Emir of Noor City enters the room, effectively putting an end to the fighting by beheading all four of the maharajah's guards within half a minute of his arrival. More soldiers pile into the room before the Emir says one sharp word and everyone comes to a standstill.

CHAPTER 35

When Bhavya was a little girl, long before the Shayateen Massacre, she was caught in a storm while traveling in the forests of Asur with her parents. She remembers the ferocity of the storm, the savagery of the wind as it made toys out of trees, whipping them back and forth as their roots clutched at the earth. Her father had wrapped his arms around her and held her close, keeping her safe. Another storm is raging around her right now, but this time no one is around to keep her safe.

The Emir turns and looks at her, his gaze a demand to move, to act. Bhavya gets to her feet, her legs unsteady. She stumbles her way to her brother and drops to her knees beside Aruna, who is stanching the flow of blood from the wound on his side with her hands.

Bhavya takes a deep breath. The scent of the blood, the red of it. The world recedes. A scream builds in her chest. The maharani is weeping.

A healer pushes forth through the Ifrit soldiers stationed in front of the room; she is followed by more. Bhavya moves aside to let them tend to her brother. As her shock wears off, she becomes aware of anger, a blistering anger, that makes her feel more dangerous than she has ever felt before.

"Someone will tell me why my brother is lying on the ground bleeding." It is not a request.

For a minute, no one speaks. Then Janab Jamshid steps forward. He is old, and fate has been unkind to him. His eyes are wet and his voice is full of whispers, but he speaks and Bhavya listens. She hears the things he doesn't say. When he is done, Bhavya tastes reality for the second time and finds it just as bitter as she did in Taaj Gul that afternoon with Sunaina.

"Do you have a copy of the report the investigators sent to Bhaiya?" Bhavya asks the old man. He nods and leaves to fetch it.

Bhavya turns to the Emir, who is talking to his soldiers, and waits until his attention falls on her. "Help us," she says simply. "Please."

Beyond her, the healers are calling for a stretcher to move the maharajah. They have managed to stop the bleeding.

"I will, of course, help you. The treaty between the Ifrit and Qirat is founded on the agreement of aid given to the maharajah by the Ifrit within reason as specified by Ifrit law," the Emir says.

Bhavya whispers her thanks, aware that she cannot fall apart at this moment. That no matter how tempting it may be to leave everything to the Emir, she is the one who must pick up the reins—at least until Aruna can start making decisions.

Janab Jamshid returns with the report, and Bhavya reads it slowly. The extent of the conspiracy opens up, and she wonders what Aarush must have felt when confronted with the truth of the people he has been calling his own.

With her face pale and a shimmer in her eyes that no one will mistake for tears, Bhavya hands the report to the Emir. He glances through it but does not seem surprised by its contents.

"Locate Rajkumar Aaruv," Bhavya says. Her voice has an odd flat quality to it. "As fast as you can." Janab Jamshid nods and bows. "Is there anyone we can trust in Southern Aftab? Is the army compromised?"

"I do not know, huzoor," Janab Jamshid says. "There are some soldiers, certainly, whose loyalty is, without question, to the maharajah."

"Send them to guard the Rajmata's rooms. Jayanti Bua should be with Amma right now. Make sure neither of them leaves the rooms. They are allowed no visitors, not even maids." Bhavya pauses and thinks. She looks around but the bodies of the four traitors have been removed from the room. "Parade the heads of the traitors throughout Southern Aftab. Let them be a warning to all servants and workers of the fate that awaits those who betray their king and country."

The Emir nods approvingly. "Contain the flow of information. No one, apart from those here, must know the extent of the rajah's injuries. The traitors' next move depends on whether the assassination attempt was successful. If they try to take over Southern Qirat while the rajah is still alive, the masses will revolt."

The corridors are cleared, and the maharajah, accompanied by Aruna and a host of healers, is removed to his suite of rooms. When they are gone and only the stain and the scent of blood remains, Bhavya asks Janab Jamshid, "Have you found Rajkumar Aaruv?"

Janab Jamshid apologetically reports that the prince of Qirat appears to be missing; no one has seen him since the previous afternoon.

"What do I do? How do I know whom to trust?" Bhavya asks the Emir, hating the frailty in her voice.

"You pretend that their loyalty is a given. You smile brighter and you laugh harder and you observe who laughs with you and who laughs at you."

"What if the rebels attack Noor?" she asks in a smaller voice.

"Leave the safety of Noor to the Ifrit. We will defend her." It is a promise. "I will go arrange for heavier patrol in and out of Southern Aftab. For the meantime, I think it best if Ifrit soldiers relieve human ones of their duties. Are we in agreement?"

"Yes." The weight of the storm presses down on Bhavya, and the desire to either scream or weep returns.

"Please send me news of any change in the rajah's condition," the Emir says, and excuses himself.

Zulfikar leaves the room and comes upon Sunaina standing outside. "Did you see Fatima Ghazala last night?" he asks her, even though he knows her concern lies elsewhere at the moment.

"No. I came straight to the mahal after the funeral," Sunaina replies. Zulfikar frowns but decides to keep his counsel.

"The rajkumari could do with a friend right about now." Zulfikar nods at the figure visible through a crack in the door; she is crying in gasping sobs.

Sunaina nods and enters the room, closing the door behind her.

Zulfikar strides away, a niggling sense of worry tormenting him. He reaches for Fatima Ghazala, but she feels distant and the only emotion he can sense through their bond is a determined calm. Zulfikar dispatches a carriage to pick her up from Taaj Gul, wondering how safe the city is and how much longer it will remain that way.

Fatima Ghazala looks around the room she was rudely abandoned in some hours ago. The door is locked, so she is . . . not a prisoner. Fatima Ghazala breaks the lock more easily than she thought possible. The Shaitan came for her at exactly midnight. Fatima Ghazala retained her equanimity with a determination that impressed even her. Even as they traveled through the forest, a shadow-drenched forest full of smells and noises Fatima Ghazala didn't have the least intention of decoding, she was calm. Even though the hiss of snakes, and who knows what other horrors live in the greenery that seems to have its own malevolence, plagued her all the way through, she was calm. The mountain path they traveled up was treacherous, but the Shaitan was nimble-footed and went ahead without waiting for Fatima Ghazala, who took her time ascending, as she was not especially inclined to break her neck by falling down. Often she stood and stared at the forest-filled vista shimmering under the sickle moon.

The Shayateen have made their home in an abandoned haveli built at the top of a mountain. The air inside is musty and smells of rot. The atmosphere is hardly like the perfumed halls of Aftab Mahal, but Fatima Ghazala supposes that perfume might be too much to ask from the Shayateen. They reached the hideout after five hours of traveling, because Fatima Ghazala refused to let the Shaitan touch her, as he would need to in order to travel quickly. The only man allowed to touch her is Zulfikar; Fatima Ghazala considers it best that she makes this clear from the very beginning.

Now she is farther from home than she has ever been before with not even a sign of the desert in this overly verdant landscape. Even the air smells green. Fatima Ghazala isn't exactly afraid of the predicament she is currently in—she has faith in her fire and her blood. But still, she would much rather be at home, where a layer of grime and dust doesn't cover all surfaces, where mold isn't growing with glee in the windowsills and what looks like rat droppings doesn't litter the floor. Fatima Ghazala wonders if the Shayateen intend to feed her and whether, on the off chance they do, she should eat the food prepared for her.

She prayed Fajr in one corner of the room, filthy though it was. Zohr comes and passes. Neither food nor drinks are forthcoming. Fatima Ghazala is tempted to leave but calms herself. Briefly, she feels a probe from Zulfikar through their bond and thinks calming thoughts. He is going to be supremely angry when he finds out what she has done, but Fatima Ghazala didn't exactly have a choice, no matter what the Shaitan said.

Her stomach issues a complaint that will not be ignored, so she moves to the door. She is nobody's prisoner.

Zulfikar knocks on the Raees's door and is given permission to enter. His superior is seated in her chair in the middle of the room, which has been emptied of all furniture except for a coffee table on the side. On this table is a pile of books gathered from the mahal library. Zulfikar looks over the Raees carefully. Her face is more fatigued than it was the day before, and there is a tremble to her movements. She looks up, and Zulfikar takes a deep breath. A thin band of black has appeared around her irises.

"What has happened, Zulfikar?" The Raees's voice is still sharp.

"There was an attempt to assassinate the maharajah. He is wounded, but the human healers are hopeful he can be saved," Zulfikar reports.

The Raees sits up at his words. She closes the book she was reading and lays it carefully on the coffee table beside the chair. "Who will take the throne if the rajah dies?"

"I believe there will be a war. The crown prince is but a mere babe, and the landowners won't tolerate the rani, a foreign female, as their leader. Besides, the rajah's younger brother is the one colluding against him."

"This brother is the one allied with those wanting the Ifrit to leave Qirat, no?" the Raees says. Zulfikar nods an affirmation. "Does the new desire for freedom have anything to do with the discovery of gold in the desert city of Sabr?"

"I can't think of any other reason the humans would suddenly discover their patriotic sides," Zulfikar replies.

"Hm." The Raees looks thoughtful. "We will, of course, help keep the peace until such time that our treaty with the humans breaks irrevocably. I trust you will direct the army as necessary?"

"Yes, Raees," Zulfikar replies.

"Should the rebels win the war, we will fight for our right to remain in Qirat. We have invested too much of our people and our fire in this country to simply leave when the humans decide they no longer need our help. Besides, we must fight the inevitable chaos." The leader of the Ifrit gives Zulfikar a narrow look. "Anwar told me that there is no progress in the investigation of Firdaus's death. I expected better from you, Zulfikar." The castigation is expected, but it still stings.

"My apologies, Raees." Zulfikar bows his head. "We have hit a dead end, and until we can capture a Shaitan alive, we will not be able to get any new information."

The leader of the Ifrit sighs, looking weary. "Where is the new Name Giver? Is she still with her family?"

"I sent a carriage to pick her up from Taaj Gul," Zulfikar replies. His anxiety grows at each passing moment without Fatima Ghazala.

A knock sounds on the door at that moment, and Zulfikar moves to open it. On the other side is the soldier he sent with the carriage to Taaj Gul. He is alone.

"Where is she?" Zulfikar asks, his voice low and calm.

"The family she was supposed to be with gave me this note to pass on to you, sayyid." The soldier hands over a piece of paper.

The note is mercilessly brief. Fatima Ghazala writes that she has gone to meet with the leader of the Shayateen. She tells Zulfikar to be wary because they speak of an upcoming war in which they are allied with the rebels. She doesn't promise to return.

Zulfikar grips the note tightly and dismisses the soldier.

"Has something happened to the Name Giver?" the Raees asks from her chair.

"She has gone to meet the leader of the Shayateen," Zulfikar says flatly. "I need to go after her."

"You know you cannot do that. You are the Emir of Noor. You have obligations here." The Raees's reprimand is gentle.

"She will die. They will kill her, Khala." Everything in Zulfikar demands for him to give in to his heart, which wants him to find Fatima Ghazala and keep her close, keep her safe.

"I would like you to calm down and remember that the Name Giver is not a helpless human though she might appear that way. She is far more capable than you give her credit for." The Raees's eyes are piercing. "You do her a disservice by wanting to cosset her. She has the full right to act on her decisions. Would you have let her go if she had told you about it?"

"Of course not!" Zulfikar replies immediately.

"Then don't blame her for not telling you. All you can do right now is fulfill the purpose for which you are present here and trust her to return. Surely that is not too much to ask."

"It is when there is no guarantee she will be back," Zulfikar says bitterly.

When Fatima Ghazala steps out of the room, she finds the same Shaitan who brought her to the haveli standing outside with a silver tray in his hands. On the tray is a plate of mithai and a glass of water. The glass is smudged with fingerprints.

"Food?"

"This is all we eat."

"Where do you get it from?"

"A village at the foot of the mountain. Not on the side we came up."

"I see." Fatima Ghazala takes the tray from him. She walks along a corridor, conscious of the following Shaitan. Spotting a chair that doesn't look like it has a decade's worth of dust on it, she drags it near a window. The haveli is located at the very top of the mountain, so the views are astounding. Of course, no matter which direction you look in, the only things you can see are trees.

Fatima Ghazala eats the mithai, savoring the almond laddoo in particular, and drinks the water. "Now what?" she asks the Shaitan, who has been waiting silently for her to finish her meal.

"Now we go see the Qayyid." The Shaitan's reverence for his leader is obvious.

"All right." It occurs to Fatima Ghazala as she follows the Shaitan farther into the haveli, down a flight of stairs and into the basement, that she is being rather blasé about the entire venture. Perhaps it would behoove her to be more afraid, but rather than fear, she feels the welcome heat of anger. The Shayateen do not intend to kill her, but even if they did, Fatima Ghazala has thorns that will not make killing her easy for them.

The room the Shaitan leads her to is dark and smells strongly of decay. No light is allowed to pass through, no flame burns. Fatima Ghazala wonders if she is going to have to talk to the darkness, when someone strikes a match. Two candles are lit. Someone hisses at the sight of the wavering flames. Fatima Ghazala reaches for her fire and feels it come to life and cover her skin with an orange sheen. This leads to some growling, but Fatima Ghazala has always been a contrary sort and keeps her fire out and burning.

When she sees the score of Shayateen glaring at her, however, she wishes she had stayed in the dark. All of them have that frozen beauty common to the Shayateen, though some of the faces look more brittle than the others. They are all so pristinely dressed that Fatima Ghazala, for one wildly inappropriate moment, wonders where they do their laundry. The menace emanating from them is strong. One of them takes a shuffling step closer to her, and Fatima Ghazala draws out a dagger she swiped from Zulfikar what seems like an eternity ago.

"Control yourselves," a voice says from deep in the gloom. The Shayateen immediately subside. They part in the middle, and Fatima Ghazala gathers something momentous is about to occur. And sure enough, in the next moment, a Shaitan steps into the light. He is immense, this Shaitan, and yet a strange sense of fragility clings to him. His skin is pockmarked and hangs off his body in folds. His face is actually decaying. But it is his eyes that concern Fatima Ghazala the most. If all childhood nightmares gained intelligence and evil intent, and congregated in one area, they would look like this Shaitan's eyes.

Fatima Ghazala looks at him with the Name Giver's eyes and finds his name covered entirely with the black taint. She takes a deep breath, belatedly realizing that coming with the Shaitan might not have been the best idea, but as she reminds herself, she had no choice.

Fatima Ghazala meets the Qayyid's eyes. Her heart thunders.

CHAPTER 36

Gripping the dagger tightly in her hand, Fatima Ghazala lifts her chin. If the Qayyid so much as even looks as if he is going to attack, she plans to slice her arm and douse the Shayateen with her blood. A cold pulse of fear beats in her neck, her throat is completely dry, and she cannot quite contain the tremble in her hands.

"You are the new Name Giver of the Ifrit," the Qayyid speaks. His voice sounds like a concrete block being dragged on a gravelly road. Fatima Ghazala flinches at the sound. Another pulse of fear washes over her followed by a feeling of reassurance. Zulfikar. His fire is a reminder of her strength.

"I am," she replies even though it wasn't a question.

The Qayyid looks her over as one would a new toy. Fatima Ghazala holds on as tightly as she can to her courage.

"What do you know about the Shayateen?" the Qayyid finally asks.

"I'm afraid we didn't cover anything after 'evil,'" Fatima Ghazala replies.

The Qayyid makes a rumbling sound. It takes Fatima Ghazala a while to realize that he is laughing.

"Typical of the Ifrit," the misshapen Shaitan growls. The Shayateen echo his anger. "Listen well, little Name Giver. We cause chaos. That is our very purpose. Without disorder, there will be no order. But do we ever get acknowledged for the part we play in the universe? No!"

A whole round of *nos* accompany his disavowal. "The universe moves toward chaos. Chaos is natural," the Qayyid continues. "*We* are natural. The unnatural ones are the Ifrit, who create order when there should be none, who go against the universe. And yet *we* are the ones vilified!"

"Perhaps you should stop killing people, then," Fatima Ghazala says, her fear spiced liberally with anger now.

"What greater pleasure is there than ending a life that was once full of possibilities?" The Qayyid sighs dreamily.

"Why have you brought me here?" Fatima Ghazala is abruptly sick of being in the same room as these monsters promenading as people.

"Do you like stories, Name Giver? I'm afraid this is not the kind that comes with a happily ever after, but even so, it is worth the telling. Fifteen years ago, we killed an Ifrit child in the desert in Al-Naar. It shouldn't have mattered; Ifrit are vermin. But our act of mercy, our cleansing, divided our people. The majority of our people, cowards all of them, decided that our actions were too extreme, so five hundred of my followers and I were exiled to earth for five years as punishment. First, we despaired. The sun is too cool and the air dirty. Then we discovered humans. Oh, delicious humans with their candle-flame lives and desperation to live, to matter. We chose our victims, stalked them, and blew out the candle flames here and there. Then we discovered Noor City." The Qayyid shivers as if in delight.

"So many people in Noor City. So many candle flames. We couldn't resist . . . In fact, it would be a lie to say we even tried. It rained the day we attacked Noor. We killed so many people. There was blood, screams, tears, and pain. It was glorious." Nostalgia softens the Qayyid's voice. Fatima Ghazala shudders. "All we did was indulge in our nature, fulfill our purpose. Yet the Creator punished us for doing what we are created to do. We were cursed by a God we refuse to believe in."

"And so?" Fatima Ghazala cannot keep the horror out of her voice.

"We are all that remains of the five hundred we once were. The Ifrit killed us. But that was not enough. The Creator tainted our Names and froze our fire. We cannot reach our fire, so we cannot change our forms, and because we cannot change our forms, we cannot leave earth. We haven't been home in eight years. We had almost given up hope of ever seeing it again. Then you came along." The Qayyid looks at her.

"The Ifrit asked us to abduct you. We waited for our chance and found it when you went into the desert. Little did we realize that you, an abomination, are also a hope. You Un-Named one of us in the desert that day, so you can Un-Name the rest of us too. We will be free to return home at last."

"Ifrit?" Fatima Ghazala repeats. "Who?"

The Qayyid gets a crafty look on his face. "A traitor among you. Surely you suspected. He hasn't exactly been circumspect."

Fatima Ghazala thinks back to the Shaitan she killed that day when her life changed so drastically. She is certain that she killed the Shaitan when she Un-Named him and removed the name from his fire. Why these Shayateen think they will return to Al-Naar when she Un-Names them is beyond her. As for the traitor, only one person comes to mind, but surely he wouldn't fall so low. Fatima Ghazala laughs at herself. Of course he would.

"I have no reason to help you," she says to the Qayyid. "I don't *want* to help you. Why should I?"

"The humans are planning to restage the events of eight years ago. Apparently, they want to rid Qirat of her Ifrit overlords." The Qayyid sounds wistful. "We have been asked to provide our assistance."

"What? You are lying." Surely no human would ally with the Shayateen. Surely not. The screams of the dead still echo in Noor City. The massacre of eight years ago has yet to become memory.

"I do not deny that I have lied on occasion, Name Giver, but in this instance, I am telling the truth. The traitor Ifrit brokered the alliance," the Qayyid says.

"You will not succeed. The Ifrit are present in much larger numbers. You will all die." Fatima Ghazala is conscious of the shrill note in her voice, conscious of her helplessness. Her anger deepens.

"Oh, but we do not offer our help in order to succeed, Name Giver. We will kill as many as we can before we die. It will be a pleasant way to go, with spilled blood still hot on our hands." The Shaitan pauses. "Unless you help us return to Al-Naar, that is."

"I don't know if I can do what you are asking me to," Fatima Ghazala chokes out, realizing she didn't have a choice. There is never a choice.

"Afroz!" the Qayyid barks.

The young Shaitan who brought Fatima Ghazala to the haveli steps forward. "Try Un-Naming him," the Qayyid commands.

Fatima Ghazala smells the damp and the decay; she feels a bone-deep weariness mixed with fear. Her lips tremble, and she presses them together. There is no way out of this, so she straightens her shoulders and lets her vision go blurry. The Shaitan's name is covered with the black taint, but Fatima Ghazala can see where the pieces are joined together. She pokes at one joint and is unexpectedly assailed by the Shaitan's memories. Most vivid are the memories of a caravan, corpses in the desert, an Ifrit woman hold-ing on to an oud, and a baby.

Fatima Ghazala wrenches away and returns to herself, breath-ing hard. "Fourteen years ago, did you attack a caravan?" she asks the Shaitan.

"Yes," the Shaitan replies with a smile, as if remembering some-thing pleasant. "We fought an Ifrit woman. We didn't yet know their blood is dangerous to us."

Fatima Ghazala wets her dry lips. "Why did you attack the car-avan? Why did you kill those people?"

"They were there," the Shaitan replies.

"No other reason?" Fatima Ghazala asks disbelievingly.

"What other reason would we need?"

"Can you Un-Name us, Name Giver?" the Qayyid interrupts. "Can you send us home?"

The question is not *can* she, but *should* she? What right does she have to play God with these creatures? On the other hand, how can she let them live? They killed her parents. Twice. They killed the city. If she lets them go now, they will kill again. But if she takes their lives, what will that do to her?

"Well?" The Shaitan leader is impatient.

"First, I need a few hours of uninterrupted sleep, a proper meal, and water." Mostly Fatima Ghazala needs time to think.

The Qayyid, as if certain of her decision, smiles. His decaying teeth fill her vision. "You shall have them."

Zulfikar thinks of the one hundred and one things he will say and do to Fatima Ghazala once he finds her, once she returns to him because she will; she *has* to. He will not accept any other alternative. He is standing at the entrance to Northern Aftab not sure what to do next. He knows what he most wants to do, but his obligations will not permit him to do that. Frustrated, he drags a hand through his hair and considers his options. Ah, he needs to visit Achal Kaur and ask her help with locating the traitorous rajkumar.

"My mother doesn't look very well today," Anwar's oily voice says from behind him.

Zulfikar tenses, but the Wazir seems oblivious to his hostility and smiles serenely. "It hurts my heart to see her in pain." His words are at odds with his expression.

"Is there something you need to report, Wazir?" Zulfikar keeps his voice chilly.

"The Ghul are back, Emir. Seventy humans were killed in the city of Baaz yesterday. The Emir of Baaz sent a message requesting aid," Anwar says, handing over a letter.

"We can't spare soldiers right now," Zulfikar says. "All of them are needed to help with Noor's defenses. Send our apologies to the Emir of Baaz and ask him to request aid from one of the other cities."

"As you wish," the Wazir replies, and turns to go. He stops as if a thought has just occurred to him and turns around again. "I heard that you misplaced your new wife. I do hope you find her again." He smiles sweetly and leaves.

Zulfikar bites down a curse and moves toward the stables. He does not have time to engage in hostilities with the Wazir, but once everything is returned to its proper place, he plans to talk to the Raees about her son.

It has been a scant five hours since the attempt on her brother's life, but Bhavya feels like an eternity separates her from the girl she was this morning and the person she is now. She looks down at her brother's sleeping form and some of her tensions ease. His color looks much better now than it did before.

The healer rises from the bedside. Both Aruna and Bhavya accompany him a little ways to the other side of the room. "The wound, while deep, is not dangerous. The sword did not cut through any organs, so given time and proper care, the maharajah, barring any complications, should regain good health."

The maharani staggers, weeping her relief. Bhavya puts her arm around Aruna. She turns to the healer. "Please remain here until the maharajah wakes up. Should you have a need for anything, one of the maharani's companions will provide it for you. Do not leave the room, but if you do, speak of the maharajah's health to no one." The healer nods, bows once, and returns to Aarush's side.

"Bhabhi." Bhavya gives Aruna a hug, and the older woman wipes her tears, a gritty determination in her eyes. "You will need to go down and talk to today's petitioners. Sanchit Goundar, especially, is clamoring to see Bhaiya," Bhavya says. "I would talk to them but . . ."

But they both know that the men would not take Bhavya seriously. She is, after all, only a rajkumari. Aruna nods grimly. "I will handle the ministers and the landowners if you will talk to the general . . . and the Rajmata."

"Oh yes, I would have insisted on speaking to them even if you didn't ask me to," Bhavya replies. "And Vihaan?"

"I will leave him here with my companions." Aruna looks at one of the companions, a tall girl who came from Darsala with her.

"Indra, I know you do not need to me to spell out these things, but I will anyway for my peace of mind." Aruna clenches her hands into fists. "When we leave these rooms, do not let anyone else in until we return. If the healer demands to leave, let him, but do not allow him to reenter for any reason. Trust no one. Not even those who claim to be our allies. Keep my husband and son safe."

"I will, sahiba. I will defend them with my life," Indra solemnly promises.

"Thank you."

"Are you ready to face the monsters?" Bhavya asks Aruna.

"You mean the men?" Aruna grimaces. "I am. First, though, I need to send a message."

"I wish you luck, Bhabhi." They exit the room guarded by no less than eight of the maharani's companions. Bhavya turns to leave.

"Bhavya." Aruna, accompanied by four of her women and Janab Jamshid, stops her sister-by-marriage. "Think with your head and not your heart."

Bhavya nods smartly and walks down the corridor. She is followed by another four of the maharani's companions, who are proving themselves invaluable. Bhavya's first meeting is with Vikram Khatri, the general of the Qirati army. The man is in his midthirties with a lean face and piercing eyes. He is always well groomed; his uniform is decorated by the medals he has been awarded in his illustrious military career. Because Qirat is not currently involved in any wars, most of their military effort is confined to border patrols. The majority of the soldiers are on base in the Southern grounds of Aftab Mahal. The palace guards and the king's guards fall under the purview of the general.

Bhavya sees the man's surprise followed by his contempt when she walks into the maharajah's office though he schools his expression quickly. Bhavya walks to Aarush's chair and sits down in it.

"Rajkumari—"

Bhavya cuts him off. "Are you a traitor, General?" She has the pleasure of seeing his face slacken with further astonishment.

A moment later, he springs to his feet. "What are you accusing me of, Rajkumari Bhavya?"

"This morning, there was an attempt on the maharajah's life by his guards," Bhavya relates with much more composure than she feels.

All the color rushes from the man's face, and his eyes widen. Still on his feet, he pivots as if to leave.

"Sit down, General. I have not dismissed you yet," Bhavya reminds him.

"I swear to you, Rajkumari Bhavya, my loyalty is and will always remain with Maharajah Aarush."

"Can you prove this loyalty you speak of?"

"I will do whatever it takes."

"Bring me the traitors in the army. Bring me the traitors among the palace guards. Bring them all to me within two days, and I will consider it proof enough. Until then, the Emir of Noor City will be in charge of all military affairs. You are to acquiesce to his authority and provide him with any assistance he may need. You are also to listen to and obey him as you would any superior."

"I will, Rajkumari. Upon the honor of my father, I will," Vikram Khatri vows. "If I may ask, what has happened to the traitors?"

"The Emir of Noor City happened to them, General." Bhavya looks at the man straight in the eyes. "Their heads were paraded around Southern Aftab as a warning. I hope, for your sake, that you find all the colluders in this conspiracy."

Zulfikar watches the maharani precede him into the grand hall of Southern Aftab, where the maharajah usually hears the petitions of his people. When the maharani requested his presence in Southern Aftab, Zulfikar worried that the maharajah's health had dangerously deteriorated. He will never admit it, but he is rather fond of the young ruler.

After thirty seconds has passed, Zulfikar follows the maharani into the hall and is gratified to see several richly turned out men go green in their sherwanis when they see him. Not all of them recognize him, of course. Zulfikar has maintained a low profile ever since he assumed the Emir's office, not being as extroverted as the previous Emir. Those who recognize him as the Emir are quick to inform those who don't. Soon the grand hall is abuzz with speculations. Whispers try to decipher the reason for the Emir's presence and the maharajah's absence.

Aruna sits on the throne while Zulfikar is seated in an empty chair usually reserved for the royal family. Janab Jamshid signals to the guards to close the doors to the grand hall. All conversations cease. The atmosphere inside the room becomes anticipatory. The maharani gestures for the white-haired advisor to proceed with the petitions. The first one to approach the throne is a short squat man wearing an excessive number of necklaces and rings. Without waiting to be introduced, the man, who is somewhere in his late fifties, demands brusquely, "Where is the maharajah? My petition is of utmost importance, and I want the maharajah to hear it."

The maharani doesn't respond. She looks at him silently. The quiet presses down on the man from all sides. The maharani's expression is pleasant, not censorious at all, and yet a flush of shame creeps up the man's neck, turning his cheeks florid. The man loses all his bluster and speaks again after a minute of strained silence. "My apologies, sahiba. I forgot my place."

"The maharajah is currently indisposed. He ate something the night before that appears to be sitting ill with him," Aruna says graciously. "Until he is well enough to present himself before you, I will complete his responsibilities."

Sanchit Goundar steps forward at Aruna's words. "Forgive my impertinence, huzoor, but your words seem untrue. We demand that you allow us to see Maharajah Aarush and ascertain his health for ourselves."

"You *demand*?" Aruna repeats. "Shall I make some demands too, Sanchit Baba? Shall I demand to send my ally's soldiers to your house? Shall I demand they search through your rooms so we can see what you are hiding in your cupboards? Shall I demand to know what the printing machines in your warehouse on the outskirts of the city are for? What pamphlets do you print there, Sanchit Baba? Shall I *demand* to know that?"

The man, stiff with anger, opens his mouth. Zulfikar chooses that moment to clear his throat and watches as the man swallows whatever he was going to say. He bows, muttering a sullen apology, and stalks out of the room.

The petitioning goes much more smoothly once people realize that the maharani is not so easily intimidated. Zulfikar is impressed with the way the maharani uses her silence and her grace as weapons. She brings those who would spread discord to heel by letting them languish in this silence.

Later, when the petitioning is finished and the hall is empty but for the maharani, her retinue, and Zulfikar, the Emir smiles at the petite woman with real warmth. "It was a pleasure seeing you handle your more difficult subjects. You didn't need my presence to bolster yours."

Aruna shakes her head. "Your presence helped immensely. People now know we count upon you as an ally. Plus, I was able to observe which of the landowners reacted negatively to you. Jamshid Chacha did give me the investigators' report, but I wanted to check in case there are more than those named on its pages. Thanks to you, I have a fairly good idea of who not to trust."

"What do you plan to do next?"

"I am not sure. What would you advise?"

"Wait. Let the traitors play their hand. A plot of this magnitude is rarely simple."

"Thank you. I will send word if anything changes with Aarush's condition. I hope Fatima Ghazala is doing well."

Zulfikar winces, and the maharani notices. "Is everything all right with her?"

"Let me just say, Maharani, you and I are in similar straits where our partners are concerned. Till tomorrow." Zulfikar takes his leave.

CHAPTER 37

Bhavya pauses outside her mother's rooms. Her anger feels like the first bite of something spicy. That initial taste overwhelms the senses. Later, tears will flow, but at this moment, all she can feel is the heat. Bhavya is both looking forward to this confrontation and dreading it. The former because her anger demands release, and the latter because one of the women inside is her mother. She looks at the Ifrit soldiers standing guard on either side of the door. "Has anyone tried to enter or leave the room?"

"No, sayyida," one of the guards replies.

Bhavya motions to the companions standing behind her. "You may enter first. If either of the two inside attempt violence against me, you have my permission to defend me even if it means hurting them." The companions nod sharply.

Steeling herself, Bhavya enters the room. As soon as the Rajmata sees her, she stands up from the chair she was sitting on and marches over. "Bhavya, what is the meaning of this? How dare you confine us to this room? Are we prisoners? Criminals?"

Bhavya looks at the woman who gave birth to her and feels the first cracks in her resolve. This is her *mother*. "Why do you not ask what has happened, Amma? Surely you must be curious? Or did you already know of the plan? Is that why you didn't come to breakfast? Blood is difficult to get out of clothes, I hear." Somehow Bhavya finds her voice. Somehow she finds the courage.

The Rajmata flushes. Jayanti, who has thus far been cowering behind the Rajmata, steps forward. "Is he dead?" she asks with indecent eagerness.

Bhavya does not consider herself a violent sort, but it is all she can do to stop herself from clawing her aunt's face. She takes a step back and asks her question again, this time formally. "Did you know about the plan to assassinate Maharajah Aarush prior to the attempt on his life, Rajmata Ekta?"

Bhavya sees her mother start at the question and reads the answer in the older woman's face. "Why, Amma? What could make you sentence a child of your womb to his death? What has Aarush Bhaiya done to deserve death?"

"Your brother has forgotten what it means to be the maharajah. He married the daughter of a concubine and muddied our bloodline. He refuses to see that Qirat has been severed in two. He fraternizes with the Ifrit, not seeing that he is but a pawn to them. He even keeps one of those creatures in the mahal! He sees no difference between himself and the peasantry!" Spittle flies off the Rajmata's lips.

"*Bhaiya* doesn't know what it means to be the maharajah?" Bhavya laughs a little hysterically. "And *you* do? Tell me, did you never talk to Baba? It was he who taught us that there is no difference between people no matter their origin or economic status. *He* was the one who sought out the Ifrit and begged them for help. I don't remember you stopping him then. Are the Ifrit only to be tolerated when we need their help?"

Her heart is made from glass and currently in pieces, but Bhavya will be damned if she will cry. "You are our mother. We are supposed to respect and protect you, but, Amma, we are also the raj. Our obligations to the people of Qirat take precedence over our duties to you." Bhavya takes a deep breath and meets her mother's eyes.

"You and Jayanti Bua will be exiled to the ashram in the mountains of Northern Rupikala," Bhavya says, naming a neighboring country, an ally.

"You have no authority here," the Rajmata replies, sounding amused. "I have strong allies, Bhavya. Once they get word of my imprisonment, you and your supporters will have no chance."

"Apparently, I do, Amma. Did you think I would wait timorously on the sidelines and allow you to arrange my life? Did you think I would play doll for you after you and Aaruv killed my brother? I'm my father's daughter, Amma." Bhavya looks at her aunt, who has the grace to flush under her gaze.

"Aaruv will not let you send us off anywhere!" Rajmata Ekta asserts coldly. "You have no idea what you are dealing with."

"Aaruv will find out about your departure long after you are gone." Bhavya smiles thinly. "Surely you didn't think I would announce my plans to the world before executing them. I studied strategy with the same tutors as Aaruv, though I think he absented himself when the teacher covered ethics and morality."

Bhavya watches her mother realize the sincerity in her words. The first sign of panic: the sheen in her eyes; the second: the tremble in her lips. And yet, she still has not asked even once about her older son.

"Amma, if you go willingly and without making a fuss, you might get a chance to come back some day. Maybe Aarush Bhaiya will find it in himself to forgive you for the betrayal. I won't, but he is the nicest of us all." Bhavya looks at her mother and once again feels that sensation of something within her shattering. "If you and Bua protest, we will have you gagged and tied." Bhavya looks over her shoulder, and the companions hold up the gags and pieces of rope they have been carrying. "I do hope you choose to keep your dignity, but the decision is entirely yours."

"I should have married you off as soon as you turned sixteen," the Rajmata spits out, and turns away.

"I am very glad you didn't," Bhavya replies. "I won't stay to see you leave."

Sunaina stands in her dark workroom, watching little rays of light that have entered through the crack under the door gleam off the glassware she uses to create her concoctions. The room smells of roses; Sunaina has been trying to perfect her recipe of the infused oil she creates with the flower. She idly wonders why Fatima Ghazala hasn't come around yet. Surely the Emir has told her about the events that occurred earlier this morning. Was it just this morning?

The door to the workroom opens, and upon recognizing the silhouette, Sunaina lights a lamp, illuminating the glassy-eyed raj-kumari standing in the doorway. Bhavya is freshly dressed in a pale yellow sari with pink and blue embroidery all over it. Her hair is perfectly coiffured and her jewelry is tasteful. Her face, though, is frozen, and she moves jerkily. Sunaina watches her silently.

Bhavya pulls out a chair at the worktable and arranges herself on it. She studies the tabletop as if it contains all the solutions to her troubles. "I just sent my mother into exile."

"Can you do that?" Sunaina asks, surprised.

Bhavya shrugs. "My word is law because I do not consider the alternative viable. If she remains here, her allies will rally behind her, adding their support to my younger brother's claims to be the rightful maharajah of Qirat."

"Are you certain your brother is part of the conspiracy?" Sunaina asks softly.

"No," Bhavya admits. "I have read the reports, though, and his recent actions make more sense now. He doesn't realize that he is but a pawn for the people behind him. He will be a puppet king."

"Have they located him, then?"

"The Emir said that Achal Kaur's messengers will find him for me." Bhavya sighs suddenly. "I am so exhausted, Sunaina. I want to pretend today didn't happen. I want to turn back time to when I was oblivious to this world and these people, but I can't, can I? I can't leave my bhabhi to weather this storm by herself." She wipes away a few tears that stubbornly resist all her efforts to maintain her composure. There is a catch in her voice when she asks her next question. "Do you know where I can purchase monkshood?"

Sunaina opens her mouth to ask why but stops herself, suddenly wary. She doesn't want to know why the rajkumari wants to purchase a deadly poison. Her throat goes dry, and she swallows. A brief but thick silence springs up between them before Sunaina names the proprietor of a small shop that carries rather esoteric items, among them deadly poisons.

The rajkumari thanks her and gets up from her seat.

"Can I help?" Sunaina asks before she can stop herself. At this point, Bhavya reminds her of Fatima Ghazala when her sister is trying to hide the hurt she feels.

Bhavya looks startled. "With what?"

"Whatever you are planning."

"Thank you. But this is something I have to do alone. I am the rajkumari of Qirat, after all."

Zulfikar is in the weapons room in the barracks, looking over the available blood-edged swords, when one of Achal Kaur's messengers shows up with the address at which the traitorous brother is to be found. He sends the messenger to Southern Aftab with strict instructions to deliver the address to no one other than the rajku-mari. He has no idea what the princess is planning to do with the address. Nor does he want to speculate. He has been impressed by the steel in the young girl's character as she shouldered part of the maharajah's responsibilities, maintaining a cool head in the face of what could have nearly been a tragedy. Zulfikar wonders for the hundredth time whether he will be dealing with a tragedy of his own. He sends a swift prayer to his Creator for Fatima Ghazala. Though he is constantly trying, he can barely feel her through their fire bond.

As soon as Achal Kaur's messenger leaves, one of the patrolling units returns in a state of excitement. Zulfikar finds out that three warrior Ghul have been sighted outside Noor City. Hearing this, Zulfikar gets into his armor and saddles up his horse. At least hunting Ghul will distract him from worrying about his missing Name Giver.

Fatima Ghazala watches the night arrive through the spaces in the forest canopy, creep out from between the trees and run, fleet-footed, up the mountain. She sees the night arrive at the haveli through the smudged glass windows in the bedroom she was moved to, and with it comes the end of her respite. This room is in a marginally better condition than the one she was originally placed in. It has no dust. Though Fatima Ghazala spent the hours she asked for thinking, she can see no other way out of this predicament than through death. She cannot, should not, has no right to act as judge and executioner but life has left her with no choice. At least no other choice she can live with.

A summons comes for her not one minute after she finishes praying Maghrib. The mountain air is cold, and the scarf she wrapped around herself less than twelve hours ago feels flimsy now.

Shivering, Fatima Ghazala follows a Shaitan down to the basement, her steps less uncertain this time around. She calls her fire as soon as they descend into darkness and uses the glow cast by it to navigate her way to the room where they are all gathered.

The same rotting smell, the same sounds of breathing, air sucked through thick throats, and the same encroaching darkness. Before anyone else can speak, Fatima Ghazala breaks the silence. "If I am going to Un-Name all of you, I need light and space."

She is provided with both. There are sixteen Shayateen in the room. The plan is that they will be Un-Named individually with the Qayyid going last. Fatima Ghazala has concerns, of course she does. Doubts fester, but she can see no other way through this. So they begin.

To Un-Name a Djinn, whether Ifrit or Shaitan, Fatima Ghazala has learned, all she needs to do is pull apart the Names that were joined to give the Djinn a shape in the human world. Without a joined name, the Djinn will revert to smokeless fire and return to Al-Naar.

Fatima Ghazala sits in the middle of a small room off to the side of the main room. As the Shayateen are not inclined to trust her, the Qayyid accompanies her. He breathes loudly, wetly, sitting in a corner of the small room, filling it with his malodor. Fatima Ghazala wonders how many nightmares she will have of this moment.

The first Shaitan enters the room. He is tall and thin with a perfectly symmetrical face and eyes the complete black of the Shayateen. He doesn't appear to be more than an adolescent. He stands in front of Fatima Ghazala, looking eager and excited. She looks at him and tries to see past the illusion of humanity his shape offers. For one panicked moment, she cannot.

"Do it, Name Giver. Set him free," the Qayyid growls from behind her.

Fatima Ghazala takes a deep breath and lets her vision blur. However, instead of Un-Naming the Shaitan, she removes the tainted Name from its position in the chest of the Djinn. The Shaitan's physical form immediately changes into that of smoke-less fire. The blackened Name pulses on Fatima Ghazala's palm. She closes her hand around it, crushing it until all that remains of it is ash visible to no one except her. It takes a moment for the Shaitan who is now smokeless fire to realize his end; he screams, just like the Shaitan in the desert did, just like all the people in Noor City did when they were killed, but the shrill sound is heard by no one except Fatima Ghazala. Not even the Qayyid breathing loudly behind her hears his subordinate's scream. Terror threatens Fatima Ghazala, the death heavy on her conscience, but a bite of Zulfikar's fire keeps her going, keeps her in the moment. The smokeless fire fades with the silent scream, and the Qayyid calls the next Shaitan in.

As Fatima Ghazala removes the Names of the Shayateen, she gets a taste of the horrors they have committed against the humans, the Ifrit, and even each other. Her world becomes smokeless fire and screams only she can hear. In the Shayateen's memories, she relives Laali's last minutes and feels the desire a Shaitan had to kill Adila. Her hands burn from the heat of the Shayateen fires that fight her attempts to extinguish them.

Fatima Ghazala finds the traitor Ifrit littered in many memories of different Shayateen. He shares in their chaos. Not a single mem-ory of a single Shaitan is redeeming. The taint doesn't affect her, but with every Name she removes, Fatima Ghazala feels her soul darken. No matter how she justifies her actions, she knows that one day she will stand before her Creator and answer for the lives she is ending.

Finally, it is the Qayyid's turn. Fatima Ghazala's hands are blistered. She looks at the Shaitan in front of her with a sense of dulled astonishment.

"What are you waiting for?" the Qayyid demands, obscene in his eagerness.

"Were you never once sorry for what you did?" A naive question, Fatima Ghazala knows, but the human part of her cannot comprehend the magnitude of evil in the being in front of her.

"Is a stone ever sorry for being hard?"

"Are you not afraid of facing our Creator?"

"I don't plan on dying just yet, Name Giver. I still have some blood left to spill." The Qayyid makes an impatient sound. "Get on with it."

Fatima Ghazala lets her vision blur for the sixteenth time. She looks at the shimmering black word in the Qayyid's chest and exhaustion nearly robs her of her consciousness. Even his fire has shades of black. Fatima Ghazala plunges her hand into the fire and wrenches the Name out, crushing it in her hands. It dissipates in the air, leaving behind a foul stench. The Qayyid gives a roar of surprised pain that is abruptly cut short when the universe reclaims him on behalf of the Creator he rebuffed till the last minute.

Fatima Ghazala sinks to the floor, shaking. The stone is mercifully cold against her burnt hands.

CHAPTER 38

An eerie silence envelops the streets of Northern Taaj Gul. This part of Northern Noor is usually never at rest. While the residential areas deeper in the city fall into slumber after the clock strikes eleven, Taaj Gul, due to its proximity to the northern gates, is always bustling with pedestrians and hawkers peddling their wares. Restaurants are always open and chai wallahs always have kettles steaming with milky tea ready for the thirsty. Tonight, all of that is missing.

Zulfikar and ten of his soldiers, all on horses, ride down the empty streets. The shops have closed their doors and doused their lights, though Zulfikar is sure the inhabitants are awake and aware. No peddlers on the sides, no voices to disrupt the night. Danger stalks the streets, and the people of Taaj Gul know to heed its footsteps.

Moonlight skims off the dusty buildings, turning them ghostly in the hour before dawn. The Emir of Noor City has been on the hunt for the Ghul for a while now. There has been no sign of them, but a toxic scent lingers in the air, marking the places they have been. Zulfikar still doesn't understand why the Ghul, creatures who have previously never ventured into cities, have begun to do so, but he fears their presence augurs more ill for the city than they can currently afford.

"Sayyid, this way!" a soldier whispers, turning into an alley between two buildings much like the one Fatima Ghazala used to live in. Zulfikar follows him. The alley continues for a ways until it opens up to a street. Stench from humans and stray animals fight for dominance, but there's a rank smell that is as familiar as it is disgusting. The Ghul have been here.

The part of him that is a soldier, that will always be a soldier, remains alert while the part of him that is learning the prickly undersides of love wonders if he will ever see his Name Giver again. He reaches for her through their fire bond, and for the first time since her disappearance, he feels her emotions. She is distraught; something has wounded her emotionally. He can taste her despair.

It is just for one second, but Zulfikar is distracted and a second is all it takes. Something slams into him from the side, knocking him off his horse and onto the ground. The soldiers yell behind him, but it is too late. The Ghul rakes its claws down Zulfikar's front, piercing his skin. Zulfikar pulls out his scimitar, not heeding the pain, and manages to defend himself from further mutilation. His soldiers surround the monster, but the creature climbs up the wall and is gone before they can do more than jab at it with their swords.

"After it!" Zulfikar calls or at least he tries to. His vision starts to swim, and he can feel himself sway. Darkness claims him.

Fatima Ghazala waits for the morning in the room on the third story of the abandoned haveli. The chill is in her bones, and she shivers violently, feeling as if she has been dirtied by the—she doesn't know what to call it. Was it— Is she a murderer sixteen times over? Could she have chosen differently? How will she face her Creator? Fatima Ghazala feels Zulfikar's concern through the fire bond and she folds in on herself, wanting him desperately. How much more does she have to lose? Suddenly, a sharp pain rips through her. She screams, the sound echoing through the empty haveli. In the next second, she realizes that the pain isn't hers. It is Zulfikar's. Something has happened to him. She reaches for him, but she can no longer feel him through the bond. It is as if he no longer exists. Fatima Ghazala gets to her feet and runs.

She remembers the Shaitan telling her about a village at the foot of the mountain. The sky is getting lighter, but it is a while before sunrise. Fatima Ghazala doesn't care. In the absence of a path, she forges one herself. She falls down often and is covered in scrapes and bruises by the time she reaches the bottom. The sun has yet to make an appearance in the sky, though what little she can see of it through the canopy of the forest is rosy. She finds a crude path through the trees, calls her fire, and lets it light the way to a tiny village. Ten houses stand in the middle of an area clear of trees. She knocks on the door of the first house she reaches. The door is wrenched open a minute later by an irate man who takes one look at Fatima Ghazala and stumbles backward.

Fatima Ghazala realizes her fire is still visible and pulls it back, but the damage has already been done. The man looks at her fearfully.

"Let me borrow a horse from you. I need to go to Noor City." Fatima Ghazala speaks brusquely, no longer caring about the sensibilities of the human in front of her.

"I only have one horse, sahiba. Our livelihood d-depends on it," the man stutters through his fear.

"The horse will be returned, and you will be compensated for your help," Fatima Ghazala says impatiently. "You can come find me at Aftab Mahal." Her desperation is obvious, and her fire unpredictable. It races along her skin, lighting her up again, and the man steps back again.

Ten minutes later, Fatima Ghazala is on that horse, riding toward Noor City, praying as she does that she reaches it in time.

꧁

Southern Noor in the morning just after sunrise is soft and green. The city wakes in degrees. First, the cats slink back after a night spent caterwauling. A little while later, those who work outside leave their homes, their footsteps pulsing through the sidewalks. The milkman makes the rounds and the kitchen staff wakes up in the rich houses. The inhabitants of these rich houses sleep on, having little idea of the catastrophe brewing, along with their chai, in the darker places of Noor City.

Bhavya notices that the hem of her brown sari, borrowed from Sunaina, is wet from the morning dew. She wonders how much the cosmetics chemist will mind if she burns this sari later. She knocks on the front door of the modest little house she is standing before. No response is forthcoming, so she knocks louder, harder, longer. Two minutes later, the door is pulled open by her brother, who stands in the doorway gaping at her. He looks beyond her fearfully, but his expression eases when he sees that she is alone.

"What are you doing here?" he demands. "How did you find out about this place?"

"Aren't you going to invite me in?" Bhavya asks pleasantly.

"I don't particularly want to see you." The rajkumar of Qirat yawns. Unshaven and red-eyed, he looks a far cry from the figure he presents at court every day.

"Amma sent me." The lie slides off Bhavya's tongue smoothly. Her mother and aunt were smuggled out of Southern Aftab in the wee hours of the morning and should be well on their way to the ashram in the mountains by now.

The rajkumar's face brightens. "Come in, then."

Bhavya spares a glance at the interior of the house. It is shabby. The pack she is carrying bangs against the narrow hallway. Bhavya holds it closer. Aaruv leads her to a small living room in the back.

"Are you alone here?" Bhavya asks.

"Obviously."

"What do you do for food?"

"Sanchit Baba brings it."

"They are using you, you know." Bhavya looks at her brother and, despite her dislike, feels a spurt of pity for him.

"And what would you know of politics?" Aaruv scoffs. "You should leave these matters alone and get married as you are being told to do." He looks at the pack eagerly. "What did Amma send?"

"How could you agree to the assassination plot? Do you not love Bhaiya? He's your own blood!"

Aaruv's shoulders stiffen, but he doesn't try to deny Bhavya's words. "He is a fool. The crown should have been mine."

"Why? What makes you think you are entitled to it?" Bhavya is genuinely curious.

Her brother turns to her, a stranger suddenly. "Because clearly I am the only one who knows what it means to have royal blood. We do not consort with commoners. Bhai is smitten with Aruna Bhabhi. He doesn't realize the taint she brings to our name. She will dirty our bloodline! She *has* dirtied it. You already know how I feel about the Ifrit."

His words are almost exactly an echo of their mother's.

"Did you plan to have Bhabhi and Vihaan killed too?"

"Did?" Aaruv laughs. "I still do. Some losses are to be expected. What do *you* know of ruling a country?"

"You cannot expect to win against the Ifrit, Aaruv."

He smiles. "We have a plan and some unexpected allies. The Shayateen have promised their aid against the Ifrit."

Bhavya freezes. She even stops breathing. "Who?"

"Ah, I shouldn't have told you. But it's not like Amma will let you tattle."

"Amma knows?"

"Yes. She gave her approval."

"And what about our people?"

"What about them?"

"Surely you don't think the Shayateen will only kill the Ifrit?"

"As I said, kaddu, some losses are to be expected." Aaruv shrugs easily.

"I see." Bhavya looks at her pack for a moment before handing it over to Aaruv. "Amma told me to give you this."

Aaruv grabs the pack, opens it, and takes out a jeweled box. His expression changes to one of avarice and awe when he sees it. Before he can open it, Bhavya stays him with a hand on his arm. "Will you not reconsider your path, Aaruv?"

He shrugs off her hand without even looking at her, his attention on the box. He opens it to find the crown of the maharajah of Qirat glittering inside. It is made of solid gold and adorned with precious stones. More of a symbol than for daily use, it was worn by Aarush maybe twice in the entire time he has been maharajah.

Aaruv stares at the crown, his face flushing pink with happiness. Then, licking his lips, he wraps his hands around the crown and hefts it up from the box, holding it as if it is the most precious thing he has ever held.

Bhavya witnesses the moment he realizes that something has gone terribly wrong. His expression changes from happiness to horror in one blink. The poison is fast-working and lethal on contact.

"Like you said, Aaruv, when running kingdoms, some losses are to be expected." Bhavya gets up and lets herself out of the house. She does not stay to watch her brother die.

Fatima Ghazala arrives at Northern Aftab to find the courtyard swarming with Ifrit soldiers. She dismounts from the horse without hesitation and stalks through the soldiers, who move aside to let her pass. She walks through the entrance of the mahal and feels for Zulfikar through the bond. Taking the stairs two at a time, she arrives at a previously unoccupied suite of rooms on the second floor. The entrance of the room is, like the courtyard, crowded with Ifrit soldiers. The atmosphere is thick with dread, and Fatima Ghazala feels fear, cold and immediate, slow down her steps.

She moves, as though fighting her way through a sandstorm, to the entrance and looks inside. A wordless cry escapes her. The soldiers melt away, and Fatima Ghazala walks to the bed in the middle of the room, conscious of nothing and no one except the figure in it.

She kneels down beside the bed, her breathing coming in gasps, and picks up Zulfikar's hand. His eyes are closed, and his skin is gray. His breaths are shallow. "What has happened to him?" Fatima Ghazala whispers.

"A Ghul attacked him, sayyida. It didn't manage to injure him seriously, but the monster's talons were tipped with poison. Poison of a kind we are not familiar with," Mansoor says somberly.

A commotion at the door precedes the entrance of the Raees, who waves away the concern of her soldiers to come and sit on a chair beside the bed. Attending her are several Ifrit healers who are unfamiliar to Fatima Ghazala. She rises to her feet and stands looking at the gaunt leader of the Ifrit.

"How do I save him, Raees?" she asks. "Can't I give him my strength, my power?"

"No, that will not do anything against the poison," the Ifrit leader replies. Fatima Ghazala feels the rent in her a little more sharply. She is made of sharp edges, and even breathing feels like a bloody affair. "The healers have managed to freeze the poison's effect on Zulfikar's fire but only temporarily. Send him back, Name Giver. Send him back to Al-Naar. He has a better chance of surviving there."

The Raees's calm breaks through Fatima Ghazala's despair, and she wipes away her tears. She looks down at her husband and nods.

"Someone will need to go with him," the Raees says, and an Ifrit healer volunteers.

"Before I Un-Name him, I would ask you a boon," Fatima Ghazala says. She tastes charcoal on her tongue and wonders if this is what endings taste like.

The Raees raises an eyebrow, and Fatima Ghazala steels herself. "Can you remove the Emir's fire bond?"

"The marriage bond?" The Raees looks surprised by her request. Fatima Ghazala nods. "Why?"

"Zulfikar forged the bond without any idea of its effect. His feelings for me were the result of the bond . . . The bond is not the result of his feelings. I do not want someone who loves me because he has no choice but to do so. I want someone who loves me out of his own free will. Please, set him free from this union."

"And what about you, do you want me to remove your bond as well?"

Fatima Ghazala shakes her head. "No. I loved him long before the bond was forged. It just took me longer to recognize the love."

"Very well, then," the Raees says. The room is cleared apart from the Raees, the healer, Fatima Ghazala, and Mansoor. Before they proceed, Fatima Ghazala asks for a minute with the Emir. She presses a kiss in the palm of his hand and whispers her farewell. She is made of losses, and she would much rather he find himself someone who is not always in the shadow of death to love. He will find love with someone who has not killed, someone whose soul is not blackened by murder. She steps back from him.

The Raees reaches out and untangles a knot in Zulfikar's fire. Fatima Ghazala's fire returns to her, and Zulfikar gains his freedom.

Later, much later, Fatima Ghazala sits alone beside the bed on which Zulfikar had so recently lain. The room is empty, and her hands are bandaged, not that Fatima Ghazala is aware of that. A numbness has descended upon her, leaving her impervious to pain and emotion. A glass-walled relief, of sorts. She had supposed that after losing so much she would become inured to loss. She had thought grief familiar and found it simple, if not easy, to speak its language. She had thought wrong.

Fatima Ghazala gets to her feet, her anger blooming like the sun at dawn. She will meet the architect of her grief.

CHAPTER 39

*A*arush, the maharajah of Qirat, opens his eyes and for a moment doesn't understand where, or even if he still, *is.* The pain, when it comes, is welcome. An insistent throbbing on his side reassures him of his continued state of existence. He flexes his fingers and feels the cool bedsheets underneath them. A scent of incense lingers in the air; someone prayed for him. From his vantage on the bed, he cannot see anyone in the room.

He tries to sit up and fails. His heart has become heavier. His guards tried to kill him. That they failed is obvious, but what happened after it is not. A thought occurs to him, and he tries to sit up again and manages this time.

The pain becomes sharper when he disturbs the wound, but he endures it. He becomes aware of someone staring at him and looks up. Sitting very still on a chair at the foot of his bed is his sister. Of his wife and son, there is no sign. Bhavya is looking at him, her face devoid of any emotion, her eyes blank.

"Bhavya!" Aarush says, fear giving him strength that he does not truly possess. His sister starts, and some awareness returns to her eyes.

"You are awake," she says flatly. "Let me call for a healer."

"Wait!" he beseeches her. "Where are Aruna and Vihaan? Are they safe?"

"Yes, of course," Bhavya replies, in the same flat tone. "Bhabhi is attending to Vihaan in her rooms. He developed a mild fever."

Aarush sags against his pillows. "What happened?"

"The guards tried to kill you. The maharani's companions saved you. Sunaina overheard some servants talking about the assassination attempt and called the Emir, who helped the companions take care of the would-be assassins," Bhavya narrates. Aarush frowns; there is something wrong with his sister. She sounds broken.

"Bhavya—" he starts, but she speaks over him.

"You knew Aaruv was conspiring against you, didn't you?" Aarush freezes. "Yes, I had Jamshid Chacha give me a copy of the same report he gave to you. You have known for a while now, haven't you?"

"I . . . yes," Aarush admits.

"Why didn't you do anything about it?" Bhavya asks softly. There are dark shadows under her eyes.

"I was thinking about my next course of action!"

"You took too long, Bhaiya. Do you know they planned to kill Bhabhi and Vihaan as well? Because you were too scared to be thought of as bad, they nearly killed our entire family." Bhavya bows her head, her shoulders stooped as if from some great weight.

Aarush wishes he could go to his sister. "Listen, Bhavya, I will take care of this. You do not need to worry."

Bhavya laughs disbelievingly. When she raises her face, Aarush sees the tears in her eyes, a sheen of sorrow. "We are the raj, Bhaiya. We do not have the luxury of sentiment. Our people come first. You forgot that, but I didn't. *You* do not need to worry, Bhaiya. Because you were too weak to take the actions necessary, I did."

"What did you do?" Aarush demands.

"I exiled Amma and Bua. They are gone," Bhavya replies. "Both of them were fully aware of the assassination attempt." Aarush flinches, though whether from relief or pain he doesn't quite know.

He immediately feels ashamed at being happy for not having to deal with his mother.

"And Aaruv?"

"I gave Aaruv the thing he really wanted." All emotion slips from his sister's face, making her into a stranger he barely recognizes.

"Bhavya . . ."

"Don't you dare blame me for what I did, Bhaiya. *I* kept us safe; *I* kept us alive while you were lying helpless in your bed. Don't blame me for your weakness, and perhaps in time I will learn to forgive you for it." Bhavya gets to her feet and leaves the room without another word. Aarush watches her go, unable to say a single word to defend himself.

The world is colored with shades of red and black: red for the fire that rages within her, and black for the sorrow and the anger that pull at her in equal parts. Fatima Ghazala is aware of the storm at her shoulders and the crackle in the air as she stalks from the room that broadcasts Zulfikar's absence to the Raees's suite one floor below. She knows she is one spark away from an inferno, and she is too far gone to care.

The Raees's doors are closed. Fatima Ghazala knocks once and opens it without waiting for an answer. The leader of the Ifrit is in a meeting with Mansoor, the interim Emir of Noor City; Fatima Ghazala remembers hearing that sometime in the past hour. They both look at her warily as she comes into the room and closes the door, none too gently, behind her.

"Where is the Wazir?" she asks the Raees. Perhaps it is the silky tone of her voice or the menace in her eyes, but the matriarch frowns.

"What need have you with my son, Name Giver?" the Raees asks.

"Your *son* is a traitor, Raees. He must answer." Fatima Ghazala speaks through her fury. "He must pay."

"What proof do you have?" the Ifrit woman demands.

Fatima Ghazala laughs, a sound stripped of all its humor. "Let me tell you where I was yesterday, Raees. Let me tell you what I did yesterday." She takes a deep breath, remembering the foul odor of the Qayyid. She swallows, taking comfort in the anger that immediately rises to resist the sorrow. "I killed sixteen Shayateen yesterday, Raees. I took their Names and crushed them in my hands. I became a murderer so they wouldn't kill any more innocents." Fatima Ghazala breathes, the sound a gasp. "And in their Names were memories. Memories of *your son*. Making deals with them on behalf of the humans, sowing chaos, laughing while damning himself. While damning us." She stares at the Raees, abruptly calm. "You should have had him executed when he killed Shuruq."

"What do you know of Shuruq, Name Giver?" the Ifrit leader roars. Mansoor starts, but Fatima Ghazala is unfazed.

"What do *I* know of her? She dies anew every single night in my dreams, Raees! The memory of her is in Ghazala's fire, the loss of her is in every spark of the flames I carry. The feel of a warm child in my arms, the way she smelled right after a bath, her voice when she called for Ghazala. I know more about her than *you* ever will.

"My entire life has become a dirge." Fatima Ghazala's voice trembles. She turns around and leaves, not heeding the Raees's strident calls to stay. She climbs the stairs to the rooms she shared with Zulfikar, wanting the scant comfort of being surrounded by his things, by his scent.

The fifth floor of Aftab Mahal is deserted. Fatima Ghazala can hear no servants cleaning or otherwise engaged, but the door to the room she shared with Zulfikar is ajar. An oppressive weight presses down the air delineating the subdued atmosphere of the mahal.

Fatima Ghazala pushes the door open and enters, only to come to a stop when she sees the person sitting in a chair in the sitting room. He is holding her oud.

She closes the door behind her. The Wazir smiles sweetly as if her presence is all that he has been waiting for. Her first instinct is to look away, but Fatima Ghazala, with an effort, keeps her eyes on the Ifrit. Her vision blurs. The Wazir's name is entirely black. The air suddenly smells of smoke.

"You have always loved this oud," the Wazir says, and Fatima Ghazala tenses. "You took it everywhere with you. It has spent more time with you than even I have." He breaks the oud in two and throws it on the ground before getting to his feet with a flourish.

Yet another loss.

"Come closer to me, Ghazala. Let us be reunited," the Wazir croons. "Do you know how much I have yearned for you?"

Fatima Ghazala does not move from her spot, so he takes a step closer. "I would keep your distance if I were you, Wazir."

"Would you hurt me?" The Wazir raises his eyebrows. "You wound me, Ghazala. I am the only one you love and I love you. More than you can imagine."

"Love?" Fatima Ghazala scoffs. "Was killing Shuruq an expression of your love, Wazir?"

"You loved the child more than you loved me. That was unforgivable," the Wazir replies simply.

"And you? You didn't love the child? She was yours, Wazir." Fatima Ghazala cannot understand him. She doesn't want to understand him.

"You know what else is unforgivable? Someone else trying to claim you when you are *my* wife. How dare he?" The Wazir ignores her question. "I am friendly with the Ghul, you know? Most of the

Ifrit think they are just animals, but they are much more than that. They are *very* receptive to trading." He smiles secretively.

"What did you give them?" Fatima Ghazala knows she is going to regret asking, but she cannot help herself.

"I didn't *give* them anything so much as I took away something." The Wazir glances at her and pouts. "Oh fine, I just removed protection from a couple of caravans to allow them easier access to the people. I let them into some cities for the same reason. There are so many humans; the death of a few cannot be of much consequence. The peace was grating on my nerves.

"I might as well tell you now. I also had Firdaus killed. And my mother's taint?" the Wazir chortles. "That was me as well."

"Why?"

"They took you away from me, so they had to pay." He comes to stand before her. She looks at him in the gloom of a day almost captured by dusk and shivers. "You were a surprise. I had almost given up hope of finding you again."

"I am not Ghazala." Fatima Ghazala's hands clench into fists. She prays to her Creator for control. For strength. For the ability to see this through.

He raises a hand, perhaps to caress her cheek or grasp her shoulder. Fatima Ghazala steps back. "We will leave this city. Go to a different one where no one knows us. We will be happy, you and I."

"I do not love you. I never will," Fatima Ghazala tells the Wazir as clearly as she can. But he doesn't seem to comprehend her words.

"I am sure Zulfikar will try to find us. It is too bad you got back before he died, but you made things easier by removing the fire bond."

"*I* am still bonded to him," Fatima Ghazala says, fiercely glad that she hadn't asked the Raees to remove her fire bond.

"You are lying." This seems to penetrate the Wazir's delusions, and he frowns.

"I have no reason to."

"I have removed all obstacles between you and me, Ghazala. No one will protect you from me anymore."

Fatima Ghazala's eyes narrow. "I can protect myself, Wazir."

"Call me Anwar."

"I will never call you by your name."

His eyes flare black, and Fatima Ghazala's hackles rise. "Since when have you been tainted?" she asks him.

"It happened in a fight with the Shayateen in the desert, three years after I was Named. It is easy to hide it. I thought *you* would see it, but you wouldn't even look at me." He smiles, friendly again. "I am a bit sad that you killed the Shayateen. They were going to help the humans with their war, but I guess the Ghul can do that."

"You are assisting the rebels?"

The Wazir shrugs expansively. "It is so easy to poke at the fissures in a relationship and cause them to break. I talked with the young rajkumar, mentioned how unfair it was that the Ifrit will be getting rich off the gold mines in the desert cities. How unfair it was that his older brother got to be maharajah while he, more suited to the role, is nothing but a moneyed prince. Nudged some landowners here and there. Humans are always eager for war. I just helped them find a reason for one."

"Why would you do that?"

"For the chaos, my love. The glorious chaos." The Wazir shudders as if in ecstasy, then suddenly straightens, all emotion leaching from his face. "We should go now."

"I am not going anywhere with you, Wazir." Fatima Ghazala turns her back on him, knowing the action will enrage him. He grabs her forearm, and she lets her fire burn him. He retreats, and she turns. "I do not need any man, Ifrit or human, to protect me, Wazir. Have you forgotten who I am?"

The Wazir hisses. His pupils spill into the whites of his eyes and turn black. "Do you think I am afraid of being burned?"

"If you aren't, you should learn to be," Fatima Ghazala replies, calling her fire to burn on the surface of her skin.

"Ghazala," the Ifrit hisses.

"For the last time, Wazir, I am not Ghazala. I do carry her fire, though, which means I know the amount of hate she had for you." Fatima Ghazala holds herself ready, her body instinctively poised to defend itself.

"You lie!" the Wazir roars. "She loved me!"

"Love?" Fatima Ghazala spits out. "You wanted to own her. You wanted to control her. Your attention was suffocating, and your jealousy knew no limits. She loathed you at the end."

The Wazir rushes at her, his rage overpowering his cunning and restraint. Fatima Ghazala braces herself for the impact. She needs just a moment to retrieve his Name. Just one moment to destroy it. But she never gets the chance. Hot blood sprays on her face, in her eyes, and the Wazir's head falls to the ground. Before she gets a chance to even scream, the Ifrit's head and body are set on fire. Fatima Ghazala falls to her knees, shaking, and raises a hand to wipe the blood away.

The Raees stands before her, the Wazir's burning body between them. She is holding a sword dripping with the Wazir's blood. Fatima Ghazala watches the sword fall to the floor, followed by the Raees, who keens as the body of her only child burns.

CHAPTER 40

The pihu of the koyal bird in the tree; the sound of the River Rahat when its waters meet the quays. The red dupatta fluttering in the wind; the small mirrors on it making stars out of sunlight. The sizzle of the meat at the kebab wallahs. Someone flying an orange kite from a rooftop. The azaan five times a day; the hymns on Sunday. The peal of bells at the mandir; the smiling faces at the synagogue. The khejri trees strive on while the date palms are full of grace. Red, pink, and purple bougainvillea leading riots on whitewashed walls. Noor, of the thousand faces, colors, and languages. Noor, where she will always belong, and Noor, which is no longer enough for her.

Sunaina has been saying goodbye to both her city and her ghosts for the past three months. Not forever, no, but at least for the next long while. She opens the door to the bookstore on Kalandar Street that her sister now runs, and enters. The first person she sees is Rajkumari Bhavya, curled up in a chair in a corner of the store, staring into the distance. The rajkumari prefers the dark now. Mirrors make her scream, and her lips no longer know the shape of smiles. Whatever she did, whatever happened three months ago, left her ensnared in sorrow and in silence. Strangely, the only person who seems to speak the same language as her these days is Sunaina's sister, which is perhaps why the rajkumari spends her days ensconced in the bookstore with little regard for her social status and the obligations accompanying it.

"You are here, didi." Fatima Ghazala appears in the doorway leading to the back room. Her sister has lost weight. Her cheekbones stand out in stark relief to her hollow cheeks. A universe resides in her gold eyes. But still, she wears her sorrow more gently than the rajkumari. "Has Jung Sori told you the departure date, then?" Sunaina had thought Fatima Ghazala would be opposed to her plans to travel and had been prepared to argue about it, but to her surprise and consternation, her sister had not just agreed but even encouraged her to leave the city.

"We leave in two weeks," Sunaina reports with a flutter of nerves. When her Han friend invited her to accompany her family on their annual trip to their homeland, Sunaina immediately jumped at the chance. The walls of the city feel less constrictive now that she will be leaving them behind soon.

"Rajkumari," Fatima Ghazala says, sitting next to Bhavya. The princess gives no indication of hearing her, so her sister pulls her cheek. Sunaina gasps at this impertinence, and Bhavya scowls.

"Pay attention to me," Fatima Ghazala says shortly.

"What is it?" Bhavya glares at her.

"Didi is leaving in two weeks. Did you know?"

The rajkumari looks confused, then uncertain. "I . . . maybe?"

"You should go with her," Fatima Ghazala says without warning.

"Go?" the rajkumari echoes. "Where?"

"Away."

"From Noor?"

"From Qirat." Sunaina tries to catch her sister's eye, but Fatima Ghazala won't look at her.

"I can leave?" The rajkumari sounds as if she hasn't contemplated the idea even once.

"There is more to life than the ghosts you are spending it with," Fatima Ghazala says, as if she is intimate with the ghosts she refers to.

"You think I can escape them?" Bhavya raises hopeful eyes to her.

"You owe it to yourself to try," Fatima Ghazala replies gently.

"Fatima!" Sunaina hisses. "I would have appreciated some warning before you brought that up!"

Fatima Ghazala shrugs. "You care for her. Why would you say no?"

"Because she is the rajkumari!"

"She's only a rajkumari in Qirat, didi. Besides, look at her."

Sunaina turns and looks at Bhavya, who is contemplating her hands with a disturbing intensity. Sunaina capitulates. What else can she do when presented with this picture of misery? "Fine, I will talk to Sori for you, but, Rajkumari Bhavya, you will need to get the maharajah's permission."

At her words, Bhavya flinches and gets to her feet. "I need no one's permission to live my life, especially not my brother's. I have decided. I *will* go with you." She walks out of the store without saying anything else. Sunaina throws Fatima Ghazala a look that promises retribution and hurries after her.

A tribunal composed of the maharajah and the somewhat less corrupt members of his court find Sanchit Goundar, Vinod Rathod, and a number of other wealthy landowners guilty of treason and murder. Though the murder charges are hotly contested, the evidence is undeniable. Rajkumar Aaruv's body was found at a small house in Imli Nagar, the deed to which names none other than Sanchit Goundar as its owner. As to the motive behind the murder, though the perpetrators insist they weren't the ones to bring about the rajkumar's end, speculations from the general populace agree that it was a result of the prince's refusal to participate in the planned assassination of the maharajah.

The royal family is in mourning. From all reports, the Rajmata was so struck by her son's death, she suffered a breakdown and has retreated to an ashram in an undisclosed location. Due to the maharajah's request, the rajkumar's funeral was a quiet affair, the attendance limited to immediate family members. Funeral rites were assiduously observed, and evening prayers for the prince continue to this very day.

"Enough," Aarush says, and Janab Jamshid stops reading from a paper that records in flat detail the events of three months past. "Leave me," he says, and the advisor removes himself from the room. Ifrit soldiers stand guard outside the door to his office. This should have made Aarush feel safe, but the sharp twinge in his side every time he moves reminds him that he is never safe from betrayal.

Aarush signed the orders for the execution of the traitors the morning after the general of his army delivered the cleaned crown to him. Though the general made the delivery without comment or censure, the implications were obvious.

A knock on his door makes him straighten. A second later, his wife enters the room carrying a tray piled with food. "I'm not hungry," Aarush says shortly. A new silence has crept in between them. A silence choked with blame and guilt.

His wife closes the door behind her and places the tray on his desk. She stands there, the maharani of the kingdom, and regards him quietly for a moment. "It has been three months, Maharaj. Isn't it past time you stopped sulking?"

"Sulking?" Aarush echoes disbelievingly. "My brother is dead!"

"No"—Aruna raises her chin—"the traitors are dead."

"You could have stopped her, Aruna." Finally, Aarush gives voice to the thought that has been festering in him for three months.

"Why would I have done that, Maharaj? The man planned to kill my husband. My child. I would have killed him myself had Bhavya not been brave enough for both of us."

"Aruna!" Aarush rises to his feet, knocking over the inkwell on his desk. The writing paper on it is dyed black.

"You know that I love you, Aarush. More than my life. But I will defend my child against everything and everyone that threatens him—even if it is you." She pauses, turns to go, and stops, as if changing her mind. She faces him again and looks into his eyes. "I understand that you may not have wanted to be the maharajah, but the fact is, you are one. If your country didn't cling to its misogyny and forbid women from ruling, you could have passed the crown to Bhavya. She has more than proved her ability to rule. As it is, you can't, so you are the maharajah. You need to behave like one."

"You think I am not? What am I supposed to do, Aruna? How else am I supposed to behave?" Aarush reels. He hadn't expected such words from his wife of all people.

"You were given the information about the rebels; you were warned about the rebellion. The report revealed the instigators, and you did nothing. You ask what are you supposed to do?" Aruna meets his eyes. Hers are clear and unafraid. "You are supposed to make the difficult choices, Aarush. You are supposed to act for your people. No, not just for the glittery, perfumed masses who fawn over your every action, your every word. I'm talking about the people you rule who do not get invited to the same parties you do, who cannot afford to eat three meals a day. I am talking about those people whose voices are taken from them by those with power and wealth. You are the maharajah, Aarush, you are supposed to serve the people no matter what personal sacrifices that requires."

"Why are you saying these things to me now? Why not before?"

"Because I was trying to be the perfect wife, the perfect maharani. I was trying to be more royal than my blood is. Because you didn't want to hear these things before. No, in fact, you still don't want to hear them, do you? But, Aarush, when I almost lost you, almost lost everything that I love, I decided to stop pretending. I decided to stop saying only the things you want to hear. I love you too much to do that." Aruna turns away. "Please eat your food."

Alone again, Aarush sits down heavily in his chair and broods. Aruna's words hurt him, but he can't help but admit the truth in them. He sighs deeply, and his eyes fall on the tray in front of him. He hadn't even thanked her for the food.

One week after his conversation with his wife, Aarush has lunch with the leader of the Ifrit in Northern Aftab. She reached out to him when he was convalescing, and Aarush was surprised by both her strength and the depth of her military knowledge. Somehow he has gotten into the habit of lunching with her once every week—something he enjoys more than he had thought he would.

As a measure of respect and sensitivity to the maharajah's diet, all the dishes served at lunch are vegetarian. Also present at the table are Fatima Ghazala and the interim Emir of Noor, Mansoor. From what Aarush has been told, he understands that Zulfikar sustained an injury during a Ghul attack, which necessitated his removal to the Djinn world. The Raees and Mansoor seem certain of his return; Fatima Ghazala does not.

They eat outside at a table set in the shade of a tree, enjoying the fine weather and a benevolent breeze. Aarush glances at Fatima Ghazala and is surprised anew by the changes wrought in her in the scant amount of time that has passed since he saw her last. Though her youth remains undiminished, she holds herself with a confidence usually visible in a much older person. But along with the confidence is a complicated sadness that Aarush recognizes simply because he has seen the war his sister wages with the same emotion.

"So, Rajah, what ails you?" the leader of the Ifrit suddenly asks.

Aarush puts down a piece of naan dipped in spicy hummus and takes a sip of cold well water. A bird sings in the branches somewhere above them. Fatima Ghazala awaits his response with a benign curiosity in her remarkable eyes while Mansoor seems distracted by his own food. "I don't know how to be a good king," he finally admits. "My maharani says I need to learn to make difficult decisions."

"She's right, your maharani," the Raees interjects.

"I try, Raees. But what if I make the wrong decision? What if instead of making things better, I make them worse?" Aarush feels ridiculous. The maharajah who doesn't know how to lead.

"You cannot always be right, Maharajah, but if your intention is pure, you won't be too wrong. You should talk to your maharani more. Get her advice. Let her make some of the decisions," the Raees replies. "Good leaders are not just those who make good decisions but also those that know how to take good advice."

After the meal concludes, the maharajah returns to his side of Aftab Mahal and Mansoor to his duties. Fatima Ghazala is left alone with the Raees. They are still outside, lingering over cups of liberally sweetened coffee.

"How are your nightmares, Raees?" Fatima Ghazala throws the opening gambit.

"Endurable. Yours?" The Raees takes a sip of her beverage.

"Sometimes I wake up screaming," Fatima Ghazala replies, contemplating the tabletop.

"I told you to move back into the mahal, didn't I?" the Raees snaps. Fatima Ghazala insists on staying in the apartment on the second floor of Firdaus's bookstore.

"I can't. Not while he isn't here." There is no need to ask who Fatima Ghazala is talking about. Only one man, Ifrit or human, matters to her.

"Do you want to send him a message?" the Raees asks.

Fatima Ghazala gives her a sharp look before shaking her head resolutely. She drains her cup and gets to her feet. "Come, Raees, let me cleanse your Name. I have someone to meet later."

The Raees's taint lessens a bit more every time Fatima Ghazala scrapes it off her Name. Neither of them know if she's going to be able to remove it entirely, but Fatima Ghazala is certain she can scrape off enough to return the Raees to her original strength. This ability has won her many proponents among the Ifrit elite, who were divided on the Name Giver being of human origin. Fatima Ghazala's power to destroy Names is something the Raees keeps secret, a weapon in times of need.

For Fatima Ghazala, daily cleansing the Raees's fire has an unanticipated benefit. Her fire is much stronger now than it was three months ago. She can, and has, easily Named the Raees's many advisors in the last month.

Fatima Ghazala makes her way to Achal Kaur's haveli an hour later in a carriage the Raees insists she use. Achal Kaur is waiting for her outside and sweeps her up in a hug as soon as she alights from the conveyance.

"Sat Sri Akaal, Beeji," Fatima Ghazala says, beaming at the woman who has been filling the void left by Laali.

"You are much too thin, chanda," the matriarch says, chucking her under the chin. "Doesn't that Raees of yours feed you?" The leader of the Ifrit has continued Zulfikar's arrangement with Achal

Kaur and her messengers. The two matriarchs have a somewhat frictional relationship.

Fatima Ghazala grins, wrapping her arm around her adopted grandmother. She knows that stuffing her with food is the old woman's sincerest expression of love and accepts it happily. They make their way to the rooftop, where a group of people is gathered.

"They are all new to Qirat and anxious to share their tales," Achal Kaur says.

None of these people have much in the way of material wealth, but all of them are rich with stories. Over the next few hours, Fatima Ghazala listens to them. She records each story, sometimes through translators. She learns the different tastes of the homes they left behind: a briny seaside, a fertile valley, a city with cobbled streets where the air smells like sugar. She hears about the roads, the twists and turns, these people took to get to Noor. She listens to the accounts of what they left behind: a small yellow house with a front yard full of roses, a pawpaw plantation, a ten-year war, and always a family. She sees through their laughter to the tears they think no one notices, and she writes it all down. All stories are precious, but these ones, because they aren't found in any books, are infinitely more so.

When the carriage drops her in front of the bookstore, the sky is streaked with orange. Any moment, the azaan for Maghrib will fill the streets. Fatima Ghazala dashes inside and upstairs to the two-room apartment. She lights a lamp and washes up quickly. After praying, she looks at the food Achal Kaur packed for her and decides that it will do for her dinner. She could easily nip outside and buy dinner from the nearby restaurants and street vendors, but now that she is away from others, the mask she hides behind has disintegrated. Fatima Ghazala doesn't have the strength to pretend anymore.

She has just sat down to eat when someone bangs on the locked door of the bookstore downstairs. Fatima Ghazala freezes for a minute before she grabs a lamp and makes her way down.

"Api!" It's Azizah. Fatima Ghazala opens the door, and the youngest Alif tumbles in. Her eyes are streaming, and Fatima Ghazala goes cold, remembering all too clearly a similar incident three months ago.

"What's the matter, Azizah?" she asks anxiously.

Azizah raises eyes full of hurt and wails, "I've been betrayed!"

It is only twenty minutes later, after a storm of weeping has passed, that Fatima Ghazala is able to make sense of the situation. Earlier that evening, Bilal the muezzin came to visit the Alifs, bringing with him his parents and a rishta . . . for the wrong sister.

"My sister has betrayed me. I will *never* forgive her." Azizah crosses her arms and looks mutinous.

"But she hasn't done anything that requires you to forgive her," Fatima Ghazala points out.

"Of course she did!"

"What did she do?"

Azizah opens her mouth, then closes it.

"If you have to hate someone, you should hate Bilal," Fatima Ghazala says patiently.

"Why would I hate him?"

"Why would you hate Adila? Did she do anything to seduce Bilal?"

"No!"

"Did she do anything to attract his attention?"

"No . . ."

"Does Adila even want to marry him?"

"I don't know!" Azizah gives an injured sniff. "Stop making sense! I'm going to stay here tonight, and that's that!"

"Of course," Fatima Ghazala says, feeling old and wise.

She has only just settled Azizah on a futon with copious amounts of desserts, when there is another knock on the door. Fatima Ghazala has an idea who her next visitor is, and her expectations are fulfilled when she pulls the door open to reveal the oldest Alif. Adila looks absolutely furious, with color in her cheeks and eyes full of spark.

"I am angry!" she says.

"So I can see," Fatima Ghazala replies calmly.

"Absolutely furious."

"All right."

"How dare he?"

"Who?"

"Bilal! How dare he?"

"Dare what?"

"Ask his father to ask Abbu for my hand! In marriage!"

"Because he likes you?"

"That's not how it's done."

"It's not?"

"No! First you talk to the person you want to marry. If she indicates interest, then you talk to her parents. That's the protocol!"

"Oh, is that so? I didn't know." Fatima Ghazala makes soothing motions.

"Now Azizah thinks I have betrayed her," Adila wails.

"Um, about Azizah—"

"She thinks I seduced Bilal!"

"No she doesn't. But, Adila, about Azizah—"

"What are you doing here?" Azizah asks, standing on the first stair leading to the second floor.

"She's my friend! I have more right than you to be here!" Adila flares up.

"She likes *me* better!" Azizah's hands go on her hips.

"Before I have to start refereeing your fight, where's Amirah?" Fatima Ghazala asks wearily.

"I'm right here, Api."

They turn to see the middle Alif in front of the entrance to the bookstore.

"I think both of you should be ashamed of yourselves for letting a man ruin your relationship. And while you are being ashamed, you should go home so Ammi and Abbu know you are alive and haven't killed each other." Amirah turns to Fatima Ghazala. "Can I stay here tonight?"

Fatima Ghazala looks at the three imploring faces and smiles weakly.

In the end, a message is sent to the Alif parents, and the Alif sisters settle in Fatima Ghazala's new home. Azizah tearfully confesses that she has known for a while where the muezzin's interests lie, but she didn't want to admit it. How he had been staring at Adila at the maidaan during Deepavali, how he had rushed over to their side during the Ghul attack later that night. She tells them how he had been peeking at Adila during Fatima Ghazala's wedding—Adila hadn't seen because she had been too busy berating Azizah for staring. Azizah had spied him pacing outside their building when Adila was hurt by the Shayateen. He had bribed one of the kids in their building to send Adila her favorite mithai. Azizah had eaten the dessert he had sent.

Fatima Ghazala loses herself in the drama of her friends' lives. She slips into the space that exists for her, that is precious to her, and keeps her darkness at bay for a little longer.

A week later, the oldest Alif and Fatima Ghazala are in the back room looking over the new books delivered earlier that day. It is late in the afternoon, and soon Adila will leave. The oldest Alif wears the glow of a woman newly in love, not that she is ready to admit it. Adila works with Fatima Ghazala in the bookstore; they are united in their efforts to provide recreational, accessible literature to the poor of Noor. Adila's intended, Bilal, is an apprentice at a bookbinder's, and Fatima Ghazala is entertaining thoughts of recruiting him into their business.

"Should I stay over?" Adila asks suddenly.

"You are welcome to stay over whenever you want, of course," Fatima Ghazala says automatically.

"Why do you do that, Fatima Ghazala?" Adila looks hurt.

"Do what?" Fatima Ghazala looks at her friend in surprise.

"Create distance between us!"

"What distance?" Fatima Ghazala can hardly tell her oldest friend that she feels too dirty for the people around her. That killing the Shayateen may not have given her the taint but has blackened her soul anyway. That knowing her is dangerous.

"You know very well what I am talking about, Fatima. You hold yourself apart from everyone now. You insist on living alone, eating alone. You don't even come over for dinner unless we force you to!"

"I'm hardly alone, Adila. You are with me during the days. I talk to Achal Kaur and the Raees. I walk around the city and talk to even more people. I am not alone."

"What about during the nights?"

Fatima Ghazala doesn't respond. The nights are her purgatory.

"I will stay over—"

"No. Bilal's parents are coming over for dinner tonight. Have you forgotten?"

"Ah. Then I shall send Azizah."

"It's fine. I would much rather be alone. I am all right, Adila. Sometimes I am sad, but can you blame me? I am healing. Slowly. I will be better. I promise."

Adila gives Fatima Ghazala a hug, holding her close. "You know I will come to you whenever you call, right?"

"I do."

Adila leaves a little while later, and for the first time since the morning, Fatima Ghazala is alone. It is easy to pretend that the dark places in her are full of light during the day or in someone's company, but away from everyone, the cracks in her become gapingly obvious. She is a composition of losses. She has lost her parents twice and her goodness seventeen times over. Knowing her means being at risk. Fatima Ghazala has lost too many of the people she loves to risk those who remain. So she will learn to be alone, learn to tell everyone else's stories, and refuse to tell her own.

Besides, how can she tell her story when half of it is missing? The fire bond still exists, but Fatima Ghazala hasn't been able to feel Zulfikar at all. All she knows is that he is still alive. Alive and hopefully well. Free from her. Safe from her.

Fatima Ghazala has learned the vagaries of love in the absence of it. Though much of it is still a mystery to her, she has become intimately acquainted with the helpless yearning love songs are usually full of. Whether Zulfikar returns to her or not, he will always have a slice of her heart. Fatima Ghazala refuses to give him all of it. She would much rather he didn't return. That is the truth, no matter how much it hurts. Isn't freeing him from the bond, from their marriage, the greatest expression of her love?

An hour before midnight, Fatima Ghazala is in the back room of the bookstore, on an old divan she dragged in as a place to rest. She tries to concentrate on the book she is reading, but her eyes keep closing. Sleep means nightmares, so she resists but it is a los-ing battle. When she has almost given in, she feels the tickling sen-sation that precedes a Naming, a signal that an Ifrit wants her attention. Fatima Ghazala frowns, not wanting to Name an Ifrit in the bookstore. She usually Names Ifrit in front of the fire pit behind the barracks on the grounds of Northern Aftab. The Raees hasn't sent a message informing her about an upcoming Naming, hasn't requested her presence. Is this an unplanned Naming? The sensa-tion repeats, an imperative quality to it.

Fatima Ghazala gets to her feet with a weary sigh and stumbles when her fire bond comes to life. Her vision blurs, and in front of her is an expanse of smokeless fire, a fire that feels as familiar to her as her own. Her mouth goes dry at the thought of Naming Zulfikar. How will she deny him when he stands in front of her? But what if he only wants to return to his position as the Emir and no longer has any interest in her? Can she endure that pain? Does she even have a choice?

The sensation repeats. He is impatient. Fatima Ghazala takes a deep breath and moves closer to the fire. The flames reach out to her, soft on her skin. She shivers, unprepared for the unintentional seduction. His Name is in four pieces. The pieces read: loyalty, honesty, courage, and . . . one more. Fatima Ghazala picks up the last golden piece. Her name. Her name is one of the pieces of his Name. Her eyes are wet. His memories are all of her, as if before her, without her, he doesn't exist.

Somehow she manages to join the pieces of his Name together. Somehow she finds the courage to press the golden Name into the region of his chest. She steps back and watches his fire flow into the shape of a man. She blinks, and he is there: flesh, blood, and fire. Oh, and anger. He is gloriously angry.

The urge to touch him, to reassure herself of his tangibility, is so strong that Fatima Ghazala has taken a step forward without realizing. She retreats, her eyes not leaving his face. His lips are still full, his cheeks are hollow, and his eyebrows are dark wings. He is breathing fast; a pulse tics madly in his throat. An oud, incongruously, is slung over his shoulder.

"You," Zulfikar says, his voice low and full of anger. He steps toward her, and Fatima Ghazala tenses, ready to flee. "If you run, I will chase you. I will chase you until I catch you," he promises.

Fatima Ghazala reaches for calm and cannot find it. Her nails dig into her palms. "Welcome back to Noor, Emir." Her voice shakes slightly at the end.

For one charged moment, Zulfikar doesn't react. Then he strides forward and wraps his arms around her, pulling her flush against the length of him. His hands slide down her spine, molding her body, as if reassuring himself of her. Fatima Ghazala savors his closeness, allows herself one whole minute of his heat before pushing him away. At first his embrace tightens and she thinks he will refuse to let go, but then his arms fall away and he steps back. Fatima Ghazala is immediately bereft.

"We are no longer married," she tells him through a thick throat.

Zulfikar tilts his head, an eyebrow raised. "Whatever makes you think that?"

"You said that once the fire bond breaks, the marriage is dissolved," Fatima Ghazala reminds him.

"Indeed I did, but, habibti, that only works when both fire bonds are broken, mine *and* yours. You may have stolen my bond, but yours still remains. You are still mine as much as you ever were. And I? Well, I have always been yours. Not that you have ever cared to claim me."

"I will ask the Raees to remove mine as well." She will not let him persuade her otherwise.

"I will petition against it."

"You do not understand, Zulfikar!"

"The Raees sent me daily reports about you, Fatima Ghazala. She told me that you think you are bad luck. Cursed. That if you allow yourself to love me, I will die."

"You almost did!" Fatima Ghazala folds in on herself. Zulfikar catches her before she can fall. She weeps at the memory of his gray face, his still form, her fear, his helplessness.

Zulfikar, still holding her, sits down on the divan. Fatima Ghazala feels his fire envelop them. She pulls away from him but does not move out of his embrace. "I am not so noble that I distance myself from you for your sake, Zulfikar. I do it for my own. I don't think I can handle any more loss."

"Death will not be denied, Fatima Ghazala. I cannot promise never to die, habibti. But before death, there is life. No matter how short our hours are or how swiftly time flees, there is life. And since there is life, habibti, let us live. Let us not squander even one second of it."

"You do not understand," Fatima Ghazala whispers. The memory of Firdaus, of Laali, of her parents, the memories of the Shayateen filled with the people they killed, among whom were surely her birth parents. How can she let herself be that vulnerable again?

"Of course I understand! You left me without warning. I didn't know if I would ever see you again, if you were even alive! I was attacked and didn't regain consciousness until I was back in Al-Naar. When I opened my eyes, I couldn't feel you, Fatima Ghazala. I thought you were gone." His voice cracks. "Don't you dare tell me I can't understand the fear of loving someone. Of losing them."

"I killed those Shayateen, Zulfikar. Their deaths weigh on me. How can I ask you to love me when I am a murderer?"

"Do you think you are the only one who has killed, Fatima Ghazala?" Zulfikar asks. "Will you not love me if I tell you of the lives I have taken in the name of protecting my people?"

"I can't forgive myself, Zulfikar," Fatima Ghazala whispers.

He cups her cheeks, his eyes full. "That is what makes you good, habibti. Only monsters kill without regard to the life they are taking. You are not a monster."

Fatima Ghazala breathes out. She has been waiting for so long for someone to tell her that. She looks at the Ifrit in front of her, his beauty pronounced in the way he looks at her. Reaching out, she brushes away the lone tear that escapes him. His eyes close under her ministrations. She touches his cheeks gently and skims her fingers over his lips. She buries her face in his neck and breathes in the scent of him. She feels his heart racing in his chest.

Unable to resist him any longer, helpless against her own desire, she presses a soft kiss on his lips. His eyes snap open, and she reads the hunger in them.

"Give me your fire, Fatima Ghazala," the Emir of Noor demands. Then relents. "Please?"

Fatima Ghazala knows that her arguments hold. He is precious to her and losing him will destroy her. She knows she should walk away from him, but no matter how scared her mind is, her heart has made its decision. She calls her fire forth, and a flame dances on her palm. "I don't know how to tell love stories, Zulfikar," she warns him.

Zulfikar breathes in her fire and shudders. He pulls her closer to him and tilts her chin up.

"We'll learn together, habibti." He lowers his head and kisses her with a heart forevers are made of.

THE END

GLOSSARY

Abaya: A loose over-garment usually worn over clothes in the Muslim world when praying.

Abba/Abbu: Urdu. Formal/informal. Father.

Adab: Urdu. Respect.

Allah hafiz: Urdu. Literally "May God protect you." Used as a farewell.

Ambi: Punjabi. A mango-shaped pattern.

Amma/Ammi: Urdu. Formal/informal. Mother.

Angrez: Urdu. The English.

Apa/Api: Urdu. Formal/informal. Elder sister.

Asaan: Kalaripayattu instructor.

Asr: Muslim prayer performed before sunset.

Assalaam wa alaikum: Arabic. Literally "May the peace and greeting of Allah be with you." Used as a greeting by Muslims.

Azaan: Arabic. The Muslim call to prayer.

Baag: Urdu. Garden.

Baba: Used in several different languages as a kinship term for "father."

Baji: Urdu. Elder sister.

Banarasi sari: A silk sari made in the Indian city if Varanasi. Known for its high quality.

Beeji: Punjabi. Grandmother.

Beta: Urdu/Hindi. Son.

Bhabhi: Urdu/Hindi. Sister-in-law.

Bhaiya: Urdu/Hindi. Brother. Can also be shortened to bhai.

Bua: Hindi. Paternal aunt.

Chacha: Urdu. Paternal uncle.

Chanda: Hindi/Urdu/Punjabi. Moon. Sometimes used as an endearment.

Charpai: Hindi. Traditional woven bed.

Chaunk: Hindi. Cooking technique where spices and onions (sometimes whole, sometimes ground) are added to hot oil briefly in order to release flavors and essential oils.

Choti: Urdu/Hindi. Literally "younger" (feminine). Sometimes used as an endearment.

Chulha: Urdu/Hindi. Traditional stove made from either bricks or mud.

Deepavali: Hindu festival of lights.

Dholak: Drums. A folk instrument.

Didi: Hindi. Elder sister.

Diya: Earthen lamp.

Dua: Urdu. Prayer. Performed at the end of the Muslim prayer by raising cupped palms as if to receive something.

Dupatta: Hindi. (Usually) diaphanous material worn with a shalwar kameez most often as a veil.

Eid: Muslim festival that follows the month of Ramadan.

Fajr: Muslim prayer performed just before dawn.

Gajra: Flower garland usually made of jasmine flowers worn in the hair by Indian women.

Ghagra/Lehenga choli: Traditional Indian outfit worn by women. It comes in two parts: the tunic/top (choli) and the skirt (ghagra/lehenga).

Gulaab jamun: Dessert made from milk and flour.

Gulgula: A pastry much like a doughnut made from dough and fried. Usually eaten as a teatime snack.

Gurdwara: Place of worship for Sikh people.

Haar: A long necklace usually very expensive and made from gold or other precious stones/material.

Habibti: Arabic. My love (feminine).

Halal: Permissible in Islam.

Haveli: Mansion.

Huzoor: Hindi/Urdu. A title of respect for a person of high rank.

Iftar: The breaking of the fast during Ramadan.

Imam: Religious leader in Islam.

Isha: Muslim prayer usually performed late in the evening.

Ittar: Scented essential oil made from different kinds of flowers.

Jalebiyaan: Urdu/Hindi (singular: jalebi). Dessert made of dough that is fried and then soaked in sugar syrup.

Jali: Perforated stone or net-like screen found commonly in Indo-Islamic and Islamic architecture.

Jama: Outer garment with a flared skirt and long sleeves worn by males. Introduced in India by the Moghuls. Usually embellished with jewelry and made from costly material.

-ji: Suffix attached to a name to denote respect.

Kaba: A small square building located in Mecca, Saudi Arabia. It contains a stone sacred to the Muslims and is the point (north) to which they turn when praying.

Kaddu: Hindi/Urdu. Literally "pumpkin." Colloquially used to describe a plump/fat person. Usage can be either affectionate or malicious.

Kalaripayattu: A type of martial arts that originated in Kerala.

Kamarband: Jewelry. A long chain worn around the hips/waist.

Karta: Used to refer to the head of a Hindu family.

Khala: Urdu/Arabic. Maternal aunt.

Kmemu: A word ancient Egyptians used to refer to themselves.

Koyal: A species of bird.

Kunafeh: Palestinian dessert. Cheese pastry soaked in sugar syrup.

Maghrib: Muslim prayer performed right after sunset.

Maharajah/rajah: King.

Maharani/rani: Queen.

Maher: The obligatory gift, usually jewelry or money, given to a bride by the groom in Muslim weddings.

Majnun: Allusion to star-crossed lovers Layla and Majnun. (Comparable to Romeo.)

Mandir: Hindu temple.

Masala chai: Chai flavored with spices.

Masjid: Muslim place of worship.

Matha patti: Jewelry. A headpiece.

Mausi: Hindi. Mom's sister.

Meethi: Hindi. Literally "sweet." Sometimes used as an endearment.

Mithai: Sweets.

Mitti ittar: Essential oil made from clay.

Muezzin: The person who recites the call to prayer in a mosque.

Nathni: Jewelry. Nose ring with a chain attached to it.

Nautanki: A play composed of different forms such as songs, dialogue, etc.

Nikah: Muslim marriage.

Pagadi: Turban.

Pallu: The loose end of a sari.

Paranda: Jewelry braided in hair. Usually has tassels and bells.

Parchin kari: A method of decorating houses using stones, cut and polished, to create images/patterns.

Patiala pants: A type of billowy trousers.

Peda: Milk-based dessert.

Pihu: A sound made by a bird.

Puja: Hindu prayer ceremony.

Pujari: Hindu priest.

Purdah: A barrier between men and women.

Puttar: Panjabi. Literally "son." Colloquially used to denote anyone younger in affectionate terms.

Pyali: A small bowl that usually functions as a cup.

Qayyid: Arabic. Leader.

Raj: Hindi. Literally "royal."

Rajmata: Hindi. The mother of the king.

Rakat: A unit of prayer in Islam.

Rangoli: Drawings made usually on floors with powdered color during Hindu festivals like Diwali.

Rishta/Rishtay: Singular/plural. Literally "relationship." It can mean an offer for an arranged marriage.

Sahib/Sahiba: Urdu. Masculine/feminine. Term of respect. (Comparable to sir/madam.)

Sambar: A dish with origins in Tamil Nadu. It is made from lentils, vegetables, and tamarind.

Sat Sri Akaal: Used by Sikh people to greet each other.

Sayyid/Sayyida: Arabic. Masculine/feminine. Term of respect. (Comparable to sir/madam.)

Shalwar kameez: Outfit consisting of two pieces: a pair of pants and a long tunic.

Sharbat: A drink made from fruit juice. Served cold.

Shatranj: An old form of chess.

Sherwani: A long coat worn with pants. Usually embroidered or featuring stone work.

Shubh Deepavali: Happy Deepavali.

Shukraan: Arabic. Thank you.

Sikhye: Sweet Korean beverage made from rice.

Silambam: Weapon-based martial art that originated in Tamil Nadu.

Taqiyah: Arabic. A white hat made of woven material usually used by Muslim men during prayer.

Taqsim: Arabic. A musical improvisation.

Tava: A flat metal pan used for making roti.

Tikka: A mark worn on the forehead between the eyebrows by those practicing Hinduism.

Tulsi: Hindi. An herb. Also known as holy basil.

Wa alaikum ussalaam: Arabic. Response to "Assalaam wa alaikum." Literally "And unto you, peace."

Wagashi: Traditional Japanese dessert made from mochi or fruits.

Wudu: Ritual cleansing of face, hands, etc., performed by Muslims before praying.

Ya binti: Arabic. My daughter.

Zardozi: Embroidery done with stones and metals (usually gold or silver).

Zohr: Muslim prayer performed at midday.

ACKNOWLEDGMENTS

In all the languages I know, the words for "thank you" are the sweetest ones. Still, they are only words that cannot quite encompass the extent of my gratitude. I will say them anyway.

First, thank you to Allah (SWT). Then, thank you, Ammi, for everything. Seriously, *everything*. From the hugs to the cups of chai. For listening to me talk about my characters as if they are real people. For assuring me that I can do this. Thank you for the flowers and the love. I do not know what I did to deserve you, but I am so glad you are my mom. I love you. Thank you, Abbu, for your enthusiasm. Thank you for being proud of me.

Katelyn Detweiler, thank you for taking a chance on me. Nothing I say will ever be enough. Lisa Sandell, thank you for seeing the beauty in Noor and her people. Thank you for believing in my words and the story they tell.

Living with a writer requires a lot of patience. My brother Izaz, thank you for encouraging me. My bhabhi Robina, you rock. Thank you for the library trips. To my little monsters, Zara and Ruwaiz, thank you for playing with me. I love you. My brother Ishraaz and my bhabhi Farzana in Fiji: The conversations on Skype keep me going. Thank you. Pakeeza and Waiz, I <3 you and other cool things like that. Sabrina, my cousin and partner in foodie crime, you are my Alif sister. Thank you. Thank you, Teng, my other partner in foodie crime, for the adventures and the laughter.

Thank you, Beth Phelan, for founding #DVpit. You forged a way for us on extremely rocky terrain. Thank you to my #DVSquad for cheering me on. In particular, Roselle Lim and Karen Strong, thank you! Axie Oh and Kat Cho, thank you for the enthusiasm, the squeals, the impromptu K-drama chats, and the advice. You are wonderful. Karuna Riazi, Runa, what can I say? You are my soul sister and the world needs your beautiful words. I can't wait until people meet Tam. Sailor Scouts forever.

Yashaswi Kesanakurthy, thank you for being there for me all the time. Thank you for listening. Janet Eastwood, Zulfikar would have been a very different person without you. Thank you for telling me the things I didn't want to hear. I am a better writer, and this book a better book, because of you. Jane Whittingham, thank you for your enthusiasm and friendship. Here's to more dates at Metrotown.

Thank you, Dr. Kat, my bookstagram buddy from the Philippines, whose enthusiasm for "the Djinns" kept me writing. Thank you, Ausma Zehanat, for being so lovely. Thank you, June Tan, for the GIFs and the conversation. Thank you especially to Rossi Hyunh, who has been keeping me tethered to reality since our dark days (which we shall not speak of). I couldn't have done this without you. Thank you, Jasdeep Deol, for the late-night texts and the coffee dates. Thank you for listening. Thank you also, Azeem Maamu, for your long-distance encouragement.

I have been immensely lucky to meet teachers who have encouraged me in this journey. Thank you, in particular, to Aruna Krishna, who was the first person outside my family to encourage me to write. Your words meant the world to the fourteen-year-old me, and Maggie de Vries, my thesis supervisor, who taught me so much about the craft. Finally, thank you to that professor who told me I couldn't. Look, I just did.

ABOUT THE AUTHOR

NAFIZA AZAD is a self-identified island girl. She has hurricanes in her blood and dreams of a time she can exist solely on mangoes and pineapple. Born in Lautoka, Fiji, she currently resides in British Columbia, Canada, where she reads too many books, watches too many Korean dramas, and writes stories about girls taking over the world. She loves libraries, chai, and languages. She is a fierce advocate for diversity in literature. *The Candle and the Flame* is Nafiza's debut novel.